THE LONGVIEW CHRONICLES

The Complete Saga

HOLLY LISLE

one more word

The Longview Chronicles

The Complete Saga

HOLLY LISLE

Published by OneMoreWord Books

The Longview Chronicles: The Complete Saga

Cover Design: Holly Lisle

Cover Art: © Forgiss, 3000AD, from BigStockPhoto.com

Holly's Author Photo: © Holly Lisle

Copyright © 2018 by Holly Lisle

Content Editor: Matthew Turano at MattContentEdits.com

PRINT ISBN TRADE PAPER: 978-1-62456-065-1

EPUB ISBN: 978-1-62456-063-7

KINDLE ISBN: 978-1-62456-064-4

Introduction

The Longview Chronicles consists of six separate stand-alone stories:

- _Born from Fire_
- _The Selling of Suzee Delight_
- _The Philosopher Gambit_
- _Gunslinger Moon_
- _Vipers' Nest_
- _The Owner's Tale_

These stories are all available separately, and can be read in any order.

However, when read in the order in which they were written, they turn into one large novel that is its own stand-alone book.

At the same time, when read as a stand-alone novel, this is ALSO the story of what's going on around and with Cadence Drake during the time between the end of _Warpaint_ (the second stand-alone novel featuring Cady), and the upcoming third Cady novel, still tentatively titled _The Wishbone Conspiracy_.

If you're familiar with Russian nesting dolls… well, *this* is that concept in book form.

Welcome to the adventure.

Holly Lisle

Born from Fire

from

TALES FROM THE LONGVIEW

HOLLY LISLE

For Matthew

Chapter 1

This Criminal

Down the darkness, down the line of standing cells, three words rippled urgently and under breath. "Death Circus here!"

In the dark, this criminal had waited long and longer for death to come. This criminal could not lie down, could not sit down—its captors had made certain its cell, and the cells of the others like it, permitted only standing.

With its bandaged knees pressed into one corner, its spine jammed into the other, this criminal drifted in that lightless place, never certain whether it was waking or dreaming. When it ate, it ate maggots. When it dreamed of eating, it dreamed of maggots. When it pissed or shit, it pissed or shit down its legs. When it dreamed, it dreamed of the same.

In one thing only this criminal knew a dream was a dream, and that was when it touched We-42K again, or saw its wondrous smile.

That could only be a dream, for We-Above had taken this criminal out of its cell to watch beautiful We-42K volunteer its death and the death of the unlicensed-but-born that We-42K and this criminal had made. We-42K had stood above the flames of Return to Citizenship with the born in its arms, and had turned to smile at this criminal. It looked thin and starved and filthy standing there, and the born looked dead, and as if it had been dead for a while.

The born had been beautiful when this criminal had first seen it, when this criminal and We-42K had hidden in the hills and held each other at night, had accidentally made the born, had brought it into the world together. The born had the bright red hair of We-42k, and eyes that looked at this criminal with strange knowing—and this criminal had thought for a little while that life could hold more than work and duty.

That ended, and after the end, the capture, the sentencing, the imprisonment, this criminal watched the flames and knew that the We are right to say Only Death Forgives.

This criminal has no right of judgement, but this criminal will never forgive.

The We asked this criminal if it would volunteer for redemption as We-42K had done. This criminal spit in the face of We. It refused forgiveness and Return to Citizenship—though it cannot say why—and thus it has been judged Willful, and sentenced to Death Without Citizenship, Redemption, or Merit.

And now that death has come.

"Death Circus here!" this criminal whispers down the line.

The metal doors bang open, and light trickles down the corridor. This criminal hears the first cells at the front opening, and the thwack of the prod on naked flesh, a sound this criminal knows well, a touch it feels often.

"We offer last chance to volunteer for Return to Citizenship. Will the nameless willful thing repent?"

"It will not," the Willful at the head of the corridor rasps. This criminal thinks it recognizes that voice, unheard above a whisper before now, and it is encouraged. It puts a face to the voice and sees another like itself, another that once thought life might be made better. That Willful held strong. This criminal will be able to hold strong too, will be able to face the unknown death rather than accept the known one.

Both We say, "Then it goes to the Death Circus now."

This criminal cannot say why the Death Circus seems better than the Return to Citizenship, with its quick leap into the lake of fire.

But an unknown, unvolunteered death is a better death. This criminal has had little more to think about than that question since the immolation of We-42K and the born.

The cells open and close, the Willful, the Blasphemers, and the Infidels make their choices to volunteer death or to take death by force, and at last this criminal's cell opens, and the We stand there and drag it out into the corridor and say, "We offer last chance to volunteer for Return to Citizenship. Will the nameless willful thing repent?"

This criminal spits into the face of the guard that asks, and takes its beating, and is surprised that the beating is so light.

Then it remembers that the Death Circus buys its creatures, and that it once heard whispers of guards sentenced for Willfulness for damaging criminals so badly the Death Circus refused to pay the Tithe to the We to acquire them.

Inside, this criminal laughs just a little, and tries to work up enough fluid to spit into the face of the other guard.

Kagen

Kagen, sitting in the Verimeter desk beneath the flapping cloth of the red-and-black Death Circus tent, muttered, "I hate this filthy little moon."

Burke looked over at him and raised an eyebrow. Burke would be doing disease screening—testing blood and saliva—on every criminal offered to the Death Circus, which meant he had to get within arm's reach of the strange mixture of people sentenced to death by the owners of Fair Bluff. The town was regional center for the half-dozen settlements on The People's Home of Truth and Fairness 14-B, so it was the contact point for all Death Circuses.

"Why do you hate this moon? It looks normal enough to me."

Burke was new. Provisional Crew Three. If he could get through this screening without going to pieces, he would be permitted to take the final portion of the Provisional Crew Three entrance exam and he'd earn a paid place at the bottom rung of the *Longview's* crew, as Three Green.

Kagen had been Crew Three for just under four years, and in that time had pushed through four promotions to reach Crew Three Gold. He held the record for fastest time and most grades skipped to reach Three Gold.

He'd already taken his Crew Two entry levels. Had already achieved all of his promotion points to reach Crew Two. He had his future planned, his goal set.

He hadn't received word that he'd passed the exam, yet, but if he had—and if he could rise to Crew Two, it meant more than just the possibility of a bigger, quieter room away from the engine noise to him. It meant better pay—he'd save every extra rucet, just as he'd saved everything he'd made in the last few years.

And it meant keeping The Dream alive. There were no accelerated promotions in Crew Two, but he was sure he could still make an impression. He *had* to make an impression.

There were rumors of a promotion at the top. Unsubstantiated, but plausible.

Had been for weeks, which was what had pushed him to take the Crew Two entry levels. He wanted to be ready when opportunity arose.

Burke, Kagen thought, looked to be a slow riser. The man had only cursory interest in what he was doing. To Kagen he seemed flat and bland and far too slow. Kagen suspected Burke hadn't hurt enough to see the opportunity provided by the *Longview*, that he wasn't hungry enough to ever rise past the automatic promotions in Crew Three.

Kagen, though, had been hungry all his life.

"If there is such a thing as pure evil, it lives here," Kagen muttered.

Burke said, "How is this worse than any other Pact world?"

Kagen looked around the still-empty tent and said, "This is a PHTF franchise. If you have thirty million rucets and want to be a god, you too can own a People's Home of Truth and Fairness settlement on your own little moon. There are a couple hundred of them now, I think, and they all run on the same rules. I come from PHTF-36. I still have nightmares." And he laughed.

To show that he was over it.

Burke glanced over at him with an expression Kagen saw as bovine curiosity. "How did you get out?"

"The We sentenced me to exile in the Needle, with the reminder that I could jump at any time and be forgiven for my crime."

"You were a Mule?"

Kagen forced a grin. "Indeed. I kissed a girl, and gave her a nickname. My Sentence was Willful and Blasphemer, but I hadn't done quite enough for the Speakers for We to put me in prison. Being a Mule exiled in the Needle is supposed to be the same outcome as if you're sentenced to death... but because of the *Longview*, you know how that is." Kagen tipped his head up to the invisible point of the Needle, where the *Longview* was currently docked. "Since I didn't end up dying for my crime, it was worth it."

Burke nodded. "The secret rooms."

The rooms in the Needles were only secret to those who despised the technology that created them and the men they'd had to hire to build them. All Needles required someone to work in the top, to greet the spaceships making their rounds through their routes, to accept or reject docking.

The PHTF worlds chose to send lone criminals into exile in the Needles. Those they didn't deem valuable enough to sell to the visiting Death Circuses, anyway.

Which was what brought Kagen to this world he despised so much. Kagen, Burke, and the rest of the ground team from the *Longview* were set up to start screening candidates for purchase by the Death Circus.

The We were supposed to have had their criminals in front of the tent an hour ago, but as usual they'd managed to get a string of last-minute conversions from the ranks of the criminals sentenced to death, and the We of the People's Home of Truth and Fairness 14-

B were busy burning them—or rather, having the criminals burn themselves—out back of the tent in their nasty little lake of fire.

Every PHTF world had a lake of fire, and they all looked the same. Kagen suspected it was part of the franchise.

Kagen could hear the announcement of the crimes of the volunteers: Willfulness, Blasphemy, Infidelity, over and over. Could hear the screams as the sentenced threw themselves into the flames rather than meet their fate with the Death Circus. Charlie, who was not a member of the crew but a mandatory passenger, was doing her duty in her role as official Pact Covenant observer. She was out in back testing all the volunteers to make sure none had been drugged, and that none were forced to jump into the lake.

Because she had gone renegade, Charlie would also watch for, and enforce removal of, anyone who gave any sign whatsoever of having second thoughts.

Nineteen out of every twenty prisoners on a PHTF world would fling themselves into the lake of fire and die in agony rather than allow themselves to be purchased by a Death Circus.

So the smell of burning human flesh was strong in the tent, and the intermittent sounds of screaming were loud. Equally horrible was the cheering of the throng of observers pulled from their work and made to chant, "You're forgiven! Welcome home!" as each volunteer stopped screaming.

For an instant, Kagen was back among them. Pressed up against the fence, feeling the stares of the Speakers for We focused on him and the others with him, he cheered and screamed with the rest as the pretty young woman, sentenced for the crimes of Property of Beauty and Apart of Love, threw herself into the fire. Kagen had not been the only boy who had kept his face forward so the guards could not see the tears streaming down his cheeks as he watched her die.

Not cheering was a sign of being Apart. Everyone cheered, because Speakers for We would note those who did not, and would investigate them for other crimes.

Each did what All did, or Each found itself locked away beneath the earth, or burning in the lake of Return to Citizenship.

He shuddered and was back in the red-and-black tent, back in someone else's horrible little world.

At last the We ran out of volunteers, and the sound of marching feet approached the tent flap of the Death Circus. Those prisoners ineligible for volunteering to repent—the murderers, rapists, pedophiles, and thieves—would come in first. They were Pact World Class A prisoners, meaning their sentencing and treatment fell within the Pact World Convention guidelines. They would be clean, well fed, well rested, and clothed, because if they weren't, The People's Home of Truth and Fairness 14-B would lose its charter, and with it the steady infusion of licensed charter world grant money from the Pact Worlds Equalization of Opportunity Committee that kept it alive. Once the Class A prisoners had been tested for diseases, Verilized, and categorized by health to determine the price the Death Circus had to pay for them, they would present their paperwork to the Death Circus judge, who would decide whether they were guilty or innocent—and would then determine whether they would be taken aboard the *Longview*, or left behind.

The Longview had to accept and purchase at least 33% Class A prisoners from those prisoners presented by the worlds it serviced in order to keep its Death Circus license.

Class B prisoners were sentenced under local jurisdiction, for anything considered a crime on that world, but not necessarily held to be a crime elsewhere. Because they were still covered by the Pact World Covenants, which ruled that no member world could carry out a death sentence, they could not be executed.

But the Pact World Covenants charter for Death Circuses was that any prisoner taken aboard a Death Circus ship must have a death sentence carried out, but only outside the Pact World borders.

It was up to the discretion of ship owners and ship captains on how these sentences would be carried out, but they had to be carried out, because each world that handed over a prisoner to the Death Circus had a written guarantee that the prisoner would die in a timely and appropriate fashion.

Class B prisoners were almost always criminals of a political or religious nature. And they always arrived at the Death Circus barely breathing: starved, caked in their own excrement, covered in sores. The only rules for Pact World members regarding Class B prisoners was that they could not be allowed to die while imprisoned, and that they had to be able to walk to and through the Death Circus under their own power.

The *Longview* crew had additional rules. The owner of the *Longview* insisted that each Class B must be showered until clean and dressed in fresh, dry, disposable clothing before entering the Death Circus tent. Nor were the PHTF guards permitted to do the washing. Members of the Death Circus crew were to do it, gently and with good soap and soft towels.

Kagen suspected the owner, whom he had never met or even been permitted to discuss, had once been a Class B prisoner on a PHTF world—one who had escaped, and who had then vowed to somehow help those still trapped.

It was a romantic notion, and considering the vast expenses of running a Death Circus, and the equally vast profits to be made for running one well, it was probably a silly one.

Nevertheless, he held that possibility as his truth until proven wrong, and occasionally assigned himself to prisoner cleanup duty. It was good for his unit's morale to see him do so, and it reminded him that, though he had escaped *his* PHTF home, many still remained.

Chapter 2

This Criminal

Two Evils from the Death Circus wash this criminal in warm, falling water, and are not unkind. They use soft cloths and something that froths white and bubbly as they rub it over this criminal's broken skin, and the white substance numbs the places where it hurts. Where its skin bleeds, they spray a bitter-smelling substance that closes the wound. This criminal wonders at the Evils that do kindness before killing.

This criminal finds the process of its death at the hands of the Evils increasingly less alarming. It listens to them talk together, easily, in terms it does not understand. As they talk, they laugh, and do not look over their shoulders to see if they have been overheard.

It thinks if it must die today, it would rather die at the hands of these.

They are Apart. Not We. They do not carry the mandatory posture of *Submission to Duty* in their backs and shoulders. They do not have the cautious speech or wary eyes of *We Report Or Are Reported*. They act in a fashion this criminal can barely comprehend

—they carry themselves as this criminal did when it was Apart secretly with We-42K, except without the constant fear.

Fear justified, in fact, for We-42K finally reminded itself of the requirements of *Submission to Duty* and *We Report Or Are Reported,* and brought this criminal's time with it to an end. It rejoined the We in death by choice.

This criminal cannot choose death.

Duty is life.
Life is dying.
Dying is duty.

THAT IS part of the *Truth of We.* It is the *Truth* this criminal failed in its every thought, in its every dream, in its every waking moment.

This criminal dared to imagine some other better truth might appear. That was its first and worst crime.

On this, the day of its death, this criminal thinks somewhere else must exist, where people stand with shoulders and backs straight, with eyes forward, where they laugh aloud and don't look around to see who might have heard. This criminal thinks in the place that gave these Evils birth, a different truth already lives.

When all are washed, this criminal is led to the front of the tent with the other criminals. It can read the sign painted above the flap:

Welcome to the Death Circus
Enter and be judged.

THIS CRIMINAL AND all with it have already been judged and sentenced. All that remains, it thinks, is the form its death will take.

"We who are about to die enter the Death Circus," this criminal murmurs, and realize it has committed Blasphemy by naming itself We.

That is another crime for which it will never be charged or sentenced. This criminal can only die once.

It laughs and steps through the tent flaps.

The tent is not filled with torture devices, with spears or knives, with huge Evils crouched over criminals, ripping out the insides of their still-living victims with their filed teeth. The stories are lies, then. The tent contains a mesh-sided walkway with one-way gates that will fit Each Apart singly. When Each steps forward, a handless touch at the back pushes all forward. The gates swing open. The gates snap closed. This criminal stands always alone, as fits the nature of its crime.

But this criminal sees that not Each Apart bears scars. The criminals far in the front of the line are all healthy and well-fed and dry. And clothed in a blue version of the clothes worn by the We. Those in front of this criminal, as well as all those behind it, are gaunt and beaten and dripping from being cleaned, and they are dressed in the clothes of the Evils. Otherwise they would have been naked.

Each Apart moves through the walkway—a step, a pause, a step, a pause—and then this criminal stands before the first of the Evils. The Evil presses something white and smooth against the arm of this criminal and holds it in place for an instant.

"No diseases," the Evil says, and marks something on a white, rectangular sheet. The texture of the sheet is exquisitely smooth, its color is unblemished. This criminal recognizes the markings on the sheet as words, though they are not words from the *Truth of We*. The evil holds the sheet out and this criminal takes the sheet and holds it carefully, and the line moves again.

"Paper," the one at the next station demands. This criminal has seen all criminals before it pass the white sheet through the small opening in the mesh. It passes its sheet through.

"Hand through the opening, hold this ball."

The ball is smooth and gray, strangely cold, slightly damp.

Holding it makes pulling this criminal's flesh back through the opening impossible.

This criminal finds holding the ball and having its hand trapped in the grate uncomfortable and frightening.

"You are accused of the crime of Willfulness, with the specific charges of being alone; of sharing aloneness with another; of making an unlicensed infant; and of failure to volunteer to rejoin the We. Are you guilty?"

This criminal glares at the Evil, and says, "Yes." The ball in its hand glows the yellow-gold of summer sunlight.

The Evil looks from the ball in this criminal's hand to its face, and smiles. "Good for you. Is the other who shared your crimes here?"

This criminal does not understand the smile or the words that accompany them. This criminal has heard mockery before—if the Evil mocked, the Evil did it wrong. This criminal says, "The unlicensed born died. We-42K volunteered to rejoin the We in Return to Citizenship."

The smile leaves the face of the Evil, and the Evil shakes its head. "I'm sorry. Truly."

"Why? This criminal is guilty. We-42K did what the We say is right."

"Do you think the We is right?"

"This criminal does not know 'you.' This criminal does not believe the *Truth of We*. But that is because this criminal is criminal. It is broken and evil. It thinks Apart, it thinks Willful, it denied We in word and deed. When it was We..."

This criminal begins to cry, then forces itself to stop.

"When it was We, it called itself We-39R, and even then, it knew it was lying."

The Evil stands up and stares into this criminal's eyes. The Evil's skin sheens with sweat, and its expression is fierce. "I was once We. Things change."

It marks the criminal's paper and adds a second sheet, hands both through the grate, and sends this criminal to the next station.

This criminal, Apart and Alone, walks forward—step, gate, step, gate—and sometimes the line pauses, and this criminal turns to look back, and sees the Evil that was once We talking to another criminal.

I was once We. Things change.

This criminal cannot get those words out of its mind. There is We, or there is death.

Things change.

The Evil was We, but it lives.

The final gate, and the final Evil, stand at last before this criminal.

The final Evil takes the papers, reads through them, and says, "Your sentence of death is complete. Go to Door B. Stand on the identity plate. The door will open for you. Walk forward, go through the door at the back, step through the next door, turn to your right, walk through the paddock, and stand in the corral with the others who have been sentenced.

"You have been purchased by the Death Circus."

Kagen

The *Longview* ground team had already packed the Death Circus tent, and all the team members were waiting beside the landing pad for the last two shuttles. The final shuttle would pack the tent back to the hold.

Before it returned, the shuttle Kagen and Burke waited for would remove the last of the Condemned.

The Condemned stood in the corral. Each of them waited in a separate gated control cell within the corral—the last twenty-two men of a haul of over two hundred. Darkness had come, and the We who had shouted curses through the fencing at the Condemned and the Evil, as well as the guards and Speakers for We who had kept them shouting, were gone. In worlds lit only by fire, darkness brought monsters, but chased away mobs.

The quiet around the landing pad was a pleasant reprieve from the grim work of the day, and Kagen was enjoying the silence.

But Burke, who was new, wanted to talk. "No women. Why do we have no women Condemned?"

Kagen said, "PHTF settlements almost never sell off women. Any place where people live beneath the *Truth of We,* young women go to the breeding factories as soon as they're fertile. Once they lose their fertility, women can claim guilt for taking pleasure in their work in the breeding factory, and volunteer to throw themselves into the fires of Return to Citizenship, or if they swear they took no pleasure, they can volunteer for the Room of Release."

"Which is...?"

Kagen shuddered. He closed his eyes and was back where he was born, on the last day of his freedom, where he and five other older boys—he guessed he'd been about fifteen at the time—were tasked with stocking the Room of Release.

The first woman who came through was one he recognized, though she did not appear to remember him. She had been kind to him when he was small. Had sought him out, had smiled at him. She had not seemed terribly old when he was young, but a decade had aged her terribly. Her belly and breasts sagged, her face was etched with pain, and her body was scarred from repeated beatings. She looked at the boys who led her into the room and connected the chain on the floor to the collar around her neck and locked it as they had been instructed to do. She looked at them, but she didn't seem to see them.

The boys went to stand in the hall beside the door, and a line of twenty men filed into the room.

Kagen told Burke, "They're chained to the floor, alone, and packs of men who are not permitted to touch women at any other time are sent in together to Release themselves. The men are told they are experiencing the Filth of Apart, and that they must all stay together and do whatever they have to do together, so the Filth of Apart will not destroy them. What they do together is horrible."

Burke frowned. "That's not right."

"No. It isn't. When the first woman in the Room of Release dies, or when she starts screaming that she wants to Return to Citizenship, Speakers for We drag her out and throw her into the fires—

alive, dying, or dead—and a group of boys not old enough to be required to Release chain a new volunteer in her place."

The morning after he'd finished his first day working in the Room of Release, he decided he would never do that again. During the recitation of the *Truth of We*, he'd looked over at the pretty girl who always stood next to him, at whom he had never directly looked before, because looking at girls and women was something the Apart did. She was a tall, slender girl with pale skin and dark, curling hair. He leaned over and pressed his mouth to her mouth, which one of the men in the Room of Release had done when he saw one of the volunteers. And he called her "Love," as that man had done before the Speakers dragged him away.

And one of the Speakers for We saw him do it, and two guards dragged him to the House of Fairness right then.

The advantage of living on a Pact World was that the Speaker didn't kill him right there.

His sentence, handed down minutes after that single kiss, however, and directly from the Speaker for We who'd heard him say it, had exiled Kagen to the Needle on his world to serve as a cargo slave. He was to live alone in the Needle, transporting cargo from spaceships docking at the Needle to the surface. He was to do this until he died.

If the Needle worked the way the Speakers of We believed, he would have been up there with only the small supply of water and food with which they'd exiled him.

His options, when he ran out of water and food, were to volunteer to die of thirst or starvation, or to volunteer to throw himself out the airlock.

It was only because the Needles did *not* work the way Speakers for We believed that Kagen breathed as a free man.

Burke said, "Rooms of Release. That's rough. There are rooms a lot like that on the Pact pleasure worlds. I ended up in one when I ran up a gambling debt I couldn't pay on Cheegoth. I was sentenced to work there until I had paid off my debt plus the interest—and the way it was set up, I would have never made enough money to pay off the interest. If I hadn't pissed off one of the establishment's clients and gotten myself dumped into the Indigent Lockup for the next passing ship to haul off, I would have been in there until I died or some client killed me. Cheegoth doesn't have any fairness, or any *Truth of We* to protect people."

Kagen looked at him sidelong. "Fairness isn't justice. Fairness is making a pretty girl volunteer to step into a lake of fire because not everyone else can be as pretty as she is. And there is no *truth* in the *Truth of We.*"

Burke shrugged. "What is it?"

Leaning against the temporary shuttle gate, Kagen once again felt the cold dark before dawn, when shivering and hungry, shoeless and wearing his light cotton uniform, in rain or snow or blistering heat, he'd recited the Words with every other man, woman, and child in his block.

"We speak the Truth, and the Truth speaks Us," Kagen said, keeping his voice low.
"We live by the covenants, We abide by the Words."

NEVERTHELESS, more than Burke heard him. Unbreathing silence fell behind him. The Condemned had stopped their pacing and nervous fidgeting to stare at him, bodies frozen and faces suddenly slack with animal fear. The hope that had been in all their eyes before—hope for a chance of escape, or for a chance to fight, or just for a chance at a quick, merciful death—vanished with those two soft lines.

Kagen kept going, though. He wanted Burke to understand.

"That none may laugh until All can laugh,
That All sleep on dirt until none sleep on dirt.

Dirt is Our birthright. Hardship is Our glory.

Hardship strengthens Us. Hunger feeds Us.

The Known is All. The new is Willful.
Welcome Pain. Pain is Knowledge. We are WE."

HE REALIZED the men in the line were whispering the Words with him. He turned and snarled, "Stop it. Now. You are not We. You're men, and every single one of you will face the justice and the death you *earned.*"

He turned to look at Burke again, and continued,

"Self is selfish. One is none.
All are All. We are We.

Each flesh belongs to All.
Each thought belongs to All.

Children are duty. All tend All.
Duty is life. Life is dying. Dying is duty.
We die for Duty. We are WE.

Within Each hides Evil. Be All, not Each.
In Aloneness is Willfulness. We will never be Alone.

We share, We do not own.
Property is an abomination.

Beauty is property. Property is crime.
Passion is property. Property is crime.

Love is property. We out love and lovers.
Secrets are property. We out secrets and secret-keepers.

All is Sharing. Sharing is Duty.
We serve Sharing. We are WE.

We speak the Truth, and the Truth speaks Us.
We live by the covenants, We abide by the Words.
The Will of All is all of Will. We are WE.

BURKE STOOD THERE FROWNING when Kagen finished. "None can laugh until everyone can laugh? Hunger feeds us? Beauty is crime? What sort of shit is that?"

"That's the *Truth of We*. If you laugh, you're a criminal. If you want a single thing for yourself, you're a criminal. The instant you realize you are not the same as everyone else—that you're thinking your own thoughts inside your own head—you are a criminal.

"And because sooner or later everyone realizes the thoughts in their heads belong to them, every single person in every single settlement is a criminal. And the Speakers for We, who do not live under the *Truth of We*, are the biggest criminals of all. They buy these marginal worlds and grubby moons and the franchise constitutions that make them PHTFs, and send out advertisements for new settlers to get a better life, all expenses paid."

Burke was staring at him. "How can these worlds be legal?"

"The same way the world you were on was legal. As long as the people in charge of these worlds don't ever try to claim the right that they can execute someone on a Pact world, or kill any registered citizen intentionally, they can do anything they want."

Chapter 3

This Criminal

The sky ship drops toward this criminal, silent. Speakers say the burning flesh of the Apart feed it, which may be true, but nothing else the Speakers say has proven true.

No. This criminal lies. *Truth of We* said this criminal would be sold to the Death Circus, which must guarantee that each criminal it purchases will have the Sentence of Death carried out. This criminal was sold. Death will come now.

Still, the ship touches the ground, noiseless. The ship does not smell of burning flesh, which is a smell that will haunt this criminal until his last thought. This criminal tries to find comfort in the absence of a scent.

In the darkness, in the silence, this criminal stands shivering, for no matter how the Evils do not seem cruel, the ship has arrived, and life now ends.

This criminal thinks—which is its first crime—of what life might have been if We-42K had remained criminal. If it had not brought the Speakers and the Guards to the hiding place. This criminal imagines a life without *Truth of We*.

But if such life exists, it will not exist for this Apart.

The sky ship's doors are open, and the line moves. The unseen hands behind push Each Apart through the tall wire corral, into the next gate.

The first criminal steps through the gates, up into the ship. The Apart does not run.

This criminal thinks when it steps through the gates, it will run. It is not ready for Death.

There is no sound as the ship doors close behind the first Apart. Just a moment later, the doors re-open and the Apart is gone. It was big, tall and strong-looking, clean and fierce, and it had shouted anger at the Evils when it waited.

The Evils have a quiet Death. It is not like the death of Return to Citizenship, which is screaming and writhing, body arcing long, then curling inward, arms and legs twisting, with skin peeling away from flesh, with flesh peeling away from bone, with bone blackening until it bursts into flame and at last is gone.

The quiet Death may be quick.

But this criminal wants to live.

The line moves too quickly. Each Apart moves forward without resistance, steps up to the ship and through the doors and is gone.

Each Apart, and then this criminal is two places away from the final corral, and it feels a sharp, quick, bright pain in its arm, and looks to see a tiny ice dart melting into its flesh.

And all its fear goes, and its anger, and its desire to live. The face of We-42K fades, and the solemn gaze of the born disappears. This criminal is washed empty inside, and steps up into Death.

Kagen

Kagen and Burke lifted the last body into its private suspended-animation unit and sealed the unit.

Kagen said, "You do the paperwork this time."

Burke nodded, took the papers from Kagen, and started to shove them into the unit's feeder slot.

Kagen said, "You weren't watching what I did. *Learn to watch.* If my head didn't already hurt, I'd have let you put them in that way. And then I'd have let you deal with the alarm and trying to get the papers sorted out on your own. Because you've watched me do twenty of those, but you evidently didn't see a thing."

Burke said, "What did I do wrong?"

"The sheets go in numerical order, print side up, all facing the same direction. If you put them in any other way, the unit alarm goes off loud enough to wake the dead."

"Why? I don't even understand why we use paper," Burke grumbled. "This whole process could be shortened to minutes with a single data thread."

"Paper can't disappear when a unit shorts," Kagen said, "and the hermetically sealed document compartments resist tampering. You should have had that information in your Preliminary Crew Three study guide."

"I skimmed that," Burke said. "I still tested high enough to be here."

Which marked Burke as exactly what Kagen had thought he was. Light crew. Barely above deadweight. Kagen decided he would pass on Burke's application and see if he could find someone better from the passenger ranks.

Annoyed, he said, "For a ship to maintain its lucrative Death Circus license in the Pact worlds, the status of every Condemned must be available to the Pact licensing body at all times. The instant the *Longview* passes a Spybee or comsat, the ship's Pact module sends a burst packet that relays our Condemned update to the Pact Core, who then distributes our list of available Condemned to all subscriber worlds. If you in any way screw up the unit's ability to identify the Condemned in the box, you screw up the system that keeps the Longview in the air."

Burke watched Kagen with puzzlement. "Wait. They're not dead?"

Kagen was pretty sure at that point Burke had done less than skim the study guide. While he sorted the paperwork correctly, making sure Burke watched him, he said, "No. Sometimes the owner decides to carry out Final Sentencing on the ship as soon as we're beyond the Pact World borders. But there's no real profit in that. And the *Longview* is the most profitable Death Circus registered."

"So we make a good living from killing people." Burke frowned. "If I hadn't managed to get passenger status on the *Longview*, I could have been one of the people in the boxes."

Kagen shrugged. "Everyone on the *Longview* has a story like that. We all have ugliness behind us. The trick is to not let that ugliness get back in front of us."

Burke raised an eyebrow.

Kagen had decided Burke was one breath above worthless, but gave him the same spiel he gave every potential member of Crew Three. "If you don't screw up on the *Longview*, you can get training all the way up to captaining your own ship. You can earn more money with us than with any other ship crew I know of. But if you want it—and I want it—you have to keep your record spotless, work hard, and study hard. And you can't make enemies. Or mistakes. It's a small crew, and almost everyone is trying to stay on it."

"Why? Because you all love the smell of burning bodies? Love taking people to their deaths?"

"We transport people who have already been categorized *Dead, Still Breathing* to places that have uses for people like that. If we didn't, someone else would, and we keep all our Condemned clean and safe and healthy until they get where they're going—which cannot be said for any other Death Circus out there. *The Longview* is different.

"When we hit some of the big buyer worlds, you start talking to crew from other Death Circuses. Most of them just shove Class B prisoners out the airlock as soon as they hit the Pact perimeter, because all Death Circuses have to buy at least 10% Class Bs, and feeding what you can't sell costs money. Class Bs are just about impossible to sell. Every other Death Circus out there buys 90% Class A Condemned and 10% Class B Condemned."

Burke said, "And Class A Condemned are the rapists, pedophiles, murderers, and... one other..."

"Thieves," Kagen told him. So Burke had at least read *something* in the study guide.

"Right." Burke considered that for an instant. "And the Class B prisoners are basically the ones who just pissed off somebody important."

Kagen nodded. "You. Me. Half the damned universe, it seems."

"And worlds *want* to buy rapists, and pedophiles, and murderers, and thieves, but don't want to buy people who didn't actually commit real crimes..."

Kagen said, "Have you ever heard of gladiators? The Shorgah Arena?"

"No."

"It's big on slaver worlds. Slave owners buy men other people want to see die, and they pit them against each other in a ring. They get rid of problem slaves that way, too, but there have been a couple times that policy turned around to bite them. So they like to get bad guys from much tenderer worlds. Pact worlds breed tender bad guys because they never come up against any real resistance."

"That's vile."

"It's a polite way for the Pact worlds to get rid of their worst citizens without ever having to get their own hands dirty. The slaver worlds buy women, too, of course. Women are easy to sell—the younger and prettier, the better, but slaver worlds usually have reju, so they can turn and old woman into a young woman, and keep her young and healthy and unmarked as long as they want."

"And we're a part of that. I'm not sure I want to go for Crew Three. I might just get off on the next non-Pact, non-Slaver world we come to."

"Always an option," Kagen said, shrugging. "There's more to this than you're seeing, I think—but there are also plenty of other people desperate to get the job you don't think you want."

Chapter 4

Kagen

Kagen was heading into the mess hall with the rest of Crew Three when Melie, who was Crew Two Gold, pulled him aside and waved the rest of his unit on.

"Congratulations," she said. "You passed Crew Two eligibility, and I've chosen you as Crew Two Green. You're the first person I've seen in ages who passed Crew Two eligibility the first time through."

He had just finished decontaminating the shuttles after unloading the final twenty-one units from each of them, and had showered the stink of burning humans off of his skin. And had been trying to decide whether to give Burke another chance or to tell him he'd failed and wait for another passenger to pass the eligibility exam. It had been a brutal day.

And suddenly it was better.

"Someone moving up, or someone moving out?" he asked.

"Both." She grinned. "Willett passed his Captain's exam and got his license while we were on Cairefon, and the last Spybee we passed had a stack of offers for him. He's going to captain a TFN starcruiser for a salary that makes my eyeballs bleed. So everyone whose tests and promotion points are in order step promotes. You were short your time in grade for promotion, but you did well as Three Gold and the captain himself approved my request to move you to Two Green."

The captain himself. This was the sort of attention Kagen had been working for since the first day he worked as Three Green. If important people noticed him, and sided with him, The Dream would become real.

"Thank you," he said. "Are you staying on as Two Gold?"

"Not a chance. Mash goes Gold tonight." And then she said, "You're the first one we've had in a while who got through the exam on the first try. I'll bet you're aiming for higher."

"Captain," Kagen said. "I at least want to qualify on the captain's exam. I want to get my own ship."

"Me, too." Melie smiled. "Skip mess with Three. You'll eat next hour with Two. Right now I have just enough time to introduce you to the Sleepers."

They left mess together, and for the first time Kagen found himself facing the always-locked exit to the top-level private ship gravdrop. Melie palmed them through.

"I still find the Sleeper bays unsettling," Melie told him. "You've only seen them from the shuttle bays below. Looking up, it's all darkness and the bottoms of walkways. You won't understand how... big... this all is until you've seen it from the inside."

He'd never been through the second doors before, so she pointed out landmarks he needed.

"Crew One duty room," she said, and pointed down the corridor to the left. "Don't go in there. It's the jump room for whichever Crew One pulls third-hand standby when we're on alert. And on your right is the owner's quarters," she said and pointed to a dimly lit corridor. "If you so much as walk down that passage, you're out on the next world we hit, no matter what sort of world it is. Don't get curious, don't forget."

They reached a crossing passage with signs saying SLEEPERS LEVEL ONE, and Melie pointed to the palm-lock that opened the Sleeper bays.

"As soon as you accept the crew position, your palm code will be added to Level Two areas," she said, and pressed the palm-lock, The door slid open.

Before him lay rows of containers stacked floor to ceiling on either side of narrow corridors. They were, he realized, more complex versions of the storage units he'd been using for the last several years to bring the Condemned up from the surfaces of the worlds with which the *Longview* contracted.

"What are all the extra connectors on the containers?" he asked.

She turned and gave him a long stare and a slow head-shake. "Don't. Ask."

"You know and can't tell?"

Her voice dropped so low he had to move his ear to just centimeters from her lips to hear what she was saying. "I don't know. Nobody knows. Not even the captain. I think they're something the owner invented for sorting the Condemned, figuring out which ones will be the most valuable where, and then marketing those people directly to the worlds that will pay the most for them. According to a name I can't mention, the *Longview's* owner is the richest Death Circus franchisee in existence. My source says by about twenty times. And the *Longview* buys the most Condemned, but percentage-wise sells the fewest. So the ones the ship sells have to be going for unbelievable prices. *Have* to be. Because this is also the biggest and most expensive Death Circus ship in existence. And it pays crew the best."

Her lips pressed against his ear. "In here, if we're quiet, we can mention this," she told him. "If you're not in the Sleeper stacks, though, say nothing. Ever."

She pulled back. "We're gravdropping down to Level Ten. I'm just going to show you Ten Port and Starboard today. It's the smallest level, and you're new. You and I will do status sweeps on Ten together twice. Then you'll do ten on your own, and your Gold will make sure you didn't miss anything. Then you'll do Ten on the first day of the week and Nine on the third. You'll have a lot of other duties, too, but this is the most important one."

They gravdropped slowly down through the rows and stacks,

and Kagen spotted green lights on some, yellow lights on a few, and red lights on many. He pointed them out.

Melie said, "Green means we have at least one bidder for that unit. We off-load those to the world that has bid the highest by the time we reach it. Yellow means the individual in the unit is new. Those will go red or green eventually. The study guides say going red means no one has bid or signaled interest... but sometimes they go red within a few hours of the Condemned's arrival, and sometimes they go green, *then* go red. And sometimes they're red for years."

"So green is usually Class A, red is usually Class B?"

"Good. I didn't have to tell you that. You did the extra levels of the exam study."

He nodded. "Figured I might not need them for Class Two, but that I'd need them for captain."

She grinned. "Actually, according to the captain, that part of the course you only need to qualify for owner. That and having just buckets of money. But I studied them, too."

"Is the owner considering selling?"

Melie shrugged. "I don't think so. And I don't know anyone who's bought a Death Circus franchise. But the captain said the owner added ownership training to each level of the testing so we'd understand what we were doing. The captain said as far as he can tell, no other Death Circus franchisee offers this."

Kagen filed that information away.

They hit Level Ten and pushed out of the gravdrop to the lowest walkway. All the way down, Kagen had been watching the rows upon rows of long containers disappearing into the darkness, and he'd been trying to count. Trying to get a sense of how many Sleepers the ship carried. He couldn't. Not even a rough guess."

"How many are there?" he asked her.

"I don't know. None of us do, and we all want to. That is another piece of information the owner keeps off the records."

"You could always count the units."

She laughed. "No. We couldn't. And if you decide you like being here, and you want to earn a captain's license without having to sell your soul and indenture your body, you'll leave this alone. It's one of the stipulations of service, which you'll get later today. You get to see this first so you'll understand the scope of your new duties. And then you have two options. Agree to the terms and accept Crew Two, or move to passenger status and get off the ship at the first world that fits your Acceptable Alternative stats."

"That seems extreme."

"Remember when I said the owner is doing something different here?"

"Yes."

"The stipulations you'll agree to regarding sharing information about this ship and what's on it are part of that. And realize that the owner is *not* playing. We veridicate after every off-ship we do, and if we don't pass veridication, we're not allowed back on the ship. We sleep in whatever Needle we end up in until some other ship will take us."

"That's harsh."

"It is. Don't count, don't dig for information you're not permitted to have, *never* get drunk or drugged and run your mouth when you're on an away team or on leave. Crew positions on the *Longview* pay five times more per level than pay on any other Death Circus ship, and officer positions pay ten times more. But that's just the start. If you do the owner's recommended investments, you can increase your pay way over that." She glanced sidelong at him. "And before you ask, you'll get the information pack with the recommended investments if you accept Crew Two placement. I've been Crew Two for my full six years now, I've done the recommended investments, but went in for more than the recommended amount, and with my Crew One raise—even assuming I wash out of captain training—I'll have enough money to buy a small in-system personal ship by the end of my Crew One minimum term. I can do better if I stay the maximum, and much, much better if I make officer."

Kagen heard the screams of the burning behind him. Before him, though, lay the clean, silent deeps of space. The possibility of his own ship within reach in twelve years, if he could make the grade, get the promotions, and keep his crew record clean.

Freedom, space, a way to get away from the regulated worlds and move out from under the ever-watching eye of the Pact, and away from slaver worlds, and maybe set up on an indie world as a transport. Or a privateer.

The Dream, and everything it took him away from, was sliding into reach.

"THIS IS YOUR QUARTERS," Melie told him. "As the Crew Green, you get 3-B. You've been Crew Green before."

Kagen nodded. "For two months. But I remember the drill. First out of bed, scrub the head before anyone else is awake, respond to all alarms, make sure the crew unit is secure; if there's an emergency, make sure everyone in the unit is in shipsuits. I am Green, I am expendable."

Melie said, "You and me both. When you're crew, you never get to forget what it means to be Green."

"You're doing Green duty in Crew One?"

"That's not the half of it. You're probably going to be Green for six months, until one of your current Blues decides not to stick it out for the next promotion. At which point you'll bump up and the new Three Gold will jump at the chance to be Two Green. But me? I'm looking at up to three years as One Green, because Joze is only two years in as Two Gold. And there are only two of us. With three years left on his eligibility, he's not going to leave until he makes first mate or runs out his clock. And I don't move up until he makes officer or leaves."

"And we have a brand new first mate who has five years to promote to captain, and a relatively new captain."

Melie nodded.

"But you're Crew One."

She grinned. "That I am. And you know I'm sticking. I want to make captain here. But either way, I'll qualify as captain and do the licensing, and if I run out my clock, I'll buy my own ship. And I *could* be the one who's in the right place at the right time to be captain here."

"So you did the full Crew Two run," he said.

She nodded.

"Any advice?"

"Probably not any that you need. Most of the crew in Two is not pushing for captain. Most of them haven't done the investments. They love spending time in rec, and spending their downtime on the fun worlds having fun. So you study like a beast for the exams, and you take them every single time you're eligible. Aim to step-promote every year—if you go faster, you won't have as much money saved up. Do all the owner-recommended investments, live cheap, and at bare minimum you'll get out of here with enough money to make a good down payment on your ship. What you do from there is up to you."

"And best case..."

"Best case, you become my first mate, and when I move on to my own ship, you become *Longview's* captain."

Other members of Crew Two started coming in. They would wash before their meal, then go up to the Mess Hall to eat together.

Kagen knew the people in Two, but only as an underling. As Green, he was still an underling, but now he was *their* underling.

Mash was the new Two Gold, Taryn was the new Two Silver, and Lindar, Porth, and Aya were all Blues. Each of them touched fingertips with him as they came in, and each said, "Welcome to Two, greenie." Each then touched fingertips with Melie and said, "Do well in One."

It was the way all crew got welcomed into a new unit, and the way all promoted crew left. It always seemed casual, but it wasn't. The words were precisely the same, and they hid the motivations, prejudices, and passions of those who said them.

Incoming crew frequently knew—or at least knew about—their seniors. Existing unit crew knew about the reputations of incoming juniors. But living with them in the close quarters of the unit, eating with them at every meal of every day, spending recreational or study time with them, they would be forced into a closeness that Kagen found difficult to manage.

He had dealt with the issue by burying himself in study, working for promotion points, and taking every grade exam the instant he became eligible. It let him avoid people as much as possible, and the distance he kept had made it easier for him to keep the distance necessary to be effective in Gold. He'd never had friends he had to discipline, because he didn't have friends. No one ever accused him of favoritism, because he didn't have favorites.

He hoped that same would work to his advantage in Two.

Mash, as the new Gold, said, "Present your connector."

Kagen reached out with his right hand. The pale circle of luminescent ink—something exclusively used by the crew of the *Longview* —marked the location of embedded data-transfer nanoclusters that allowed the instant exchange of information.

"Your Level Two Green Packet and Orders," Mash said, and the two clasped right hands. Their connectors linked up, and Kagen instantly had full access to his orders, his room assignment, the crew-level promotion sheets of the people in his unit, and his schedule.

"I'm missing my list of recommended investments," he said.

Mash's face darkened, and his gaze flicked from Melie back to Kagen. "You'll get them when you need them, greenie."

Mash, he realized, was a man who needed to be the biggest bull in the room.

Kagen didn't miss the expressions on either Melie's or Mash's face as they stared each other down.

"So. You're sticking me with your... *protégé?*" Mash asked, and his emphasis on the word suggested a relationship considerably less professional than mentor and student.

Melie stared right back. "Are you already failing at your job requirements as Two Gold?"

She outranked him. She clearly didn't like him. He clearly didn't like her—this was information that had never filtered down to Crew Three.

If Melie had time to force the issue with Mash, his dislike for her would get itself transferred to Kagen with the same speed that his Green packet had arrived.

And Melie wasn't going to be around to help him deal with Mash. She was going to be in her own unit, busy dealing with her own stint as Green.

The Dream flickered before his eyes. Mash could ruin him— Kagen had never sabotaged anyone in Three, because he didn't like or dislike his underlings. But he knew how sabotage could be accomplished easily within any portion of the three years Mash could remain as Crew Two Gold.

Kagen had to side with his crew leader, no matter how much he didn't want to.

"Not a problem," he told Mash. "I wasn't planning on wasting my money gambling on something speculative anyway. I just wanted to see what was on the sheet."

He saw the look of shock on Melie's face, the look of satisfaction on Mash's.

And in the moment he said it, he realized that he had no other way to get the recommended investments if Mash didn't pass them to him. Packets were coded. No crew member could share his or accidentally pass it to someone else.

Mash would hold Kagen to his word... he'd said that he wasn't interested. Mash—biggest bull in the room—would remind Kagen of his words if ever he tried to recant. So Kagen would lose up to three prime years of building his capital to buy his ship that he could not get back, and the early years were the most important. Compound interest made early investments vastly more profitable than investments made late.

And just as bad, if the look on Melie's face was any indication, he had just murdered all hope of her recommending him again as the two of them moved up the promotion ladder. He'd just spit on her for championing him in front of a man who was not just her subordinate, but her enemy.

Third, he'd put himself on the wrong side of the career fence, marked himself to those others in his unit who were on the promotion track as light crew who didn't understand the value of *this* ship, *this* job, *this* opportunity.

Worst of all, he knew why he'd done it. The pathetic voice of We that still wailed inside of him, that still bent before trouble rather than standing against it, had cried out that he was about to be destroyed.

And he had listened.

He'd betrayed his ally, had sided with his enemy, had claimed We over I.

He would have done anything to have that moment back. But the moment was gone, the damage done.

He'd made an unrecoverable mistake.

A man who could not hold onto his principles against the threat of disapproval was not a man who would ever be captain. Not of this ship.

Not of any ship.

Chapter 5

Kagen

Alone, Kagen worked his way through the stacks on Level Ten. The place made his skin crawl. It wasn't as bad when Melie had done the first two rounds with him, though those rounds hadn't been pleasant.

She'd spoken to him only when she absolutely had to as she showed him the process of keeping each Condemned core connected into the system and fully charged.

She made sure he understood that any disconnect or unit failure would mean his job—that every active core unit was valuable to the owner and the crew responsible for the few units that had ever failed had been dropped off at the Needle of whatever world was next on the circuit and left to fend for themselves.

Core integrity was the number one priority of every member of Two. *Everything* else came second.

But while she did her job well, that was all she did. She didn't hear him if he offered a personal remark or tried to apologize. She gave him the two days of training he needed, and then she was gone to her own duties as Crew Two Green.

And he was left with Mash, who went through after he had made his rounds and claimed to have found errors Kagen had made, even though Kagen knew he had not made them. Three weeks into his stint as Two Green, Mash still treated him like a complete waste of skin.

Kagen worked his way alone through the dimly lit stacks, feeling the ghosts of his past and the ghosts of his future crowding in on him, and he tried to focus on the work he was doing.

The still bodies in the stacks made it hard for him to maintain his romantic notion of the owner as some escaped Class B prisoner made good and determined to save his fellow Class B prisoners. The endless rows of the officially dead stored in cold, hard storage units spoke of some horrific purpose that he could not begin to comprehend. He did his best not to look at their faces through the transparent inspection covers. The people inside did not breathe. They did not move.

They were not dead, but they were the same as dead. They had been reported dead back on their home worlds, with the terms of their executions fulfilled.

Officially dead, but not entirely dead—stored, with large amounts of energy expended in storing them.

All of the cores—the storage units with their locking seals stamped Death Sentence Carried Out and their heavy-duty power cables and complex end-caps that performed functions no one could guess at—were full in Level Ten. All of them were red-lighted. All of them would always be red-lighted. Level Ten was designated permanent storage.

Each person in each core had been passed over for purchase, had been categorized as unsaleable, and had been sentenced to eternity within the chamber that held him. Or her.

Men and women, young and old, lay motionless, eyes closed, lungs forever stilled, captive forever, with enormous amounts of power running through their units, not alive but not dead either.

Kagen's imagination ran wild. To store the not-entirely-dead in such a fashion, the owner had to be doing something with them. Had he discovered a way to use them as filters to process vast quantities of designer nanoviruses? Had he discovered that souls were real, and found a way to sell theirs? No one would spend the vast fortune it had taken to store the bodies of countless nearly dead for as close to eternity as technology could reach unless there was some tremendous payoff for him. It was entirely too cheap and easy to simply kill people and dump their bodies into space.

So why did this place with its red lights exist?

He rounded the corner in the narrow aisle, asking himself that question, and this one time, his head was up and he was looking directly at the ident screen on the core directly in front of him as he came around the corner.

It said *We-T74G*.

He froze.

He stared at the screen, frowning, trying to look at the letters and numbers and see a different combination, to make it clear to himself that his mind was playing tricks on him.

But below the identity designator, he read, "Origin: The People's Home of Truth and Fairness 14-B."

The date was right around the time he'd been exiled to the Needle, sentenced to work alone until he was ready to starve to death or throw himself into space to rejoin the We. She might have come aboard in a transport unit the same day he'd been taken in as a passenger by the *Longview*. He had worked his way past her and checked her unit half a dozen times without seeing her.

But this time, he found himself frozen, staring at a face he could not believe he was seeing. She was the girl of his memory—unchanged—though he could no longer see the little grin she'd aimed at him when the two of them were doing Weeding Duty, separated by the wire mesh that kept We First apart from We Second.

Her dark hair curled up around her face as if gravity meant nothing to it, as it had always done.

Her lips were full and perfect. Her brow arched. Her jaw was smooth and firm. She would never have been sentenced with the crime of Property of Beauty.

She was the girl he'd kissed and called "Love" during the morning recitation of the *Truth of We.*

She'd been Condemned when he'd been exiled.

He had never before considered that she might be sentenced to death for what he had done. But she would have been. There was no justice on a People's Home of Truth and Fairness.

Her crime would have been Property of Love. He looked lower on the ident screen.

"Murder Grand, four counts."

That was impossible. They'd lied about her to make an example of her. To make sure she would never kiss another boy—and to make sure, as well, that anyone who saw what happened to her wouldn't either.

So they'd sentenced her for murder, which meant she could not be offered Return to Citizenship in the lake of fire.

Then they'd sent her away so some rich ship owner could flip a switch and turn her off forever.

On another world, the two of them could have been together. On some sane Pact world, they could have been friends. Could have been lovers. Could have been together their whole lives.

He rested his fingertips on her core. He whispered, "If you had known it would end like this, would you still have done it? Would you still have kissed me back? Locked away in a storage unit in the bottom of a spaceship for the rest of forever, never knowing what you were being used for, what precious commodity was being drained from your body and sold..."

Her still, frozen face haunted him. "No," she seemed to say. "Of course I wouldn't have kissed you. Look what they did to me because I did."

He looked at the future that lay before him. He had sold his future among the stars because he'd been unwilling to stand firm against Mash—just as he had sold the girl whose smile he had loved to Death for the price of a kiss.

He had failed, and failed again. His dreams were dead. His future was ruined

Only one path remained to him.

Melie

When the emergency panel went off on Level Ten, Melie was asleep.

But she was Green, so she dragged herself upright, threw on her shipsuit, and gravdropped to Ten with the suit accelerating her passage.

The units on Ten were usually stable. She'd seen Mash's reports about Two Green making mistakes, but as Level One crew, she had access to the process flows from Level Ten, and Kagen hadn't made any mistakes.

Someone had come along after him, had tampered with what he'd done, had played with the public time-set to make it look like the mistake had been made when the unit was checked, and had then signed himself into the unit as himself and had corrected the error and sent notification to the captain.

She suspected this time Mash had set one unit low enough to drop to alarm status before Kagen did his next rounds—which would put Kagen before the captain, the first mate, and the owner's representative, unless the owner himself decided to weigh in.

She hit Ten fast and followed the overhead running lights and the directional signal on her wristcom through the stacks.

And there she found Kagen. With him stood a girl who was touching his face with a mixture of joy and dismay—and beside the two of them was the shattered Sentence Seal that had once secured the core unit of We-T74G.

"I do remember you," the girl was saying, running her fingers across Kagen's cheeks and lips and jaw.

"Oh, hell," Melie whispered.

Kagen turned to stare at her. He stepped in front of the girl. "Before you say anything, I'm taking her place in the box. She did nothing to deserve a death sentence, and I'm the reason she was sentenced. If I can't be the captain of my own ship, if I can't fix what I've done wrong here, I can at least fix what I did to her. Just help me get into the core, lock it back, figure out a way to reseal it..."

And the girl looked from Kagen to Melie and said, "He didn't know, and he doesn't understand. But I have to go back in. As much as I want to be with him, I can't stay here."

Melie said, "Kagen, you idiot. You screwed up everything. You — We... whatever your number is. I'll help you into the box. Maybe we can still fix all of this."

The girl said, "Just call me Lithra."

And then, behind Melie, the owner's representative, Shay, said, "Unfortunately, We-T74G's unit has already reported re-activation."

Melie cringed and turned to face her.

Shay continued, "No one can go into that core now. We're going to have to file an incident report with the Death Circus administration about one of our official executions appearing to return to life... and all three of you are going to have to stand before the captain and the first mate. You will probably have to face the owner, too, instead of me. He was furious when the alarm went off in his quarters."

The security detail came around the corner, and snapped restraints on Kagen and Melie. Lithra walked between them, unrestrained but cooperative.

Chapter 6

Kagen

The captain sat at the big chair in his private mess. On his right sat the first mate. The chair to his left was empty. When everyone came through the door, he looked past Melie, Lithra, Kagen, and the security detail to the owner's representative. "He says he's too angry to deal with them rationally. You're in the third seat, Shay."

Kagen had never seen the owner's representative before. She was stunning. Long, straight red hair, impossibly green eyes, incredible body. He wondered what her story was—how she'd ended up among the *Longview's* misfits.

Shay sighed heavily. "I don't know why he does this. He's never happy with what I decide."

Then she took her seat and said, "I have the comlink open to the owner's quarters. He may or may not comment, but he'll get the full recording. So go ahead when you're ready."

The captain nodded. "He have a preference in which one we interview first?"

Shay murmured into her shipcom and came back with, "Lithra. He wants to know why the idiot took her out of the box."

The captain muttered, "I'd ask the *idiot* that question," but Lithra had already stepped forward.

"When I was We-T74G on The People's Home of Truth and Fairness 14-B, the man behind me was a boy. And he was my only friend, even though we never dared speak to each other. You know how the PHTF worlds are. And one day he kissed me, and did it in front of Speakers for We. He was exiled to the Needle, where he was to stay until he died, while I was sentenced as a criminal of Property: Love, and handed to the Speakers to be their plaything.

"I did not want to have them touch me," she said. "I decided I would rather die—so I attacked the first man who came into the cell where I was held, and was lucky enough to kill him. I took the weapon I found on his body, and used it to kill the next three men who entered the cell. One of the men was the Head Speaker, and the fact that he was dead and that I had killed him made it mandatory that I be sentenced as a Class A prisoner. And because I was a Class A prisoner, I was untouched until I was sent to the Death Circus.

"If he had not kissed me, I would never have survived to escape PHTF 14-B. Even if the Speakers had not taken me before I became an official citizen to be one of their toys, to be abused and killed as so many other women were, I would have spent the rest of my life in one of the breeding factories. If unending cycles of pregnancy and childbirth didn't kill me, volunteering for the Room of Release or Return to Citizenship when I could no longer bear children would have.

"I request that you absolve him for the actions he took tonight, even though there will be problems that arise from them. He acted out of love and great courage—he was willing to go into my box and take my death sentence to give me my freedom."

"We cannot let him go unpunished. He destroyed the owner's property, acted against the rules he had agreed to obey, and has put the charter of the *Longview* at risk," the captain said. "He cannot remain in his current position as crew."

"I agree," the first mate said.

The girl looked from captain to first mate, clearly frightened. "I do not understand."

The owner's representative said, "He will be sentenced based on his actions. He must be. Otherwise, there can be no justice." She gave the girl a long look, and eventually the girl nodded. "You faced the same justice he faces. Think on that. And now it is time for you to return to your core. It's been repaired."

"No!" Kagen shouted. "You can't condemn her to nothingness again! She did nothing wrong!"

"We must," Shay said. "This ship cannot maintain its charter if we do not."

Lithra turned to the crew who were on security duty, and said, "I'll go with you, and I won't cause you any problems." And then she turned to the captain. "May I thank him before I go?"

The captain said, "Yes. I suppose."

Lithra came to Kagen, and reached up on her toes and kissed him once, passionately. "Thank you for trying to save me. I have always loved you. And I always will."

She wrapped her arms around him and held him tightly, pressing her head to his chest. "I will remember the sound of your heart beating. Always."

He pulled against the ungiving restraints around his wrists, desperate to hold her close to him. He could do nothing. With his eyes filling with tears, he whispered, "You were my only love. You are. You'll always be." He swallowed hard, and she pulled away from him and walked between the crew members who took her back to her core. Back to nothing, forever.

"Melie," the captain said, "I'll hear from you next unless there are any objections."

Both the owner's representative and the first mate shook their heads, indicating they had no objections.

So the captain said, "Do you have any idea what caused this behavior by your choice for Two Green?"

Melie winced on hearing Kagen described in that fashion.

Kagen didn't blame her. He'd certainly not turned out to be the man she'd chosen to move up to Two.

She said, "I've been investigating Mash for the last three months for intimidation of other crew members, and for attempting to fill all crew positions with his people. I admit that I somewhat misused Three Gold Kagen when I brought him into Two as my choice for Green. I'd previously made sure to mention Kagen among my Two unit as my best guess for eventual captain of the *Longview*, and while this was in fact true, I made sure to state it more than once in front of Mash."

Kagen watched her looking from face to face across the table. He could see her trying to figure out how all three listeners were taking this information. "So Mash was already inclined to hate Kagen. When Mash step-promoted into Two-Gold the same day Kagen became Two Green, Mash saw Kagen as a better-qualified rival for the job he planned to get, and further, as someone he needed to take down."

She sighed. "I could not warn Kagen about what I was doing without damaging the credibility of my investigation. I have not been able to explain my treatment of him to him—and I have not been kind.

"So he'll have to confirm this for you, but I suspect he took his treatment by Mash and me as signs that he had made an unfixable mistake, and I further suspect he thought he had lost his future on the *Longview*.

"You see, Mash has been going behind him, sabotaging his work on Level Ten while ostensibly checking after him. He's been writing Kagen up for every mistake he claims to have found. I was waiting for that noxious..." She stopped herself from saying whatever she had been planning to say, and started over. "I was waiting for Two Gold to submit his formal *Request for Dismissal of Crew* on Kagen before I sent my own results to you. I wanted you to be able to independently compare Mash's documentation of errors with mine."

She pulled her shoulders back and lifted her chin. "One of my associates from Two says Mash has just about completed his dismissal request form. My informant expects it to go to you..." her gaze flicked to the clock, and she sighed, "...in six or seven more hours. Once Mash submits that request, I can bring forward everything I've found out about what he's been doing. This will include falsifying records on three other talented subordinate crew members, which resulted in one crewman being removed from crew and left without recommendation in the nearest Needle on our circuit, and the other two leaving the *Longview* before he could create his reports on them. I cannot prove the cases on the two who quit, but if you can search Mash's private files before he can delete them, you will probably find falsified documentation."

Kagen tried not to look as stunned as he felt.

Melie had been working to get rid of Mash.

She'd still thought he would have qualified as captain eventually.

He was truly an idiot.

"And your attempt to get the girl he'd liberated from her core back into her box before anyone found out?" Shay asked Melie.

Melie dropped her head. "I was hoping to save both his career and my investigation."

"Because...?" the owner's representative prodded.

"Because I thought both of these actions would be in the best interests of the owner, the crew, Kagen's career, and my own career."

"Both the owner and I are inclined to agree that they were," Shay said, and glanced over at the captain. "The owner wants your first thoughts."

"If that damned report were in my hands already, I could simply demote her back to Two Gold and let her serve there for an extra year without counting that as overage on her time in grade."

"I'll be happy to get the report in your hands within the next five minutes," the first mate said. "I'll simply go to Mash, let him know it looks like One Green may be opening up, and ask him if he has anything he can present to suggest himself as a suitable candidate for the opening."

"Do it," the captain said, and the first mate shot out of the room like a man on fire.

He was as good as his word.

He wasn't even back when the captain's wristcom whispered to him, and he nodded.

He turned to Melie. "That's his report. Can you bring up yours?"

She nodded. "If you can remove my restraints, I can transfer it to you from here."

He nodded to the crew member standing guard behind Melie. "Take them off her."

Kagen watched the crew member tap her wristcom and an instant later, the captain's wristcom whispered to him again.

He flicked a finger, and both reports appeared in the space in front of him, reversed from Kagen's perspective. He flipped through each at tremendous speed, and after just moments, he said, "All right. The security detail is going to be delayed here just a bit longer. When I've finished with you and Kagen, I want night security and day security to go together, armored and armed, and pick up Mash and move him to the brig. I'll come with you to get him out of his room without giving him the chance to destroy his private files, and to present the charges once you have restrained him.

"Melie, you have two choices. You can either take what you've earned and cash out now, or you can be demoted to Two Gold with no promotion for one year, but no disqualification for the time spent."

She looked a little pale, but she said, "I'll stay."

And then the captain turned to Kagen.

"Do you have anything to say for yourself?"

Kagen considered. "I did what seemed to me the most just and proper thing I could, based on the situation I believed myself to be in and on what I knew of the girl in the core unit." He paused, still thinking, then decided to add, "Because of who Lithra is to me, and because she should never have been sentenced to death, I would do the same thing again if opportunity presented itself."

The captain sighed. "Thank you for your honesty, no matter how damaging to your case it happens to be."

He stared down at the table, drumming the fingers of his right hand on the surface in an irritable, quick pattern.

He sighed again. "You have done a brilliant, irreversible job of destroying what has been one of the most promising careers I've seen anyone put together. You have demonstrated an impulsiveness that makes you impossible to keep on as a crew member. You have destroyed the shipowner's property, have released a convicted criminal from a mandatory death sentence, and have allowed emotion to sway you into dereliction of duty.

"By any standard of space law, I have the absolute right to drop you off at the nearest Needle with no papers, no recommendation, and no money, and let you fend for yourself. Furthermore, that is the sentence that best fits within my guidelines as *Longview* captain."

Kagen braced himself.

The captain looked at the ship's representative. "Does the owner wish to involve himself in sentencing?"

Kagen watched Shay listen to her shipcom, nod, murmur something he could not hear, and then say, "As you wish."

She turned to the Kagen directly. "The owner wishes to pass sentence himself, if the captain will defer." She turned to the captain.

"I'll defer. Happily, in this instance."

"Very well. Kagen, you have been given two choices. Because the owner was moved by Lithra's story of her love for you, and by what you tried to do for her—ignoring the criminality of what you did—he has chosen to impose a lighter sentence than what the captain would have to make.

"Your first choice is to select a world on our circuit on which you'll debark. You'll take with you all money you earned on the *Longview*, and will leave with only your record up to the end of your stint in Three Gold. No mention will be made of your promotion, your test scores or points toward promotion. You will go out as a Three Gold who chose to terminate with the *Longview* in search of other employment, and who became a passenger when you made this decision so that we could train your replacement while you were aboard."

He looked at her and swallowed hard.

"You wish to say something?"

"That's... very generous."

"Yes," she agreed. "It is." She stared into his eyes, and he felt himself wanting to squirm.

"Your other option is... very different. The owner has offered to make a core unit available to you. If you choose to take this option you will wait, exactly as Lithra is waiting. At some point in the future, the laws under which she has been sentenced to death may be changed, or the government that sentenced her may cease to exist in its current political structure, or the Pact may change its ruling on the death sentence, at which point her sentence will be negated, and she will be freed. If this happens, you will be freed along with her. Neither of you will be any older than you are now, and you will at that time be able to pursue whatever relationship you may desire."

She was still looking into his eyes, searching for some truth about him that he could not begin to guess.

"Understand," she continued, "that there is no guarantee she will ever be released, and hence, no guarantee that you will ever be released. There is no guarantee that you will still love each other if you are, and no guarantee if you do that you will have any sort of future together. Your current existence will stop when you are in the core, and may never resume. Your money will accrue for you— the owner will treat it as a Level Two crew investment, since this appears to have been the point of contention that caused your dispute with Mash. But there is no guarantee that you will ever claim it."

He stood there, feeling Lithra's arms around him, feeling her lips pressed to his once more. She was still alive—if only after a fashion—and she had known him, had loved him.

He could make it in the universe with what the owner had generously offered to him. He could find another ship, become part of another crew, and someday he might once again have the chance to own a ship and captain it through the stars.

But he was on a ship in which the woman he loved loved him back. She was locked away in one of those cores... and she had not been afraid to re-enter it. She had almost seemed eager to go back.

He had earlier been willing to go into the core without any hope of ever seeing her again.

How could he turn down the chance to go in with the hope that one day the two of them might be together?

"I'll take the core," he said.

The owner's representative nodded. "I thought you might."

Chapter 7

This Criminal

There was death. And now there isn't.

This criminal wakes—but the waking is all wrong. Sunlight blinds its eyes, and it cries from fear and shock, and arms hold it, and a voice comforts it.

This criminal has a body it cannot control. It cannot speak. It cannot ask.

It remembers what it was, but that is no longer what it is.

Yet the voice comforts it. The arms hold it.

After a while, this criminal stops fighting.

And it sleeps.

Afterword

This series wasn't born in the usual manner. Most of the time, if I come up with a series idea, it's because I sat down and intentionally brainstormed concepts until I figured one out.

But I would have sworn the only stories I was going to write in Settled Space would have Cadence Drake as the main character.

Here's how I tripped over *The Longview.*

I was writing *Warpaint,* the sequel to *Hunting the Corrigan's Blood.* And I was having an awful time getting the scale of the ship in my head. I'd done a ship layout on quad paper, and had my scale figured out. I knew where things were. But the drawing was about seven inches long from nose to tail, and Cady's ship was about 280 feet (about 87 meters) from nose to tail.

I was having trouble looking at that tiny line drawing and visualizing Cady and her crew moving around inside the ship, and, as frequently happens when I'm struggling with a story problem, I had this crazy idea.

I thought, *I can just build the damn thing in Minecraft, and go inside it and walk around and then I'll know what it's like in there.*

So I figured one block for one meter and I carefully laid out the ship, following my schematic. Built the whole thing, furnished it, filled it with secret areas and notes to myself about who went where (stuck on signs.)

And then, because it was so incredibly useful to stand in the middle of the ship and know exactly what my characters could see and do, where they could go, and how they could get there, I built the other two ships from the *Cadence Drake* series so far.

And then I built the *Bailey's Irish Space Station* for the upcoming third novel in the series, *The Wishbone Conspiracy*.

I was hooked, you see. Having these places that I could walk around in was fun...but better than being fun, the places I'd built were talking to me. They were telling me stories.

But then I ran out of things to build.

The little voice in my head whispered, *How about building an ancient, mysterious spaceship from the days before TFN travel, when people were trying to colonize space in giant sleeper ships? Just for fun. No pressure. You aren't going to use it. You'll just build it.*

I may have an odd idea of fun, but I started building that mammoth ship. And floating through its vast reaches, feeling the dark and the weight around it, I realized its first inhabitants never reached their destination. I understood that when it was salvaged, the person who bought it and retrofitted it was going to have to be someone odd. Someone with a secret plan, and a hidden past.

Someone with a use for a ship that big that had absolutely nothing to do with the ship's apparent purpose.

Suddenly I wasn't building a spaceship for fun anymore. I had to know what was going on.

And here we are. I hope you'll accompany me through the next episode, when we'll rejoin the crew of *The Longview* as they deal with the extraordinary interstellar ruckus caused by *The Selling of Suzee Delight*... and look a little deeper into the lives of the folks from this tale.

Holly Lisle
Thursday, April 3, 2014

THE Selling of Suzee Delight

TALES FROM THE LONGVIEW

HOLLY LISLE

For Matthew

Chapter 1

Transcript: Suzee Delight—Preliminary Death Sentencing
Interview #1

Danyal Travers, SPORC Capital Offenses Interviewer, Cheegoth: Prisoner, you have stated your professional name and ident. For the record, who are you?

SUZEE DELIGHT, First Courtesan, Court of the Diamond Dome, Mariposa Pleasure City, Cheegoth: *What* I am was chosen for me when I was nine years old, when the Educational Selectors discovered that I could sing and dance and play musical instruments and draw pretty pictures—and when they also discovered that my aptitude for science and mathematics was even stronger than my aptitude for the arts. Wishing to suppress my mathematical and science interests and to encourage my entertainment abilities, my Selector removed me from the General Consumer cohort, named me Tawny Girl, and placed me on the Introductory Arts and Pleasures track. I was trained to be a consort.

Because I exhibited superior skills and ability to learn and equally because I was obedient, when I was twelve I was placed into Advanced Arts and Pleasures and renamed Sweet Silver. Along with my physical and entertainment training, I began learning languages, courtesies, and what the Pleasure Masters refer to as Polite Observational Skills.

DANYAL (INTERRUPTING): Spying.

SUZEE DELIGHT: I've heard it called that. I do not think that is the correct word. My training teaches that as a consort and courtesan, my service to my profession must consist of equal parts information gathering and recording on my clients, and the providing of entertainment and pleasure for my clients.

THIRD VOICE: Suppress that, Travers. That does not go into the public record.

DANYAL: I've deleted that. Prisoner, please continue.

SUZEE DELIGHT: By the age of seventeen, I had learned so far beyond the rest of my Pleasure cohort that I was moved into Masters training in Arts and Pleasures. At that time, I was renamed Suzee Delight, and for the past six years I have been the First Courtesan of Diamond Dome. I have served at the direction of the Pleasure Masters, and at the pleasure of my clients.

DANYAL: While the information you have given is true, it does not answer my question. *Who* are you?

· · ·

SUZEE DELIGHT: I'm sorry. I don't understand your question.

DANYAL: You murdered the Administrators of the five most populous and powerful Pact Worlds. You did so during a seduction dance performed for all five men at once, using a knife that you could not possibly have had, hidden beneath your costume and... on... on...

(The sound of the interviewer taking a deep breath is followed by a long silence.)

(Audio resumes.)

You killed all five of them before any one could warn the others. Our holos show that you never hesitated, that you never missed a step, that not one of the men had any inkling of his danger or made any move to protect himself when you killed him.

SUZEE DELIGHT: Yes. I am a remarkable dancer. And I killed them quickly because I wished to be merciful. I had always considered them dear friends.

DANYAL: Prisoner, I want an answer to the question I *asked* you. Someone planted you in the Diamond Dome, someone gave you the order to kill the Administrators, someone gave you the knife, someone put you up to this. *Who are you really?*

SUZEE DELIGHT: You are mistaken in several ways. First, I am not a *who*. I am a *what*. I am the product of my training. Every moment of my life since I was tested at the age of nine has been recorded; every action I have taken with every man and woman who has paid for pleasure from me is available to you in full holographic detail. Second, in every encounter with every client, I have acted on my training, and I have done exactly what that training has dictated I do—including the encounter for which I am now here.

· · ·

DANYAL: You're saying that you acted on your own—that you murdered the five Pact Worlds Administrators because your whore training required that you do so?

SUZEE DELIGHT: I am a courtesan. I don't know what training whores receive. My lifetime of training as a *courtesan* required that once I learned and verified the truth about my old friends and long-time clients—Radiva Kels, Stannal Bregat, Nethamatnu Ha, Soth Smithe, and Kiero Chenzwa—I had to stop them before they could commit the crime they planned.

AND THE ONLY way I could stop them, because of the enormity of the crime they were planning and how close they were to committing it, was to kill them. They were going to legalize sla—

THIRD VOICE: OH, GOD! Delete, delete, delete! Stop the interview, get her out back to her cell, and delete that entire last bit.
(The sound of someone pushing buttons while warnings sounded, and then a long pause.)

DANYAL: Prisoner, we'll resume this interview at a later time.

Suzee Delight

I LIED TO DANYAL TRAVERS. I know exactly who and what I am.

A courtesan is a whore with a good education, and what I am is the best-educated whore in the Pact Worlds—and the most famous one. I'm Suzee Delight, and from my original songs and dances and my *Paint Beautiful Pictures as Suzee Delight* Senso series, on through my instructional pleasure moves and positions, and right up to my studio-recorded personal full-Senso sessions with famous clients, my mass-appeal products sell to more than three billion men and women across Settled Space. The Pleasure Masters make a great deal of money off of me.

As for who I am...?

Well, I'm the woman who, as a little girl, wanted to be a scientist and design custom nanoviral augmentations for GenDaring on Bailey's Irish Space Station.

When, during my Wish Conference back when I was nine, I told my Educational Selector that I wanted to leave the Pact Worlds and become a citizen of Bailey's Irish so I could make tiger people and pony people, he should have let me go.

Now—because he didn't—I'm going to destroy the whole poisonous, corrupt Pact Covenants system and every power player in it.

The five great men who had entrusted me with their pleasure and privacy had come to the Diamond Dome to make use of me... but also to write law—to modify the final language of the Covenants of the Pact.

They had a clever plan to become even richer and more powerful, though at the expense of the people they supposedly served.

And that's where I come in. The life I wanted to live was taken away from me when I was nine.

In truth, it was taken away from me when I was born, but I did not find out that I was an Assisted child and that my government would choose my life path for me until my ninth birthday.

My life—the life I wanted—was over a long time ago. My execution—if that is where I end—will be the conclusion of my long humiliation and pain.

But if I die, I'm going to bury the people who did this to me right along with me.

How?

It starts with my comment during my interview about me being nothing beyond the thing their training created.

I put that into the interview with Danyal Travers because I knew the new Administrator of Cheegoth was listening in, as were my

Pleasure Masters, the Educational Selectors, and everyone else in the whole corrupt Personal Skills and Educational Tracking and Optimization system.

By stating categorically that my training required me to kill my clients once I knew and had validated that they were planning to commit a crime against the Pacts of the Covenant, I sent everyone responsible for my education back through every bit of it from the day I was old enough to toddle into General Consumer training at the age of two.

While they task ever more resources into dissecting those stored holos and figuring out where I came up with my justification for murder—and at the same time put more resources into searching for outsiders who might have somehow implanted in me a trigger they could use from afar—I have both the time and the means to contact an old client who promised to help me out should I ever find myself in a situation where I had to do something that was both right... and criminal.

Chapter 2

Charlie

C harlie, the *Longview's* Mandatory Pact Covenant Observer, sat in Passenger Room 5, her *Longview* quarters, and on split screens watched what was being billed as the holocast of the century, presented by ever-smiling Danyal Travers, who had been covering the story for days. Each of Charlie's two screens showed a different datastream of the same event.

On the left screen, she had the official Pact Worlds coverage of the public confession and sentencing of Suzee Delight, First Courtesan of the Diamond Dome, superstar goddess of a thousand Sensos—some actually suitable for general audiences—and reputed simultaneous murderer of the Administrators of the five most important Pact Worlds.

On the right screen, she had the raw, siphoned, underground version of the same feed. If Charlie's Pact Worlds controller ever discovered that she watched unofficial feeds of anything streamed from the Pact Worlds, he would recall her and drop her citizenship level to F-10: Permanently Unemployable, Sentenced to Minimal Survival Assistance Only.

However, as long as she was assigned to the *Longview* and had Passenger Room 5 to herself, she was safe. If she did her job and made sure the Pact Worlds received a steady stream of money in exchange for their sentenced criminals, she could hope to remain aboard the *Longview*, where she was treated better than she'd ever been treated in her life, for at least a couple more years before she received mandatory rotation orders.

Charlie's only objective where her controller was concerned was to remain unremarkable—to do an average job, turn in average numbers, and in all ways be an invisible cog in the Pact Worlds' massive machine.

So she was content that the *Longview*, rumored to be the most profitable Death Circus franchise in Settled Space for its owner, only managed to stay in the middle of the pack where its profits on criminals bought and sold was concerned. How its owner made his *other* money was officially none of her concern.

Unofficially…

…Well, anything she knew, she might be able to use to her own benefit. And she'd made it her business to know a lot.

Until she found a way to use what she knew, Charlie had decided that if she received rotation or recall orders, she planned to defect. Her defection details were fuzzy, but she was getting them together.

Meanwhile, however, she was in a position to make a difference for people the Pact Worlds considered fodder.

So she watched, tense, anxious, and at the same time hopeful.

Left-side Suzee said, "I am ashamed of my actions. I betrayed the trust of five men I loved, and used my position of trust to murder them because I envied them their power."

Right-side Suzee said, "I am not ashamed of my actions. These five men betrayed the people they served. They planned to use their positions of trust and power to destroy the autonomy of the citizens they claim to represent."

The cutwork on the official version had been skillfully done. Charlie couldn't see or hear the blending between the segments that were actually Suzee's words, and those that had been inserted.

Most of Settled Space would see the raw version, would know the venom in Travers' voice as he asked her the questions, would see his eyes glitter as he envisioned her eventual fate.

Most citizens of the Pact Worlds, however, would only have access to the official version, which had little truth in it.

Left-side Suzee said, "I failed my government, my educators, my selectors, my trainers, my clients, and my profession as a courtesan —the highest calling to which any woman can aspire."

Right-side Suzee said, "I accuse my government, my educators, my selectors, my trainers, and my clients for creating laws that make being a courtesan the highest work to which any woman can aspire."

"Damned right," Charlie muttered. "You tell 'em, Suzee."

Charlie had been lucky enough to be born homely and lacking in any discernible entertainment skills—she had been channeled into a low-level government job from which neither her intelligence nor her competence would ever elevate her. But her other government-designated career track had been D-3 Convenience Prostitute, and only the the shortage of PCOs caused by the higher suicide rate in the D-3 Pact Covenant Observer career field had saved her from that fate. The people she had to watch burn themselves to death on People's Home of Truth and Fairness worlds haunted her. The executions she had to certify haunted her. She didn't question for an instant the reason D-3 PCOs had the highest suicide rate of any career field in the Pact Worlds.

Her plan was to disappear from her job before it devoured her, too.

In front of her, left-side Suzee said, "Because I am guilty of five murders of men designated A-1, and because I freely confess that I committed these murders by intent..."

Right-side Suzee also said, "Because I am guilty of five murders of men designated A-1, and because I freely confess that I committed these murders by intent..."

Left-side and right-side Suzees both said, "I waive my right to trial in order to save the Pact Worlds the cost of such trial when the outcome is already certain, and instead elect to sell my death to the highest-bidding Death Circus, where my execution will be streamed for all viewers on all Pact Worlds. All Pact Worlds citizens need to be able to see me receiving the consequences of my actions."

Charlie didn't the hear Suzee's last few words, however.

She was out the door and shooting herself onto the *Longview's* passenger bridge transport, screaming, "I need to speak to the owner, I need to speak to the owner now!"

Shay, the owner's representative, was on the bridge waiting for her when the passenger transport unlocked.

"Suzee Delight is selling herself to the highest-bidding Death Circus now," Charlie shouted.

Both the captain and first mate looked back at the two of them.

Shay looked startled, then pleased. "Oh, that's excellent. You and I will go to the owner's quarters, Charlie. His condition is bothering him again, so he won't meet with you personally, but you and I will talk, and he'll watch us and relay suggestions to me." She paused. "I'm assuming that you've brought this to me because you hope the owner will buy Suzee Delight's execution."

"Of course."

"Because you want to be the one to witness it?"

Shay's suggestion was as far from Charlie's truth as it was possible to get.

But Charlie shrugged and nodded. "That... is as good an explanation as any."

The corners of Shay's mouth twitched. "You have good entrepreneurial instincts. Come with me, then. I'll let the owner know we have an investment opportunity for him."

Suzee Delight

I'm locked inside a large Senso recording studio with four moleibond walls, a moleibond ceiling, and a moleibond floor. My captors are recording every instant of my captivity, and are selling the feed at several price-points, the least expensive being "Suitable for all viewers," and the most expensive, which does not include any blurring or decency shielding, and which does include full-Senso connectivity, being "Live Suzee Delight's Last Days: Credit Rating A and above only."

My cell contains a luxurious transparent bathtub and non-bubbling body wash; a Nestor Insta-Dress wardrobe programmed to instantly create any of thousands of exotic costumes for me—all of them see-through; a silk-sheeted bed; my musical instruments and art supplies and the necessary equipment to use them; a transparent dining table and chair; a small but elegant reconsta unit with Bailey's Irish Reconsta—because the Senso viewers would complain and rate the Senso badly if they had to taste sub-par reconsta while living inside my skin with me—and a set of specific instructions on what I am to do with myself while I wait to be sold.

Before I was locked in my cell, my final Pleasure Master told me exactly what will happen to me while I'm waiting if I do not obey that list. It will not be pleasant, but there are certain Senso buyers who will pay a premium for the experience, should I decide to indulge them by being disobedient.

They are not the buyers I ever hope to entertain.

So I am still doing the work I hate. Making prison Sensos for Suzee Delight fans—and making one last fortune for the Pact Worlds.

Because it amuses the Pleasure Masters who have caged me to let me know how much money the Pact Worlds are making from my imprisonment and will make from my execution, they've placed a sales board for the feed and Senso on the control corridor. I can always see it, but the viewers and Senso fans cannot. To people looking at my world through my eyes, it will be edited to read as a pretty wall.

Three hours after the Death Circus bidding opened, my imprisonment recordings are already outselling everything else I've ever done.

It hurts me that the same people who claimed to love me are leaping at the opportunity to indulge in my destruction.

I entertain them as I've been told to do, and I watch the boards.

The Death Circus bidding has already started, too—three hours in, low bids from small Death Circuses I've never heard of have given way to bigger and more profitable circuses.

The name of the ship I'm hoping to see has not yet flashed across the board, though. Three hours in, twenty ships have dropped out of a field of over a hundred. His ship is not among them—and wasn't even in the showing early on.

He told me his ship was a successful Death Circus, but I have no idea how successful. Perhaps it will not be able to afford to bid on me.

He told me if I ever found a need to escape, he would find his way to me. And maybe he meant that, but something is standing in his way.

Unlike many of my clients, he never made a pretense of love. But he expressed great admiration for my skill and intelligence. Perhaps he was only being kind.

Perhaps—like the words of so many others—his words had nothing behind them.

Perhaps he wasn't as important or powerful as he claimed to be, and now that I had put myself in his hands, they were tied, and he could do nothing to get his ship to me.

Perhaps I believed him simply because he never hurt me.

And perhaps I'll never know the truth.

I murdered the five chief Pact Worlds Administrators because it was the right thing to do. I do not regret it.

But in the back of my mind, I held as my private reward the promise that I would escape punishment for my crime.

And perhaps—like every other part of my life but one—this last piece of my existence will betray me.

Chapter 3

Charlie

Charlie sat across from Shay at the owner's table.

Shay was still arguing that the execution of Suzee Delight would be profitable enough to consider as a major investment, and though Charlie couldn't hear the owner's end of it, Shay's reactions demonstrated that he wasn't convinced of the value of this expense.

Charlie was looking through the Pact rules for some sweetener that would get him involved. She had her reasons for wanting him to win the bidding, none of which were what she'd claimed to Shay. But her incentive was enormous, so even though the cause seemed lost, she kept digging.

Digging through the two-hundred-screen subsection of the Selling Of Execution Rights amendment of the Pact Covenants addenda, she finally struck gold.

"Shay!" she whispered, "I've got it. If he bids in the top one percent of all prisoner execution bids ever, he'll get exclusive control over the content, packaging, formatting, distribution, and reselling of the entire execution, plus relevant explanatory or investigative content produced or repurposed by bidders' contractors."

Shay said, "Wait, mado, we've just discovered the perfect investment format for you." And to Charlie, she mouthed the words, "How much?"

Charlie was streaming the numbers even as Shay asked. "The aggregate of the top one percent of bidded executions right now is $753,884,600 rucets. Rounding up."

"Less than a billion rucets total, then. So a one-billion-rucet bid will force the execution into a private rights situation, mado," Shay said. "If you win this bid, you will acquire all presentation and resale rights of the entire execution, from start to finish, in whatever format you wish to offer it, along with related content you wish to have created." She listened, then turned back to Charlie. "He wants to know if rights include choice of location of execution, type of execution, and disposal of remains? He's asking about her genome rights, physical copyrights, and possibilities for entertainment cloning."

"It's an all-rights package," Charlie said after a quick search. "The remaining Pact Administrators won't love the idea of him offering physical copies of her—her being a five-strike murderer who killed their kind—but if he pays the money and wins, he gets the rights."

Shay passed that on, and a big smile spread across her face. "He's bidding now. One billion rucets. It may not be the final bid, but he's determined to have her. He'll pay whatever he needs to pay to get her." Shay paused, looked thoughtfully at Charlie, and said, "Helping us like this isn't going to create a problem between you and your employers, is it?"

"I just got a minimum one-billion-rucet bid on a criminal for my controller, who gets to claim income I generate as his credit. In no universe would that get me in trouble."

She kept her mouth shut about the thing that would.

Kagen

The last think Kagen remembered was the faceplate of a core unit on the *Longview* sliding shut above him, and the captain standing over him saying, "Inhale slowly and count backwards from ten."

He awoke in a bed. An uncomfortable one, with a hard, thin mattress, worn sheets, and a view that consisted of water-stained acoustic ceiling tiles.

His nose itched.

Drowsily, he tried to scratch it, and discovered that his hands were tied to the bed.

He was instantly and fully awake. Scared, he began shouting, and voices to either side of him bellowed, "Shut up, you lunatic!"

He tried to turn his head, and discovered that he couldn't do that either.

"Hey!" he yelled. "Hey! Someone! Help me!"

That elicited a response. He heard footsteps, and after a moment a woman dressed in gray striped coveralls moved into his field of vision.

"Did you shout?"

"Yes," he said. "Where am I?"

She didn't answer his question. Instead she spoke into a bead implanted on her wrist. "305-C is conscious."

The voice on the other end of the bead said, "Combative?"

"Not this time. Seems like he might have come out of it."

"Get a history if you can. I'll be down in five."

"On it." She turned to him, and stroked her finger across the bead. It began to glow. She dropped her wrist and said, "Ellah Tan, adding to case history on Jondo-305-C-K7491-Smithside." Her eyes focused on him and she said, "My name is Ellah Tan. I'm your repair rep. State your name and ident."

"I'm Kagen..." He paused. Kagen was his crew name, and went with his ident as *Longview* crew. But he'd lost his place on the *Longview* over a woman he'd known as We-T74G, whose new name was Lithra.

He had volunteered for long sleep in a core unit just to have a chance at being with her again.

To the best of his knowledge, he no longer had a crew name or ident—but his original name and ident would connect him back to People's Home of Truth and Fairness 14-B, the world that had sentenced him to volunteer his own death either through starvation or by stepping into the vacuum of space.

The woman was studying him. "Jondo, now that you're awake I need your name and ident to clear you and get you back into the real world. I can see in your eyes that you know who you are, but if you don't tell me, you're stuck here with no ident. Someone found you on a side street down in Smithside, and as far as we can tell, you don't exist. Until you exist, you stay with us. So. Do you want to stay tied to this bed?"

He didn't. He decided an out-of-date ident was better than none. "Name: Kagen. *Longview* crew ident: Rebus-47-Cargo."

"Kagen R-47-C, that's a short ident."

"Not a lot of crew on the *Longview.*"

"Thank you." She told him, "You're in the Smithside Emergency Center. When you were found, you had no drugs or intoxicants in your system, you had no money or ID on you, and whoever you ran into took the time to pound you into a pretty fine paste. What were you doing in Smithside?"

"I don't know. I've never heard of Smithside. I don't have any idea where I am. I was supposed to be in a sleeper unit on the *Longview.*"

"And the *Longview* is...?"

"A space transport for convicted capital-offense criminals."

"It's a good thing *Longview's* dock records confirm you as crew. We'd hate to have to treat you as a capital-offense criminal." She shrugged. "All right. I'll check to see if the ship is docked, and if it is, we'll get you back aboard. But if it's gone, you're going to be marooned here on an indigent pass. We don't keep indigents. Which means the city will give you temporary room and board, but from the day you move into quarters, you have exactly thirty days to start earning enough money to cover your room rent and your food, and six months from there to get out of temporary housing and into your own accommodations. If you fail, you'll be put aboard the first spaceship that docks that's taking strays."

Kagen knew all about his odds if he ended up being designated a stray. Bad, and worse.

"I'll find work. I have skills," he said, then asked, "Where am I?"

"You got lucky," she said. "Whoever dumped you didn't hate you. You're in the City of Furies."

He couldn't believe what she'd said. "There really is one?" He sounded like an idiot, and he guessed the expression on his face made him look like a man who'd just discovered he'd won his own spaceship in a contest he hadn't even entered. But... "Really?" he whispered.

The woman—Ellah—smiled for the first time. "Good reaction. You might do all right here."

Ellah returned just moments later to tell Kagen the *Longview* had left a few days earlier, and that it would not return until the ship had another special delivery for the Pinnacle. She told him no ships were permitted to include the City of Furies on a regular route, so it could be weeks, months, or years before the *Longview* came around again.

He was classed as Visitor, Trial Period 30.

Ellah told him he wouldn't be charged for his Medix repairs because the city had been unable to identify and arrest the person or persons who had damaged him. So to his benefit, at least he had no starting debt.

She turned him over to the indigent liaison for the Emergency Center. He set up Kagen's housing, fused a temporary com bead onto his left wrist and embedded an eario, and provided him with a thirty-day provisional pass to the city. Then he called transport for Kagen, and told the vehicle to use Tour Guide mode before taking him home.

The sleek red one-seater floated Kagen up into the traffic lanes, above a small but glistening city, colorful and complex, surrounded by an octagon of shining gold walls.

He realized he had seen a painting of the city during a recreational leave. He couldn't remember where he'd been at the time, but he remembered stopping to look at it, to trace its broad walk-ways and admire the details of its airstream traffic and the artist's focus on the beauty of its buildings and landscapes. No one had suggested the little city was real.

"Welcome to the City of Furies," the Tour Guide said. "We'll begin at the Pinnacle, and spiral outward through the Eight Arms, and I'll tell you about the most important buildings below us and how they affect the operation of the city as we pass over them. Should you miss important details, you may access this program again at any time during your stay via your com bead, and take a walking tour or hire an aerovan to see each location. On your right..."

Kagen lost the voice, let the words flow over him without hearing any of them. He was in the City of Furies, which was cred-ited as the home of many of Settled Space's most controversial artists, musicians, writers, scientists, engineers—hell, anyone who created anything that didn't fit with some government's or religion's Truth was rumored to end up there.

But no world claimed the City of Furies. No ships booked passage there. Most people—and Kagen had numbered himself among them—believed the city didn't exist. Reasonable people assumed it was a name concocted by the wishful downtrodden, who needed to believe there was some place in the universe where people were truly and fully free and where someone gave a damn about them.

"To your left, the long alabaster building is the Open University of Unconventional Studies..."

People said that the City of Furies manufactured and exported free thinking—and those products, stories, songs, holos, and other creations rumored to come from the city were always better-made and better-functioning than products from known origins. They were also always subversive in one way or another.

They required that users look at themselves and their lives differ-ently in order to make their purchases work—and those new ways always reminded users that their lives and desires were meaningful and valuable to them. That the skills they'd learned belonged to them to use for their own survival first. That their thoughts were worthwhile even if they mattered only to the individual thinking them.

City of Furies products told people they mattered, not as parts of some bigger whole, but as individuals. Not as cogs in a machine, but as people.

Kagen had thought it was a clever marketing scheme. He had not been a believer.

And now he was in the city.

"The bright red building below and to your right is the Howert Building. It began manufacturing..."

The City of Furies wasn't some imaginary place, a figment of wishes and dreams. It was real, with real deadlines and real demands—and his first deadline was to pull himself together, understand how this place worked, and then advance within its rules toward... something. Maybe something that could someday let him earn his way back to his dream of becoming the captain of his own TFN transport.

He needed to get on track quickly, because the kinds of ships that took on strays usually sold them to slavers. He'd found freedom too wonderful to conceive of losing it again.

He did a mental inventory of his skills. He was intelligent. He was competent. He was willing to work hard, so long as he was able to reap the benefits of his work.

He didn't let himself linger too long on the question that was first in his mind: Why had the *Longview* dumped him?

He had no sense of time having passed, but he realized that ten minutes or a thousand years could have gone by while he was suspended in the core unit, and it would have been the same to him.

If significant time had passed, perhaps Lithra had died.

Or perhaps she had been freed.

Most likely, she was still in her core unit on the *Longview*. Most likely, he had been offloaded because the owner needed his unit for someone else.

But when he was on his feet, he would search for Lithra. Maybe he could find a way for them to be together.

Chapter 4

Shay

"We're looking for the following criteria: public execution with paid observers present; subject awake and alert until the moment of death; subject able to speak clearly until the moment of death; no face or head mutilation because she still has to be beautiful when she's dead; process of execution causes visible pain and suffering sufficient to cause distress to a significant portion of the observers; process of execution lasts at least twelve hours and up to several days," Shay told Charlie, and watched her eyes go wide.

"Days! That's horrible," Charlie said. "Why do we need to make it so… awful?"

The two of them were going to be studying case histories of all the high-profile executions of Pact Worlds citizens, looking into the setting up and marketing of the ones that had been carried out directly by Death Circuses instead of being sold to third parties.

"We're going to make sure people can see it's horrible because it *is* horrible," Shay told her. "Because Suzee Delight is a celebrity even outside the Pact Worlds, and there are people from all walks of life who know who she is, and who will watch her execution.

"And many of those people know her in a way they have known few other human beings—they have *been* her through her Sensos.

"Those Sensos, and her music and dance and paintings, and her famous clients from everywhere in Settled Space, they all create a connection. Her death will command the attention. And we need to prolong the execution in order to make room for sponsor messages, and keep Suzee awake and alert and able to communicate for the entire conclusion of her life, in order to keep the audience connected to her for the longest possible time. Minutes are money."

"You're talking about torture."

The look on Charlie's face as she said that told Shay that Charlie was closer to breaking than she had suspected. The average tour of duty of a Pact Covenant Observer on the *Longview* was about three years, after which they started hunting around the ship, looking for ways to kill themselves.

Charlie had already lasted twice as long as the average PCO, but Shay knew that Charlie had a sharp and clever mind, and hope. And most importantly, a secret plan. Shay liked people who had secret plans.

She said, "There might be other alternatives, which is part of what we're looking for. But it's probably going to come down to torture. Mado Keyr did not open his bid at one billion rucets to kill Suzee Delight in one minute. If he wins the bidding, he needs to recoup his enormous investment, and make a profit on top of that. This has to be huge."

Charlie closed her eyes. She looked both sick and exhausted.

"Consider," Shay said. "Her many fans and admirers will want a spectacle because they imagine that they loved her, and they'll want to understand how she could have done what she did, and then see her come to a memorable end for doing it. If we can figure out a way to give them Suzee's life in a meaningful way, they'll want to participate. To have *their* say in what's happening.

"Meanwhile," she continued, "the Pact Worlds' many governments will want a frightening spectacle with moral overtones, because Suzee Delight held a position of deep trust, and used it to slaughter five of their top men. Nearly every Pact Worlds Administrator or high-level official uses women or men like Suzee, and some of them will have used Suzee herself. They'll want to be sure no consort or courtesan or citizen will ever consider doing what she's done. They'll want their citizens to see what happens to pretty young women who do such wicked things—and they'll hope to make sure that what their people see will deter future murders.

"Finally," she said, "Mado Keyr will want a spectacle because he's already hired a major production company at considerable expense in order to tie them into an exclusivity deal. For the money he's already paid, as well as the money he'll pay if he wins the bidding, he'll be getting 90% of the proceeds on every minute of every subscription sold to the locked data-stream feed of her execution. Plus income from the after-death marketing of any private holos, Sensos, or other materials found by his investigation team before her death and published afterward."

Charlie shuddered. "You're so calm about this. So... unbothered."

Shay sighed. "I'm not. I have my own thoughts about this, and my own issues. But the owner didn't hire me for what I feel. I'm going to make sure he gets his money's worth out of the execution, because that's part of what he pays me to do. Suzee Delight has to be executed. She chose to be executed via Death Circus. In order to keep its franchise, whichever Death Circus wins her is going to have to kill her publicly, and is going to have to have one of you folks in place to verify her death. All we can do within those limits is the best job we can do."

"You mind if I ask you a personal question?"

"No."

"What is your definition of *the best job we can do?*"

Shay gave her a sidelong glance. Charlie was a thinker, a closet subversive who hated the Pact Worlds. Charlie hid this, because she didn't know whom on board she could trust—but at some point, she'd started to trust Shay a little. So Shay gave her an honest answer. "I think the best job we can do is to let people see who the real Suzee Delight is during the execution—and give her an opportunity before she dies to say everything she wants to say in a forum that the Pact Worlds cannot manipulate."

Charlie stared at her own hands, considering that. And then a broad, startled grin spread across her face. "The locked feed. Everyone pays to see it, and everyone sees the same thing."

She was, Shay thought, a bright woman. "Exactly."

"So the Pact Worlds won't have any official feed. They'll be able to cut off transmission, but they won't be able to manipulate what's sent."

"The contract between Death Circuses and the Pact Worlds goes two ways," Shay said. "If they sell a prisoner to us, and then interfere with our profit from the sale, they will be in breach of contract, and will become liable for every rucet we lose because of their actions. The Pact Worlds aren't rich. They cannot afford to cut transmissions."

"Oh, my…" Charlie whispered. "Then… what does she have to say, do you suppose?"

Shay leaned back in her seat and locked her hands behind her head. "She killed five of the richest and most powerful men in not just the Pact Worlds, but all of Settled Space. I think it would be interesting to hear her tell everyone *why*."

Charlie was watching her with narrowed eyes. "And the owner… what does he want?"

"Much the same thing. For his own reasons—controversy sells, and is immensely profitable; he does not like the Pact Worlds or the slavers or the fact that executions are an entertainment business; and —this goes no farther than you and me—I suspect he knows Suzee Delight personally, and was in love with her at one time. May be in love with her still."

Charlie murmured, "Oh. I'm so happy to hear that. He loves her, so we'll *pretend* to execute her. I'll verify her faked death. I'll be happy to do that. Though if you can hide me afterwards, I'll be grateful."

Inwardly, Shay smiled. "I wish we could do that," she said. "But, no. We have to execute her. She has to die, and die for real. Her death cannot be faked. The people who buy tickets to see her execution live at the execution site must know that she is truly dead. And the people who ordered her execution must know she's dead as absolute and inarguable fact.

"So she will die, and you will certify her death by the method required by Pact Covenant law, and she will be gone from this world in all but memory. What we have to do in order to make her death meaningful is make sure that her memory lingers."

Charlie froze, staring for a long moment at Shay. Then she hung her head. "I'd hoped that we could save her somehow."

She gave a good performance, Shay thought. Woman Whose Hope Has Been Crushed By An Ally. But Shay's instincts told her Charlie's hanging head and crushed expression was *just* a performance. "She's an incredible human being," Shay said. "She deserves better."

Charlie nodded, still not looking Shay in the eyes. "Killing her would be the real crime."

Suzee Delight

I was amazed when the bidding hit a billion rucets two days ago—an enormous jump from the twenty-four million rucet previous bid.

At that point, the Pact Worlds announced that the new bid forced a rule change. All bidders from that point on had twelve Standard hours in which to present their next bids, and each would present them at the same time—2400 Standard.

All bids would show on the board, each marked with the name of the Death Circuses bidding. From the hundreds competing when the auction opened, only eighteen were still in the race once the bid hit one billion.

But I no longer cared. *His* bid was the billion-rucet bid. I didn't know why he waited so long to bid, but knowing that he was coming for me, I could breathe again.

Only, the situation has changed again.

Two days later, I'm watching five remaining circuses. They're *Rage Of Angels*, *Bone King*, *Joy of Vengeance*, *Slaughteress*, and *Longview*.

The next bid is due in two minutes. The current bid is over three billion. At this moment, I'm trying to imagine what the bid winners can do to me that will be worth an investment of more than three billion rucets.

I'm not naïve. I know the Death Circus that wins the bid will gain tremendous promotional opportunities from broadcasting my death.

My imagination is good, and well practiced in going into dark places. My life has taught me to foresee horror and understand how events can always be worse than the worst I could imagine. I've been trained to endure pain, and have endured worse than my training many times. I've been pushed past my breaking point more than once.

And I cannot imagine I will comport myself well when enduring more than three billion rucets worth of pain.

At this point, knowing that I have a friend aboard the *Longview* becomes increasingly less valuable. The price is too high to give me a clean escape. I'll have to suffer publicly and greatly to repay my benefactor for saving my life.

So I wait for the next bid, hoping that this time it will be over— and that the *Longview* will win.

The board goes dark, and the new results start to appear, one each minute, from the lowest bid to the highest. The first bid lights up, only it is not a bid.

Slaughteress: DISQUALIFIED

I wonder what that means. What could someone offering to spend fortunes do to be disqualified from spending them? This is something I may never know. I have one full minute to consider it, and cannot even come up with a theory.

The next bid appears in the top slot, pushing *Slaughteress* and its mystery down.

Bone King: R4,250,000,000

That's a high bid. Far higher than I'd anticipated. It might be the last bid. I might be going to the *Bone King*. I have no friends there.

But a minute later, *Bone King* is pushed down the board, and the next bidder lands.

Longview: R4,500,000,000

It is an extraordinary bid. I hope it is the winning bid. I find myself standing, my knees locked, unable to move. I breathe shallowly, clench my fists, stare at the board, will it to remain unchanged for the next minute.

But no.

Longview slides down one space, and the next bid appears.

Rage of Angels: R6,735,800,000

I shudder. And wait. The next minute rolls past, but *Joy of Vengeance* does not appear.

Only three bidders remain in this round, and *Rage of Angels* had made an all-out bid—nearly seven billion rucets. It is unprecedented. In the next round, I expect to see only one bidder remain.

The same one. The wrong one.

Kagen

It was impossible to escape Suzee Delight in the City of Furies. Feeds in every quick-eat and business lobby carried stories of the three Death Circus franchises that were still in the bidding to get her.

"If we had a space fleet, we could wait until they finished bidding, then attack the ship that won her, rescue her, and bring her back here," the man who processed one of his many work applications said, looking past him to the streamed discussion on the screen at the front of the lobby.

"If we had our own privateers, we could attack the world where she's being held and break her loose before anyone purchased her," one of the business owners who interviewed him for work remarked. The woman then added, "It would be more ethical that way, because then the government that is doing this to her would not be rewarded with billions of rucets for the evil it's doing."

"She killed monsters," the man next to him in line at the Happy Hunan quick-eat said. "Those administrators were playing fast and loose with the lives of Pact Worlds citizens. What she did wasn't a crime."

"It wasn't?" Kagen said, but the Happy Hunan diner had already moved on.

In any other place he'd been, Kagen guessed that the people around him would have been speculating on the manner in which she'd die, and cherishing the details of the spectacle to which they would be treated when she did.

But every citizen of the Furies who talked about Suzee Delight finished with some version of, "I wish we could get her here. She'd fit right in."

She'd killed five men, seemingly without provocation, and the citizens of the Furies apparently approved. Nothing he'd seen suggested this was a city of happy killers.

Nothing anyone did suggested anything other than that these were the hardest-working people he'd ever met—excluding himself.

He knew the Pact Worlds were corrupt.

He knew that citizens could only be classified as Order A if each parent and grand-parent back four generations had also been Order A; that Pact Worlds governments were hereditary, run by the great-great-great grandsons of men who had once been elected; that each franchised moon and space station could be purchased by *only* an Order A citizen, or by a rich outsider who first had to pay an enormous kickback to the members on the Pact Worlds Committee of Finance to own that franchise; and all legal businesses were owned by Order A citizens and rented by people of lower orders who had to bribe the Committee to keep their doors open.

He knew that bribery and cronyism were the true laws of the Pact Worlds, and had been for a very long time.

But when a woman dancing on a table-top suddenly murdered all five men who were sitting naked around that table sharing a three-hundred-year-old bottle of Tooki Scotch, people generally didn't say, "Good for her. I wish she was my next-door neighbor."

Granted, the City of Furies had been built by Pact Worlds refugees and was exclusively inhabited by Pact Worlds refugees. This was the reason that only a few trusted ships were permitted to orbit the hidden planet that contained the City of Furies, and that the city offered no way for people to leave or arrive except via shuttles from those occasional trusted ships.

Kagen realized that, although he'd only been a part of the city for a few days, if he could not become the captain of his own spaceship, he would be happy becoming a transport captain for the Furies.

He didn't know, then, what he thought about Suzee Delight and her confessed murders.

But he did know what he thought about the City of Furies. He wasn't even a citizen yet, but he knew he'd come home. These were his people. They'd been persecuted on their home worlds—every single one of them. They knew what it meant to be punished for their thoughts, to be beaten for their actions, to be silenced, to be forced to work for the exclusive benefit of others, to be turned into people they had no desire to be.

Here, they worked for their own benefit, every single one of them. They did what they loved, what they were passionate about, what mattered to them—and whether they did it full time as their paid work, or on their own time while they were developing their skills, they were alive with their goals and their desires.

Breathing the air in the City of Furies was like inhaling energy. The question one Fury asked another was never, "Where did you study?" or "Who is your family?" or "Where do you come from?" or "What is your rank?"

It was always, only, ever, "What do you do?"

And in the lower city, filled with new immigrants like him, the answer was, "I program transport routes, but at night I'm working on a new self-terraformer—you drop it onto a moon or lifeless planet and it spins out its first dome, starts breaking down existing elements to create free oxygen, nitrogen, and water, builds another bubble, connects the bubbles..."

Or it was, "I teach new immigrants basic Standard, but on my days off, I'm developing a way to upgrade pingball data transfers to work with old-style Spybees, so that even people living in tech-blocked systems will be able to receive live datastreams using primitive equipment."

Or it was, "I'm doing construction on new immigrant units on the periphery, but at night I write songs and on my days off, I perform at this little club over in Westside. Here's my card. You should come hear me."

For Kagen, as he walked from business to business through the crowded tech district, his answer to that question became, "I'm still looking for work, but at night I'm using my room terminal to continue studying and testing toward my spaceship captain's license."

But when he walked past the Anja Mayre Holographic Recording and Datastreaming building, he thought about the people in the Furies, and about their comments about Suzee Delight, and an idea flashed in front of him.

It wasn't anything he could claim experience with, but it was... well, he thought it was magnificent. On impulse, he walked into the studio, where a young woman in casual clothes and with her arms full of papers took his name asked him what he did.

When he told her, she said, "I'm Anja Mayre. This is my place. How may I help you?"

"It occurred to me that most of the people in the Furies don't want to see Suzee Delight executed, and that many of the citizens here are famous across Settled Space. And that someone might be able to make a real difference if he were to sit down with the people who want her to live and record interviews of them telling the universe *why* they want her to live."

"What experience would this hypothetical interviewer have, and what budget would he need to create these recordings?"

"In answer to your first question, I have no experience whatsoever," he told her. "I'm still trying to get off my 30-day indigent listing after being dumped here with nothing. But as a crewman on the space transport *Longview*, I was in firefights during pirate attacks, and under attack when things went bad on the ground, and I was in command of men and women who had to depend on me to get us out of those bad situations alive. I made my way up the ranks to a command position, and carried the highest rating throughout my tour with the *Longview*. I survived being born on a People's Home of Truth and Fairness world, and being sentenced to volunteer my death there. I escaped alive.

"I don't get flustered, I don't panic when meeting important people, and I want to make Settled Space understand why the brilliant, hard-working, creative people in this city want to see Suzee Delight survive. And most importantly," he said, "I'm willing to work for the lowest possible wage that will get me off the indigent list and let me start earning my citizenship.

"On your second question, I will make this happen with whatever budget you give me. I suggest asking citizens to come in and talk to me without payment, so that there can be no hint of corruption attached to these interviews."

She studied him with narrowed eyes. After a long, thoughtful silence, she grinned.

Just under an hour later, Anja had finished walking him through her recording studios. "You're going to be dealing with some of the most famous people in Settled Space," she said. "I'll contact them, ask them to let me know when they can come in to talk about the pending execution of Suzee Delight, and you'll do the recording."

She walked into an empty studio, past a plain white chair set dead center in a standard holocorder cube, and through to the control panel on the other side.

"This will have to be basic stuff," she told him, "because if we're going to do any good with these protests of yours, we need to get them into the datastream as quickly as possible, and as many out there as possible. So you won't add image ghosts or sound effects, or sweetening, or play with the lighting. These will have to go out raw, as one-takes."

"Will famous people do this if they know that?" He thought of the rich and important people he'd crossed paths with during various leaves, and suspected that famous people would want all the sweetening and special lighting they could get.

Her sidelong glance and low chuckle told him she'd come across people of the same sort in her previous life.

"We're *all* immigrants here," she said. "Including our famous citizens. When the oldest of them got here, they had to build their own first homes—little prefab domes. They had to set up their own reconsta stations. They had to live hard and thin."

She leaned in and said, "The famous folks here escaped torture and imprisonment and censorship and death sentences to get here. Just like you and me. And just like us, they'll want Suzee Delight to get here too."

She showed him the buttons for starting and stopping the recording, for presenting the interview questions that would appear on the transparent screen between him and his speaker, and the one that would package the entire interview and send it automatically into the datastream.

"Try to keep each interview to between ten and thirty minutes— but if you're getting something amazing, let it run," she said. "Try to complete twenty interviews per day."

"May I work longer than your regular hours?"

She grinned again. "You definitely belong here. Yes, you can work extra hours, but at the same hourly rate."

He was fine with that.

He signed her contract, she marked his "Employed" voucher and told him to request a housing transfer to Westside Best Rooms to eliminate his commute, and said she'd cover his first month's rent.

And just like that, he became an official resident of the City of Furies.

Chapter 5

Melie

Aboard the *Longview*, Melie—the Two Gold crew on monitoring duty on the bridge—was watching transmissions to and from the ship. The owner, transmitting unencoded, was setting up a meeting in his quarters with someone planetside, and was offering to provide transportation for his guest.

There was the standard encrypted stream setting up a banking link for the upcoming transactions between buyers and sellers. They were docked above a Pact World, so the *Longview* would be the buyer, and the various prisons would be the sellers. No one was selling people, of course, or buying them. Not on a Pact World. The Covenants demanded that no human being could be sold to another —but was fine with selling commodity wrapped around people. The commodity here was Packaged Criminal Transport and Capital-Crime Disposal Options.

On the slaver worlds, the commodity was slaves who could be executed. No fancy product labeling, no capital letters.

The hypocritical conversion of neat, tidy Options into slaves purchased for torture and slaughter with the simple crossing of a border gave Melie nightmares.

She knew most of the people purchased by the *Longview* would never be sold, and she believed that overall, her ship and job were not about trading in slaves. She believed the *Longview* was part of something secret. Special. Good.

But the *Longview* still purchased some people that it later resold for execution. If its turn-around time on any given purchase was twice to three times that of any other Death Circus ship, it did not change the fact that some people purchased were in fact executed by slavers and those who bought from slavers.

The *Longview* was docked above a People's Home of Truth and Fairness moon and in the process of buying Options at that moment, so she was monitoring transmissions.

Crew never took leave on PHTF worlds, so usually the owner's transmissions and banking details were the only traffic until the Death Circus began and the owner started running records on prospective purchases and began buying those that fit his needs.

This time, however, two burst packets went from ship to surface and from surface to ship immediately after the banking stream closed. They were fast and they were encoded, and they almost looked like the banking stream had hiccuped while closing transmission—which sometimes happened.

If it hadn't been that the first message was outbound, Melie would have ignored the two blips entirely.

Instead, however, she rolled the ship's log back to the two transmissions, and pushed them through the standard decode algorithm.

Her screen flashed FAILED.

At that point, she went on alert.

"Shipcom," she said, "run marked transmissions against all possible encryption algorithms, and use any cracks necessary."

The ship said, "Working."

She contacted the captain. "Sir, I have a possible security issue on the bridge," she said. "Can you come take a look?"

"Right there," he said.

The shipcom was still working on breaking the encryption when he arrived.

Melie walked him through what she'd seen and what she'd done.

"Isolate the origins of both transmission for me," he told her. "Meanwhile, I'm going to ask the owner if he had anything going out that we shouldn't look at."

She nodded and went back into the log. Tracking back from the transmission port, she was able to isolate the origin of the outgoing burst to Passenger Room 2. Room 2 held five people, and was full at the moment.

She then pulled the pulse map from the log and did an overlay of coordinates. A building not named in the datastream popped up.

The owner's representative, Shay, arrived on the bridge. "He sends his regards," she said, "but is preparing to meet with an important contact. What do you have for him?" And then Shay looked at Melie. "You found something *else*?"

The last time Melie had met Shay, Melie had lost her coveted Crew One position. But she'd still come out of the encounter with a job, and with savings and investments intact—and for that she had Shay to thank.

Melie said, "You can't imagine how I wish someone else had found this right now, believe me."

And she walked Shay through what she'd discovered.

When she finished, Shay said, "What did the messages say?"

"Shipcom is still working on them."

Shay looked stunned. "Shipcom, how long have you been working on unencrypting those messages?"

"Seven minutes, thirty seconds at the tone," the ship said. A chime sounded.

"What the hell do they have in there?" Shay whispered. She told the ship, "Turn all but critical resources over to unencrypting those messages."

"Working," the ship said.

More than a minute later, the ship said, "Messages unencrypted. Estimate of time to completion at regular speed rounded to three days."

"Thank you," Shay said. "Hold results until deck is need-to-know only. I have now linked to the owner's com. Please connect him to audiovisual and data."

"Completed," the ship said.

Shay looked from the captain to the Crew Three man doing routine maintenance testing on the docking controls. "Please tell your Three to leave the deck," she told the captain. And then she looked at Melie. "You can stay."

The captain asked Shay, "Are you sure you want her here?"

"The *owner* wants her here. Twice now she's demonstrated both a laudable suspicion of small wrong details, and twice has captured information meant to be kept from your attention, the owner's attention... and mine. So while she might have only rooted out someone's overprotected invitation to a surprise party, Mado Keyr wants to let her see what she's discovered."

Melie felt a little thrill of pleasure at that comment. "Thank you," she told Shay.

The crewman left the deck, and the hatch locked behind him.

"Let's see what you found," Shay said. "Shipcom, report."

"The send transmission contains lists of Mado Keyr's investments, properties, and financial holdings, and a note that states the estimated maximum bid he will be able to offer for Suzee Delight. These files are extensive, though incomplete. The received file notes that the Pact World administrators who are backing the bid of an unnamed Death Circus can only go a billion higher than Mado Keyr's highest estimated bid, and asks for access to Mado Keyr's larger accounts so that these can be sabotaged."

The silence on the bridge stretched agonizingly after that announcement.

Shay had her finger pressed to her right ear. She stared off into space, nodded several times, then said, "Yes, Mado. I'll take care of that."

Her hand dropped to her side and she turned to the captain.

"The owner has several requests. First, he asks that you block all transmissions to or from the ship *except* for those originating from or destined for Room 2. When you close off transmissions, please give notice to ground and Needle that we are upgrading to a Convex 8 system, and may be out of touch all day."

"We already have a Convex 8 system," Melie said.

She glanced over at Melie. "We do. But neither ground nor the Needle has any way of knowing that, and it makes a nice excuse."

She returned her attention to the captain. "Mado Keyr is also setting special priorities for the shipcom, and will require that you leave resource optimization off, in spite of the fact that you will see some periods where some of the ship's functions push critical. He notes that, because we are docked, this should be a minor inconvenience."

The captain said, "I'll leave things alone."

"He further requests that all passengers in Room 2 be invited to join you for dinner tonight in your quarters, and he asks that he be permitted to attend as well."

"Of course," the captain said. "I'll be delighted to oversee this particular dinner."

Lastly, Shay turned to Melie. "The owner has instructed me that you are to be given a significant reward for intercepting these transmissions. Captain, she is to come with me. Do you need time to cover her position before she leaves the deck?"

"If shipcom is taking over all communications, then her position is covered until we resume regular operation. She can leave with you immediately."

Shay said, "Melie, come with me."

Heart suddenly racing, hope rising, Melie followed her.

Kagen

"...And Suzee Delight cannot be held accountable for these five deaths. Individuals who are not free to direct the courses of their own lives cannot be judged or sentenced as if they were. Responsibility for any actions they take lands on the heads of those who claim the right to control them. The deaths of the five Pact Worlds Administrations are therefore the fault of those same Administrators. They are guilty of their own murders."

"Thank you, Berramyn Chase. Berramyn Chase is a citizen of the City of Furies, and the inventor of the Modix, which is an internal cellular regeneration implant that should become available within the next one to two Standard years to individual residents on worlds that permit it. It will be an emergency backup for in-box Medix treatment—people will survive even massive trauma and self-heal from any injury that does not destroy the brain. This implant, like Medix treatment, is already banned on all Pact Worlds to citizens of Order B status or lower under the Legend War Act, Section B: Mandatory Natural Lifespans, and Section C: No Augmented Self-Healing."

Kagen finished the recording, and as he had done with every one before it, hit the Send To Stream button on his screen.

Then he walked out to shake hands with Berramyn Chase. She was young and attractive—but because the Furies made access to Medix tech a priority for every Furies citizen, all citizens stayed young and healthy, and any who chose to be so were attractive. Berramyn's true beauty was internal: she was driven, obsessive, ferocious, passionate, and joyful in an oddly intense way.

"Thank you for taking the time to speak for Suzee Delight," Kagen said.

"I've never met her personally, but it's impossible not to be aware of her work. Whenever I've needed to close out the world and focus on regenerating neurons, I've looped her *Birds Flying* instrumental series—it's incredible music, mathematically perfect but deeply emotional. I cannot believe anyone will really allow her to be executed."

"I hope they won't," Kagen said. "If she's somehow saved, the story you told will play a part in saving her."

"I would do more if I could," she told him. "We all would."

He'd found himself crying, listening to Berramyn's story of her own life before the Furies, of how she had managed to find love on a PHTF world, only to have the man she loved ripped away from her and sent to his death before she managed to escape.

He'd heard more than two hundred variations of that story, and as the bidding war to buy Suzee Delight dragged on, he had interviewed once-persecuted, still-hunted luminaries of the sciences, technologies, mathematics, literature, arts. But along with the powerful and famous, he was also recording the stories and protests of general entertainers, traffic controllers, food processors, farmers, city programmers, construction workers, science technicians, full-time parents, shopkeepers, small business owners, and other ordinary people who had fallen afoul of the Pact Worlds' ever-more-restrictive "protective guidelines" for citizens.

People like him.

Berramyn was his last interview of the day. He was grateful. He was pushing himself harder and harder, working eighteen Standard hours a day and sometimes even more, keeping Anja's front studio open just so he could make himself available to everyone who wanted to speak for Suzee Delight. Fighting to save her life had become his obsession—drawing the best out of every single guest he interviewed had become his goal. He was directing the interviews, but the interviews were changing him.

After each one, he studied whatever he could about his next guest and wrote down questions—and for people who had no available information, he had a standard set of questions he started with, and he worked out from there.

He ate from the studio reconsta machine, slept on his studio floor, and made use of the WashAll down the street to keep himself and his clothes acceptably clean.

All he could think of was to keep the interviews going out, to flood Settled Space with them, so that someone who had the power to do something would hear the one story that would make him change his mind and let Suzee Delight live.

Suzee Delight could only receive justice from those who shared the same rights she had, and lived under laws they had created jointly, consented to voluntarily, and held in common.

But Suzee Delight had no rights, including the right of consent, and those who sentenced her were bound by no laws. Those laws they created were only to constrain the actions of others.

By that standard, every action the Administrators of the Pact Worlds took had no legal value. Was, in fact, criminal.

His head hurt.

He was tired.

But he dreaded the idea of slowing down. This thing he had put together meant much more than he'd thought it did when he walked into Anja's studio—and he suspected that he still only understood a part of how much it meant.

When Berramyn left, he started to turn out the studio lights to catch a few hours sleep before his next interview, but saw Anja standing in the corridor waiting to speak to him.

"You're doing amazing work," she said. "Incredible, nearly impossible work, actually. So... did you once meet Suzee Delight? Is she a friend?"

He laughed wearily. "Not a chance. At no point in the universe would her circle and mine ever intersect."

"Are you... a big fan of her work?"

He grinned. "Not that, either. I'm one of the fifteen percent of people who have an aversion reaction to Sensos—I am completely incapable of letting my body relax into someone else's neural pathways."

"Then, and please don't take this the wrong way, Kagen, but..." Anja slid her hands into the pockets of the coverall she was wearing, and narrowed her eyes to study him. "Why are you killing yourself on this project? You've lost weight, you look like hell, the dark circles under your eyes are starting to look like someone punched you."

"It's simple. It's about getting the truth out. Suzee Delight took an aptitude test when she was a child, and that aptitude test said she should be a whore. She turned out to be a very talented whore—but she didn't choose to be a whore. Some little functionary in her school or her dorm or however they did it where she comes from chose that future for her. She couldn't quit, she couldn't protest, she couldn't walk away to do something else."

"But that's true for every person in the Pact Worlds who isn't

Order A. It's true for nearly every person who lives in the Furies—it's what we all escaped from. Everyone knows it's the truth."

"YES!" he said. "That's exactly it, but no one has questioned it. Only now, the famous Suzee Delight has murdered five of the most important Order A men in Settled Space, and she says what she did was required by her training. Right now, people are questioning her training, they're questioning how no one ever considered her a danger to those five powerful men—and they're questioning how she managed to become the most famous courtesan in Settled Space.

"People out in Settled Space are listening now, so while they're listening, I'm putting the stories of every Fury I can get my hands on in front of those listeners. People who escaped from worlds where someone else chose their lives for them, people who are now something entirely different than the things they were forced to be back home. I'm connecting each of these people to Suzee Delight, and they're telling me how they're like her—and why she needs to live, like they needed to live, and what they had to do to get away.

"I don't know if Suzee Delight killed those men because they deserved it, or because she lost her mind, or for any of a million other reasons, but I know this: She is not the person who put herself in that room with them. She is the one person who was in that room who had no choice about being there.

"So that's what I'm focusing on in the interviews—and that's what I'm getting from the people I'm talking to. None of them chose to be where they were before they were sentenced to death, or before they escaped. They support Suzee Delight because they know where she came from, and the rules she lived under. She got away. They got away.

"And somewhere out there, someone in the Pact Worlds is looking at the stories that are coming from here, and thinking, *I can live my life if I get away from this place, too—if I can just get through the people blocking me.*

"At the same time, some functionary or official or administrator out there is thinking, *I'm the person standing in the way of the next Suzee Delight, or Mettor Helmyn, or Berramyn Chase, and the minute that person real-*

izes I'm the obstacle, I'm dead. And I'll never see it coming. And his next thought will eventually become, *I need to get away from here and get my hands off of other people's lives before somebody kills me.*

"Every story I can get out there is one more voice from here talking to one more person out there who didn't take the *other* stories to heart because they weren't like his story. Or her story. But *this* story is. Anja, right now Settled Space is listening. But I don't know how long it'll keep listening. And I don't know, if I lose this opportunity, if it'll ever listen again. And this matters. So I can't rest. I can't slow down. I'd give up food and sleep entirely if I could."

Hands in her pockets, Anja stood staring at her feet, swaying a bit from side to side. Kagen watched her, waiting while she worked out whatever was going through her mind.

"Right," she said after a moment. "I'm taking you on full-time at full pay starting tomorrow morning. I'm getting you a crew of nine more people, because that's all the studio space I have, and I'm plastering the city with, "Fight for Suzee Delight" signs that send people here to tell their stories. There are going to be lines out this building from now until Suzee Delight's story comes to whichever end it comes to, and you and the people you and I train tomorrow are going to interview as many of them as you can before we run out of time. Meanwhile, I'll ask the people to whom this matters to pitch in for studio and datastreaming costs, and I'll eat the rest of whatever this costs, because what you've turned this into matters to me, too. It matters to all of us.

"When it's over, we will have done what we could do—you and me and the Furies—and one way or the other, our lives will move on. We will not come to our own ends knowing once, long ago, we could have mattered but we chose not to. Thank you, Kagen, for seeing a way the Furies could fight after all."

Melie

Melie entered the owner's quarters for the first time, and took the seat at the small table that Shay indicated. Shay sat opposite her and said, "Mado Keyr regrets that he cannot meet with you personally, but he will monitor the conversation while you and I discuss your future with the *Longview*. I will convey his gratitude and his wishes regarding your reward for the service you have provided him."

Melie nodded. Her mouth was dry and her heart raced. She had stepped into the den of the lion, and it was a frightening place. The entire room, including the table and four chairs that were its only contents, were black. Everything gleamed. She could not locate the source of light, but it was muted and indirect. One oversized door punctuated each of the room's walls; all four arched like identical gaping mouths, glossy black with keyed ident locks. She realized that if she stood and walked around the table, she could easily lose her direction and not know which door she'd used to enter.

She looked at Shay. "How do you know which door is which?"

Shay smiled. "That's a secret I cannot share with you. And it isn't what we're here to discuss." She settled into the chair to Melie's right. "If you could ask for anything from the owner, what would you request? Think about it before answering."

Melie didn't even have to consider this. "I'd want to be reinstated into my position as One Green."

Shay laughed. "You do understand that you have done a service for the mado that is worth billions of rucets to him. Reinstating you to your former position would cost him nothing."

"I'm not interested in costing him money. I want to captain my own ship someday. To do that, I need my TFN pilot's license, and I can only get that by earning it. You know how I came to be here. Outside of the *Longview*, I will never have the opportunity to earn that license, or the money to buy my own ship."

"Would you request anything else?"

"The only other thing I would request, the mado cannot offer."

"Which would be...?"

"To get my family out of Sunray City and off of Targa."

Shay raised an eyebrow and cocked her head. She studied Melie, an expression on her face that Melie couldn't identify. "We didn't get you off of Targa."

"I stowed away in the hold of an outbound freighter, got dumped on the nearest needle when I got caught, and managed to hang on there until you arrived and took me on as a passenger."

"You've heard from your family? You know they're still in Sunray City?"

Melie shook her head. "I don't dare contact them. My leaving the planet was a crime, but their being in contact with someone who left the planet would be a bigger crime. I'm sure my family reported me missing as soon as I left. If they tried to hide what I'd done, they'd be..." She closed her eyes and shook her head. "You know what happens. So they reported me. But they—we—were all Order D. So nothing will have gotten better for them, though it certainly may have gotten worse."

Shay was staring through Melie, seemingly frozen. Melie realized she was listening to the owner. After a moment Shay said, "Yes, mado," and then focused her attention back on Melie. "You'll give me the names of your family members and their last known addresses, and the mado will contact allies who will remove them to safety for you. They will be set up on a free world with full identification, housing, and work. And when this is done, you will be given leave to go visit them."

Melie blinked back tears and swallowed hard until the lump in her throat let go enough that she could speak. "Please thank him for me," she said.

Another pause. Then Shay said, "He says you thanked him when you discovered and reported those messages. He also conveys to you the following: You will not be raised to Class One until your year has passed, unless the captain, first mate, or One Gold leaves the *Longview*. However, you will receive payment as if you were one One Gold, and as long as you have completed both the One Gold and First Mate certifications by the time your year is up, you will be jumped over the current One Green into the One Gold position."

"He's going to jump-promote me over the crew in one of those positions?"

"No," Shay said. "But the offers coming in for one of his top three people have reached astronomical levels, and both Mado Keyr and I are nearly certain that a position is going to open up in One Gold soon."

"I'll be ready," Melie said.

"I know." Shay stood and smiled. "You always have been."

Chapter 6

Captain Shore

The dinner would be interesting, Captain Dermet Shore decided. In the three months since Captain Willet stepped down and he took the helm, everything about the job had proven interesting. From the moment he signed his final nondisclosure agreement and opened the sealed papers that explained to him the objective of the *Longview*, the universe had come to look entirely different to him. He could not imagine that he would ever again have a job that would be so dangerous, so challenging, or so worthwhile—and yet, the only people with whom he could even speak about what he did were Werix Keyr and Shay.

And mostly he could only speak to Shay, who for reasons he could not explain made his skin crawl just a bit.

But in just a few minutes, he would be entertaining Werix and an unknown number of spies, and he would get to see how the owner dealt with them.

Interesting. Possibly dangerous.

His first mate, Laure, would be armed. He would be armed. And Werix, who suffered from a degenerative condition not even

Medix sessions could overcome, would be tucked inside his molei-bond flexsuit, impervious to anything that might go wrong.

Over the com, Laure said, "I have arrived with our guests, Captain. Are you prepared for them?"

He said, "Bring them in."

Room 2 held five occupants, and all five berths had been filled when the messages went out.

The five filed in, and Laure introduced them. "Captain Shore, meet Celdica, Peret, Ersero, Jorje Ness, and Deesa. Celdica and Peret were in the PHTF-112 needle when we took them on. Ersero was a toss from Clewmass. Jorje Ness tried to stow away in our shuttle when we were down on PHTF-28, and because we had a berth, we brought him with us as a ride-along in the shuttle. Finally, a crew member who remains anonymous to the other four smuggled out Deesa in his carry-on when leaving Caynute Pleasure. Deesa was a C-8 consort. You've had full reports on her—we ran the most recent records worm at twenty-thirty-five Standard, and her back-trail remains clean, though activity on Caynute Pleasure continues as her employers attempt to locate her."

Dermet nodded at each, and pointed them to their seats. "Welcome," he said. "I am Captain Dermet Shore, and it is my pleasure to welcome you to my table as my guest. Joining us will be the owner of the *Longview*, Mado Werix Keyr, who has asked to share a dinner with you before you move on to your destinations. Whenever he can, he joins a small group of his passengers for dinner: he likes to meet them and hear their stories."

This was a pure lie—as best he could tell from studying previous captains' logs, the owner had never before met with escapees. Werix would occasionally request a dinner at the Captain's table if one or two of the paid passengers were especially interesting—when Dermet had been first mate, Willet had told him about getting to meet the dissident holomaker Falstaff Shottley, who he said had been the most interesting man Willet had ever met. Dermet had not yet entertained a celebrity.

He was doing something different.

He was entertaining a spy.

And he wondered what role he would play in the owner's plan to uncover the identity of the one who had betrayed his generosity in providing rescue, room, and board.

"Before the owner arrives," Dermet said, "I will go over protocol with you.

"The owner has a condition that requires special consideration. When he arrives, the lights will be lowered. I will introduce each of you to him. You will not touch him, though he may touch you. You will not speak to him unless spoken to. You will not raise your voice when speaking to him or to each other—his hearing is incredibly sensitive.

"He must wear a special suit at all times in order to survive—his condition is not treatable by Medix. Please do not stare at him."

His guests nodded. While they had been cheerful and excited on entering Dermet's quarters, they became increasingly subdued as he laid out the restrictions on their actions.

The shipcom said, "Mado Keyr requests permission to enter."

"Permission granted," Dermet said.

The room lights dimmed as his door slid open. Werix passed from the corridor into Dermet's entertainment room. As soon as the door closed behind him, the corridor lights would brighten again. Dermet found it strange to contemplate the owner's life, always surrounded by a ring of darkness that followed him everywhere.

And yet, in spite of the difficulties he faced, Werix had managed to accomplish things no one else ever had.

The captain stood as Mado Werix Keyr walked in, and each of the guests followed his lead.

Werix went from guest to guest, studied each for a moment, introduced himself, and before he stepped away, touched the arm or shoulder of each. "I hope you are enjoying your stay," he said each time before moving on to the next.

When he took his seat, Laure—acting as waiter—brought covered plates and presented them, first to Werix, then to Dermet, and then to each guest in turn.

As they ate, Werix entertained them with a story of his visit, when he was a young man, to the vast city of Meileone. "I went to

Oldcity," he told them, "though I did it against the advice of my guide. And my guide proved himself a fool. Oldcity was the only place I ever visited that had the perfect amount of light for me, and it was endlessly graceful, lit by man-made stars, and filled with gentle breezes and night gardens. It was lovely—but far too crowded. Still, if ever a cure is found for the illness that devours me, it's the place I would love to call home."

He looked at his guests, and said, "Deesa, you're from Meileone. Did you ever visit Oldcity?"

"Frequently," she said, and then froze. "I didn't... I've never... I'm not from Meileone."

"But of course you are. You were there as recently as a week ago. Tell us all about your trip."

Her eyes opened wide. Her whole body had gone rigid. "I... met... with..."

She acted as if she were fighting herself—as if her mouth were moving against her will.

"My dear Deesa, if you keep that up, you'll hurt yourself. Simply tell us. I'm sure it was a fascinating trip."

The muscles of her jaw bulged, and sweat broke out on her forehead—and then she slumped.

"I met with representatives from the Pact Worlds who have set up a consortium that is bidding against you through *Bone King*."

"Of course they are," he said thoughtfully. "*Rage of Angels* dropped out when it couldn't go over seven billion. But *Bone King* kept bidding, always managing to stay close to my bid, going over often enough to avoid the three-sub-bid disqualification..."

Dermet felt a chill run down his spine. In the dim lighting he could not see Mado Keyr well, but he could feel the man's rage as clearly as if sheets of electricity had wrapped themselves around him. No one else spoke. No one else moved.

"Someone found a way to track the movements of my money into and out of my bidding account. It wasn't you, was it, Deesa?"

"No."

"But you know who it is, Deesa."

"... Yes..."

"And who is helping you, Deesa?"

Veins stood out in her neck, her muscles locked tight, and the sweat beaded on her forehead ran down her nose.

Dermet's body locked in sympathetic struggle—he wanted to answer for her, would have if he could have, but of course he didn't know whatever she knew.

"You want to tell me the truth, Deesa," the owner said softly. "You know you do."

The little crunch that followed sounded like an explosion in the dead silence.

Deesa's eyes rolled back in her head until only the whites showed. She began to twitch, bloody foam poured from her mouth and nose, and her limp body toppled sideways from her armless seat. She thudded to the floor.

The instant she hit the floor, Dermet's muscles unlocked. Without needing to think, he was out of his seat, his hand hitting the button on the wall that brought the Medix out of its hidden panel.

He lifted Deesa, dumped her into the unit core, and set emergency auto-repair before anyone else had done more than gasp.

Werix murmured, "She thought she had a plan for everything, didn't she? Silly girl. Well done, Captain. Your skills and reflexes do you tremendous credit. Unless I'm mistaken, that was a *tatuka* nanovirus she had embedded in one of her teeth. She might not yet survive—but if she does, it will be because of you."

Dermet said, "I'm... glad I could help."

Werix tipped his head toward the ceiling, "Charlie? Did you witness all of that?"

Dermet heard Charlie's voice over the shipcom. "Every bit. I wish she'd implicated the worlds involved in the bidding, and the person who'd leeched your banking data. But I have enough to file a fraud suit against the *Bone King*."

"Please do that, then. I'm rather enjoying this dinner, and I'd like to see it through to the end."

Dermet took a deep breath and sent Laure for the second course.

Charlie

Charlie had always known the trick to maintaining her post on the *Longview* was to avoid attracting attention.

And more than anything, Charlie wanted to keep her job—because any other job she would have as a servant of her world would be worse.

Yet she had willingly, as a favor to Mado Keyr, witnessed and recorded the confession of Deesa at the captain's dinner. She had voluntarily filed suit in Werix Keyr's name against *Bone King* and the half-dozen worlds Deesa had named, as well as Deesa and the crewman who had provided her cover story aboard the *Longview*.

She had set up the Verilamp and tamper failsafes, and once Deesa recovered from her suicide attempt, had obtained both Deesa's full confession and that of the *Longview's* Two Blue ex-crewman who'd helped her. And then she'd streamed these holographed confessions to her controller in unencoded files over open public datastreams, and had tagged the files as exactly what they were.

As a result, every entertainment and news source in Settled Space acquired the information for free, in unadulterated form, and had it up for broadcast at the same time that the involved Pact Worlds were discovering in their own datastreams the files that implicated them in a massive criminal cover-up.

Charlie had voluntarily made herself the public face of the scandal—the single recognizable person whose actions had brought more than a dozen Pact Worlds and their governments to their knees; who had fed fuel to worlds that had been Pact Worlds trading partners and who were now boycotting the entire Pact Worlds system; and who had been the cause of the bidding on Suzee Delight being dropped back to the last legitimate bid, which had been to the *Longview* Death Circus for seven-point-five billion rucets.

Charlie was pretty certain she was attempting slow public suicide, though she was equally certain that for the first time in her life she was doing exactly the right thing—and doing it with an absolutely clear conscience.

She wondered if this was how Suzee Delight had felt, murdering the five men who'd plotted to turn the Pact Worlds into slave worlds by another name.

Charlie wasn't done destroying her career, though.

The *Longview* had reached Cantata, where Suzee Delight had been transferred following the implication of her world in the bidding scandal.

And Charlie had asked Shay for a favor.

"This call is encoded and tight-beamed," Shay said. "You'll have to enter your contact information, but you'll get Gen-ID verification before your data will go to the person you're contacting. You have this room to yourself, and when you seal it, no one will be able to hear you. Will that be good enough?"

Charlie nodded. "This may take me a few minutes."

"You're fine," Shay said. "Werix is grateful for everything you've done to help him over the past week. Without you being willing to act in your official capacity, the *Longview* would very likely have lost the bid." Shay rested a hand on Charlie's forearm. "And I know that doing what you did has put you at risk."

Charlie laughed. "I can't go back. They won't let me stay here and work this job, but I can't go back." She shrugged. "I'm not sorry, Shay. I'm not sorry for one single thing I did to help you."

Shay said, "And the owner remembers the people who help him. Don't do anything stupid, Charlie. We'll take care of you."

"I'm not going to hold you to that," Charlie told her. "Not you or Mado Keyr."

"All right. But please remember what I said."

Shay left. Charlie sealed the room, and then she called her contact down in the city of Meileone. They went through the Gen-ID verification, and then she was face to face with the one friend she had who'd managed to slip out from under the monstrous thumb of the Pact Worlds machine to hide in plain sight.

"Hi, Lee," Charlie said, and winced. "I'm hoping you can help me out."

"Oh, Charlie. I thought *I* made some trouble, but you—I've never seen anyone work so hard to self-destruct."

"I'm glad I did it."

"For as much good as it's going to do you, so am I, and so is everyone I know. But you have to know that with everything you've done on this Suzee Delight fiasco, you're going to disappear the instant you get back here," Lee said. In the year since they'd last met, Lee had changed her face, her body, even her voice—but her mannerisms were the same. "You aren't going to get a trial or a sentence. You're simply going to vanish into the grinding gears of the world, and never be heard from again."

"I know that's what they plan. I have a plan of my own. But before I carry it out, I have to preside at the execution of Suzee Delight. So I need to know if you ever made any progress with that —*project* you were working on for yourself."

Charlie saw Lee's eyes widen. "The insanely dangerous one? With the DNA kicker?"

Charlie nodded.

"I have the recipe on file, but none of it is tested. I'll have to set up a port for each subject's DNA that you want to include in the kicker. And there will be a delay before you can use the *project*."

Charlie closed her eyes. Nothing was ever simple. "How much DNA? How much time?"

Lee said, "I don't think you're hearing me. I said *insanely dangerous. Isn't tested.* Times and amounts are best guess because *no one has ever used this. Ever.* Right now, this whole thing is numbers and letters in a little file I have tucked away where no one will look for it. I can't promise that the kicker will work. I can't promise anything."

"I got that. This is the only chance I have."

On the screen in front of Charlie, Lee's hands started waving, and her face sheened with sweat. "You're insane. You are *insane*, and you are going to get yourself *killed*, and there just aren't that many people left in Settled Space that I can actually stand, damn you."

"You owe me, Lee."

Lee looked away. "Yeah, I owe you. And debts must be paid. So, I'm going to repay you by getting you and some unknown number of your friends killed. Fine. You saved my life, I'll make sure you end up dead. Helluva thanks. But I offered to get you out of the system, and you turned me down. So on your head be it."

Charlie had hoped Lee would be a little less dramatic. "It's on my head, and I just might live. Walk me through the process."

Lee sighed. "Pull out one or two hairs from the head or body of each person who gets the kicker, clip the hair roots and bulbs off the end—you know what those are, right?"

"I have hair."

"Funny. Put the hair roots and bulbs onto the DNA sieve, and shove the seals closed. Make sure you've got them tight. Shake the *project*. Wait at least six Standard hours before you use it."

"How much do you want?"

"Cash in advance. Twenty thousand for the *project* and kicker port."

Charlie exhaled. She'd received a large cash thank-you bonus from Mado Keyr when he won his suit and the bid for Suzee Delight. Twenty thousand rucets would have been impossible for her before, but now it wouldn't even dent the money in her account.

"And when I'm ready to use the *project*?"

"Open the casing, give the contents one squeeze. One. Drop it on the ground and walk away. Squeezing will activate the cells, the *project* should bloom to full strength in five minutes, hold for five minutes, and then die off completely."

"Should?"

"*Untested*," Lee repeated. "*Untested*, Charlie. Everything about this is *hypothetical*. If you don't understand that, don't do this."

Charlie thought about it for just an instant. "Untested will have to be good enough. I'm sending the money to you now."

There was a pause, then Lee said, "I have the full amount verified. I was really hoping when it came down to it, you wouldn't have the plunder. But you do, and that suggests you're into more than just doing your job. So...? Never mind. How shall I get the *project* to you?"

"How big is it?"

"It'll fit in the palm of your hand."

"Pack it inside a tourist welcome package, and send it via courier to the *Longview*, care of Roget Major. Make sure third parties can sign. I'll tell one of the crew I have something coming in that my controller can't know about, and ask her to sign for it and get it to me."

"You'll have it tomorrow."

Chapter 7

Danyal Travers, SPORC Capital Offenses Interviewer from Cheegoth, assigned to the Suzee Delight execution, in the city of Meileone on Cantata:

Suzee Delight, the Pact Worlds are deluged with holostreamed demands for your pardon and release. Cities across the Pact Worlds system are facing criminal riots instigated to cause friction among the lower classes, and demands from these under-citizens that government officials be removed from office and tried as criminals. Our Pact Worlds are being boycotted by outside systems that have been our trading partners for decades, and in some instances hundreds of years, that are now demanding that we dismantle the Covenants of the Pact or lose our status as Approved Worlds and instead be classified as rogue slavers. Are you pleased by the amount of trouble you've caused, Suzee?

Suzee Delight, First Courtesan, Court of the Diamond Dome, Mariposa Pleasure City, Cheegoth, in the city of Meileone on Cantata: We're on a first-name basis now? That's interesting. All right, then, *Danyal*. I'm twenty-three years old and I'm on my way to my execution. Pretend you're me. Is there anything in the universe that could please you?

Danyal: Don't evade the point. You murdered the five most important men in the Pact Worlds, and much of Settled Space is demanding that you be forgiven and applauded for what you did, and *we*, the law-abiding citizens of a law-abiding planetary alliance, are being called the criminals in your stead. You confessed to murdering five great and beloved men—leaders of our worlds. You said in other interviews that given the opportunity, you would murder them again. And you demanded execution through the Death Circus, when as a woman who was born in Order E but finagled your way into Order A Equivalency, you could have awaited trial and hoped for a life sentence. You are getting exactly what you asked for.

Suzee Delight: No, I'm not. I *asked* to be allowed to transfer my citizenship to Bailey's Irish Space Station to work in the field of nanoviral augmentation—

Danyal (interrupting): You were seven when you requested—

Suzee Delight (interrupting): *I was nine.* I knew what I wanted when I was nine, and I knew where I could become what I wanted, and instead, my government decided my many talents would best serve the greater good if I were employed as a sex trade worker. So for more than fourteen years, that has been my unchosen and unwanted fate.

Danyal: Courtesans are treated as members of the highest level of society. You live in palaces, you want for nothing…

Suzee Delight: You and I are both whores, Danyal. You're voluntarily sleeping with a corrupt government. I got drafted when I was nine. Did you know that the average lifespan of an Order A Registered Courtesan is twenty-nine years? Or that fully half of all Registered Courtesans commit suicide before they're twenty-one? (Voice drops to nearly inaudible.) Did you know that most of those suicides are actually murders committed by men in positions of power who like to hurt women, and who will never be held accountable for doing so?

Third Voice: Danyal, cut the interview and get her out of there. We have enough holo to work with—there isn't a single word of this that we're going to be able to use unedited, but she looks good, and you can turn this into what we need.

Suzee Delight: Remember this interview, Danyal.

And know that I wish you a short and painful career as the Pact masters' whore. I wish you the ever-louder voice of a conscience that reminds you that no matter what you choose to call it, you have volunteered to hide the evil deeds of criminals for a living, and to help oppress the people they were supposed to serve. And before I go, since I now know I'm speaking just to you and them, let me give all of you a final warning.

Alive, I can only walk and whisper. Dead I'll soar and sing. And every song from my dead lips will be another torch to burn down your twisted, subverted Covenants of the Pact and destroy everyone who gains and holds power from them.

Chapter 8

Shay

Shay hated to do it, but she could not allow any unidentified cargo aboard the *Longview*. So when Charlie finished her conversation with her friend Lee—a conversation as secure as Shay had promised it would be, with the single exception of her silent presence—she piggybacked through Charlie's connection to Lee and set a tiny worm to track and report everything Lee did.

What Lee did was both fascinating and terrifying. She broke into a government-secured nanoviral database using a high-clearance researcher's ident-encode, and broke into the agency's Class-V Restricted Nanoviral Agents Registry, wherein she connected with one tiny file coded with a non-Agency tag. Shay realized Lee was using her government's strongest security system to secure her own personal dangerous files, and doing it in such a way that the rightful users of the system would never find what she'd hidden there without a brute-force search. Lee then retrieved her chosen file using a system-override-and-trail-erase routine so fast and elegant it filled Shay with envy.

Briefly, Shay wondered if she might recruit Lee to the *Longview*, but reconsidered immediately. Lee was doing interesting things right where she was, and needed to be left to do them for as long as she could.

So Shay contented herself with copying Lee's copy.

She needed to know just what Charlie had coming.

Before she killed the connection to Lee, however, she set a little tag on Lee to let the *Longview* know if Charlie's friend was ever investigated or arrested. Shay thought she would be worth a rescue if she ever needed one.

And then Shay sat down with Lee's file and manually dissected the formula, working out by hand (but out of the shipcom's reach) what turned out to be a short-burst airborne nanoviral crowd agent.

It was a nightmare—one designed by a woman with much better bio-weapons skills than she'd let on, who apparently planned to destroy any army that came at her down to the last man.

And Lee was sending her weapon to Charlie.

Shay smiled a bit.

Charlie might have hung her head when informed that Suzee Delight had to be executed, but not for a second had she considered letting that happen.

And she'd figured out a solution. One hellish horror of a solution, granted, but looking over the formula and her own extrapolations based on it, Shay had no doubt it would succeed.

Shay's only remaining question was how Charlie planned to carry it out.

Charlie

Suzee Delight was finally only minutes and meters away.

Surrounded by armed crew from the *Longview*, Charlie waited at the exchange point in the neutral corporate space station Abdex Trade and Security, trying to ignore the incredible noise of thousands of people jammed into every available space, all chanting, "We want Suzee, we want Suzee..."

Station sporcs in green uniforms lined both sides of the outer skin of the temporary corridor through which the prisoner exchange would take place, providing a human barrier to keep the crowd from pounding on the moleibond, or doing anything embarrassing.

The far end of the corridor remained clear—the exchange was set to take place at 1200 Standard hours, and according to the chatter in Charlie's eario, set to the sporcs frequency, the procession should appear through the open doors in fifteen seconds.

She stared up through the transparent dome of the station to the small shuttles and smaller dronecams that hovered outside. She recognized logos on the hulls—the biggest news agencies in Settled Space were well-represented, as were organizations she'd never heard of. From the looks of some of the shuttles, a few members of the ultra-rich had arranged front-row seats for themselves, too.

The moleibond shielding and the sporc patrols would reduce the risk of any incidents during the transfer, but couldn't eliminate them entirely. The Human Purity shuttle directly overhead worried Charlie—that particular anti-sex group insisted that all sex was perversion, that human beings existed in a state of damnation, and that for any human to engage in intercourse even once without Divine InterVenntion™ was to invoke an automatic death sentence. Human Purity sold Divine InterVenntions™, of course—sterile programmed clones of their leader, Statius Venn, available in both male and genderflipped female versions, which followers could purchase for an ungodly fee so that they could engage in holy sex while avoiding the doubly damned sin of reproduction.

Every Impurator™—the Human Purity term for a mating or reproducing human anywhere in Settled Space—was going straight to HellVenn™. Charlie thought it funny that in the eyes of the Puritites, eternal damnation could only be truly horrible if it was trademarked.

But that particular group could be dangerous. Charlie was trying to figure out whether the Puritites were up there to take a shot at Suzee Delight with some new weapon, or if they were simply cheering the pending death of one of the most visible flaunters of their religion, when the doors on the far end of the corridor slid open and a wall of green-uniformed sporcs five across marched toward Charlie.

She swallowed hard. It was impossible to see Suzee. She was somewhere in that tall mass of green, moving forward. The roar of sound that had hammered Charlie's ears doubled, trebled, quadrupled as the block of men—only men—moved solemnly forward.

The men split off and lined the inside of the walls as they neared Charlie, and suddenly, there was Suzee, dressed in a green gown, her long black hair tumbling in curls down to her waist, her eyes dark and for just an instant startled as she recognized Charlie.

She hid it well—Charlie had been looking for the reaction, but she thought there was a good chance no one else would see it.

Charlie did not smile. Suzee did not smile.

Then the guard outside the moleibond barrier parallel with Charlie's position turned and began cutting his way through the barrier with a moleibond cutter, screaming, "Suzee Delight, I love you! I've come to save you!" From Charlie's perspective, he provided a welcome diversion. His fellow guards tackled him, and in the chaos, Suzee stepped behind Charlie, Charlie imprinted the transfer documents with her Gen-ID, and the crew of the *Longview*, skipping solemnity and pageantry, hauled ass into the *Longview* before things got any crazier.

Suzee Delight

A small, strange, dangerous client once promised me that if I ever had to take a stand—if I ever had to do something that I knew was right but that was criminal, I should do it, then demand public execution by Death Circus, and his ship—the *Longview*—would come to rescue me.

I'd done something unforgivable in the eyes of the Pact Worlds elite and many common citizens, but I had done it for what I believed to be just and compelling reasons.

And as promised, the *Longview* won the bid and came to rescue me.

But it was Charlie—my Charlie—who was standing there watching me walk toward her, waiting to take me away from my nightmare. Seeing her waiting to greet me and get me out of the reach of the Pact Worlds let me know everything was going to be all right.

I had never dared to hope that I would see her again. Discovering that my only love waited to sign with her blood to buy my freedom—that was the moment when my life became a fairy tale.

I hid my joy. If I had been able to bend the whole of the universe to my will, I could not have made that first sight of her more perfect, more wonderful, or more welcome.

Before, I had hoped. Now, I *knew*. I was going to escape. I didn't know how, but Charlie and Mado Keyr were going to save me.

Chapter 9

Charlie

Suzee Delight and Charlie marched side by side through the airlock to the ship and entered the bridge, where Captain Shore, First Mate Laure, Two Gold Melie, and Owner's Representative Shay waited to greet them. They did not touch. They did not look at each other.

They had to pretend they had no previous connection, and neither of them wavered in the least.

Shay explained to Suzee that Mado Keyr was suffering from his condition and regretted that he could not meet her in person. The captain, stunned by her beauty, stammered a short greeting, then flushed bright red. The first mate bowed and said nothing. Melie said, "You're more beautiful in person than you are in your holos."

And the two women moved on, accompanied by Melie.

Charlie, having walked prisoners to the core units hundreds of times before, thought she knew the drill, but once they were off the deck and headed toward the sleeper units, Melie said, "The owner told Shay the two of you were to complete the documentation of Suzee's arrival alone. So, Charlie, please call me when you've filed the paperwork and I'll join the two of you at the sleeper cores. If you have any problems, you only have to notify shipcom, and I'll be there."

Charlie nodded.

Melie left.

Once they were off the bridge, Charlie took Suzee's hand. As their fingers interlocked, Charlie began to smile.

They reached the sleeper unit designated for Suzee, and Charlie opened the core.

She and Suzee faced each other.

"Oh, Charlie," Suzee whispered. She wrapped her arms around Charlie and kissed her.

Charlie kissed her back. "I love you so much," she whispered.

"I love you, too," Suzee told her.

From the time they were two, Suzee and Charlie had been best friends. Their ident numbers had been Bellowary-Mews-K-42G85N and Bellowary-Mews-K-42G86N, so they'd shared a bunk in their dorm from the day they'd been taken from their mothers and put into their General Consumer cohort. As they grew up, they'd whispered all of their secrets to each other, held hands, made promises that they would be best friends forever.

They were the two most intelligent students in their cohort. Because they were girls, that was like being the two most intelligent fish in a fish tank. They were still fish, so no one cared.

When they turned nine, Suzee's beauty and entertainment skills had lifted her out of Charlie's life, and for years, neither of them had word of the other, or any idea of the other's fate.

Then Charlie, barely eighteen, was assigned to the *Longview* as a Pact Covenant Observer, and with access to open datastreams, discovered that her one-time best friend had become famous. And an Order A citizen, if only in name.

There was no way Charlie could contact Suzee legitimately. Order E citizens were forbidden to attempt any sort of fraternization with Order A citizens.

But Charlie had a plan.

From her receipt of her first payment from the Office of

Licensed PCOs, she had lived on ship rations, slept in her assigned quarters, skipped off-ship travel, and in every other way hoarded her money toward one single, impossible goal. Shay, noticing that Charlie never went anywhere and never spent any money, asked her why and Charlie had told Shay she was saving up for something special. Shay had offered to let her join the crew's recommended investment plan, and had sworn she would never tell Charlie's controller or anyone else that she was earning extra money.

Charlie had poured every rucet she made into the plan, and had rolled all her profits back into her investment... and she had profited greatly.

When she'd earned enough—which took her four years—she bought her dream.

She purchased the Ultra-Deluxe Suzee Delight Package, which was one whole week alone with Suzee Delight, with no public or client-identified purchasable Sensos of their time together, no monitoring except for vital signs (to guarantee that Suzee lived through the week), no public appearances.

One whole week.

And Charlie had purchased an Order A ident through a trusted source used by a crew member who'd escaped from Norel, a minor Pact World.

For one week, Charlie and Suzee were together. Suzee played guitar and mariole and sang for Charlie; Charlie read novels she'd loved to Suzee. They told each other everything about their lives, the bad as well as the good. They discovered they were still best friends—but more, they discovered that they loved each other.

For that one week, they pretended their dreams had come true, that they lived as permanent partners on the space station Suzie had so hoped to reach, and that Suzee designed body modifications while Charlie built hand-crafted in-system planet-hoppers.

They talked about their imaginary work, held hands, kissed, and shared each other's bodies. Woke up together. Fell asleep together.

Knew what it meant to love and to be loved.

It was the life Charlie would have given anything to have.

And then she had to leave. She'd known before she got to the

Diamond Dome that she would never again have the means to repeat that one perfect week. At most, she could hope for another year or two from her controller before she was recalled and reassigned to a different ship, or to some PHTF world monitoring the care and feeding of murderers, rapists, pedophiles, and thieves.

That one week had become Charlie's whole life.

Her time with Suzee was everything she'd wanted, everything she could have dreamed of, everything every instant of her existence had forbidden.

She loved Suzee with every cell of her being.

And she would be damned if she would let her die.

She'd tried to figure out a way to fake Suzee's death, to certify her execution, put her still-living body in the wooden box, and to get her out of the coliseum where she was scheduled to be executed with no one the wiser.

But Suzee was to be executed by Deathmasters, and Deathmasters could not be bribed, could not be threatened, could not be cajoled.

So Charlie had found another way. It would mean killing every single person in the coliseum except for Suzee and Charlie herself—but the Deathmasters would be there to kill her, the audience would be there to cheer her death, and the administrators from the Pact Worlds would be there to gloat.

To Charlie's way of thinking, they all deserved to die.

The crew of the *Longview* shuttle that took Suzee and Charlie to the coliseum were another issue—but Charlie knew what she was going to do about them.

So when their kiss ended, she put her finger to her lips, then pulled two hairs from Suzee's head. She clipped the base of each hair into the receptacle on the side of Lee's little invention. When she was done, she yanked two hairs from her own head, and clipped the important ends into the sieve with Suzee's. She sealed it, then dropped it into her pocket.

Suzee took Charlie's hand, and with a finger, wrote *What did you do?*

Charlie, following Suzee's lead, wrote, *I just saved you.*

When Suzee nodded and smiled, Charlie said, "You need to get into your core. I have to make sure your Gen-ID from the unit is logged into the database so the Pact Worlds can verify that you're confined and alive."

Suzee winked and climbed into the core. The straps slid in place over her arms, legs, chest, and forehead. She looked startled.

"Don't panic," Charlie told her. "You'll sleep until we arrive at the coliseum."

"Coliseum? How are you going to—" She mouthed the words *rescue me.* "—You know... from there?"

Charlie almost laughed. But because she knew someone was probably listening, she simply smiled, kissed Suzee once more, and said, "Dream of the future, my love. I have this under control. You're going to be all right."

Shay

Shay watched Charlie seal Suzee Delight into the core and sighed.

Charlie hadn't opened her weapon in the ship—yet, anyway. Shay, though, had become certain that Charlie planned to use it in the coliseum, to have her vengeance on the Pact Worlds Administrators who were sure to be present, and to wipe out those in the audience who had come to cheer Suzee's death.

Which meant Shay had *two* extra problems to deal with, and just less than ten hours to solve both.

Suzee first. She waited until Sleeper Level One was empty, then blocked all ship tracking on herself, went to Suzee's core, and pressed her fingertip against a hidden square tucked behind the core's data panel.

The top of the core opened without registering that it was open, without awakening Suzee, without causing so much as a blip in the core diagnostics that fed almost constantly into the Pact Worlds' monitors.

Shay took a lumpy white patch out of her pocket, peeled off the bottom protective cover, and pressed the patch against Suzee's neck. Beneath her fingers, the lump beneath the top patch quickly flattened. Shay held the edges down until the squirming stopped and the lump disappeared. Then she lifted the flat white square that was all that remained of the patch, checked for marks on Suzee's neck, and reassured that there were none, shoved her trash into her pocket.

Shay closed and sealed the core unit, then changed the settings on it so Suzee would be kept unconscious instead of in suspended animation.

Shay tapped twice against the hidden access panel. The unit gave a soft cheep. From that moment on, anyone tampering with the unit would once again set off alarms across the ship.

One down.

Shay returned to her quarters. There, datastreamed interviews from the City of Furies protested not just the execution of Suzee Delight, but the injustices that had caused it. These interviews, now numbering in the thousands, had set off a firestorm of other protests, both in the Pact Worlds and across the rest of Settled Space.

They'd sparked more than five billion unique holovid protests tagged through pingball traffic. And those protests were a fraction of the nova blast of voice pings and screen demands bombarding the Cheegoth Administrative Center, from which the planet was run.

Threats of riots on Cheegoth; threats of trade boycotts by non-Pact Worlds against *all* the Pact Worlds and systems; demands from even Order A Pact Worlds citizens for the replacement of Administrators...

...It was everything she had dared to hope for.

But it wasn't, and could not be, enough.

For any of this to matter, injustice would have to be fed.

Suzee Delight's death was the injustice that would feed it.

Shay checked ticket sales to the live event, had the shipcom vet each ticket application, then got to work on the solution for her second problem.

Transcript: Danyal Travers Reports on the Execution of Suzee Delight

Danyal Travers, SPORC Capital Offenses Interviewer, The Voice of the Pact Worlds, on assignment in the Arena of the Ritalath Free City:

Welcome to Ritalath, and to the Arena of the Kings, one of the largest coliseums in Settled Space.

I am honored to be the commentator chosen by *Longview* owner Mado Werix Keyr, the wealthy and mysterious entrepreneur whose Death Circus enterprise is only part of an empire that includes art, commerce, and industry.

We are here today to witness the execution of Suzee Delight, confessed spree murderer of the administrators of the five most powerful worlds in the Pact Worlds system.

This is the most-watched event in human history.

Above us, the dome is closing over the arena—rain, thunder, and lightning would have interfered with today's proceedings, and with the 227,450 observers who pack the stands today and who have paid tens of thousands of rucets apiece for their seats.

Thirteen Pact Worlds Administrators, including all five replacements for the men murdered by Suzee Delight, are guests invited by Mado Keyr. They have the only arena-floor box seats, just meters away from the execution.

The Administrators are waving to the holovid operators. Unlike most executions, the execution of Suzee Delight is being brought to you *only* by FurioCity Entertainment, a private production company hired by the *Longview's* owner to do all of the promotional work surrounding this execution.

Meanwhile Universtat-verified datastream purchase links confirm that more than twenty billion households are paying for the access-locked live feed, which is being simulcast by closed LokStream technology through origami points to every world capable of receiving it, for an estimated audience of nearly a trillion total viewers.

We are only minutes away from the moment when Suzee Delight will be brought to the center of the arena—

—Wait! The *Longview* shuttle is opening, and all the screens surrounding the arena have lit up. We can now clearly see Suzee Delight, her right arm bound to the left arm of the now-well-known Pact Worlds Observer Charliss Bellowary-Mews of Cheegoth.

Suzee is wearing a white gown, and her hair is loose. According to my sources, the gown is a Pertha Fyne original, valued at twenty-five thousand rucets. It is a gift from Bashtyk Nokyd, well-known dissident writer who was an Order A1 citizen of Meileone on Cantata before he broke the Covenant of Peaceful Speech, then escaped his own death sentence. The criminal Nokyd, still at large, has been one of the most vocal supporters of Suzee Delight, and one of the loudest in demanding her pardon.

Suzee Delight looks… young. Twenty-three Standard years, her birth record says—she would have turned twenty-four in thirty-seven Standard days, but right now she looks much younger.

She is stepping up to the recorders positioned just outside the *Longview's* shuttle.

CLAMOR OF QUESTIONS from news scriptors: "What do you have to say for yourself?" "Have you heard about the protests?" "Are you going to be pardoned?" "Do you think you deserve to be executed?" "Who's the last person you sexed?"

SUZEE DELIGHT: "I have been brought here to die. I chose to claim my actions, I chose to confess my deeds, and I chose to sell my death to the highest bidder.

"I accept that I will die for my actions, even though I believe that what I did was both right and just.

"I place myself in the hands of my executioners, certified Deathmasters from the Slaver world of Trabinknya. I didn't know about the protests, I don't know about any possible pardon. And those are all the questions I wish to answer."

DANYAL TRAVERS: I have just been handed the Official Order of Ceremony for today's execution. The dozen Deathmasters before you will be executing Suzee Delight by the Death of the Hundred Knives.

The order of the ceremony states that Suzee Delight will be bound to the frame assembled in the center of the execution dais, in such a fashion that she can neither move nor collapse. Bannaman Billion-Point holographic recording equipment and VanTarka audio capture is already in place, and Suzee has been fitted with InfinaFeel Sensodine neural recorders...

Chapter 10

Suzee Delight

Just before we stepped out the door, Charlie told me, "We have to get to the center of the arena. So just give them a good show, tell them what they want to hear, and once we're in position, I'll put an end to this nightmare."

I thought I would be frightened.

But I stare up at the stands of a coliseum that has seen more death than I can imagine, and I discover the crowd is not faceless. Behind the private boxes, a woman with my face on her gown weeps openly into her hands. Nor is she alone.

I see many people waving signs—mostly in Standard, but some also in Mergotte, or Kaithe, or Hannish—and they say things like, "Thank you, Suzee!" and "We'll Fight On When You Are Gone," and "You Become Infinite Today." I don't believe in the Infinite, where all our purported selves from a multiverse of infinite lives are supposed to join into one all-knowing Self. I don't believe in the multiverse either.

I believe what I can prove. I think that when we die, we are simply gone, and all that we might have become dies with us. But I do appreciate my unknown supporters' attempts to give me comfort.

I try to find the signs that call for my death, but there are none. Not one.

I try to find the faces of the people who hate me, the ones who are eager to see torture and horror and death, but except for the Administrators and their many guests and supporters in the center-front-row box, I cannot find one.

The rivers of sound pour down from the stands and batter me, too loud to be heard. They can only be felt as waves pounding against my skin.

The sound in my head is my own breathing, which is slow and steady. I find this odd. My heart always races before a performance, but for this performance, I am impossibly calm.

I am suddenly aware of smells. Sunlight on the grassy arena field. Heat-baked dirt from the flat bare patch of ground in the center where the Deathmasters have erected the frame to which I'm supposed to be bound. Sweat and food carried by coliseum vendors up and down the aisles. Charlie's hair, which blows in the little breeze brushing against my skin. From the day I was taken away from my parents, she has been the only human being I ever loved.

She is with me.

She came for me. And I don't know what she has planned, but I trust her. When we are done with this, the two of us will be together for the rest of our lives.

Charlie

The audience wasn't the screaming mob of death-worshippers Charlie had anticipated. Front and center sat the gloating Administrators, come to see the final destruction of their most famous victim. But once Charlie looked beyond their gathering of rich and powerful cronies, everyone else appeared to be on Suzee's side. Charlie could only read the signs that were in Standard, but each of those—every single one—was either calling for Suzee's pardon, or promising to carry on for her once she was dead.

This wasn't right.

Charlie knew who paid to watch executions. There were two groups. People who liked to see things suffer—who liked to hear them scream and beg for mercy before they died—they made up the big group. Family and friends made up the little group—people who sat in the stands and begged deities and fate and anything else that might move the hand of the person with the power to grant a pardon to offer a last-minute reprieve and a refund of the money paid by the Death Circus to win the execution.

Charlie knew as fact that Suzee didn't have family: all Order E children were removed to education centers and boarded in dorms when they turned two, and the breeders who gave birth to them were permitted no contact. As for friends, Charlie was it.

Only… the people in the stands suggested that Suzee had a whole universe of friends. The people in the stands were just the very rich ones.

There were over two hundred thousand of them.

The palm of her right hand began to sweat. The tiny, deadly package in it began to take on the weight of every innocent man and woman standing above her.

Beside her, Suzee walked quietly, confidently, trusting Charlie to save her life. Charlie could not be so calm. Her heart was in her throat. These were not the people who needed to die. They were cheering for Suzee, shouting, "Pardon, Suzee! Pardon, Suzee!"

But she didn't have any more time to think. She had tampered with the controls of the *Longview's* shuttle—a clumsy bit of programming on her part that had fused the hatches shut the instant they closed behind Suzee and her.

Everyone on that shuttle was competent, though, and the instant they tried to open a hatch, they would discover it was locked, and they would find and reverse Charlie's program.

She hoped she'd made enough of a mess to keep them inside the safe air for half an hour. She did not want anyone who had helped her reach Suzee, who had made it possible for her to get back to the only person she had every loved, and to the only person who had ever loved her...

The longer she hesitated, the more chance one of the crew would discover what Charlie had done. The more chance *her* people would be harmed if she went through with her plan.

If she murdered two hundred thousand plus *innocents*. That was her plan.

It was a bad plan.

She wouldn't be killing the death-chasers, the ghouls, the cheering bloodthirsty bastards who had attended every other execution she'd been required to certify.

She would be slaughtering two hundred thousand plus innocents... and if there had been only one innocent in the stands, if the only person who had come to offer comfort was the dowdy, sobbing woman just back of the Administrator's private box, wearing her shabby clothes, waving her misspelled sign that said, "I WILL ALWASY LOVE YOU, SUZEE DELIGHT!"—a woman who from her appearance had almost certainly spent every rucet she had to get here to let Suzee know her life had mattered to someone else...

It would still have been a bad plan.

If Charlie murdered *one* innocent to save the life of the woman she loved, she would be no better than those who claimed their right to slaughter innocents for their twisted visions of some "greater good."

Charlie realized she was crying, realized that her pace had turned from a steady walk to a near-standstill.

Realized in the same instant that her face and Suzee's were on every enormous screen that surrounded the top of the coliseum, and than on that screen she could see Suzee looking steadily at her.

In the instant she saw the two of them together on the big screens, she recognized the expression on Suzee's face as one of resignation.

Suzee knew.

Charlie began to cry harder, and felt the tug of the binder on her left wrist as Suzee's fingers intertwined with her own. Felt a squeeze that was meant as comfort.

Charlie realized that she had a choice. Not a good choice, perhaps—but a choice that would allow her peace of mind. She could live a monster—and Settled Space had enough monsters. She would not join them.

Or she could choose to die human.

She would take that option.

Charlie slid her right hand over her pocket, pretending to scratch an itch. The canister was gone when her hand dropped to her side again.

She looked at Suzee, and Suzee gave her the smallest of smiles, and squeezed her hand once more. In a whisper loud enough that the holocasting and amplifying equipment could pick it up, Suzee said, "Charlie, understand that none of what happens to me today is your fault. Don't blame yourself. You didn't choose your work any more than I chose mine. But... please... when this begins... stand where I can see you. I want your face to be my last vision and memory."

The holocasting and amplifying equipment broadcast Suzee's whisper to the crowd. They fell silent.

Charlie and Suzee reached the execution frame, and the waiting Deathmasters. Unable to think of anything else to do, Charlie undid the binder at their wrists, and let go of Suzee's hand. She stepped back and turned Suzee over to the Deathmasters, gave her Gen-ID confirmation on their pad, watched them confirm that Suzee was also who she was supposed to be.

Half of the recorders were trained on her—she knew everyone could see the tears running down her own cheeks. They could all see that she had allowed the unpardonable to happen. She cared about one of her prisoners.

If the Administrators had not planned to have her quietly murdered before, they certainly had reason to condemn her now.

One of the masked Deathmasters took her arm and said, "The prisoner has requested you over there where she can see you."

He placed her directly in front of the Administrators' box, blocking the view of some of the replacement Administrators.

Those men immediately and loudly demanded that she be removed so they could have a good view of the proceedings.

The Deathmaster who'd led her there turned to stare at them. The black mask he wore, featureless except for the eye holes, was a symbol of terror across Settled Space. He was Death without mercy, Death without pity, Death as pain prolonged, Death as suffering heightened past breaking.

Not even administrators of worlds were immune to that silent stare, that stare that judged them and found them wanting.

The Pact Worlds' most powerful men, who'd been standing and shouting, grew quiet and sat down.

It seemed to Charlie that the whole of the universe took one slow inward breath, waiting to see what might happen next.

In her eario, Shay's voice said, "You did well. We'll take care of you, Charlie."

Transcript (excerpted, seven hours from execution start): Danyal Travers Reports on the Execution of Suzee Delight

Suzee Delight: (sharp cry of agony, then silence)

DANYAL TRAVERS:

The Death of the Hundred Knives continues. That's six knives now, at a rate of exactly one-point-two knives per Standard hour. As a reminder, each blade has been coated in a pain agent said to be unbearable. Because Suzee has been able to maintain her silence after being run through with each knife, the head of the Association of Registered Deathmasters—to demonstrate how these knives work—has provided recordings of previous executions where this technique has been used.

Further, after a protest from the Pact Worlds Administrators present that the knives had been altered to make things easier on the prisoner, the Head Deathmaster demonstrated on the Administrator from Burnell's Rock, using one of the knives prepared for Suzee and permitting the Administrator to pick the knife to be tested. The Deathmaster merely scratched the skin of the Administrator, not even drawing blood.

The Administrator had to be removed from the arena because his incessant screaming, even after the administration of pain blockers, interfered with the recording equipment.

Blood tests of Suzee Delight have shown that she has no drugs or pain blockers in her system, and neuro-reads indicate that she feels every bit of this.

The Deathmasters have been instructed to make her death last for five days, and I can see the pain on her face. Everyone can. It's hard to imagine her enduring five days of this. But—aside from the moment when she is run through with each knife, she's not making a sound.

Because she isn't screaming, or begging for her life, or doing anything except standing there in silence, the producers of this event have been showing previously unreleased recordings of her life as a courtesan.

If you're joining us in progress, Suzee Delight has just taken another knife, and in the most extraordinary execution I have ever seen, is bearing the pain silently. Now another recording has gone up on the big screens.

The note I've just received from one of the producers says that this recording is reputed to be the events leading up to the five murders—

Look! The Administrators have just stood up, and are attempting to leave their box, but the guards around their enclosure are refusing to let them. And now the recording has started.

FROM RECORDING: Radiva Kels, Chief Administrator of Cheegoth

This is the simplest thing in the world. We just change the law to require that all citizens accept government nutritional services in order to make sure everyone is cared for equally. We have justification for it as an expansion of the No Hungry Child program, basing this expansion of services on the outbreak of Order B women across the Pact Worlds who have starved themselves to death because of body-image disorders.

It's the change of one single line in the existing law: "*mandated for the benefit of each citizen child of Orders B through E from birth to age nine*" becomes "*mandated for the benefit of each citizen of Orders B through E from birth to death*" that expands its reach to all ages and full life-spans.

FROM RECORDING: Stannal Bregat, Chief Administrator of Cantata

My God, that's brilliant, Radiva. We simply *help* them. Everyone wants help.

Meanwhile, the instant they are put on birth-to-death government support, their Order listing drops to E, though of course there's no need to point that out. We want them to keep working at their existing jobs, after all—and we'll have to change employment laws to make Order E citizens eligible for Order B, C, and D employment, though of course at Order E pay. At that point, all of their work will go into taxes to support the programs that will support them. We can lower the mandated standard of living to keep costs down.

FROM RECORDING: Soth Smithe, Chief Administrator of Third Earth

We can make this even better. By mandating lifetime nutritional coverage, we'll also have to institute lifetime medical coverage, so people like those poor women can be *forced* into medical treatment for their own good...

FROM RECORDING: Radiva Kels, Chief Administrator of Cheegoth

That *is* better. When we reach that point, we write the laws that allow us to act unilaterally for the greater good.

Within the next few years, we'll need to make our terms in office permanent just so we can ensure our programs remain funded.

We'll add additional programs as necessary to keep one hundred percent of the Order E population taxed to the point where they have no alternative but to stay on the programs. By keeping them on the programs, we can force them to do what's best for themselves.

One line of law—and we can amend that line without it raising so much as an eyebrow. Everyone loves No Hungry Child, or at least the idea of it. We're just making it a tiny bit better.

DANYAL TRAVERS:

That's slavery! Suzee Delight told me that's what they were doing, and I called her a liar. Administrators of the five most important worlds in the Pact Worlds system really were conspiring to enslave everyone in the Pact Worlds.

I'm Order B.

They were going to do that to *me...?*

Chapter 11

Suzee Delight

They see what I saw. Hear what I heard. Not just the people in the stands, but everywhere in Settled Space.

Through the weight of pain so terrible it almost stops my thinking, I find my voice, and call the nearest Deathmaster over.

"I want... to speak to them," I say. "May I?"

He does not hesitate, but moves one of the holocorders directly in front of me, then holds it up so I can speak into it easily.

"No one," I say, "no person... no religion... no government... no business... no organization... has the right to own one second... of your life...

"... Or to demand that you spend one... instant... of your precious time in any... pursuit you do not choose."

I falter, but looking at Charlie standing before me, I find my strength, and push down the pain, and aim my words at her.

"Your life... belongs only to you. Live it to... bring yourself joy. Live it... to create something... wonderful.

"Live it... so that in your last moments... you can truly say... *I have lived... I have loved...*

"And... I have... no regrets."

Shay

The feeds were locked, which meant that they went directly to every person who had subscribed. Nothing could block the signal. The Administrators had insisted on this. The Pact Worlds officials had expected the execution of Suzee Delight to be a cautionary tale for anyone thinking of acting against them.

Instead, in cities and villages across Settled Space, people had just heard Suzee's words, and now Shay was feeding them more parts of the life Suzee had lived but had never owned.

She gave them the dark side of the life of Suzee Delight.

Shay was carefully and slowly building a fire.

Across Settled Space, that fire was getting hotter. Suzee's crowds were growing and their rage was spreading.

In the stands above the trapped Pact Worlds Administrators, an ugly mood had taken the crowd; they were demanding that Suzee be pardoned, and while they had not yet moved to block in the Administrators and their cronies, their shouts were getting louder.

Every secret recording of Suzee demonstrated that, for all the unsavoriness of her work, she had been gentle and kind, talented and hopeful, young and beautiful, and it became clear with every grim segment of her private life laid bare before the audience that she'd had to fight to make the most of the life that had been allowed her. Between beatings and torture by "clients," between ordeals of humiliation and shame, she had pushed herself above that life. She'd studied the science and math she loved, even though she was not permitted to use it. She was kind to those of her clients who did not mistreat her, and did her best to create real relationships with them.

Suzee had not been exaggerating in the least when she'd described the five men she eventually murdered as friends. From her perspective they had been, though it was clear from conversations recorded in their private suites in the Diamond Dome that they did not hold her in the same high regard.

Shay pushed through half a dozen of these looks into the secret life of Suzee Delight, going ever deeper into her past, showing her as a young woman, and then a teenager, and then a young girl— showing what had been done to her every step of the way.

Outside government buildings across the Pact Worlds, mobs were trying to stop the tragedy of the death of someone who had earned a better life.

Shay had the *Longview's* shipcom feeding her constant updates— and events were happening far faster than she had anticipated.

For the first time, Suzee Delight was being made truly human to billions of viewers across Settled Space. No one could see her any longer as the pampered whore the Administrators had claimed her to be.

In the hours since the start of her execution, she had become the daughter, friend, confidante, or lover that people of both genders and all ages discovered they'd always yearned for.

And they were determined to make those in charge of the Pact Worlds pay.

Pact Worlds officials had wanted to make sure everyone everywhere knew the cost of killing a Pact Worlds government administrator.

It turned out it was nowhere near the price of publicly executing a whore.

Now, with riots in the streets, with every world that had previously threatened to boycott the Pact Worlds making good on that promise, along with hundreds of worlds that hadn't even considered boycotting before, the Administrators who had not attended the execution of Suzee Delight were fleeing their worlds if they could, or hiding if they could not find the means to escape.

And the twelve Administrators who remained in the celebrity box directly in front of the execution frame cowered, silent.

Shay had feared Suzee would have to suffer through the whole five days and the whole hundred knives for the mood of the majority of the inhabitants of Settled Space to reach this point.

But the rage of a few had become the rage of all of free Settled Space.

The time had come to show the beginning of the story in order to bring about its end.

Shay selected the recording she'd deemed the most important in Suzee's history, and placed it in the queue, so it would show immediately before the next knife. She could not tell the Deathmasters how to do their jobs.

She could only present them with reasons to do it differently than they had planned.

Transcript (excerpted, nineteen hours from execution start): Danyal Travers Reports on the Execution of Suzee Delight

Danyal Travers: Not a single person in the stands cheers as the Deathmasters convene. An ugly mood has taken the crowd as we wait for the next knife. A silent mob has now surrounded the private box occupied by the Administrators and their friends. They have not yet done anything more than whisper, "Pardon her, pardon her," in the intervals between each recording of her life.

So far, the Administrators have made no move to take their suggestions—which to this reporter seems an error in judgement.

We have a short time to go before Suzee takes the next knife, and we are now being shown her classification interview, recorded when she was nine years old. We see a little girl, dark-eyed, pretty, and cheerful, who has cut her hair very short and is wearing the uniform of a boy. She looks happy as she walks into the classification chambers.

FROM RECORDING: Educational Selector Veral Timothy: You are Order E, ungraded, age nine, Bellowary-Mews-K-42G85N. Is that correct? Your ident says you're female, nicknamed Tikka. Why are you dressed in a boy's uniform?

. . .

FROM RECORDING: Suzee Delight, age 9: The olders in the Mews say that girls always stay here, but boys are sometimes classified for space stations and other places far away. I want to do science. In Bailey's Irish Space Station, GenDaring scientists make new kinds of people, and I want to do that. So I want to be a boy.

FROM RECORDING: Educational Selector: We don't change people's genders so they can chase after nonsense. You were born to serve your world, and you will be classified where you are most needed. Science—no. We don't need scientists here, and science is the work of men, anyway. But we always have work for pretty girls. You can sing?

FROM RECORDING: Suzee, age 9: I am second in my group in singing and dancing, and fifth in drawing and painting. I am learning the guitar, though it hurts my fingers. But I am *first* in math and science. Those are much more fun than dancing or painting.

FROM RECORDING: Educational Selector: No one is going to waste an Order E girl on science. You have good thick hair, and when it grows back out, you'll be popular enough. You have bright eyes and a pretty mouth. You'll learn how to please your betters, and if you're as smart as you think you are, you'll like it. I'm placing you in Introductory Arts and Pleasures, and starting you as a consort-trainee.

FROM RECORDING: Suzee, age 9: What is that?

FROM RECORDING: Educational Selector: It's the only kind of work your sort should do. *(Speaking to someone offscreen)* See that she goes to House Tarleymin. In Stonehill Corners. Right. *(Speaking to Suzee again)* I'm naming you Tawny Girl. I'll drop in on you from time to time to make sure you're learning your work.

FROM RECORDING: Suzee, age 9: You'll come visit me? You'll be my friend?

FROM RECORDING: Educational Selector: *(Laughing)* Yes, pretty child. I'll be your *friend*.

DANYAL TRAVERS: *(Under breath, but still clear)* Someone needs to kill that bastard. Wasn't anyone *ever* there to look out for her?

CROWD IN THE STANDS: *(Blocking out all other sounds)* Pardon Suzee! Pardon Suzee! Pardon Suzee!

DANYAL TRAVERS:

Wait! Something is happening near the frame where Suzee Delight is bound.

The Deathmasters are *all* going to their knives. I've never seen this before. Each of them is taking up a knife. There is going to be no chance for a pardon. They're getting ready to finish this!

SHAY, Owner's Representative for the Death Circus ship *Longview*, over the coliseum's sound system from inside the *Longview* shuttle: The following section comes from the execution clause in the contract between the administrators of the Pact Worlds and the owner of the *Longview*.

"Against the direct request of Mado Werix Keyr, owner of the

Longview, the representatives negotiating in the interests of the Pact Worlds as regards the execution of Bellowary-Mews-K-42G85N, known as Suzee Delight, do hereby declare that no circumstances can exist in which a pardon can be granted for the aforementioned criminal, by anyone, anywhere, and that the condition of her death by execution must be met publicly and her death witnessed by a certified representative of the Pact Worlds.

"Any reversal of the death sentence by pardon, or any requested delay, if obeyed, will render forfeit the lives of *Longview* owner Mado Werix Keyr, every crew member of the *Longview* Death Circus employed at the time sentence was to be carried out, and any subcontractors hired by the *Longview* to assist in carrying out this sentence. This by order of the administrators, sub-administrators, and negotiators for the Pact Worlds Alliance.

"Three hundred seventy-two Pact Worlds representatives' Gen-ID signatures follow this clause, and copies of the complete clause—along with the contact and location information for each of its signatories—are now being made public through this locked datastream."

DANYAL TRAVERS: *(Whispering)* There can be no pardon.

The Deathmasters have their knives in hand, and are approaching Suzee Delight. They've stopped. They're pulling off their masks. Deathmasters never take off their masks, but each man present has removed his—

They're *crying?* Each man is kneeling to kiss her feet. Each is begging her forgiveness for what they must do.

They are confirming that they cannot save her. There can be no pardon. They must kill her.

The last one is asking if she has any final words...

She... *does.*

155

Chapter 12

Suzee Delight

I'm done. All hope is gone.

But Charlie is standing there, her fists knotted, her face the color of bone.

The unmasked Deathmaster holds his knife to one side, and through tears asks me if I have last words.

I do. They are only for Charlie.

I look into her eyes. "I lived..." I tell her. "I loved. And for every act I chose that I committed..."

Now I am afraid.

Now I have to fight for breath, and all the air has gone.

"...I have no regrets. I love you."

The head Deathmaster looks at me, questioning, and I nod. I am finished. I have nothing else to say.

They surround me and draw their knives.

Transcript (excerpted, nineteen hours from execution start):
Danyal Travers Reports on the Execution of Suzee Delight

Danyal Travers: They're… Oh, god, they're killing her. She's… Oh, god. Oh, please, no. There has to be some way—

I was wrong. I was wrong to say I would cheer her death. I was wrong to say she had betrayed her city, her state, and her world.

We were wrong, all of us who thought Suzee Delight deserved to die. She deserves to live. She deserves to be spared, healed, loved…

There's been a signal, the Deathmasters have pulled back, they're calling for the Pact Covenant Observer—Charlie—the one Suzee spoke to at the end.

(Audible whisper) Oh, god, I'm so sorry.

The Pact Covenant Observer faints as it looks like the execution has been… has been successful…

Three Deathmasters, still unmasked, kneel beside the Pact Covenant Observer and help her to her feet. They are bloody, they are crying.

The Pact Covenant Observer is heading toward the frame where the body of Suzee Delight will remain bound until her death is certain. The Pact Covenant Observer—Charlie, her name is Charlie—wobbles a bit, then steadies.

The crew from the *Longview* shuttle are walking toward the frame now, carrying a plain wood box, required so that there is no chance Suzee Delight can be revived by Medix.

The Observer runs her scanner over the body of Suzee Delight. The scanner readout is up on the screens…

There is a flicker. No. It's gone.

It's gone.

It's gone.

Suzee Delight is dead.

The mob and the Pact Worlds Administrators' own guards turn and attack the Pact Worlds leaders—

Charlie

Suzee Delight was dead.

Charlie did her job, certified the death, saw to the placement of Suzee's bloody, lifeless body into the plain wooden box in which she would be transported to the disposal site.

The wood box was the Pact Worlds' guarantee that Suzee could not be revived by Medix technology.

All hope was dead.

Charlie's world and dreams died with it.

The mob behind her was making sure that the Administrators and their friends would not go home.

The innocent would live. Charlie had not murdered anyone.

She held that thought close.

She was not a monster.

She had not chosen to be a monster.

She stood beneath the hot field lights under a starless sky, exhausted and broken. She stared at that wood box, and at Suzee lying face-up in it, her body bloodied and punctured by the knives of her weeping killers.

Charlie had lived through the ordeal of watching the only human being she had ever loved die horribly, in pain, a spectacle for all of Settled Space.

She became vaguely aware of one of the Deathmasters standing beside her. "I'm sorry," he said. "I'm sorry that she'd dead, and I'm sorry that I was part of her death."

"You did your job," she said dully. "I did my job. We all did our jobs. It wasn't our fault—but she's still dead."

He had pulled the knives from her body, had shoved them beneath the belt of his long black robe.

She turned her head to look at him, to offer him the same forgiveness Suzee had given her. But all she could do was look at those knives.

She thought of the feel of Suzee's still-warm skin as she'd helped lower her into the box, and whispered to Suzee, "The only part of my life I *don't* regret is you..."

...And pulled one of the knives out of the Deathmaster's belt, turned it on herself, and ran herself through.

The pain devoured her. She screamed until nothingness claimed her.

Chapter 13

Kagen

He'd resigned his job two days earlier, right after Suzee Delight's execution ended, even though Anja had not officially accepted his resignation. He hadn't gone back in to work, though, so he was pretty sure she now understood he'd meant it.

He had a week left on his rent on the room he'd never had time to live in, but he was once again unemployed, and since he wasn't going to look for another job, there was no reason to pretend he was going to make rent, or to tie up the apartment Anja might need.

He would go back to the indigent center, and he would let them ship him wherever they wanted to ship him.

He'd started out using Suzee Delight as an excuse to get the stories of the lives of people like him in front of the rest of Settled Space, but by the end he was fighting for Suzee Delight with every bit of imagination and strength he had in him. He'd given his best, had run himself on nothing but air and water the last few days, had in the end brought most of the rest of space with him over to her side—he and everyone in the Furies who had made a stand for her.

He had come to believe in Suzee Delight herself, in her innocence, in the possibility of her pardon. He had watched the execution, and had seen that he'd been right to believe.

Suzee Delight had deserved to live.

And she had still died.

Innocence meant nothing. Justice meant nothing.

He was checking drawers to make sure he hadn't left something
in one of them when someone knocked on his door.

Might be Anja, he thought, coming to show someone through
the place.

He opened it.

It wasn't Anja.

It was Shay.

"You're an idiot," Shay said.

For an instant, he lost the power of speech. When he got it back,
he managed to fake a calm he didn't feel. "Nice to see you, too.
What are you doing here? And why the hell did you dump
me here?"

Shay raised an eyebrow. "I'm here because I'm a citizen of the
Furies, and the city called a critical vote."

Then she growled, "And *dump* you? In the City of Furies? Do
you know how much people are offering to pay to come here? *Dump*
you here? I put you where you fit, you moron—and you fit perfectly.
You did something I don't think anyone else *could* have done. You
saw what it was about the City of Furies that made the people here
special, and then you took their stories, and put them in front of the
blind, complacent, oblivious masses of Settled Space and you
showed those complacent drones that every single one of their lives
mattered.

"You showed them that they had the right to live their own lives,
no matter who they were and no matter where they were, and you
gave them someone they never knew was like them. You made
Suzee Delight a real person to most of Settled Space, and you did it
by introducing Settled Space to the other real people who had lived
her same pain."

She pushed past his door, and moved closer, staring into his eyes.

"You made them care—and you woke them up to see that the people they *needed* to care about and the people they *needed* to fight for were not strangers someplace far away.

"You made them see that *they are Suzee Delight too.*

"They don't get to choose their own lives, but they'd never noticed before. They don't get to be the people they want to be, but everything in their lives was designed to hide that truth from them. Their governments and religions and schools and families and even their friends tell them everything they can't do, and make them pay for the privilege of living out their lives in somebody else's chains— and you're the one who made them see that."

Shay paused. Shook her head.

"And now they are finally fighting back—and doing it in numbers large enough that their religions can't slaughter them and their governments can't imprison them and schools can't detain them and their families can't guilt them."

Shay took a deep breath and took a step back from him. "This was *your* vision, Kagen. This was *your* project. It worked, and people are fighting for their own lives and their own freedom to live those lives as they choose...and now you're going to *quit?* When the citizens of the City of Furies voted you early citizenship with honors because of your magnificent campaign—your magnificent vision of how to give the people here *their* voice in what happened to Suzee Delight? Your magnificent appeal to all of Settled Space to wake up and live?

"You're going to quit now, when Lithra is here? When you have earned the right to be with her?"

Kagen stood there, unable to find a word to say. What she'd just told him started to sink in, and his knees got wobbly. There was a lot he wanted to know, but only one thing that really mattered.

"Lithra is *here?*"

Shay took two steps back, leaned out the doorway, and said, "He hasn't *completely* lost his mind."

And there she was, in the doorway. Lithra. His Lithra.

"You're here," he whispered.

She stepped into his arm, and rested her head against his chest. "And so are you. Please don't give up, Kagen. Please."

"I won't. But I... failed. I fought so hard. And after everything, Suzee Delight is still dead."

Behind him, Shay said, "Yes she is. And so is Charlie. And you need to help make damn sure they stay that way, because your campaign to save Suzee got bigger than anything I ever imagined. Suzee Delight made some terrifying enemies in her last few hours, enemies who would rip space apart to get at her if they ever got even a hint that she might still be alive."

He stood in the room with Lithra in his arms, and felt his heart skip a beat. He frowned, studying Shay's face, puzzling over her words.

"I...didn't fail?"

"Suzee Delight is dead. And Charlie is dead. But then, the man who was We-B93Y back on a hellish PHTF world is dead, too." She smiled at him. "And so is the woman who kissed him. And you have quite a few dead neighbors, dead guy."

He considered that, and nodded.

"There so much you're not saying. I always knew the *Longview* was different. And I thought we were better. Not like other Death Circuses. So...what's going on?"

Shay smiled. "Nothing that concerns you today. You've earned your citizenship, you've won your love. Now you have your own life to live, your own happiness to build. Focus on that."

"But...the owner—he's doing something really good, isn't he?" Kagen said. "He's a great man, with a great vision, whose mission is to help people who cannot help themselves."

Her smile died.

"No."

"No?"

"He's a monster," she said quietly, "with hands covered in blood. He is a worse creature than anything that crawled screaming out of any nightmare you ever had. And he is doing terrible things. He's simply doing those things to people who earned them."

Chapter 14

Suzee Delight, One Last Time

I wake up, and stare up into the face of a stranger who is smiling down at me like she invented me.

"I'm so thrilled to meet you, Suzee Delight. I've wanted for years to thank you personally for *Birds Flying*. It's the best music for stimulating thought that I've ever found. By the way, I'm Berramyn Chase—I invented the Modix—it was the patch Shay put on your neck that delivered the neural adapter into your... you're staring at me... you have no idea what I'm talking about, do you?"

I sit up. I'm on a stretcher in a room. Both are white—the stark, cold white of snow. The woman standing by my bed, Berramyn Chase, wears the same white, but her skin is the rich, deep red-gold of mahogany, and her eyes are a warm and wonderful brown. Her hair is thick, glossy blue-black. It falls in wild curls to her shoulders, and halos around her head.

"Charlie took me off a space station, put me into a monitored transport box, and I slept from there to the coliseum. I remember the coliseum. I thought I was going to die. I—I think I remember dying..."

"Shay didn't tell you the Deathmasters were not going to be able to kill you…" Berramyn frowned. "I supposed she had her reasons, but that must have been hell for you."

"Hell…"

I remember pain. People everywhere, the noise, the smell of the grass, and the heat, and then the stink of my own blood drying on my clothes. And Charlie—"

In the last memory I can pull up of Charlie, she is staring at me. She looks broken, and then I see grim determination come into her eyes. Suddenly, I'm afraid for her.

"Where's Charlie?"

Berramyn said, "So the two of you hadn't planned that she would kill herself? I thought that was a brilliant touch, but—"

"Charlie's *dead?*"

"Of course not. The *Longview* shuttle crew dragged her off the field and put her in one of the transport Medixes on the shuttle. She was inside and hooked up well before the four minute mark for brain death."

"Where is she?"

"She doesn't know you're alive yet. We had a—a little problem with *you.* The Modix worked, but until Shay could get you here to me, we didn't *know* that it had worked. You see, I don't actually have the Modix finished yet, but Shay talked me into giving her one of my test patches. They haven't been through human trials yet, and my simulation testing has been… imperfect. So we didn't have any signs of life on you, and you were in that wooden box. In the finished Modix, the adapted regenerating neural pathways will reconnect in mere seconds, stop bleeding, start reversing damage, and keep core systems operating under most conditions. Your system and your Modix reacted… differently."

Her expression suggests that things went very wrong. "Anyway… Shay got you to me, and I got everything working correctly. I think."

"You think?"

"You're inside the test, Suzee. You're going to have to tell me." Berramyn said, "Stand up and walk."

166

I stand. My muscles ache as if they've been beaten, but I'm alive, so pain does not distress me. I report it, and then I walk, and discover that I'm wobbly, and my balance is awful.

"It may take some more adaptation of the Modix, and another couple of Medix treatments to get everything working at their peak. Let's walk a little farther."

I tire when we reach the door, but she opens it. "A little farther."

And Charlie right in front of me. She's talking to a woman I vaguely recognize. She looks so sad.

Berramyn clears her throat, and both Charlie and the woman I don't quite know look over.

Charlie's eyes go wide, and her jaw drops, and she stands like someone who's never stood before, like she'll fall over at any minute, like she's just discovering the concept of knees.

"You're...alive."

I would run to her if I could. She would run to me if she could. As it is, we totter together and almost fall over and manage to right ourselves and each other before we crash, and then we are kissing, hugging, holding each other alive alive alive alive...

Charlie and I both have questions, and once we have assured each other that we are both really there, that we are both mostly fine, that we will be together, we ask them.

Shay, the owners representative from the *Longview*, is the stranger I almost recognized. She is also the woman who, with Charlie's help, orchestrated my purchase for the *Longview* Death Circus. And she is the woman who, behind the scenes and unknown to anyone but herself, the *Longview* owner, and Berramyn Chase, made sure I survived my own execution.

"Why?" I ask her.

"The owner knew you," she says. "Loved you. He knew that because of... of his condition... he could never be with you, that you would never be able to love him. But since he first met you, he has used every resource at his disposal to find out your true story. He collected the private pieces of your life, and the more he found out about you, the more he wanted you to win your freedom. For you to find love and happiness. He located Charlie, pulled strings, and got her assigned to the *Longview*. He told you that if ever you needed him, he would come for you. And then he waited."

"And I took the chance that he meant what he said..."

"Yes. Everything depended on you. He could not buy you and he could not steal you, but he could legally take you to your execution—and he could make sure that no one would ever come looking for you again. Not your enemies. Not your clients. Not the countless hoards of people who knew you through Sensos. He was in a position to give you your freedom."

Charlie says, "But if *he* loves her, why did he bring *me* into this? She would have been so grateful to him for saving her, she would have stayed with him if he'd asked her."

Shay says, "She loves *you*, Charlie. And Mado Keyn knows that he cannot be loved—that he is not worthy of love. He can only maintain the pretense that he is a good and decent human being for a while, until his illness overcomes him and he turns terrible." In Shay's eyes, I see tears. "He loves Suzee, so he wants her to be happy. And he knows that she could never be happy with him."

"You love him," I say to Shay.

And her smile is sad. "I hate him. He is right to think himself undeserving of love. But sometimes I do pity him. And I am willing to help him pay his penance for being what he is. It allows me to meet people like you, Suzee, and you, Charlie—and people like Berramyn Chase, and the other Furies. It allows me to be a citizen here, even if I cannot yet stay here. Someday he'll die, and on that day I'll celebrate, and move here for good. But this is not that day."

I consider the gaunt, wizened, damaged man I remember well from the few times he visited me. He can only be outside his protective suit for moments at a time, and the slightest touch hurts him. Inside his suit he can move, and the suit makes him very strong. But he doesn't like seeing the pain of others the way so many broken men do, and he never hurt me. Instead, he likes laughter.

He wanted me to sit beside him, to talk to him, to sing for him. He liked to watch me undress, but he also liked to watch me cook. To eat. To walk around my fine quarters. He loved watching me paint, and once I put a brush in his gloved hand, and told him I would show him how to paint if he liked—and he said that painting was something he remembered from before he became ill. And he painted me an amazing picture of how he saw me. He made me radiant, laughing, a dancing naked muse floating in the sunlight above a stormy sky. He gave me the painting, though I tried to encourage him to keep it. Courtesans were not permitted to keep gifts from clients.

And in private, he had been gathering up all the secret holos my... the holos my owners had been keeping of every move I made and every action I took.

"Why did so many people come to my defense?" I ask.

Shay says, "A promising *Longview* crewman ended up in this city, and discovered that the people here were incensed about your upcoming execution. He knew vaguely who you were, but it was their outrage that you were to be executed that fascinated him. He created a campaign of their interviews, and released them at no charge through the datastreams. People found them, and discovered that they only thought they knew who you were."

I consider this. I had not seen any of the interviews from people who had come to my defense—my keepers would never have permitted me to have access to such things while I was in my cell. I knew when I looked up into the crowd in the coliseum that something had to have happened to bring them there, but I couldn't imagine what that *something* might have been.

I shake my head and look Shay in the eyes. "Why would the people *here* care whether I was sentenced to death or not? I killed the men I said I'd killed. Who was I to them?"

Shay smiles. "First, every person in this city escaped from a Pact World to get here. Including Mado Keyr, and including me. Almost every one of the citizens here was under a death sentence. Many of them still are. They know what the Pact Worlds are, they have people they care about still trapped on them—and because of this, they are already sympathetic to people facing the Pact Worlds' brand of justice.

"Second, the instant Mado Keyr got notice that you had killed five Administrators, he acquired and sent me the recording of the plans the five Administrators were making. He'd already tapped into that system some years ago, and the tap still worked, so he actually knew what had happened before the news reached the surviving Administrators.

"I sent that planning session of theirs to a friend of mine here who owns a recording and datastreaming company, and she immediately streamed it to every citizen in the Furies. She kept it from indigents and non-citizens, of course, because if they failed citizenship, they would have taken with them the knowledge that we had this information before anyone else. Information like that would be dangerous to every citizen here."

I'm trying to put all of this together in my head. I ask Shay, "So Mado Keyr decided if he ever got the chance, he would free me. When I killed five terrible men based on his promise to protect me, he had you send the recording of them plotting—and I assume, of me killing them just moments later—here. They saw what I saw, and..."

"And we were furious," Berramyn says. "We wanted to do something to save you, but we had no idea what. Then Kagen—who wasn't even a citizen—went to Anja with her datastreaming company with his idea for a protest—and Shay passed on to her the request from Mado Keyr that citizens not mention the damning holo of the five Administrators, or let it leak out into the rest of Settled Space. Each of us was briefed before meeting with Kagen, or—later—with his helpers."

At this, I cannot keep silent any longer. "Why?"

"Because we wanted both of you here, and Settled Space would have demanded—and got—your acquittal and return to your life as a courtesan if anyone saw that holo too soon. You would have been locked back in the same cage you'd just escaped."

I consider this. "Everyone had to see me die for me to be free."

"Yes."

Charlie says, "You said you wanted me here, too?"

"We weren't sure about you. Shay told us everything you did to help Suzee. Everything. Including you acquisition of a nanoviral bomb that would have let the two of you walk away from the coliseum untouched, leaving nothing but corpses behind you. Character, though, isn't just what people do. It's what they *can* do, but choose not to. Before the coliseum, we only knew what you *could* do. After, we knew what you wouldn't. And refusing to buy your happiness with the deaths of innocents made you different than those who rule the worlds you've now escaped."

"So all along, Shay and Mado Keyr were on Suzee's side... and mine," Charlie murmurs.

"Thank you for my life—for both our lives," I tell Berramyn. "Dying was... There is no word."

"There's a word. Horrible," Charlie says. "Dying was horrible."

"Well, now you're reborn—and as new citizens, you'll need to come up with new names. You can't meet anyone here—ever—as your old selves."

I nod. "When I thought I might go to GenDaring, I'd picked out the name Tikka Hale for myself," I say.

Charlie says, "I always liked the name Bob." She gives me a sidelong look. "Or Bobby? So maybe—Roberta Hale?"

She looks a me, eyebrow arching upward.

"I love that," I tell her. And ask Shay, "Can we have the same last name?"

Shay laughs out loud. "If you want, you can both have identical bodies. Of *course* you can have the same last name."

"And about bodies," Berramyn says, "You both have to change your appearance before anyone but the two of us sees you. I have a U-Dezine Bodymod station in my apartment—you'll be able to change your appearance before you leave. Shay will set you up with your citizen idents."

Shay nods. "Local requirement is three names, no numbers. We'll do the citizen cards after you have your new appearances. You'll need them for work. We have offers for both of you already, by the way. Suzee, GenDaring has a satellite research branch here, and the three folks working there now are very excited to have you as a new trainee. Charlie, Dromedan Kourso is a ship designer here who would be willing bring you in as an apprentice if you're still serious about designing planet-hoppers.

We both nod. I squeeze Charlie's hand. "We're alive. We're together. We get to keep each other. We're here," I whisper, and wrap my arm around Charlie's waist. And then I stop, realizing that to me, here means together with Charlie, but that I have no actual *place* to attach to that concept. "Where is here, exactly?"

Berramyn laughs. "I'll show you. This building has a wonderful view of the city."

We step outside her door into a public corridor that terminates in gravdrop. We step in and float upward, to an outdoor observation platform at the top.

Above me the sky is a blue so rich and clear it shocks me, the air so sharp and cold and clean it takes my breath away.

The real magic, though, comes when I look down. Below me lies a little city of impossible beauty. It gleams gold and red and blue and green, purple and silver and shimmering white in the sun. Traffic races below us in floating streams, with different streams layered over and under each other in always-crossing, never-slowing lines, as if they're weaving the world together. Farther below, the dots that are other people hurry from point to point, their movements as steady as the traffic.

The city sings with energy, and I think, *I get to work at GenDaring after all.* I find myself grinning, and though I cannot explain it, I'm suddenly laughing. Then the woman I love and I are hugging each other, and the two of us fold Shay and Berramyn into our embrace.

Shay, who is helping a strange, broken man find absolution.

And Berramyn Chase—who was once just another smart fish in the fish tank—and who won her way to freedom to become the woman who has figured out to make a human body reverse its own death.

"You called the people here Furies," I tell Berramyn.

She nods.

I don't dare to hope, but I suddenly suspect a myth I have dismissed all my life as too good to be true is about to be proven real. I want it to be true. "This is the city that gives people who were forbidden to be alive their chance to live." I whisper my hoped-for truth. "Is this *the* City of Furies?"

"It is." Berramyn smiles. "And now it's your chance to live. Make it count. Live wonderful lives, both of you." She waves an arm over the glorious tapestry laid out beneath me. "Suzee, Charlie —welcome to the City of Furies.

THE
Philosopher
Gambit

TALES FROM THE LONGVIEW

HOLLY
LISLE

For Matthew

Chapter 1

Bashtyk Nokyd (The Philosopher)

"As a gesture of rage and protest, I recently bought a pretty girl a fancy dress for her execution. In retrospect, that was an error."

I keep my voice down when I say it.

Across the booth from me, a curvaceous green-eyed redhead gives me the smallest of smiles. "Everyone makes mistakes. For a man in your situation, that was a breathtakingly public one, though."

Her gaze flicks around the crowded room, filled with rough men and dangerous women, pauses at something back of my left shoulder. I see her eyes narrow, and then she's looking at me again.

"But if you hadn't bought that dress, we wouldn't be meeting now." She arches an eyebrow. "That gesture bought you… friends."

I nod. Try to smile, but fear is a tight knot in my gut. That idiot gesture bought me enemies, too. I have twice managed to escape bounty hunters, and now there are rumors the Pact Worlds Administrators have changed the rules. "Latest word through the ping is that the Administrators have contracted with assassins. I've been lucky twice, but…" I shrug. "Can you help me?"

At the bar to my left, a fight breaks out — not some rolling, swaggering fight of drunken punches by two men, but two angry women with knives, moving fast at each other. I have never seen women fight before, and hope never to again. There are no screams, no shouts, just the flash of knives, cries of pain, the thud of flesh against flesh. Blood spatters on our table, an elbow grazes my head.

Bar patrons scramble out of the way as one woman falls dying to the floor while the other stands above her, bleeding, gut-stabbed, swearing under her breath. It is over in seconds. Both women might live if someone tosses them into Medixes, but the bartender and a couple of bouncers are dragging both out into the space station corridor.

My contact isn't smiling anymore. "Place is going to be crawling with sporcs in a minute. My contact said you want transport, that you can pay."

"I can pay. But I want to get to…" I almost say the name, and catch myself just in time. "I heard that your ship contacts a *certain city*." Those are the words I was told to use. Certain city. That if I were to book passage, I might be able to get there.

She shakes her head. "Our ship never leaves its route. Can't. Our movements are public record, tracked. We have never been to the *certain city*."

"But…" I have traveled under assumed names, met with other strangers, paid thousands to get to this one place, this one moment, for this one meeting. I came here believing that this would be the end of my journey. That after this I would be on my way to safety and to true freedom.

I am risking my life just to sit across a table from this woman my gut tells me is as dangerous as everyone else in this dark and noisy bar. And this is not, as my last contact had promised me, my answer. This is simply one more middle point.

"You can book passage with us — no names, no records. I don't know how you got to us, I don't know who mistook us for something other than what we are… but we'll take you aboard." Her eyes are staring into mine. "We cannot take you where you want to go, but we will not stand in the way of you getting there. You understand?"

I don't, but I say, "Yes." Because I have no place else to go.

I don't doubt the rumors of assassins. I slapped my name, my presence, and my protest across the faces of every friend I'd ever had in the top tier of Meileonese society when I bought Suzee Delight a designer dress to wear to her execution — and then had a contact slip a copy of the receipt with my signature on it to Danyal Travers. I wanted to let my old friends know that I had not forgotten about them and their criminal actions against their own people. They'd already sentenced me to death. It was only after I rubbed my continuing freedom in their faces that they got serious about seeing me dead.

I am not going where I want, but I have nowhere else to go.

"Whatever you need from me," I tell her.

"Passage is two thousand cash," she says. "Rucets only."

I nod. I hand her the chit, she scans it and validates it. "Let's go. Once we're outside this bar, do not say a word to me or anyone, keep your head down and your eyes on the floor at all times, and stay to my right. Got that?"

I nod. I follow her out the door, down the corridor, realizing that I am entrusting my fate to a stranger vouched for by other strangers — that she could be anyone. Her shipsuit is nondescript — no crew markings, no ship's name, nothing. She could be an assassin herself. She moves the way I imagine cold-blooded killers move. But I keep my head down, my eyes on the floor. I have come this far. I cannot know that I will be safe, or that I have made the right choice. I can only know that this is the chance I have bought and paid for, and this is the chance I cannot permit myself to lose.

The corridor is crowded, and I am pressed close to the right wall of it. The thin layer of moleibond that stands between me and the death of vacuum is flawlessly clear, and I cannot help but see the black beyond, the splash of stars spreading beneath my feet. For a moment, I see once again the strellita-lit arch of false sky above Oldcity, and I feel a pang of loss. Meileone, my home, is lost to me forever.

I don't know what my future holds. I only know that it will be far from my past.

Danyal Travers

"This is Danyal Travers, Voice of the Furies, with Twenty Points: News for the freedom seekers trapped inside the Pact Worlds Alliance.

"Item One: The little men of the Pact Worlds Administration have met again. Minutes leaked to this investigator from their last meeting confirm that the criminals who rule the Pact Worlds are seeking to break another contract, this time with the owner of *The Longview.*

"Remember, *The Longview* is the Death Circus ship that carried Suzee Delight to her execution, and that, when the universe screamed for her pardon, let the universe know the Administrators demanded in their contract that if Suzee Delight was not executed, the ship's owner, all its crew, and all subcontractors for her execution would be executed in her place.

"Now these Administrators have engaged the law firm of Fenga, Ruttquivt, and Challs to lay claim to *The Longview,* all of Mado Keyr's incomes and possessions, and all rights to products related to Suzee Delight's life and execution…"

"**ITEM EIGHT**: If you are still trapped inside the Pact Worlds system, be wary of strangers offering to sell you weapons. Rebel sources have proof that slavers are using this tactic to capture new slaves — though how these slavers are managing to travel through Pact-Worlds-guarded origami points without being apprehended remains a mystery…"

"**ITEM FOURTEEN**: Well down our list, here's some good news for a change. The Madrigal system, previously a Pact Worlds Covenant signee, has revoked its Pact Worlds charter and declared its independence…"

"**ITEM SEVENTEEN**: Slaver pirates appear to be targeting systems with worlds newly independent from the Pact Worlds Alliance…"

"**ITEM TWENTY**: In spite of the ever-increasing bounty on his head, Liberation Philosopher Bashtyk Nokyd has not yet been apprehended — and The Voice of the Furies cheers him on in his fight for individual freedom and rights for every human being…"

"…AND that's the Twenty Points. If you have proof of corruption, collusion, or criminality from those who hold power in the Pact Worlds Alliance, start fighting for your freedom. Send your proof securely to Ping Eighty-Eighty-Five, Danyal Travers, The Voice of the Furies."

Chapter 2

Shay

Her lungs felt tight and the air seemed far too thin until she passed through the last airlock to *The Devil's Dilemma*.

But once the moleibond hatch sealed behind her, Shay exhaled and her knees went weak. She sagged and leaned against the deck.

Bashtyk Nokyd studied her, a puzzled expression on his face. "Are you... unwell?"

Tears were starting in her eyes, and her throat tightened. She shook her head and managed to say, "I did it. I actually got you."

"I... don't understand." She saw fear in the philosopher's eyes. She rested a hand on his shoulder and said, "I'm not some random flesh-mover, Mado Nokyd. My name is Shay — *just* Shay, and I'm the representative for Mado Werix Keyr of the *Longview*. He has been trying to get you aboard since the first announcement that you'd been given a Death Sentence in absentia and had a bounty on your head. As for me, you have been my hero since I was in —" She stopped herself. There were parts of her life she did not discuss. Not even with her hero.

So she changed the subject. "I told you most of the truth back in the bar — the *Longview* doesn't go to the City of Furies. Not directly. But we can still get you there eventually."

She could feel his emotions pouring off of him, washing over her. Elation. Hope. He whispered, "I'm... safe?"

She pointed to the seat behind the captain's chair, and held up one finger. He nodded and settled into the seat she'd indicated, and waited while it conformed around him.

Shay, meanwhile, locked herself into the command seat and said, "Shipcom — connect to Station Control. Notification Shuttle Fellows T-38 from Fellows Moon debarking from Dock 42."

There was a moment of silence. Then WheatRun Station com said, "Shuttle T-38, station-com has your signal. Follow your shipcom lock-on until you're outside of station traffic. Break lock on our mark, and proceed to exit point."

"Course set, com ackked. We are breaking seals and lock on... your... mark..." She separated from the station dock and peeled into traffic, carefully following the route set for the shuttle whose codes she had purchased.

The real Fellows T-38 would show up at the WheatRun Station in two months, just as if it were running its regular route, and had not missed one trip entirely. Mado Keyr's money had purchased that cover — that and the fact that Bashtyk Nokyd had friends in places he could not yet imagine.

She picked up her conversation by answering the question Nokyd had asked before they left the station.

"You're not safe yet. Something was off at our pickup point. Someone was following me, or watching our meeting. If it had been anyone but you, I would have dropped the pickup.

"But we're headed to safety. You and I are going to follow the shuttle route until we're out of WheatRun's range. Then we're going to change the ship ident codes, get to this system's origami point as quickly as possible, do several highly illegal things, and by doing them, meet up with *Longview* on its way to its next Death Circus. As far as the universe is concerned, though, once we're inside the origami fold, you will cease to exist. We're going to hide you aboard the *Longview* for a while. Mado Keyr wants your help on a — a project of his."

"Wait… we're going through the fold in this shuttle?"

She glanced over her shoulder and grinned at him. "This is not a shuttle. *This* is a one-of-a-kind vehicle. It is, as far as I know, the smallest fully capable TFN sidewinder ship in existence. Mado Keyr paid a fortune to have it built — and it has proven useful for him on a number of occasions."

"Such as this one…"

"Especially this one," she agreed.

The philosopher shivered. "I have been told that going through an origami point unprotected can destroy the mind."

"You'll been told correctly, but you're not going through unprotected. You're going to be in a jump berth," she said. "We have four full-Medix jump berths in the back. I'll be unshielded during the trip, but I have a high resilience rating — I deal well with the stresses of the folds."

He nodded and changed the subject. "So you know Mado Keyr."

"Probably better than anyone, for what that's worth."

"He is quite a mystery. I've been fascinated by him for several years now, since he first came to my attention when various friends of mine began noticing how rich he was and how many different industries he traded in. According to them, he's one of the ten or fifteen richest men alive, but there are no pictures of him, no public events that he attends, not a single leaked holo of him anywhere doing anything. He has no apparent past, and not much of a provable present except for the trail of money and disruption that flow in his wake."

"As I said, I *probably* know him better than anyone. But I can't shed much light on the mystery. What I can tell you is this: He hired me to work for him about fifteen years ago. Wherever he is, I must also be. My primary job has always been to be his interface with people with whom he wishes to do business. I have a number of different physical guises he requires I take when doing this — the body design I'm wearing now is what he calls Trouble Girl. In this guise I go into the sorts of places where I meet with people like you.

"My secondary job is to help him stay healthy. Mado Keyr has severe health problems that apparently are unfixable by any known means, including by Medix. I cannot even begin to guess what sort of health problems these might be. I am not permitted to ask — all I can do is follow the steps he gives me to get him into and out of his pressurization chambers, locate and keep in stock various chemicals he needs, and other activities of that nature.

"I do know — and am permitted to say — that he spends an ungodly amount of money buying research from various gen-tech companies — but I have no idea what he's having these firms study, or what he hopes they'll accomplish. And that when he is not inside his pressurization chamber, he lives in a pressurized light-blocking suit, cannot eat regular food, and cannot touch another human or breathe air breathed by anyone else.

"He loves art and science and the pursuit of all knowledge for its own sake. He reveres men and women who know how to think, and who use their minds to create wonders. He was desperately in love with Suzee Delight. He is a sad and lonely creature.

"But not to be pitied. *Never* to be pitied."

Shay had been scanning traffic on the com, and she finally spotted what she'd been looking for: a big TFN passenger liner headed for the origami point. She cloned the liner's ship codes and, disguised — if only via ping and shipcom — as one of its shuttles, raced to catch up to it. As it lined up for the origami-point passage, she would clamp under its belly and camo the *Devil's Dilemma's* skin to look like a hull bump. They would go into the origami point unseen — and then she would peel off and sidewind on to her own coordinates.

It was dangerous as hell, but it was also the perfect way to cease to exist in anyone's records. That feeling she still had of being tracked, followed, watched — this little technological dance would put an end to that.

"We're on auto," she told her passenger, and slid from the pilot seat to take a place in the seat opposite him.

Bashtyk Nokyd leaned forward. "You have no idea where Keyr came from?"

"None. And unlike you, I am not free to research the issue. The block on making any attempt to backtrack his past is one of the terms of my employment with him."

Nokyd grinned at her. "Excellent. Then that means there is a past that can be backtracked. I won't dig into it while I'm his guest. I respect Host's Right far too much to breach it with such crude behavior. But in the future, I'll put some effort into finding out what's back there. The trails his money leaves lead to some fascinating places… places that make the two of us kindred spirits in a number of ways." He gave her a smile that would have fit the face of a little boy promised a wonderful gift. "I'm excited to meet him."

"He wants to meet you, too — he is a great admirer of yours, Mado Nokyd. He will no doubt want to spend as much time with you as he can before he sends you to the City of Furies."

"I still can't believe it's real," he told her. "I have seen what comes out of there, I have watched the miracles the citizens there have pulled off — getting the whole of Settled Space to see the truth of what the Pact Worlds are and the evils they have committed…"

He stared down at his hands. "I want to be a part of that, Shay. And I was so afraid this was a trap," he told her. "I kept thinking that somewhere along the way, someone had sold me out for the Pact Worlds' bounty."

Shay laughed. "No one could have been that stupid. Mado Keyr has been offering a bounty a thousand times greater than the one offered by the Pact Worlds. That is to have you delivered safely to a meeting place of his choosing. And unlike the Pact Worlds, the mado pays his debts. The entire chain of people through whose hands you passed on your way to us has been compensated already.

"Guaranteeing," she added, "that the next time he needs to rescue someone, there will again be people willing to take the necessary risks."

Nokyd frowned. "But if they know Mado Keyr is paying them, doesn't that hand the Pact Worlds a reason to come after him?"

"While he has been offering a bounty, no one has seen Mado Bashtyk Nokyd." She gave him a look of feigned innocence. "Mado Nokyd has met with no one from the *Longview*, nor has he ever been aboard — or even anywhere near — the *Longview*. And the bounty for his rescue still stands — in some very public places, too."

Shay rested her fingertips on his arm. "On the other hand, *Mado Wong Chang*, you, a rich potential patron, hopes to buy some of the lovely things that find their way into Mado Keyr's hands. And now, rich patron, I need to get you into your medichamber before we go through the point. We'll catch up with the liner in just a few minutes, and you must be secured before we reach the origami point."

Rowse, IMAL

In the quiet deep of the *Longview*, the sudden incessant chime of the contract fabricator dragged Rowse away from happy immersion in the latest fictional adventures of Tanne Yho, renegade lawyer turned bounty hunter.

He set his reader aside and rose, grumbling, to see what damned piddling thing had come through on the ping, and discovered this time it wasn't a damned piddling thing at all.

Attullo Rowse, Interspace Master Attorney at Law, with specializations in intersystem contract negotiation and individual rights law, and with a secret sub-specialization in the fabrication of past histories for individuals whose own pasts could not be made public, discovered that he was done with Tanne Yho for the day. Probably, if he was lucky, for just a month. The deeper he dug into the stack of sheets, the more he began to suspect he and his favorite renegade had just spent their last lovely hours together.

He swore softly and said, "Shipcom, get me Keyr."

Shipcom said, "Mado Keyr is in medical pressurization, and has routed all calls to Shay."

There was a delay. Then in his earbud, Shay said, "What's wrong, Rowse?"

"Apparently everything. I've just signed in blood for a Gen-ID-locked stack of insanity from the Cantata Over-Court representing the Pact Worlds Alliance. The Over-Court has claimed impound rights on the *Longview* and all contents; has put out warrants for the arrests of Mado Keyr and all employees and crew of the ship as criminals under sentence of death; has announced as final the reversion of all sold rights on the Suzee Delight execution and all monies therefrom retroactive to the date of the signing of the initial Death Circus contract with the *Longview*; and has demanded that the ship dock immediately at the nearest Pact station to comply with their writ of seizure."

"From your first read, does any of this have teeth?"

"It's nothing *but* teeth, Shay. It's coming from the full slate of the Cantata Over-Court Supreme Justices, all of whom signed off. Which means it carries the same weight as the Covenants of the Pact. Anywhere in Pact Worlds space, we're now dead men walking."

"That's more teeth than I'd like."

"In theory, I can buy us some time. Because *Longview* is a Free Space registry out of Tatulle, the ship is technically outside of the jurisdiction of the Pact Alliance, and I can get an immediate stay of all writs pending review by the Court of Free Space..."

He heard Shay's sigh. "But...?"

"But the Court of Free Space is not the Cantata Over-Court of the Pact Alliance. It will back you on paper, but it doesn't have the necessary army to back you with guns."

"Recommendation?"

"Get out of Pact Alliance space immediately, because the instant the *Longview* doesn't show up at Haile Station on schedule, the Pact Worlds are going to throw everything they can at us to hunt us down. We need to be able to fight our legal battles when we're not sitting in the middle of enemy territory."

Shay had a colorful vocabulary, and ran through a good part of it in Rowse's right ear. "I'm four hours out, best case."

"You're not aboard?"

"I had to pick up a package for the mado. Have shipcom connect me to Captain Shore, and I'll have him reroute to meet me halfway. As soon as you've done that, file whatever you have to file to get this mess stalled. As soon as I'm back aboard, we'll have to run for the nearest non-Pact space. And since we're going to have to run through at least one Pact-controlled origami point to do it, we can anticipate trouble."

"I'm on it," he said, and cut the connection.

Attullo Rowse had started life as a slave, had earned himself a death sentence by killing his master to escape, and had managed to be in the right place at the right time to luck into a crew slot on the *Longview*.

Aptitude testing had shown him to be both highly intelligent and clever, and Shay had pushed hard with the owner to get him through general education at the fastest pace possible, and then into an accredited law school.

He had excelled. He knew that if he did well, he would have a place on the *Longview* until he timed out as crew and had to set up his own practice elsewhere, but that was not the future he saw for himself.

So he had done better than well. He had pushed himself to and sometimes beyond the breaking point. He had lived a monkish life of simple foods, regular exercise, no sex, and unending study, had taken every advanced course at an acceler-ated pace, and had graduated as the top student in his class. He had then passed the bar in his first attempt with a perfect score — one of only three students in all of Settled Space that year to do so.

He had done in five years what most students managed only half as well in ten — and he had done it not because he was smarter than everyone else, but because he was willing to work harder, to put everything else in his life aside. For five years, he made himself a pure vehicle for the transmission of the concepts of law from records to mind.

With his accomplishments, scores, and determination in hand, he had returned to the *Longview,* and insisted on a private interview with the owner himself.

It had been the most terrifying hour of his life. The owner made Rowse's skin crawl — his illness radiated off of him like the aura of Death incarnate.

But Rowse knew what he wanted, and only the owner could give that to him.

"You made me," he'd told the still, suited figure in front of him.

"You made yourself," the owner had said, "and did a fine job of it. You should be proud of yourself."

"I don't have time for pride. I did it because I want to ask an enormous favor of you, and I needed the best leverage I could get so I could twist your arm into granting me that favor."

The sigh had echoed like an escaping ghost from the owner's rebreather. "Whom shall I rescue from Hell for you? And how many? It doesn't matter — if they're still alive, I'll get them for you."

"That isn't it. It's nothing like that. I want to be made permanent crew."

"You... *what?* You have spent the last five years killing yourself in study to have a job any intern could do — and you want to be locked into that for the rest of your life?"

It was then that Rowse had laid out for Keyr his vision of what a future that included a partnership between the two of them could mean.

"You're hiring out your patent work, your contract-writing, your ID creation for crew members. You need to have someone in-house to do these things for you. Someone you know is loyal, someone you know cannot be bought — and someone you know has the skills to do every bit of legal work you need to have done.

"I have proven that I can excel. But more than that, I have proven that I can learn anything put in front of me — and what isn't put in front of me, I can go out and find.

"I have already researched three places where I could go to learn how to build airtight IDs for your crew, better than anything you've been able to get them. If you will put me on as permanent crew, I will spend the rest of my life mastering every new element of the law that you need to make yourself richer and more powerful."

The owner said, "And in return?"

At this, Rowse had smiled just a little. "You compensate your regular crew well."

"I would say spectacularly," the owner had murmured.

"So would I, but money isn't the biggest thing you give them. You give them a way to earn lives and skills they can take with them. You protect them. You earn their loyalty every day, with every action you take — and you have earned my loyalty. I want to make you richer — and I want to be compensated accordingly."

"Good for you. I appreciate the fact that you're willing to say that."

Rowse had sighed. "Also, and please never let anyone know I said this, but I'm more than a little in love with Shay."

"No man can have Shay."

He and his hand had enjoyed Shay most nights he was in law school, but he didn't think it prudent to mention that.

"I know she's yours…"

"You misunderstand me. No man can have Shay, because Shay only desires women. Her story is darker than you can imagine — far more hellish than yours — and at the back of it lies a man who was a monster. He stole her and owned her unspeakably. When she killed him, she freed her body. And over the years, she has crawled out from under the worst of her darkness. But I do not think she will ever come back far enough to desire a man again."

"I didn't know that."

"And you'll never tell it to anyone else, anymore that I'll will ever tell anyone what happened to you." The owner leaned back in his chair in the black room, the single light on the table between them glowing. "Knowing that you have no chance at Shay, do you still want to tie your future to this ship?"

"Not to this ship. To you personally. I want to be your personal lawyer, and I want to act for you, and for any of your people, in any capacity in which you need legal work done."

"We'll have to draw up a contract," the owner had said.

And Rowse had replied, "I brought one with me."

Keyr chuckled. "Of course you did."

Ten years later, for the very first time, Rowse wondered briefly if he might have made a mistake.

And then he shook it off and got to work.

Chapter 3

Bashtyk Nokyd

Rested, feasted, Medix-flushed and pampered, and left for a day to recover and refresh myself, I feel like a new man.

I spend the first portion of my morning digging through both legal news and all the freshly wormed illegal Pact World reports a truly fine Spybee hacker can provide. I am fascinated and thrilled by how quickly and furiously Settled Space is reconfiguring itself. And I'm happier to be watching these changes now that I'm out from under immediate danger of death.

Going through the current events in Settled Space, I've come to two conclusions. The first is that my host has a deep well of talent in his employ, and he has some of his people employed in interestingly subversive activities.

The second — this upon discovering that I am still being hunted, but now with the bounty raised; and that my host and the entire crew of this ship are now declared condemned criminals with death sentences on their heads — is that I am tired of the universe, and just about everyone in it.

I do have one brand new exception.

In my days here so far, I have acquired a guilty but delicious secret. To the crew and guests, my host provides all sorts of fascinating current entertainment, and I have discovered live Sensogaming — and more particularly, a wonderfully violent, delightfully raunchy game called *Old Earth Cowboys Versus The Bug-Eyed Monsters of Mars.*

After creating an account, I have occupied myself for the majority of each day as a member of a variable twelve-person unit comprised of complete strangers pinging in from elsewhere in the star system. We are brave men and women` who have banded together to shoot down alien monsters bent on taking over Lonesome City and kidnapping — for undoubtedly horrific purposes — Miss Sweetbits and her harem of ladies and gentlemen of delight. And as we earn the rewards of saving Miss Sweetbits and her harem, we can use our rewards to purchase the company of various harem members — all in full, utterly believable, live action sensory detail.

While I have passed on the companionship of Old One-Eyed Beddy, exchanging her reward ticket for extra Sarspariller and Mightee-Chili, I have twice used tickets to visit Chunky Cherri.

Oh, my!

I cannot believe I have lived my whole life without ever knowing about Sensogaming. It beats hell out of the opera.

When we are not attempting to win time with lusty beauties or eating feasts of exotic AlienFuud, or telling grand lies about ourselves, my fellow saviors of the universe and I shout instructions, plans, and happy profanities to each other, ride horses that run like the wind, and shoot weapons that splatter bug-eyed, tentacled armies of enemies with such deadly substances as water, hot cheese, small mammals called gophers, and squishy loops called rubber bands that are hard to come by, but absolutely lethal when acquired and loaded into our gaudy weapons.

My horse is a wild brown-and-white Pinto stallion I have named Hero-Hooves. He is a killer in his own right, deadly to anything that attacks me if I am unhorsed, and from no other person in the universe will he accept saddle or bit — but he is devoted to me. I have already leveled him up five times, and I frequently spend my in-game credits buying him whiskey-and-gunpowder, his favorite drink, to reward him for saving my life.

My gun is now a MultiVexxor Six, with a special side-trigger that blasts an entire twenty-pack of rubber bands in a 280 degree semi-circle of alien-withering death and destruction, and only the unbelievable difficulty in finding twenty rubber bands with which to load the chamber keeps me using my gun's five other modes, which include the ReloadingExploding Gophers — thirty little animals who launch themselves at the enemy, explode in a blinding shock wave of destruction, then race back to me and reload themselves into Cylinder Five of the MultiVexxor.

I am TheProfessorOfDanger, a Sarspariller-drinking, skirt-chasing hero from another age — and in the game, I *love* the universe and every bug-eyed monster and busty, enthusiastic woman it cares to throw in my path.

Life is glorious.

And then, in the midst of bringing down the alien captain by myself so I can revive my eleven downed comrades, the earbud with which I was fitted when I came aboard dings.

A voice I don't recognize says, "Mado Wong?"

For a moment I am disoriented. I "park" my character, and am instantly back in my quarters, once again a man without rubber bands or a horse. I am bereft.

Shay was ferocious in her instructions that my identity must be known to no one on the ship. So she had dubbed me Mado Wong Chung, one of the most common names in Settled Space.

And I have to take a moment to remember that here, as in the game, I am not Bashtyk Nokyd.

"This is… Wong."

The voice in my earbud says, "I'm Melie, the ship's Two Gold. I've been instructed to take you to a private dinner with the owner in two hours. Formal dress is being autofabricated in your quarters now. I'll arrive at eighteen-hundred-fifty hours to pick you up."

And instantly I am invigorated, excited, intrigued. "I'll be waiting when you get here."

Mado Werix Keyr is one of many Settled Space legends without a beginning. He fascinates me beyond all others, because he has succeeded so strangely.

Keyr does not use his wealth to seek fame… and did not gain wealth by first becoming famous.

He deals in the most extraordinary things — inventions and art and bits of technology and science. These things come from the most extraordinary places, the most notable of which is the City of Furies, which all of Settled Space believed to be a myth until he began importing Furies products to a stunned and delighted market.

He owns a Death Circus franchise, a dismal and horrible acquisition that is beneath him and that has caused him endless trouble for what public records show are the thinnest of profits.

And yet as far as anyone can tell, he lives full-time aboard this ancient, outlandish, oversized ship and tends his little franchise with a fanatical dedication greater than he appears to give to any of his other businesses.

He owns not a single grand estate that anyone can locate.

Has no harem of men or women, nor anyone from his past willing to appear publicly to suggest that he once did.

He indulges in no findable vices.

Partakes in no discoverable pleasures.

Purchases nothing that can be either directly or indirectly connected to any debilitating disease.

But he spends money as if it were hydrogen. The economies of any number of small worlds and entire systems in Settled Space list him as their number one client.

Melie arrives at the door at the appointed hour and minute. She's a pretty young woman with a sweet smile. She finds me dressed in the black and gold formal shipsuit fabricated for me in my quarters, ready and impatient to be on my way.

I leave behind a half-lit view of a gallery filled with the treasures of Settled Space, trading this for a maze of corridors stacked floor to ceiling with modified Medixes — individual prisons, no doubt, to keep the nightmarish numbers of Keyr's criminals pacified.

The gloom of these stacks is unbearable, the weight of the place like the tomb of the universe on my shoulders.

"How can you bear this place?" I ask my young guide.

"I'm sorry, Mado Wong," she says. "Crew are not permitted to discuss the ship with guests."

I fall silent. We float down a gravdrop, past more floors filled with more stacks of units that fade into dark pinpoints — units that are filled with Condemned waiting to die. The horror of the place bleeds into me. There are so many people. So unspeaking, unseeing, unfeeling many.

How many people were the Pact Worlds executing every year, that one ship could be filled like this?

How did no one know the number of the Condemned? How did no one care about their fates?

The number of Medixes I saw stacked in just my passage toward Mado Keyr's quarters would have represented genocide on any single world. I did not believe for an instant that I had seen them all.

So what did that number represent here?

At last Melie brings me to two rich dark-wood doors, and says, "I'll return for you once the Mado and you are finished." Aside from her greeting and her response to my question, these are the only words she has spoken.

She leaves me standing outside the doors. When she is gone, a disembodied voice says, "Open the doors and come in."

I look up and see directional sound heads. That's a relief. I take a deep breath and pass through the doors, only to find myself in a tiny, dimly lit, featureless space between four sets of identical doors.

I hear the click as all the doors lock.

I lose gravity, and float to the center of the tiny passageway, which begins to spin around me. I am thoroughly disoriented when gravity returns abruptly. though, lightly, I float to the floor, facing one of the four doors, with the uncomfortable sensation that I have traveled a very long way in a very short time.

"Open the doors to your right."

I open them. The room is painfully dark. I step in carefully, making out the shape of a large desk to my left and a vast empty nothingness everywhere else.

"Rest your hand on the wall to your right, and walk forward."

I do as instructed. The wall jags left, then right, and I follow it.

At the right jag, I face a broad staircase, faintly illuminated.

I climb the staircase, an oddly old-fashioned thing in a ship filled with gravdrops. It funnels out into a soft gray room, nearly empty except for a broad, well-upholstered couch and an expanse of polished white stone wall on which hangs an immense blank canvas.

My host, frail-looking even in his shipsuit, rises from the couch as I reach the top of the stairs, and turns to greet me. He, too, is suited in formal black and gold, but he has a fixed helmet in place, and its faceplate is darkened. Werix Keyr holds out a gauntleted hand in greeting, and I take it carefully and shake it.

"It is an extraordinary delight to meet you," Keyr says. "Yours is a mind I have admired since well before anyone knew my name. I have built much of what I do on principles I first discovered within your work."

I think of the long rows lined with boxes filled with living men and women. I think of Suzee Delight, and place what I know against what I have seen, and I realize with a start that no matter what else they are, all those people in the boxes are still alive.

And then I think that the Pact Worlds and their actions to help people into slavery are coming apart because this man put Suzee Delight in front of Settled Space, showed her to everyone as a human being who had fought and lost in her search to win the life she dreamed of.

He had given people a way to see. And many of them had dared to look, and dared to think, and dared to act.

"I am honored," I tell Keyr.

I have a sense of the man behind the mask, a shadowed glimpse of a gaze fixed with fierce intensity on my face, the overwhelming impression of a hunger so keen it frightens me. In Keyr and in this moment, I sense passion tightly chained, intelligence caged, vitality imprisoned behind walls it cannot escape.

Healthy, Werix Keyr would be a force of nature, I think. He would own the universe.

But then I reconsider. Sick, crippled, his existence and his will channeled through the broken path of his body, Werix Keyr has been forced to focus his life narrowly, and perhaps had become extraordinary *because* of his suffering.

I wonder what the man was like as a boy.

Keyr, meanwhile, leads me to the couch and bids me sit. "I have a wonder for you to witness," he says, "and I have my drone set to bring you a delightful meal while we experience it. You are an admirer of the works of Tai Kavati?"

I am startled that he knows this, and say, "God, yes! I owned her glorious *Winner of the Battle at Mattera* before I was declared a criminal."

"I know."

"You know about a painting I owned?"

"I *own* the painting you once owned. Obtaining the locations of great works I might wish to acquire has been a significant part of what I do for many years. You will have *Winner of the Battle at Mattera* returned to you when you reach the City of Furies." Keyr's voice drops, and he growls, "They should never have stolen it from you." But then he says, "In any case, sit and watch with me."

As we seat ourselves on the couch, a low table rises out of the floor in front of me, and a metal serving drone scuttles out from behind the couch carrying a covered tray.

At the same time, a soft white light begins to glow within the blank canvas in front of us.

"This will become Tai Kaviti's *Heart of the City*. We are going to watch her paint it — though much more quickly than was done by her hand."

"*Heart of the City*. I'm not familiar with that one."

"It's new."

"She's been dead for a dozen years."

The helmeted face turns toward me, and I sense amusement in the set of shoulders and the tilt of head. "No. She is simply out of the reach of the men who owned her. She lives in the City of Furies. You'll meet her. I suspect you'll like her a great deal."

The food I eat might be delicious, but I don't taste a bite of it. Tai Kavati is alive, still working — and I will meet her. On the canvas before me, I watch paint appear a stroke at a time, but quickly. I watch layers build, watch as the artist undoes parts that do not please her, as she adds and changes, chooses and creates.

She paints the backdrop first, with buildings thrusting skyward in wild abandon, endlessly patterned and detailed — architecture in a chaos of styles that speak not of disorder, but of passion and love and the dreams of individual humans shaken loose from imagination and wish, fought for, given life and form and meaning in reality.

Studying angles and perspective, I understand that she is painting from ground level, looking up at the pinnacles of these buildings far above.

Next, she places flying vehicles, representing them with brilliantly colored dabs in layered lines that speed between the buildings, weaving the sky together.

And finally she works in the foreground. Faces appear in a crowd surrounding her, all of them pleasing in their intent, radiating an inner joy that touches me and makes me yearn to be among these people in this world as they hurry to their destinations. And I understand what she's painting.

"Ahh," I whisper, watching the birth of a world I have hungered for my entire life — a world that *should* exist but never can. "That's Heaven — not the way the religious depict it, but the way I always dreamed it might be."

"It's the City of Furies," my host says drily. "Intersection of North Tech and Science — the morning crowd. It's one of my favorite places in the city, and my very favorite time of the day. People on their way to doing amazing things, greeting others doing the same. It's when the city inhales, in the moment before the inhabitants begin to create. I commissioned this painting because I almost never get to the City. And I miss it every second I'm not in it."

"It's... perfect."

Keyr chuckles. "It's a pretty good city. Every single person who lives there earned the right to be there. Every single one continues to earn the right to be there every day. The motto of the city is *No one rides for free.* Every person there lives that motto."

The glow within the painting ceases. It is finished.

"I will do anything to earn my place there," I tell him.

"Good. Help me find a way to set the Pact Worlds' people free."

Melie

She hated being on the run, and they'd been running for days.

The *Longview* tore through space, heading toward the Raythonade origami point, and toward the jump that would take them out of Pact Worlds space.

Melie knew bounty hunters were after them, and that everyone aboard the *Longview* would be imprisoned, tried, and with their guilt already declared, executed if they were captured. The owner's lawyer, Rowse, had announced the amounts of the bounties the Pact Worlds were offering for their capture — they were high enough to interest the worst sorts of hunters.

Those bounties included Class 1-A Pact Worlds citizenships, magnificent properties on Pact Worlds' core planets, guaranteed entitlement incomes, blanket pardons for all crimes committed before and during the capture of the *Longview* and its crew, and more. Every tribe of monsters in Settled Space was going to be hunting them.

But the owner said they were going to be all right. That he was going to get them to safety, that he was going to protect them, that he and his lawyer Rowse already had a safe harbor for them.

All they had to do was get there.

Melie suspected they were on their way to the world of the City of Furies.

Well, she hoped they were.

Rising through the gravdrop from the crew rec room to the bridge, Melie listened to the powerful thrum of the sub-light engines grow stronger as she neared the engine room, and then drop away again as she rose above it.

The ship had been running hard for days, staying well out of sight and reach of anyone watching the official path. If they were on schedule, they had another twenty-four hours before they arrived at the Raythonade point.

When she hit the command deck, Laure was just coming on shift, and Tagly — Melie's Two Silver — and the captain were both going off.

She sat for the report.

Captain Shore said, "Shipcom, record the report. Report is Code April Leader Four. Repeat, report is Code April Leader Four."

"Recording for Captain Shore. Verifying Code April Leader Four," shipcom said. "Go for report, Captain Shore."

"We've been clear the whole shift," Captain Shore said. "No other traffic, no hails, no scans, no pings. We're deep dark. We're going to stay deep dark, and the odds are that you are going to see absolutely nothing during your eight — that you are going to have no problems and encounter nothing unusual.

"But because of the circumstances under which we're operating right now, you are not going to be able to spell each other to nap in the crash room. You're going to have to have two on the bridge at all times, and you're going to have to call in a third if either of you has to take temporary relief.

"Who's going to be in the crash room?" Laure asked.

Captain Shore said, "I've pulled in Brian."

"A Three Gold?"

"I want to keep as much experience up here as I can, and everyone above him is either here or going to have to be here in pairs until we're clear. I've just pulled twenty hours, and I need to get an uninterrupted eight so I can do the upcoming pre-jump through post-jump.

The captain gnawed at the corner of his lip. He looked close to exhaustion. "Odds are this is going to be a tedious shift for both of you. But keep each other awake and focused, stay ready, and keep all manual monitoring on in case any sort of alert comes through. Do you have any questions?"

"No, sir," Melie and Laure said in unison.

The captain nodded. "Shipcom, report completed. Execute Code April Leader Four."

"Code executed."

The captain left the bridge, and in under a minute, the shipcom reported back.

"Crew, Shore, secured. Ship is now cleared for point jump. Origami point is not in range. Point jump is not available. Shipcom jump status on standby until designated point and coordinates reached."

Laure looked at Melie. "We have a full eight hours in which we can do absolutely nothing but sit here and watch a whole lot of nothing go by. I'd rather not spend that time imagining what is going to happen to us if bounty hunters capture us."

Melie said, "That's what's been running through my head since Rowse talked to all of us."

"Mine, too." Laure sighed. "We have to stay awake, we have to be alert and unimpaired, and we have to be available if anything goes wrong. I think our chances of fulfilling our shift duties will be better if we think about something besides what's coming after us."

"I'm in."

"You have any dirty stories you haven't told me yet?" Laure asked.

"No. You?"

"I've missed leave on two of the last three stations where I had downtime coming. I was doing re-certs. Then on Byng Station last week, where I took two hours to grab some decent ground food at Charney's, I ended up seated next to a woman who would not shut up. I barely remember what I ate — and I didn't get to enjoy it."

Melie could only nod. "Tell me about it. I'm a couple leaves short, too. I just redid my Shuttle Pilot 3 and annual TFN Emergency Protocols. Next up is TFN Ship Secondary Systems."

"Work." Laure laughed. "We love it, it devours us, and we still love it. I don't think that's an entirely healthy relationship."

"We could be guests on the next episode of *Love Gone Wrong* — call it *'The Twisted Romance of Women and Their Spaceships.'*"

"I'd watch that. Speaking of twisted romances... you have anybody *else's* dirty stories to share?"

Melie said, "Well, I just heard about Karlex and the tiger-girl body-modder."

"Heard it."

Melie sighed. "Figures. That was a pretty good one. How about you?"

Laure sat with forearms draped over the top of her head. "Meese and the caped heroes in the closet?" she asked, sounding hopeful.

"Heard it."

Laure sighed. "Figures. I think I was the last person to get that one — *everyone* has already heard it. I'm out, then. You in-processed the last group of recruits, didn't you?"

Melie nodded.

"Anyone in there worth bedding, if they last long enough to reach equivalent rank?"

"Not for *me*. There's a guy who came in from Shanxley Station *you* might like. He's a little older, a little scarred, a little dark. Has interesting eyes. Tested well, comes in with some real-world experience. Looks like he could rank-jump into reach fairly quickly."

"Name?"

"Hinks? Henks?"

"Shipcom," Laure said, "biography, holo, and status of crew members in-processed from Shanxley Station in our last pass."

"Two found. Aromenja, Belyn, female; age, twenty Standard; occupation, testing in progress —"

The holo hovered between them. A dumpy woman with hacked hair and an angry expression stared back at them, looking for all the world like she thought they owed her money.

"Not her," Laure said, and glanced over at Melie. "And... ouch?"

"If she had a great personality, I could get past her looking like... well, that," Melie said. She paused. "Probably. Maybe. If she even had any future here."

"But..."

"She's empty as null-space. No interests, no passions, no ideas, no goals. She isn't going to make it out of Three Green."

Laure was glancing at stats. "In her bio, she lists herself as Gender Three — female/female. She's about the only one right now, isn't she?"

"I'm G-5, not G-3, but close enough. She is the *only* female/female on the ship right now besides me. The fact that she's uni and I'm poly, which would be a disaster, but fortunately it's not going to be an issue.

"Confession here, though. When I hit rank clearance and got access to your rank-locked bio, I checked you out. I hoped..." Melie smiled. "Pretty and talented as you are, I'm sure everyone who hits rank equivalency hopes you might be available. Broke my heart when I saw you're G-6."

"I'm flattered that you looked," Laure said. Then the other bio appeared, and Melie watched Laure look appreciatively at his holo. "Oooh, you're so right about him. I can see that bit of dark you were talking about — he has fierce eyes. I *love* that in a man."

She read through his bio and sighed. "He's not going to be here long, Melie. He's jumped crews four times in four years. No sense getting interested."

Melie said, "Shay must have seen something in him. She doesn't put anyone on crew that doesn't show *some* promise."

Laure gave Melie a long look. *"Oh?* I beg to differ, and to prove my case, I give you one name. Burke."

And Melie winced and laughed. Burke was inexplicable. "Well... all I can figure is, Burke had to have holos of Shay in some impossibly compromising position."

"I was guessing nepotism," Laure said. "He was too stupid to be related directly to the owner, but maybe he was the backbred genetic mistake of a good friend or something."

Melie considered that, and nodded. "That might actually be possible."

But after belittling Burke, neither of them could come up with anything else to say.

Melie's thoughts turned toward the trouble they were all in, toward the hunters tracking them and to the death sentences hanging over their heads.

"It's going to be a long eight hours," she murmured after a while.

"Technically we're probably not supposed to talk about it," Laure said, "but you could tell me what Bashtyk Nokyd was like. I can't believe you got to escort him to the owner's quarters and then back."

Melie froze and stared at Laure.

"Wait. You're telling me that…"

She closed her eyes, replayed the escort she'd done from Mado Keyr's private guest quarters at the back of the ship to the owner's, and then back — to the older man in the formal shipsuit. To his voice, and his face…

She'd seen holos of Bashtyk Nokyd, of course. Most people had.

But the idea that he might actually be aboard the *Longview*, or that she might have met him…

"Oh, it *was* him," she whispered.

"You didn't know?"

"I had no idea."

"Was he wonderful?"

Melie grinned. She had not spoken with him — it was the rule that crew interacting with passengers were to speak only when necessary, and to give guests their privacy.

But she had superb observation skills, and excellent recall — and she had noticed a great deal.

She had met — and spoken to — the great Bashtyk Nokyd.

Just discussing what each of them knew about him, and what they could find out from the ship library, occupied them for a good part of the shift.

When hours later the shipcom said, "Incoming message for Laure, request private," both of them jumped and laughed nervously. "I'll take it through earbud," Laure said.

She listened for a moment, then said, "On it."

She turned to Melie. "Owner. I need to set something up for him."

"Do I need to get Brian to the bridge?"

"I've got everything from here," she said. "Keep track of the external monitors for the next ten minutes while I set this up."

That was the biggest excitement they had the entire shift.

Chapter 4

Shay

"**W**arning to all crew: Deep dark goes to ping range in ten minutes. Warning to all crew: Deep dark goes to ping range in ten minutes. All assigned crew to the bridge now. All assigned crew to the bridge now."

Shay, sitting at her desk in the office that fronted her quarters, took a deep, steadying breath. Captain Shore knew he was to call her if there were any problems during the passage. And she expected some.

She did not anticipate that any of these problems would require her on-deck presence — the *Longview* had a remarkably capable crew. But she had the owner's private gravdrop open and waiting. She could be on the bridge in three seconds if she was needed.

The Raythonade origami point was currently a low-traffic one. The Raythonade system had been one of the busiest developed systems in Settled Space and one of the most profitable before the Legend Plague.

Traffic, money, and densely populated worlds had drawn Legends — body-modders who'd used a brilliantly engineered nanovirus named Legend to turn themselves into mind-controlling, blood-drinking, incredibly attractive nightmares. These nightmares had been able to replicate themselves by injecting the nanovirus in their blood into unmodded humans. Because they fancied themselves vampires, and romanticized Old Earth vampire myths, they did this by sucking blood from their victims and having their victims drink their blood in return.

The nanovirus made those victims their slaves. Any body-modder using Legend could make his own slaves, and almost all of them did. The process of making slaves — new, enthralled vampires — had been designed by the mod developer to give the modder a sexual rush. Worse, though, the process of drinking blood, which was the only way a Legend could eat and survive, gave the drinker an even bigger sexual kick. And drinking a living human being to death was the biggest physical thrill of all.

The combination of power over normal human beings and the designed addictiveness of the nanovirus had pushed unmodded humanity toward the brink of extinction. The Legend modders, unable to survive without fresh human blood, would have followed.

And then someone, somewhere, figured out a way to stop it. Figured out how to get the Legends to identify themselves and voluntarily wipe themselves out, and at the same time to make almost all the human beings who remained instantly and inescapably lethal to any Legends who had survived.

In the aftermath, many previously bustling regions of Settled Space were achingly empty. But the Legends has become extinct, or the next best thing to it, and humanity had survived and was rebuilding.

Still, the bigger and stronger a system had been before the fall of the Legends, the emptier it was likely to be in the aftermath.

And that was the point of heading to Raythonade.

The *Longview* needed to run an origami point — to break through the line regulated by the monitoring spaceport, and to jump through the point without submitting to the required legal protocols — and at the same time, to escape the ship to be identified, boarded, and confiscated, with all crew detained and remanded into Pact Worlds custody for execution.

To jump a line, the *Longview* needed light traffic and a jump clock with some space between point insertions.

Raythonade sounded like it was in that situation.

If it was, *Longview* would jump the line and push into the origami point without even hailing the station, using coordinates to an uncharted origami point Shay had used *Devil's Dilemma* to locate. *Longview* would then immediately jump to a second uncharted origami point Shay had located on that same run. She had several more such points stored as backups in navigation.

An infinite universe meant an infinite number of origami points — most were worthless, except for ships trying to hide their trails.

The first jump would be tracked by Spybees, drones positioned at every known origami point. These instantly logged the identity, passage, direction, and destination of every ship that passed through, then disseminated this information from each origami point to all others instantly via tiny point-jumping transmitters called pingballs.

Pingballs would follow the *Longview* through its first jump, and would return to the Spybee to report where they'd been. So the *Longview* would burn its first secret origami point by using it. That location would become known throughout Settled Space instantly.

But there was no Spybee on the other end of the jump to record the *Longview's* arrival, and no pingballs from *that* Spybee to follow the *Longview* through its second jump, back through the same origami point, but on a different trajectory that would take it into a different fold in space. So the location of the second point would remain a secret, and they would be able to lose any trackers.

The *Longview* could sit there in safety. It would take forty-eight hours of off-time to allow the bridge crew to recover from the brutal strain of going through two point insertions back to back while conscious and required to function.

Once captain and essential jump crew had recovered, they would jump to their safe harbor — Bailey's Irish Space Station in the Bailey's Irish system.

Shay smiled just a little, thinking of Bailey's Irish.

Upon receiving the news that the *Longview* and all its personnel had been branded criminals by the Pact Worlds, the station's owners had sent a brief message via tight coded ping to the *Longview* that said in full:

Bugger the Pact Worlds. You and yours have shelter, dock, citizenship, and an army of mercs to cover your asses. Come on home. — The Baileys

Following that message, which had made Shay laugh and cry at the same time, they had sent to Rowse airtight legal paperwork creating the Agreement of Asylum; citizenship offers for those of the crew who wished to avail themselves of it; full pardons for any crew who did, safe passage for any guests aboard the ship for which the captain or the owner would vouch.

It was an incredibly generous offer.

The *Longview* and Bailey's Irish had a good, decades-long history.

And unlike most stations and most systems, Bailey's Irish was built from start to finish to protect its people.

The well-armed, freedom-loving folks of Bailey's Irish belonged to no cross-system alliances, covenants, or pacts. They permitted no slave traffic. They had been the first system to cut off trade with the Pact Worlds when the details of the Suzee Delight story became public.

And rumor had it that Herog, an ex-slave who had earned a deadly reputation as a slaver-hunter and freer of slaves, had moved some of his crew to Bailey's Irish, and that these most feared of men had added their own variety of protection to the system.

Shay couldn't validate much of this. Bailey's Irish actively blocked the transmission of any information about people through the Spybee/pingball network. It permitted the transmission of ship-movement data for ships tagged as criminal... if the Bailey's Irish folks agreed with the assessment.

But details on citizens of the system or those visiting legally could not be obtained.

Which, to Shay's way of thinking, made it the next best place to the City of Furies.

So she did what she was supposed to be doing. She set the coordinates for both off-the-charts origami points into shipcom, made them accessible to the crew who would be doing the jumps. Then she started toward the back of her apartment to use the private passage from her quarters through the owner's quarters and down to the private "shuttle bay" that housed *Devil's Dilemma* so she could prep the tiny sidewinder for its next voyage.

In the instant she moved, she heard a tiny pop, and hissing. Felt a damp mist on her skin.

Turned quickly enough to see mist pouring from her desk into the air.

Had time to think, "Sabotage."

Felt pain lance through every cell in her body in the same instant that her gastrointestinal tract reversed course. She vomited blood, and more blood, and then nothing at all, while her body tried to tear itself apart ridding her of the poisons that overcame her, and her world became a nightmare of pain, a hell of confusion, a wall of darkness.

Then nothing at all.

Melie

"I'm not *even* supposed to be here today," Melie muttered to the motionless, boxed bodies as she worked down one aisle of Level Ten, doing status sweeps and wanting to punch walls.

She was supposed to be up on the bridge, getting ready with the rest of the crew to do the first of the three origami-point jumps Captain Shore explained would get them out of Pact World space and to their unnamed safe harbor.

No one — not even Captain Shore — knew their final destination. No one except the owner. And Shay, certainly.

Maybe Rowse.

Rowse wouldn't talk. He'd sold his soul to the owner, and had become the owner's favorite devil in exchange.

Shay wouldn't talk. Shay had never leaked even the tiniest bit of trivial gossip to anyone. She dealt with guests, business associates, dignitaries from major worlds, the rich and the famous come to buy the mysterious cargoes the owner acquired and traded in — and as well, with PHTF world owners, Pact Worlds Administrators...and ship crew if she had to. She had to have the best gossip in the universe.

But she was no one's friend.

And the owner wouldn't talk. The owner rarely even showed himself.

So until they got where they were going, no one but those two or maybe three would know where the *Longview* was headed.

Melie had actually been looking forward to toughing out the awfulness of the jumps, of drinking terrible shipcom-doped coffee and additives, of checking both unregistered origami points for signs of human passage or of any connections to Spybees, pingballs, traffic, or feed relays, just to be the first to see whatever wonderful place it was that had given them sanctuary.

She'd been excited about being a part of the crew that got everyone to safety. This mattered so much to every single human being on the ship.

And she'd been secretly happy that the *Longview* was going to have to give up its Death Circus franchise. There were other things it could do. Better things.

She was thrilled that her job would no longer involve being close to people burning themselves to death. She *knew* getting the ones who didn't volunteer to die away from their horrible worlds was important. She *suspected* that she and the rest of the *Longview* crew were helping smuggle some of them to freedom.

But she was sure there had to be some way to do this that didn't involve breathing in the smell of burning human beings, or going to sleep with their screams echoing in her nightmares.

But something had gone wrong.

Her orders that morning had come directly from shipcom, and

had been terse. *Pending investigation of breach of confidentiality regarding the owner, you are to report to Level Ten for status sweeps on all units.*

She hadn't done anything wrong. She hadn't gossiped about the owner. Hadn't spilled any confidential material from their runs. Hadn't exposed the identities of priority passengers, because she hadn't known any.

She was in aisle five when she realized where she'd ended up in trouble.

Bashtyk Nokyd.

She had not known who he was. That had been Laure.

But when Laure tipped her off, and she realized that the man she'd led to meet the owner actually was the famous philosopher and political exile, she had happily discussed everything she could think of with Laure.

And Laure, the ship's first mate...

They were both in trouble, weren't they?

No one but the shipcom had heard them talking, but no one could mistake what they'd said.

She wondered if Laure had ended up doing status sweeps in Level Nine, or if she had some other grim duty.

Well, between the two of them, she felt confident they would manage to get it cleared up.

Laure

"We have the jump coordinates," Captain Shore said.

"Locking them in now," Laure said. She had the navigator's chair. Melie was supposed to be on communications, monitoring the local chatter, but she had not appeared on the bridge.

As Laure received their jump coordinates, she copied them into a locked info-packet and tight-beamed them to the approaching Spybee.

She then read the Spybee's ship-tracking schedule and said, "We are approximately five minutes from origami-point insertion. Traffic is very light. I am calculating the timing between individual ship jumps as approximately every fifteen minutes."

"Approximately?"

"They're not running exact-timed jumps. There isn't enough traffic, either inbound or outbound, to support them. They're running exclusively off of ping-ball communication to keep track of traffic.

Shore said, "I remember when Raythonade was running a four-second jump clock, and we thought that was pretty roomy."

"Yes, sir," Laure said. "This laxness at the Raythonade station certainly makes what we need to do easier for us."

"That it does."

"Do you have any word from Melie?"

"Still not responding to calls, Captain."

"And tracking?"

"Isn't bringing her up. It's almost…" Laure stopped before completing the sentence.

"Almost what, Laure? We don't have time to be coy."

Laure sighed. "It's almost as if she's hiding. I cannot locate her anywhere on the ship by tag, or vital signs, or through shipcom."

"I wanted her running com, dammit. She's the best communications crewman we have."

"She is," Laure agreed. "If you want to delay the jump, I can go look for her personally."

Shore gave her a look of disbelief. "Delay?"

He was studying the pattern of the jump window. Laure could see the tenseness in him — the stiff shoulders, the thinned lips, the pinched nostrils.

"It will be all right, Captain. We have time, we have surprise. All we have to do is do it."

"Something's wrong."

Laure laughed, and startled herself with the explosion of the sound. "Sir? *Everything* is wrong. Lunatics have offered an enormous bounty for all of us, for this ship, there are people out there right now hunting us, and they'll be paid more than any of us will see in our entire lives for turning this ship over to the Pact Worlds.

"We have a chance — one thin chance — to get someplace supposedly safe, but we have no way of knowing that offer is true... and damn the legal paperwork. Rowse may want to believe it, but you know as well as I do every bit of that paperwork means nothing if the place that has offered us sanctuary has secretly sided with the Pact Worlds on this. If they've negotiated with the Pact Administrators, they can legally... *legally*... use any means necessary to bring in this ship and crew in. And that includes giving us written promises of sanctuary and citizenship."

Shore looked at her with weary eyes.

"What would *you* do, Laure?" he asked.

"The same damn thing you're doing. The same damn thing the owner told us to do. Run. Because what else can we do?"

She stared out the port at the blackness of space, at the tiny speck of light that was Raythonade Station. At the universe that had been so close to being hers, in which she would have been a free captain of a free ship sailing the stars. "I just won't be surprised to see the cordon of gunships at the other end."

He didn't look at her again. "Order crew to jump berths now. We're getting this over with."

Chapter 5

Melie

Down in Level Ten, Melie was instantly awake, the chemical rush of the blood scrubbers and the chilled oxygen in the jump berth jolting her to alert consciousness even before the jump berth could slide open.

Shipcom said, "First jump complete. Clear your berth, do your physical check."

She was already on her feet. The jump berths were vertical, set for crew to pour out of them at speed in case of an emergency.

She cleared the door and rolled into the passageway, dropped into pushups and did ten quickly, jumped into squats and did twenty.

Little numbers, but they demonstrated that her body was functioning, that she had control of it.

Out loud, she said her name and ident number, and shipcom validated her. She knew who she was, and the ship's memory agreed.

The whole thing took less than a minute. Every other berthed crewman on the ship was doing the same thing at the same time.

She shouldn't have been doing it, though. She should have been on the bridge drinking coffee and shaking off the jump, checking for anything out of place on com. She should have been part of this, not down in the dark in the Sleeper holds.

She should have been…

"Non-jump crew, return to berths for second jump," shipcom said, and she swore hard and loud, and stepped back into the damned berth, raging to the darkness that she was jump crew. Jump crew.

The dark swallowed her, and the dark spat her back out.

"Second jump complete. Clear your berth, do your physical check."

She started into the process, and realized the ship was silent. No sound from the air scrubbers. No sound from the sublight engines. No sound from people doing their pushups and squats — she heard not a single scuffle of movement over the thin, grip-grained surface of moleibond flooring.

Far aft of the engines, sounds got lost in the immense, crowded spaces of the *Longview* — but she was just back of the bow, under the open gravdrop through which every sound from ten levels passed, and there, the ship echoed with life — always.

Except in that instant, she could believe the ship broken beyond repair and herself the only living soul aboard. She froze as the emotionless voice of the shipcom said, "Bridge has been breached. Bridge has been breached."

She thought, *Breached?*

She was running, she discovered, running toward the closest weapons locker on Level Ten. Starboard siding, right on her walkway.

Time slowed inside her — every step took forever, and her thoughts raced to conclusions between single beats of her pounding heart. She ran the drill through its steps at light speed. In the event of a breach, shipcom would lock all palm lock and ident access, so initially the pirates would be stuck on the bridge. They would have to bring in moleibond cutters to cut their way into into the captain's office, or into the gravdrop, or into the passenger access.

Passenger access would lock down. Until one of the four people on the ship with full access — the captain, the first mate, Shay, or the owner — passed Gen-ID as a live person offering a live-drawn blood sample, those quarters would remain locked. No one would get out. Equally importantly, though, no one would get in.

Shipcom would cut power to the gravdrops to prevent pirates from spreading through the ship quickly. They would have to use the emergency ladders in the gravdrops to move through the ship.

In the gravdrop, they would be vulnerable.

They would be above, in danger of falling.

She would be below, armed and shooting straight up — clear, simple shots that even a shaking, terrified crew member could not miss.

She was at the locker in instants, while far above, the captain shouted orders, fought, screamed…

… While One-Gold Joze, manning defense, shouted that crew berths would not unlock, that the gravdrops had not gone offline, that weapons would not respond…

… While One-Green Taryn yelled something about blowing the Blu-O seal, then screamed before she could say more…

… And Mettan yelled something Melie could not make out…

… And Melie's hand hit the palm-lock on the weapons cache…

… and the cache did not open.

She snarled "No," while the echoes of ugly deaths reached down from above and squeezed her lungs, and she slammed the flat plate with her hand, over and over, and as she did words sliced their way out of her memory into her consciousness like knives.

Pending investigation…

Hit the palm-lock.

Pending investigation of breach of confidentiality regarding the owner…

Hit the palm-lock. Hit it again.

And then stopped.

Just stopped, as the *meaning* of the words worked through her brain.

She stared toward the gravdrop, invisible from the weapons locker that would not yield to her.

Pending investigation of breach of confidentialities regarding the owner, you are to report to Level Ten for status sweeps on all units...

Only...

If she were pending investigation for breach of confidentiality — an enormous, career-threatening offense — *she would not be permitted to act as active-duty crew...*

She should have *thought*, but she'd been angry. She was furious at missing out on being a part of getting the people she loved to safety. Furious at herself for discussing Bashtyk Nokyd with Laure.

But what mattered was that if she were awaiting investigation, she would never have been given crew duties. Would not have been sent to Level Ten as punishment.

She would have been locked in her quarters.

Someone already on the ship had needed her off the bridge this day of all days.

She heard the moleibond cutters. Heard Laure screaming, "No, no, no, no, no, don't make me, no!" echoing down on her from above, and her first stupid thought was *Why wasn't Laure punished too,* and her second smarter thought was *Because she wouldn't see what I would have seen, and whoever did this just needed me out of the way.*

Then Laure's scream cut off like a silenced alarm.

"Spread out, open the crew berths, kill the rest. No survivors. Bounty's the same either way!"

Dead ran through her mind. She was supposed to have been up there, and she would be dead now.

And I'm alive.

And somehow, her berth had unlocked, when every bit of evidence she could see suggested not a single other one had.

Then a sound poured down on her that froze her thinking brain, melted her knees and dropped her to them and rolled her into a ball of pissing, whimpering flesh.

It was a roar and a scream and the shriek of the damned rolled into one — and it changed the sounds from above from those dangerous criminals in control of a situation to the whimpers of mewling animals.

She heard a monster erupting from the bowels of some primitive's hell with a rage that she could *feel* ten floors below.

It was nothing human. Nothing that fit within her experience.

But it was killing the brigands, and it was doing it quickly and horribly, with wet, sucking, slipping thuds, and terrible crashes. Some screamed. Others begged. One by one, they all went silent.

Nothing in her life had prepared her to experience the muscle-locking, mind-freezing fear the sounds she heard elicited in her — or to think through them.

Still, she managed one clear thought Whatever it was that had gotten loose up there, it was killing the enemy.

And that made it *her* monster.

She crawled back to her feet, grateful for shipsuits that dealt with piss.

From the tool belt at her waist, she pulled out a handheld moleibond sealer. It was too small, too up-close to be a good weapon, but it was all she had.

She took deep, shuddering breaths, and gathered the little courage remaining to her, and ran for the gravdrop. Though it should not have been, it was working.

She pushed hard into the upstream, and shot toward the deck, ten long stories above her.

She arrived in a new and different silence, and there found the bodies of Captain Shore and Mettan, Joze and Taryn with their throats cut, and Laure cut and burned and with parts of her shipsuit sliced away, with knife holes all over her body, some of them bloody and some not.

Her hindbrain whispered, *This would have been you.*

Intermingled with the people who had been her friends and her family, she found bits of what had once been men, all in pieces, ripped apart by something hideously strong, horribly fierce, with claws and teeth… and fury.

Whatever had killed them had been angry.

A grav shear could have left only a slightly worse mess.

At the very front of the ship, another ship was coupled to the Blu-O seal of the Longview, and both airlocks were forced open.

A trail of bloody bare footprints walked in a straight line from the *Longview's* deck into the cargo hold of the other ship — a belly-access TFN ship. From the looks of it, it was a Colson coil-sidewinder, a big one.

She started to follow the bloody footprints, then had second thoughts. She would stay on the *Longview*, monitor any communications, guard the airlock against...

The half-formed thought became the deed as one pirate trotted across the umbilical, head down, studying the blood trail, and before he even knew she was in front of him, Melie jammed the blue-hot tip of the moleibond sealer into one side of his skull and swirled it once before shoving it out the other side, then yanking it back.

He was dead before he understood it.

"Too easy for you," she shouted at the corpse. Jammed the sealer though his head again, but having killed him, she could not unkill him to hurt him.

She was furious. Her eyes filled with tears. She wanted more pirates to kill. She wanted to destroy flesh and bone, wanted to rend and crush, wanted to see the pain and fear and regret in the eyes of the men who had done this to her people. Wanted to make *someone* pay for the murders of her friends. Her family. The only family she had ever known.

Three pirates came running toward her, screaming, and she charged them, the moleibond sealer glowing blue in front of her like a tiny version of an ancient hero's magic sword.

She got one of the bastards. Ran him through the balls, the chest, the belly, the face in outraged jabs, and he fell to the floor screaming, begging, and died before she was done with him.

She turned to keep fighting, but discovered she could not touch the other two because a thing that moved faster than her mind could comprehend had grabbed both of them.

She stood, shocked frozen, her hands and makeshift weapon dropped useless to her sides while the brigands turned to fend off the monster behind them — a skeletal, clawed, fanged horror with bloody eyes, with blood-clotted hair falling out in patches, with ribs outlined against skin thin and translucent as document sheets. The naked monster — lacking genitals, lacking muscle — killed the other two men by ripping out their throats with its teeth while she stood transfixed. It let one fall to the floor. It drank the blood of the other.

And then, blood-coated, hideous, but already less gaunt, it looked at her with keen intelligence, with curiosity, with a vast and dangerous sense of... waiting.

"I know who you are," she whispered.

It walked up to her, rested a hand on her shoulder, and stared deeply and intently into her eyes.

"Yes, you do," it said after a moment. "And you're the new captain."

Tikka Hale

Outside the GenDaring building, citizens of the City of Furies were in corner coffee houses and tea rooms, at restaurants, home with families relaxing as the day wound to a close.

Inside the GenDaring building, Tikka Hale, who had once been a courtesan and a criminal, who had once borne the name Suzee Delight, was doing a live gene-sequencing read in front of her boss.

"Whatever this disease does to the person who has it," Tikka said, "it doesn't kill the victim."

"Good." Tikka's boss looked over her shoulder as she showed him her testing screen. "Give me a list the things you've figured out that it does."

In this new life, Tikka was low woman on the totem pole in the GenDaring hierarchy — a trainee. By her own measure, that made her the happiest woman in the universe. She was finally living her dream, and it was everything she had hoped. She was learning to use the gene sequencer, a process she found both thrilling and exhausting. And her boss, Jhreg Winter, had decided to see what she could do with a sample he'd pulled from Classified Storage.

She told him, "It makes individual cells live an incredibly long time. My simulation suggests this long-life quality is nonspecific to cell type. It strengthens myelin sheathes and almost triples the impulse speed of ion passage through neurons. It looks like it has the same tripling effect on receptor cells, so that any stimulus is going to be about three times as powerful to the — " She glanced up at Jhreg. "I'm having a hard time using the word *victim* here. Pain would be more painful, but pleasure would be more pleasurable. Taste, scent, hearing, vision, sensation and pressure — they all get a boost from whatever this is. Reaction times would increase dramatically, thought processes would be faster and more efficient…"

"Go on."

She had learned the dangers of jumping to conclusions before she had the evidence — every time she'd done it, Jhreg had torn her conclusions to shreds.

But she made a jump this time anyway. "I don't think this is a disease. I think it's a carefully developed genetic mod."

Jhreg pulled up a seat beside her, and turned it so he was facing her. "Give the screen a rest. You've hit on something here, and I want you to talk through your reasoning for me."

Her mind was racing. She was seeing the pieces fitting together, and the way they were coming together was ugly.

Her gut felt tight. She took a deep breath to steady herself. "Someone — someone like us, if not actually one of us — designed this."

He watched her. Nodded. "Keep going."

"It was designed to create… supermen."

He said nothing.

"Stronger. Faster. Tougher. Smarter. Much longer lived, almost unkillable. But not just that. It twists the people who take it. Does evil things to them."

He was watching her. Waiting. Waiting for her to say the next thing… the word that leapt into her mind, the word she didn't want to say.

"This is Legend," she said. "The vampire mod."

He exhaled, and she realized he'd been holding his breath. "Not quite," he told her. "But close enough. Good job. Legend is susceptible to a highly contagious, airborne, symbiotic man-made virus called AntiLegend. However, we've had reason to call the version which now lives in roughly 90 percent of the human population AntiLegend A. It has been designed as a tough airborne virus. It enters the body through the lungs, gets picked up by the blood-stream by latching on to oxygen molecules and riding on them through the plasma transformation that carries them into the blood-stream, and from the bloodstream it targets the bone marrow. In the blood marrow it multiplies, and injects itself into every red blood cell created in the marrow. The presence of this virus has nearly eliminated the Legend mod, and those body-modders who used it. A single sip of the blood of a human carrying AntiLegend A will kill a Legend carrier — immediately, horribly, and in such a fashion that other Legend carriers in the vicinity have a very high chance of becoming infected. However, the version of the mod you're looking at is not susceptible to AntiLegend A antibodies."

Tikka pulled out the name that had for a time run rampant through the feeds. Even she, sequestered in her palatial cage, had heard the rumors, though she had not seen the holos. "Legend II? I thought that was a… a trick used to kill the Legends."

"It was. But it was also real. Is real. We have a denatured sample of Legend II in Classified Storage, and like this sample, it is immune to AntiLegend A. But this isn't Legend II, either. As far as we've been able to tell, this is an independent developmental path branched from the original Legend. Much more powerful than Legend, much less *creative* — for lack of a better word — than Legend II.

"Legend II was designed to allow the modded individual to change his physical form — within the limitations of mass, of course. It allowed volitional cellular reconfiguration, although the learning path to control body reconfiguration had to be both terri-fying and painful. We've done artificial intelligence simulations with Legend II, and in every instance, the AI, once Legend II is added to the human simulation, ends up with a mindless blob of goo. Human brains are much more adaptive than artificial intelligences, and there is proof that at least some people were able to master this voluntary change of physical form. But those first attempts…. The learning curve had to be nightmarish."

Jhreg shook his head and took a deep breath.

"This sample is from a very rich client who says he was originally involuntarily infected with Legend. Who did not want Legend, but became addicted to its beneficial aspects. Who hired someone to develop a mod that would eliminate the symptoms of Legend he did not want."

"Which are?"

"The inability to derive nourishment from any source but living human blood. The involuntary response of growing top and bottom fangs when hungry and inhaling the scent of nearby humans, and the compulsion, apparently severe, to rip out the throats of these people and drink their blood. And on a lesser note, extreme photosensitivity."

"In other words," Tikka said, "our client wants to be an immortal… but not an immortal vampire."

"Yes."

"We have Medixes. Why not just find a way to revert to a normal human state?"

Jhreg raised one eyebrow. "You already listed them. Heightened responses. Faster thinking. Faster neural responses. Heightened senses. And according to the client, the big one: massively improved sexual stamina, and heightened sexual pleasure."

And that last one, Tikka thought, would have been enough all on its own. This mod could have eliminated sight, taste, hearing, smell, and made the modded individual dumb as bricks, but if it kept him hard for ten hours and let him experience multiple orgasms within that timespan, he would have called that a win. That it didn't do any of the other negative things… yes. She could see why he didn't want to go back to being a normal human being. Who would?

"So he hired someone to specifically remove the vampire symptoms. And…"

"He got moderate decreases in the worst of the symptoms — enough that he can live around normal humans most of the time without killing them. But he pays the price for these lessened symptoms by suffering regular massive buildup of cellular toxins, for which he has to spend time in a Medix having his blood cycled."

"Mado Werix Keyr," Tikka breathed.

Jhreg's big hand wrapped around her upper arm hard enough that it hurt, and his face moved in until their noses were almost touching.

"That's *classified*," he growled. "How did you know that?"

"I didn't know anything," she said, pulling her arm out of his grip. "In my old life, Mado Werix Keyr was a client of mine. He suffered the symptoms you describe. He lived inside a suit, and although he would sometimes purchase... *hire* me for a week, he never touched me. Never opened his mask, never cleared the dark filter from the face shield, never shed the shipsuit that covered every centimeter of his body."

Jhreg was frowning, studying Tikka with definite curiosity. "So you know Mado Keyr personally. Have been in his presence for extended periods of time."

She thought back. "Added together, a total of three months, spread out over six years."

"That answers one mystery," he said. "Which is how, along with AntiLegend A, you acquired the only known copies of AntiLegend B and AntiLegend C into your bloodstream. He had to have put them there."

Tikka thought back to her life as Suzee Delight, and to her strangest client. "What do they do?"

"Same thing as AntiLegend A. They instantly kill anyone modded with Legend II or this variant — which we've been calling Peri-Legend — who ingests blood containing them."

"Then he... gave me a way to kill him?"

"Him and every other Legend user of every known variety."

"He was directly responsible for me being here," Tikka said. "He had his people save my life, had them transport me here, and gave me... gave us... a way to kill modders who give themselves Peri-Legend and Legend II upgrades. But... why?"

"That would be the question, wouldn't it?"

MONSTER. NIGHTMARE. OWNER.

The naked gaunt stopped at the captain's chair on the bridge for only a second, rested a bloody hand on the captain's Gen-ID pad, and said, "Shipcom, transfer captain's access to Melie."

Shipcom said, "Confirmed, Mado Keyr."

Then it — he — turned to face her.

"Your orders are: Set up your account as captain. Wait for Shay to come to the bridge before doing anything else. She was badly hurt by the same traitor who took you off the deck. I had to get her into a Medix to save her life, or I would have made it to the bridge faster."

"Do you…" she faltered. She couldn't look at it and talk to it at the same time. So she focused on the other ship, still locked to the *Longview*. With her eyes safely on other things, she asked, "Do you know who did this?"

"No. I only know that you did not. Your third order is this. Do not touch *anything* but the captain's console until Shay gets here."

The floor of the bridge was a charnel house, the surviving crew were locked in their berths, the enemy ship was docked to the *Longview*.

"Yes… *sir,*" she managed.

And the thing disappeared into the captain's office.

Her office, but not one she wanted to step into.

She took a deep breath and sagged into the captain's chair, relieved that the owner was gone. Hoping that she would never see him — in or out of his shipsuit — again.

She shuddered. Pieces of her friends, her family, lay on the floor close to her. Captain Dermot Shore, Taryn, Joze, Mettan, Laure…

The stink of thickening blood filled the air, and because the air cyclers still weren't on, she started to catch the first hints of decaying flesh.

She had been forbidden to even cover their bodies. Melie understood. Shay had to see this. Whoever was assigned to investigate what happened had to have an untouched crime scene.

But these were her family lying there. She wanted to clean up around them, to clean them up, make it better. Make it not have happened.

She wished she could erase the horror of the scene before her from her mind.

Melie rested her head in her own bloody hands and closed her eyes for a moment. Then, with an effort of extreme will, she pushed what had just happened to the back of her mind.

She was the captain. The lives of everyone else on the ship depended on her stepping up. Being strong.

She had orders.

Order One. Set up her account as captain of the *Longview*. She could do that.

"Shipcom," she said, and cringed at the trembling in her voice, "help me set up my account as captain of the *Longview*."

Shipcom said, "It's very simple, Captain. You must select a surname for yourself. You must come up with a biography suitable for a captain that can hold up to inspection — Mado Rowse will work with you on that. And you must drink some coffee."

Chapter 6

Melie

Melie had three cups of coffee in her system — and along with the coffee, whatever the shipcom had doped it with to get her past the shock of the slaughter on the deck.

She had gone from being Two-Gold Melie to Captain Amelie FraRiveri. And she had done it not because she'd earned her way there, but because every person who outranked her was dead. And she, who should have been dead, had been tucked safely away on Level Ten, out of harm's way with an excuse not even a child would believe.

I was assigned there because I was being punished for breaching the owner's confidentiality.

The ship didn't work that way, discipline didn't work that way, and how the hell had the owner not seen that when he made her captain?

She couldn't touch anything. She couldn't find out anything. She couldn't *fix* anything.

All she could do was sit beside the bodies of people who had been integral parts of her world. Who had been friends, colleagues, and mentors. She could think about who they had been when they were alive, and how she was going to find the people who betrayed them, and how she was going to make those people pay. She could keep herself from falling apart, from becoming a weeping, useless wreck.

So she did that.

Shay announced her presence on the deck and dropped into the navigator's chair behind Melie to her left, and Melie swiveled around to face her.

Shay said, "The owner told me it was bad."

"It's bad."

Shay's gaze flicked from horror to horror, but her face showed nothing. "He also told me you… saw him."

"I did."

"What did you think?"

Melie shuddered in spite of herself. "I never want to see it… *him*… again."

Shay managed a tight smile. "Neither do I. I get to see him like that several times a month."

"*Why do you do it?*" Melie blurted out.

Shay closed her eyes. "Because there is a part of… him… it. *It* is far closer to the truth, but he chose his name, chose to call himself male, so I say him." She opened her eyes again. "Anyway… there is something about him that is good. Something right. I stay here and work with him because that part of him keeps working to create goodness, to create places where goodness can live and work and build and create free from the interference of evil."

"The City of Furies?"

"That's part of it. This ship is part of it. *You* are part of it. As he sees it, he wins with every person he pulls out of the hands of a slaver — by whatever name that slaver chooses to call itself — and sets his rescue free to become fully human, fully creative, fully passionate and able to live an individual life."

"Wins *what?*"

Shay smiled. Shrugged. "A little piece of the universe made the way he thinks it should be? A bit of redemption for himself and the...the monster he is? Some joy at second hand?" She shook her head. "Maybe all of those things."

"He is," she continued, "paying people all around Settled Space to research ways to cure him — to let him become one of those freed humans — but at the same time, to let him remain capable of being the protector of those humans he values most. The ones in whose company he chooses to live out his life."

"Us?"

"You. And those he loves in the City of Furies. And me. I'm a version of what he hopes he can someday be. And I'm here because I still believe that, as monstrous as he is, he might yet be... *saved.*"

"You love him."

Shay gave a shocked, disbelieving bark of a laugh. "I *hate* him. But I love that tiny bit of light that still lives in him. In a funny way, I want what he wants — I want to see him freed, made whole, given the chance to become the creative, loving creature he yearns to be."

"The part of him you call the protector?"

She shrugged. Said nothing.

The silence lengthened, and into it, Melie's fears came crawling.

"Shay, I was supposed to have been up here when this happened. I was supposed to be running com. At roll-out this morning, I found myself assigned to Level Ten doing sweeps, and I swear on my life shipcom said I was there because I was being investigated for breaching the owner's confidentiality — and I was so angry at being pulled off com for menial work that I didn't even *think* I would have been confined to quarters for what I was accused of doing."

Shay smiled. "I already know that. But thank you for telling me."

"The owner —"

"The owner doesn't know who is responsible for all of this. But, Melie, he knows you didn't do it. The way he is lets him see the truth in people. He knows that you are absolutely innocent of all of this." She looked at the bodies and her brow furrowed. "But he has no idea who is guilty."

"Then what do we do?"

"We lie for just a bit."

"We... *lie?*"

"You are captain of this ship, both by legitimate succession and by showing extraordinary courage and intelligence in the face of the unspeakable. Including meeting the owner, who is the very definition of unspeakable. That you didn't melt into a puddle of piss on the floor when that happened impresses the hell out of me."

"This shipsuit gets credit for preventing the puddle of piss."

"You get credit for getting to your feet and coming to fight. That was you, and that was what mattered."

Melie said, "Thank you."

"As captain, you have access to every place in this ship except for the owner's and my private quarters and storage. You have full access to the records of every crewman who has ever worked on the *Longview*. You have access to all of Rowse's records except for those locked as *Owner-Confidential*."

Melie nodded and waited.

"You are now captain in fact, and as captain, you have this access free and clear of shipcom alerting anyone else that you are going through their records. Including Rowse, including all the Golds, who would otherwise be locked to you.

"And you can reach all of these records from any console on the ship." Shay stopped and looked over the deck at the bodies scattered there — bodies of enemies and friends alike. Melie could see anger burning in the owner's representative's eyes. "But we are not going to let anyone know — not just yet — that you are the captain. I'm going to create a scenario that gives you a plausible promotion, but not the ultimate promotion. You're going to ostensibly be One-Gold behind Kagen, whom I'm going to talk into coming back as First Mate until we can fill out our ranks with qualified people.

"The story with Kagen will be that he jumped you in rank because of the tremendous work he did on the Suzee Delight situation.

"Meanwhile, I'm going to take on the role of Acting Captain. From that position, I can keep an eye on the bridge, and have a legitimate reason for always being here or in the office.

"While I am so engaged, you can use captain's access plus your remarkable skills in digging the truth out of well-hidden communications to find out who is going to pay for this. And you won't have everyone looking at you and wondering if there's a connection between the deaths of everyone who outranked you and your promotion to captain."

Melie nodded. She was happy to be left alone to ferret through com until she could find the truth.

"We won't be able to keep Kagen on the ship long," Shay said. "Things have changed for him. But he'll help us out for a while."

"How long will it take for him to reach us?"

"We're right beside an origami point. He's close to the City of Furies point. Neither is monitored by Spybee, so I should be able to make the trip safely. If I go and get him, I should probably be back in…" She closed her eyes and thought. "Probably under two hours, if he is made to understand the urgency of the situation."

Melie nodded. "It sounds like a solid plan. So what do we do now?"

"We unlock all the jump berths and let the crew out. We touch nothing on the bridge until we have our people rated highest in security go over our crime scene here. Meanwhile, you and I go into our attackers' ship, make sure everyone there is dead, and then go through their records to see what sort of information they received from the *Longview*, or elsewhere, that allowed them to find us after two jumps through unregistered origami points. We'll figure out what comes next after we've done that."

Melie stood. Shay stood, too, and in spite of everything, their eyes met, and in the moment that they did, Melie noticed the fall of Shay's long, curly black hair, the curve of her waist, the swell of her hips, the fullness of her breasts in her shipsuit, and in spite of herself and the situation, she felt a pull.

She turned away and stared at the hell around her and took deep, stinking breaths of the bridge air to drag her mind away from that inappropriate attraction.

It was in that instant that Shay said, "Melie, what did you do that made you think you might legitimately be under investigation?"

"I talked about Bashtyk Nokyd with Laure," Melie said, caught off guard. "Laure and I were bored out of our skulls during the deep dark, and we were stuck up here on the bridge together — just the two of us — for a full eight. She asked me what he was like. I hadn't even known Mado Wong *was* Bashtyk Nokyd."

The stillness behind her made her turn.

Shay looked stunned. "Of course you didn't," she said. "But how in all the hells humanity ever created did she?"

Chapter 7

Captain Amelie FraRiveri

The pirate ship *Manshark* was well-armed — but had used none of its weapons against the *Longview*. It hadn't needed to.

The traitor on the inside of the *Longview* had crippled its defenses, controls, and other systems, unlocked the *Longview's* docking umbilical, and welcomed the pirates aboard.

Melie found the codes. She found the records.

She had all the evidence anyone could ask for. What she didn't have was the truth.

Melie manually overrode *ManShark's* shipcom, and sent her voice echoing through the ship. "Shay, I found what we're looking for. Get up here when you can. This is... really bad."

Shay didn't get back to the bridge immediately, and when she did, there was fresh blood on her shipsuit. "They weren't all dead," she told Melie. "They are now. They got their information from an insider on the *Longview*, but these were not the ones who knew the insider's identity."

"Dammit. You're sure?"

Shay's flat *yes* did not welcome any other questions in that direction.

"I wish they'd given you a name. I found the following messages: notification that Bashtyk Nokyd had come aboard the ship; notification that the *Longview* had signed for and received its summons from the Cantata Over-Court; jump coordinates to both unregistered origami points sent to a relay that bounced them to this ship; a system override code that allowed *ManShark* to prevent *Longview* shipcom from taking the security measures it would have when the ship was breached, even though shipcom knew we'd been breached. And finally, an outbound message that the recipient's cut of the bounty would be one full share, or one ninth, as previously agreed."

"Eight crew on this ship?"

"That's what the roster says."

"I got them all, then." Shay studied Melie. "You look like hell. What's the thing you're not telling me?"

"Every one of those transmissions went through my account."

Shay considered that for a minute.

"That makes sense. That was at least a part of why you had to be off the deck today. You would have noticed the transmissions coming from your own account while you were running com, and you would have known you weren't sending them."

"Why do you think I didn't?" Melie shook her head. "I was in a place of safety where I had no business being and where I had no reason to think I should have been, I had access to shipcom from Level Ten, I survived when everyone above my rank died, and all the evidence points to me."

"One, all the evidence points to you — and you are far too intelligent to send incriminating evidence from your own accounts. And two, if you had been doing this, there would have been no incriminating evidence. You have delved deeper into signal transmission than anyone else currently on the ship. And you're good at it — far better than I am, and I'm not bad. *You* would have set the records to disappear after they were read, among other things."

Melie nodded. She would have done exactly that.

"This was someone who thought she was being clever. It wasn't someone who *was* clever."

"She?"

"It had to have been Laure."

"No! Absolutely not. Why would you think that? Laure loved the *Longview* as much as I do!"

"Even so, it was her."

"How can you say that? She's dead along with the rest of our people, and she died fighting just like the rest of our people."

"It was Laure," Shay said, "because she told you Bashtyk Nokyd's identity."

Melie said, "Why would that prove anything?"

"Bashtyk Nokyd is the most important passenger we've ever carried, and getting him safely to the City of Furies has been the owner's biggest goal since Mado Keyr and the citizens of the City of Furies first started trading. Mado Keyr talks about Nokyd being the perfect Fury. He sees Nokyd as the man who, when he lends his voice and his philosophy to the City, will give it the words and actions it needs to lead every individual in Settled Space to freedom.

"*No one* knew we had Bashtyk Nokyd on board, save the mado and me. Not the captain, not the first mate, not Rowse, not anyone. I knew who he was because the owner sent me to get him, and if I didn't have to validate Nokyd's identity before bringing him aboard, Mado Keyr wouldn't have told me. That information was not on the ship database, it wasn't in the owner's records, it wasn't anywhere. Mado Nokyd did not meet with any of the crew or any of the guests. You were the only person entrusted with meeting him, and he did not speak much to you."

Melie frowned. "Then how did Laure know?"

Shay whispered, "I don't know. *I. Don't. Know.*"

She sat down in the deck chair opposite the one Melie occupied, and Melie realized that she was seeing fear on Shay's face for the first time ever.

She tried to imagine where that fear might come from.

It took her no time at all to guess the source.

"Shay," she said. "The owner won't… *hurt* you for having missed information on Laure, will he?"

Shay looked startled by Melie's question, then shook her head. "No. But this oversight, this disaster, is on me. I vet every person who comes aboard the *Longview*, know each history, know everything anyone anywhere has ever known about every single human being aboard.

"Every crew member is tested frequently for honesty, integrity, and loyalty as well as skills — and though I use the guise of the shipcom interface to do it, I test them personally. Our cargo is so precious the owner has never taken the slightest chance with any of it.

"Are the captain and first mate subject to the same testing as the rest of the crew?"

"Yes," Shay said. "We trust. But we use the complete veridicator process. Laure passed her last test, which was days before this happened."

"Right. When she came back for short leave on Byng Station," Melie said.

Shay's eyebrow rose.

Melie continued. "We were talking about her leave, which was just for one meal, and that meal was ruined because her seatmate in the eatery would not shut up."

Shay nodded. "You and I will run through her chip data and go over that encounter in detail. It may give us a direction to pursue."

"Her…chip data?"

"This is confidential. It goes no further than the two of us, ever — but every member of the *Longview* has a high-density doppler chip embedded on bone when that crew member is accepted as ship crew. This chip constantly records everything that happens around the crew member within a thirty-meter sphere, and can record and store twenty years of sequential data. In circumstances like these, the owner will remove and review the chips of any crew, living or dead, who may have essential information. Most chips are removed and destroyed without ever having been seen when the crew member leaves the crew."

"So... *I* have one of these chips."

Shay studied her and nodded slowly. "Trust," she said softly. "But veridicate. This way, even the dead can have their day in court and be assured of a just trial."

Then Shay shrugged. "But we'll listen to the stories of the dead later. First, show me what else you've found here."

Melie ran the data on the bounty the Pact Worlds were offering for the *Longview* with Shay, and said, "One ninth of the price on our heads — one share of the blood money for bringing this ship and its crew in, dead or alive, is over three million rucets. Do you think that would have been enough to buy Laure's loyalty?"

Shay snorted. "Laure was an enthusiastic participant in the owner's investment pool. Between her daily and investment accounts, she has — had — about three times that much, truth be known. She also owned property shares in the City of Furies for a home there when she was ready to retire — and those cannot even be bought by anyone not already a Furies citizen. They must be earned. Nothing the Pact Worlds could have offered her could hope to match what she already had. The owner *earns* the loyalty of his crew."

Melie said, "I know that. And yet this time he didn't."

She dug through the scant, poorly organized records on the *ManShark*, hoping to find anything that might link Laure to the crew. There was nothing.

Melie finally said, "This is garbage. They kept sloppy records. If anyone was behind them, that information isn't in here. If they had a bigger plan, that isn't here. All we're doing on this ship is wasting time."

Shay sighed. "Then we'll go to Laure's chip, and if necessary the chips of the others on the bridge when this happened."

MELIE SAT in the locked conference room with Shay. So Shay could keep track of what was happening with the *Longview*, she had live screens of the crew members who were cleaning up the bridge, and of those who were stripping the *ManShark* of records and salvage.

Meanwhile, Shay was showing Melie how to run a doppler chip reader — a piece of technology Melie hadn't even suspected existed.

They were in the center of a gray-on-gray universe in which Laure was a visible figure who existed inside a sphere sixty meters in diameter when viewed at full size.

The commands were simple. Shay could touch any point in the image to make that the center of what she was looking at, could squeeze her thumb and index finger together to make the image smaller, or spread them apart to make it bigger. Saying the date and time she wanted to see moved the hologram to that date if it existed. The words *go* and *stop* started and stopped movement. The words *open* and *close* brought the image up and turned it off.

By default, the doppler reader centered Melie right inside of Laure, so that she would see what Laure saw from Laure's own perspective.

Shay had Melie forward to the moment when Laure left the ship to take leave on Byng Station. But that was horrifying. It was utterly intimate, personal — there was no censor to anything Laure did. No buffer at all.

"I can't stand this," Melie said.

Shay said, "If you're inside your own image, it's bearable. If you're inside someone else's, it will make your skin crawl. It does mine, anyway. Fix it by making the image half size and by moving Laure to the tabletop on your right."

Shay did as she was told. It helped a little.

"Now make her smaller still, but keep her in the same place. We want to be able to get a clear view of her as she steps off the *Longview* and out into Central Processing."

They watched the world move around her as Laure walked off the ship, through the personnel scanners, and into the open-stall marketplace that waited on the other side. Laure headed toward the station corridor on the other side that went to ByngTown, the part of the station that had upscale shops, restaurants, and other forms of personal entertainment.

"Wait," Melie said, and then realized that was the wrong word. "Stop, back at one third speed."

Laure walked backward, but slowly.

Melie said, "You see that?" A woman had stepped out from behind one of the market stalls as if she had been waiting, and took the same path as Laure, at the same pace, but keeping well behind her.

Shay nodded. "The timing is suspicious. Go ahead and mark the woman. Just put your finger on her and say 'Mark.'"

Melie did that, and the woman turned green.

"You can change the color if you want."

"Green's fine," Melie said.

"Go," Melie said, and they began walking again.

Laure was heading toward ByngTown's restaurant row when all of a sudden the woman following her accelerated, caught up with Laure, and Laure stopped as fully and completely as if she'd been frozen.

"She was waiting for Laure," Melie said.

Shay nodded.

The woman wrapped her hand around Laure's wrist, and Laure followed her, not saying anything, not giving any sign that she was awake or aware of what was happening to her.

"What's going on?"

Shay said, "Trouble of a kind we don't need."

Melie's heart had sped up, and her breath had quickened. She was afraid, deeply and completely afraid. She watched the stranger lead Melie into a locked, closed storefront, watched the stranger lock the door behind them, watched as the stranger turned Laure to face her, lifted Laure's chin with her index finger, and began to kiss Laure on the lips.

"Laure isn't G-5."

"No," Shay agreed. "But that woman isn't kissing her. Stop." she said. "Back up ten seconds. Stop." The doppler image dropped back to just after the start of the kiss.

Shay reached out, touched the point where their lips met, flicked her thumb and finger apart rapidly, and suddenly she and Melie were inside Laure's mouth; Laure's jaws were forced apart by the stranger; Laure's tongue was the size of the conference table; and the stranger's four sharp fangs were embedded top and bottom into that tongue.

"Legend," Shay said grimly. "And not one worried about dying explosively from AntiLegend, which Laure's blood is full of. So this one may be a Legend II monster. Or it may be something else."

Which was too much for Melie. She vomited for the second time in the same day. One of the little autoscrubbers shot out of the wall to clean up the mess, and brushed Melie's ankle, and she jumped onto the tabletop and swore before realizing what had touched her.

She wiped her mouth on the back of her hand and looked at Shay, embarrassed. "I may not be the best choice for captain."

Shay gave her a crooked smile. "I was just thinking that was a pretty good vertical jump for someone launching from a sit-and-puke position." She rested her fingertips on Melie's wrist and said, "Relax. You had a healthy, normal human reaction to something that is horrifying. You're the right choice for captain, Melie."

"You didn't react that way."

"I don't have normal human reactions to Legends anymore. I deal with the owner as my primary job. Remember? I knew this woman was a Legend — or something a lot like one — the instant she took Laure's wrist and Laure didn't resist her. I knew what we were going to see before I enlarged the image."

"You've seen that before?"

"I've *experienced* that before. The fact that I'm even alive is something I find myself disbelieving about half the time. You don't want to know my story, Melie. It's dark and ugly and tied to a man I hate and cannot leave. The only light in my life is the fact that I get to be here, on the *Longview*, with good people I care about — and that *sometimes* I get to go to the City of Furies. If the best thing in the world happens, someday I'll get to live there." She touched the image of Laure and reduced it in size. "I'm not holding my breath, though."

It was a moment of nakedness from Shay, and Melie had never seen that before. She slid off the table and back into her seat, and turned to face Shay. She put her hand atop the hand Shay rested on the table, and said, "You'll get your freedom. You'll get to live in the City of Furies and have the life you want there. Hang on, and stay strong. I'll do anything I can to help you get there."

They stared into each other's eyes, and Melie *saw* Shay. Saw her as a woman like herself, saw her as someone else who wanted love and was sure she could never find it.

Could never have it.

Would never deserve it.

"Someone will see who you are," she whispered, "and love who you are. Someone will be worthy of loving you — and where the two of you are won't matter, as long as you're together."

Shay's eyes went wide. In them, Melie saw both desire and fear.

She pulled her hand back. "I'm sorry," she said. "I — that was inappropriate. I didn't mean to make you uncomfortable."

Shay put her hands in her lap and stared down at them, and for an agonizingly long time, she said nothing.

Melie wanted to crawl under the table and hide there. "I can go," she said, "to give you time to go to your quarters. And then I'll come back in and work on this on my own."

With her head still down, Shay said, "You didn't make me uncomfortable. You...woke me up. Made me remember what it was like to want to be with someone. I haven't let myself feel that since — well, a couple years before I ended up in the employ of Mado Keyr."

Melie's breath caught. "Is there any way you...and I...?"

Shay said, "My association with Mado Keyr leaves me dirty. I am trapped by his secrets. I know that no one else can do the work I do for him. And I have been alone for so long, and assumed that I would always be alone."

She studied Melie.

"But for the first time, someone on this ship besides me knows what he is."

"The other captains haven't known?"

"No. Just you."

"Why me?"

Shay stared down at her hands again and shook her head. "I don't know. He could make you forget. He always made them forget before. Always. I don't know why you're different."

Melie considered that. "Maybe he wants you to have someone. Would he think I would interest you?"

"He knows me," Shay said. "And you interest me. You have since you first walked aboard this ship. But that doesn't...it's not..."

Melie found this fragile human side of Shay both uncomfortable and confusing.

I'm the captain, she thought. Captains make command decisions. "We have work to do," she said, "and many people counting on us to do it well. I'm not going anywhere, and neither are you. So for now, nothing changes between us. If at some point in the future you want it to, I'm here."

Shay nibbled the corner of her lip. "Thank you."

Melie gave herself half a second to inhale and to refocus. She resumed the doppler image at the point where the kiss that was not a kiss ended. The Legend in the image injected a liquid into Laure's upper arm; injected a small oval into the tissue at the base of her skull that, when the image was backed up and expanded, looked like a slow-release nanoviral mod pad; and inserted a microbead into the palm of Laure's right hand.

When she finished, the Legend said, "You went from your ship straight to Low Rose's Eatery for a meal, where you found yourself seated next to a woman who talked constantly about her recent vacation, and while the food you had was adequate, the company in which you were forced to eat it was so awful it has driven specific details of your meal from your mind. You know you ordered favorites, but are understandably vague about what they were."

The woman then walked Laure to a seat in the room. "In one hour, the door here will unlock and open for you. You will return to your own ship. You never met me, you never came here. Until you hear my voice again, you will act in every way on your own free will. Only when you hear my voice will you remember that I own your body and your mind, and you will obey everything I tell you instantly and without question."

And then she walked away.

Melie followed her into the crowd, but she didn't go to a ship. Instead, she wandered deeper into the station and vanished from tracking.

Shay stopped the recording. "Find everything," she said. "Go through every instant of Laure's life from this moment until her death. Find every change she made to the ship, backtrack every person she contacted, walk through every action to every consequence you can. We will hide until you finish, no matter how long it takes — but only you can do this. We cannot be sure of a single other person on this ship but you, the owner, Kagen, and me until you have done this.

She rose, her eyes not meeting Melie's gaze. "I have urgent work to do in the meantime. When you have everything, though, call me over shipcom and I'll come."

Melie asked, "How can we be sure we can trust ourselves? Either of us might have been tampered with."

Shay smiled. "The owner read you and vouched for you. Had he been looking for an attack from one of his own kind, he would have looked at Laure, and would have seen what was done to her. In the wake of the attack, he used every ability he has to look at you. You're fine."

"And you?"

"I'm under his scrutiny every day, and every moment. There is no part of my life he does not see, or know."

"I don't know how you bear it."

Shay looked Melie directly in the eye and said, "It is the price I pay to make my life matter."

Shay was at the deck's aft hatches when Melie realized they had another problem. "What do we tell the passengers about what happened?"

Shay stopped. Exhaled loudly, and muttered something under her breath. "Right. I'm clearly not at my best right now. We tell them nothing. They were safe, they were locked away in the passenger berths front and aft, and they were in Medixes. As far as they're concerned, nothing happened. If one of them is involved in this, 'nothing happened' might flush him out. It's done, it's dealt with, and all we're doing right now is hiding until we get a ping that tells us it's safe to go to our new destination, from which they can book passage anywhere they choose."

Melie nodded. "You'll let the crew know? Or have Kagen do it?"

"I'll take care of it. I'll take care of the passengers, too. You… just find that bitch."

"On it."

Bashtyk Nokyd

I am not meeting with the owner, and I am grateful for that. He was not comfortable company.

Shay is. Shay is, in fact, delightful.

"Here is the problem for which the owner has spent several fortunes tracking you down," Shay tells me. "He wants to free the people trapped in the Pact Worlds. But people who are freed from corrupt and repressive governments without a philosophy to guide them to better lives usually duplicate the corruption they just escaped."

We sit at a table together in her private quarters — Shay, the infamous lawyer Rowse, who looks like the pirate gossip and speculation say he used to be, and me.

Rowse is swarthy, muscular, dressed in a shipsuit with dozens of little skulls on the left breast; he has glittering black eyes and black hair worn long and braided down his back. He is not a man who would have fit comfortably in the A-1 salons in Meileone's Silver Cathedral.

I like this about him. But having heard rumors of him, I had expected to like him. Rowse is not a surprise.

Shay is. Shay's private quarters are decorated at considerable expense to look like a cabin built of logs from any of a number of Old Earth settlements — this is an anomaly I cannot explain. This place is a paean to a primitivism that is far removed from any element visible in the woman who hosts our little talk. If ever a woman did not fit her surroundings, it is Shay in this place.

Shay now has long, curling black hair, honey-gold skin, the same astonishing green eyes. I liked the red-head Trouble Girl look better on her — but this is good too.

I think long, deep thoughts about Shay, and keep them to myself. There are women who, alone, walk through all the throngs of men as though guarded by guns and turrets and flamethrowers; who smile warmly yet never for an instant smile suggestively. Shay is one of these. Were she not, I would have shamelessly used my fame and her obvious admiration in an attempt to bed her. Every line and curve of her haunts me.

Rowse looks at Shay the way I wish I dared to look at Shay. Clearly he is much less afraid of invisible guns and turrets and flamethrowers than am I.

Every time I look at her, I see her naked in my bed.

But Shay wants to talk about freedom, and philosophy, and governments.

So I consider the problem she has presented. "The choice to force others to do what you would have them do — the thug choice — requires neither intelligence nor planning. It requires only a bigger stick and the willingness to use it. It is the animal choice, and thus it is always the easier choice. Most of Settled Space, most of the time, operates in thug mode."

"Slaver worlds, for example," Shay says. "And what so many of the Pact Worlds have become."

Rowse is thoughtful. "The monarchies are such — they're run by thugs who won their territories, then legitimized their rule by claims of Divine Right."

"Dictatorships," Shay says. "Obviously. But… less obviously, democracies run by pure majority rule — such governments are nothing but mob rule when there is neither protection nor permission for those who hold the minority point of view."

Rowse glanced at her, nodded, looked back to me. "Add also those religions that present God-as-Thug, and those believers who threaten any who disbelieve with torture and hell in an afterlife, and as often deliver torture, grief, and even death to believers and non-believers alike in the current life."

They both fall silent.

"All true," I say, "but far, far too limited. Thug rule is not the purview of religion or government or a mob alone. Thug rule originates in the mind of the individual, and in the desire of the individual to *make* other people do things his way, for his benefit, or *for their own good*. Doing something that forces change in the life of another for his own good is Thug Rule just exactly as much as doing something that forces changes in his life for your benefit.

"Every time you hear someone say, 'There should be a law for that,' you are hearing the voice of a thug saying, 'I should be able to make government force people I disagree with to do things my way.' And every time there is a law made to do that very thing, thugs rip another inch of individual freedom away from the individual."

"But law is the way by which free humans retain their freedom," Rowse says, and Shay nods.

"Are all laws created equal?" I ask.

"Of course not," Shay says, and Rowse, a beat later, says, "Some are certainly better than others."

"So what do you think of the Broad Identification Law on Cantata? This law currently requires that any human being with a citizenship level lower than A-1 must be Gen-ID'd, tagged with full bio-ident data, and tracked at all times, so that this individual can never enter an A-1 area without a purchased pass — even accidentally — without setting off an alarm."

"It's a terrible law," Rowse says.

"Of course. But why?"

It takes Rowse only a second to consider. "Because in the guise of protecting life and property — both inherent rights of the individual — this law forces the vast majority of the population to be put into access arrays that can give their complete personal information and location to anyone, anywhere, at any time. And these tracking devices, because they're tagged at the genetic level and powered by the individual's own physiological electrical conduction system, will allow any live individual to be tracked anywhere on any planet — not just in A-1 restricted zones, or just on Pact Worlds, but anywhere. And with the improved sensitivity of ping-based tracking systems, any planet with ping and a Spybee or a feed becomes a relay station for that individual's signal.

"One tracker sitting anywhere in Settled Space, searching the feeds for a specific individual, can locate him to within one-hundred square meters in any system that is within reach of the ever-expanding feed. And do it in about ten minutes real-time."

I stare at him, astonished. "Is it truly that bad already?"

Rowse shrugs. "Technology expands. The benefits get us what we want — and smart men hide the worst of the side effects that give our enemies what they want. I've had to do a great deal of research on this particular issue when dealing with removal and destruction of cell-level Gen-ID tracking in our recruits."

"Then individual rights within all of Settled Space — not just the Pact Worlds and the slaver worlds — teeter on the brink of destruction, and what you have tasked me with becomes more urgent and more desperate than I had ever imagined."

I stare down at my hands. They're knotted into tight fists, and it takes an effort of will for me to relax them.

"The animal instinct to force others to do what one wants them to do is the enemy of free will, of individuals pursuing lives worth living, and of all creativity. Government tries to make humanity better, and in doing so, destroys everything good that people might do. People can only be better because they choose to be — and those who choose other paths can be punished for the actions they decide to take that cause harm, but not for their choice to be some-thing other than good people.

"The *only* way I can help you is to figure out a better way to show individuals the values of their individual choices. I will not take part in anything that attempts to force people's paths to be better — even if they choose paths that will take them to harmful actions."

Shay looks at me, eyes intent to the point of being frightening. "I understand this. Every individual must have absolute choice over the path of his own life. Please just help us figure out how to show people that a Thug Universe is not the only choice. Every resource I can get for you, you will have. Tell me what you need and it will be yours."

I *need to bed you*, I think. "Access to the feed," I say. "Access to someone who can search the feed well and without leaving any tracks behind. Access to anything you know about the way the City of Furies is organized —"

Shay stops me. "The City of Furies is a dead end. I cannot tell you how I know this, but *I do know it.* It is… not finished. Not yet. You must find a way to show people the value of individual choice without using the City of Furies at all."

I want to argue, but I find that I believe her. Something in her eyes, in the tension in her shoulders, in the line of her mouth, convinces me that she is telling me truth absolute. Whatever the City of Furies is, it is *not* the answer to my life-long quest to make possible a universe that offers self-directed and universal freedom.

My heart breaks quietly inside my chest.

Chapter 8

Melie

Melie needed ten full days, sleeping only an hour or two at a time, to pull every bit of information she could find out of Laure's data. When she had it, though, she called Shay over shipcom.

"Owner's Representative to the Conference Room," she told shipcom, and heard her request echo through the mostly-silent ship.

Shay's voice, which she had not heard once since their uncomfortable conversation ten days before, was instantly in her earbud. "You have your report?"

"Everything," Melie said.

"I'm on my way."

When Shay arrived, Melie occupied the place in her mind where the captain of a TFN ship lived. She nodded Shay to a seat, then started into her presentation.

"This is flat-imaged," she said. "It eliminates nonessentials and distractions, and allows us to focus on data."

Shay simply nodded.

"This first image is the microbead injected into the palm of

Laure's hand. It was a data collector. The instant Laure's hand touched the palm-lock on the ship, it read Laure's complete palm-lock data and transferred it at that instant to a tightly controlled feed. I cannot locate the recipients of the feed, or crack its contents — whoever she is, the Legend who put this attack together either has tremendous skills on her own, or someone working for her who does government or corporate high-level security. This is layered, bounced, mirrored, and folded. I found it and broke it in the *ManShark*, and got through half a dozen steps backwards, but in the end I simply don't have the power to brute-force my way through the protection on this.

"However, I got far enough to tell you that the feed had two purposes. The first was to permit the pirates of the *ManShark* to unlock the *Longview* before they even reached us. Laure's codes allowed them to set up exactly the configuration they needed to keep the crew locked in jump berths, to turn off the majority of our systems while leaving the gravdrops operational, and to open the doors once the umbilical connection was complete.

"The second," Melie continued, "was even worse. From the day this connection was established, everything in Laure's access became instantly accessible to the Legend who tagged her. All this woman had to do was to pick up the information from any of thousands of dead drops she has set up. After that, the ship simply opened everything to which Laure had access via a locked code in the feed. Every time we passed a Spybee or gave ship codes to pingballs, the feed also passively collected whatever new information was available to Laure."

"How much did the bitch get?"

"Everything Laure could touch," Melie said. "Absolutely everything. Because she didn't have access to the owner's private information, or yours, or Rowse's, none of that was compromised. She didn't get any of the crew's private-personal information — diaries, logs, personal communications. But she got all their records. She got all the records from the Sleepers. She got all public documents such as contracts. She got all ship logs, all origami-point logs, all station stops..." Melie shook her head. "Just about everything we have that matters, she has. Assume that any crew member or registered guest can now be blackmailed. Assume that any secret routes you've put into shipcom are now in her hands."

Shay sat down. "Anything else?"

She didn't look as worried as Melie had been. Maybe she hid it better.

"Search records, contents of any research done over open channels, receipts for payments and purchases through non-secure accounts, details and contents of open feed use as well as any secured feeds to which Laure had access, crew and guest feed chatter — a lot of non-specific garbage. What she got that really matters is personal information about crew and official guests."

Shay considered that. "Bashtyk Nokyd isn't an official guest. He's back in the buyer/client quarters, he's under an assumed name, and his presence aboard the ship isn't recorded anywhere. So where does this connect to Laure asking you about him?"

"That's where the injection she did at the back of Laure's head comes in. The injection was of a classified programmed nano-augment called Third Ear. It's designed for military use and remains accessible only to people with deep military connections in those armies that use it."

"She's a Legend," Shay said in mild tones. "Her skills are extremely well-developed. If she wants military access, she'll have it without anyone even knowing they gave it to her."

"Right." Melie felt her skin flush. She should have remembered that aspect of Legends as it related to this situation. "Third Ear creates a tiny skin-and-bone middle ear at the base of the skull that wires directly into the neurological system through the foramen magnum — the hole in the skull through which the spinal cord connects to the brain. This would be useless if it didn't have a way to gather sound, though. In this case, it has a tympanic-membrane-analog — the part of the ear that collects sound waves — that is set up to read auditory signals connected from a coded feed. The person on the other end of the feed can transmit through a subvocalizer, a standard voice-to-feed connection, or anything else someone wants to rig up."

"So our Legend wasn't just getting information. She was also sending it."

"Yes. And to keep things simple for herself, and to make sure Laure was always within reach, she send her transmissions through a narrow, locked band she threaded into our shipcom feed."

Shay swore.

Melie waited until Shay wound down. "So, as I understand the abilities of Legends, this woman could give Laure specific commands, and Laure would have no choice but to do what she said."

"It's possible to resist some commands." Shay dropped her gaze from Melie's face to her own hands. "To resist, though, the victim has to know she is being controlled, has to recognize the order she has been given as coming from outside of her, and has to have the strength to fight it. The only commands the individual has any real chance of resisting are those things she would never, ever, under any circumstances do on her own."

Melie watched the way Shay's body had gone rigid while she explained that, and she could not help but wonder, *What did the owner do to her? Or try to make her do?*

But of course she did not ask. Instead she said, "I have proof that Laure resisted at least once. Successfully."

Shay looked surprised when she raised her head. She looked oddly hopeful. "Really? How?"

"I'll get to that when we go over the Actions and Consequences in a second. First, I want to tell you about the thing the Legend did to Laure."

"All right."

"She did the injection in Laure's upper arm."

"She did that injection first."

Melie nodded. "If it had worked, I would have covered that first. But it was the thing that broke."

"Did that matter in the end?"

"Yes. The failure of this mod was fifty percent of saving the lives of everyone on this ship at the end."

"What was it supposed to do?"

"It was supposed to create hardwired connections through Laure's body that would have allowed the Legend to take over physical control of her body — the same way you would control a character in a Sensogame."

"Right." Shay nodded sharply. "I understand how that works. So what happened that broke this adaptation?"

"It was a black-market one-off mod. I suspect the Legend had this developed specifically for gaining control of the Longview. According to the GenDaring analyst who read all this stuff for me, this was a long-shot prototype, done to fit to the broadest general human DNA compatibility profile. This means this Legend had no prior connection to Laure, and no way of testing for compatibility. She had no previous access to the ship, crew, or known passengers."

"Lucky us," Shay snarled. "A break at last."

"It was. Laure came from an established small-population PHTF settlement that suffered horribly from Founder Effect. The majority of pairs on her genes were rare or matching, or both. She looked normal because she used her Medix to give her a normal appearance. But she was both reproductively sterile and would have had a number of internal and external deformities without Medix adjustment."

"I remember," Shay said. "She was a horribly deformed toss who managed to get into her settlement's Needle, and hang on up in the cabin until we arrived on our Death Circus rounds. We took her on as crew during that stop, and she changed herself into a pretty girl and worked her ass off when she wasn't busy being admired by pretty boys."

"That fits. That fits, and that tells me how she managed to beat direct orders she got from the Legend." Melie took a deep breath. "So here are the actions and consequences you asked for: One-Action: Laure asked me about Bashtyk Nokyd during deep dark.

"Consequence: I tell her.

"Two-Action: The Legend sends her to poison Nokyd.

"Consequence: She visits the official guest quarters — the only ones she has access to — and none of the guests are Bashtyk Nokyd. The Legend tells her to come to you to steal codes the Legend believes you have, but this Laure will not do. She successfully resists. The Legend decides to wait and get Nokyd another way.

"Three-Action: The Legend has Laure send me to Level 10 during the jumps to keep me from monitoring com and seeing the *Longview* sending docking codes to an enemy ship, and shutting down our protection.

"Consequence: I am out of the way when the rest of the rest of the crew is killed.

"Four-Action: Laure can read the *Longview's* status as the other ship begins to dock, and tries to shut down the overrides. She can't — except for me, because she manually set my status. She unlocks my jump berth, fighting the Legend's orders about what she was to do during the boarding to do it."

Shay said, "No. That cannot be. The Legend could not have been giving her direct orders. We were in an unregistered origami point, and we had no communication with pingballs or Spybees — oh..."

"Right. The pirates had Spybee-equivalent technology attached to the back spine of their ship. She probably put it there, just like she probably controlled all or most of them. They probably didn't know they were dragging spyware. When we found it, our crew shut it down, disassembled it, sealpacked it, and stored it as salvage. So she doesn't have direct communication now. But she did then."

Shay sighed. "That's a lot of probablies."

"It is. But the consequence of Laure's fourth action is that I was free to fight. She took one more action after that."

"Which was?"

Melie showed her final 2-D image. "When directly commanded to help the invading pirates attack her crewmates, she instead turns her weapons on them and kills two of them before they grab her and stab and cut her to death.

"Consequence: She delayed them long enough on the bridge to give the owner time to get there. Had she not done that, more of us — and possibly all of us — would have died." Melie swallowed back tears. "She loved this ship, she loved her shipmates, and she never betrayed us. Never.

Melie leaned forward. "I have tracked every breach in our system that I can find, and to the best of my knowledge, I have presented you with a full assessment of our vulnerabilities, and a complete report on how those vulnerabilities were used in the past and might yet be used in the future."

"We may still suffer losses from this breach, and take harm from directions we may not be able to foresee or to protect against." Shay rubbed her eyes with the back of her hand. "As for Laure, I'll see that her will is honored in full, and that she gets a ceremony and honors on her record. It isn't much. It's never enough. But it may give some comfort to those she named as her heirs." She started to rise, and said, "You've done well."

"I've done a little better than that, if you can give me another moment or two," Melie said.

Shay sat back down. "Really?"

"The Legend has no way to know I've discovered her breach of our data. It was well-hidden, and I was very careful breaking into it. So I tampered with the feed she's getting. Any crew or guest files she had not yet read have been modified to provide real-looking data with fine-grained false details. Any of these she has read will be gradually updated to provide the same false details.

"Further, I have put something into the feed that, with your permission, will reach her the instant we pass our next Spybee, and which is so tempting she'll almost have to take it."

"Go on."

"I've dumped direct personal contact information with the owner into a private contract that appears to have been accidentally misfiled as public by Rowse. The information will allow her to connect to a special feed I built for her alone. If she never uses it, it will be useless for us."

"But if she does?"

"If she attempts to contact the owner through this feed, she will get a shipcom message telling her that Mado Keyr is in his pressure chamber, and temporarily unavailable, but that she is being forwarded to his personal representative. While she is receiving that message, we are doing a backtrace through our invisible connection. It will give us her location and voiceprint instantly, and then dig in and gently parallel her own system. We'll be doing to her what she did to us — but we won't be leaving big footprints."

"I love you," Shay said. "That is simply brilliant. Thank you, and yes. Go ahead and set it up. That's the all-clear. I'll go let the owner know we've done what we can, and are ready to move on. We'll announce you as Captain once we're safe in our new home."

SHAY HAD the captain's chair, Kagen ran back-up on the first's seat — which he would hold until the *Longview* had time to acquire a ready first mate, or to train up one of the jumped-up crew members to take the chair.

Melie settled into her station and monitored com. Vogert, jumped into Two-Gold, held the defense chair. And Stwrak navigated.

Everyone not on deck was in a jump berth. Everyone who was on deck braced themselves, because there was no way to get used to the instant of sliding along the origami fold.

The ship made the first jump, and Melie was for an instant and an eternity thrown into the mind of her otherself, overself, and in that instant both saw and felt every other life she might have lived, all the places where she did not escape the hell of her past, where she was still a slave, where she was dying, broken, twisted. Saw every place where she had failed to connect with the *Longview,* where she had missed her one chance, and felt all at once all the pain of all those other lives as one infinite full-body scream of terror and grief and loss — and then the *Longview* tore itself free of the hell of the multiverse and Melie was on the ship, on the Longview, once again the one who got away.

She threw up, and wept, and shipcom scuttled a cleaner beneath her feet to take care of the mess and pumped a coffee-plus-vitamins-plus-regenerative-fluids cocktail into her built-in workstation cup. She drank the mixture straight down, doing her best not to taste it.

She wound down. Ignored the post-jump distress of the others on deck, caught their sounds of their own frantic gulping of coffee.

Her job was to read com. She read com.

Nothing had come in or out, there had been no pings, no contacts, no attempted contacts. There was nothing waiting outside the point, nothing lurking outside their hatches.

One down.

"We're green on com at Insertion Point One," she said. "No Spybees, no pingballs, no feeds, no leaks. Everything is clear out there, and everything and everyone is locked down in here."

Shay said, "Prep for second insertion."

"Ready on First."

"Ready on Nav."

"Ready on Defense."

"Ready on Com."

"Insertion Point Two now," Shay said, and hell returned.

And then was gone, replaced by a sight that was as welcome to Melie as beautiful as sun-grown food and friends around a table.

They were not in another unregistered origami point. They were running toward the north-east corner of Bailey's Irish Station, with the iconic moleibonded solid wood Colson Traders tower growing larger in their forward screens and viewport. Ship traffic around them was heavy.

"This is Longview hailing Bailey's Irish Station Tower Control," Melie said. "*Longview* hailing Bailey's Irish —"

"Tower Control here. Got you locked in on Tower Control Two, *Longview*. Gantry Couples South 3 and 4 Outfacing are reserved for you. Your docking couple will be Gantry 4. Do you have our beacon?"

"Have your beacon on the board and locked on," Stwrak said.

"Follow the beacon — I'm sending you the long way around to keep you out of main station traffic. The *Longview's* size will foul things up otherwise.

Shay said, "Affirmative. We'll keep your path clear."

"I have you set up for a Blu-O Four docking ring. That still work?"

"We're good for Blu-O Four, Tower," Stwrak said.

"Then let's do this. Guidance crosshairs are extended, and we're standing by to bring you on station."

"Tower acknowledged," Melie said. "We're coming in."

"And by the way," Tower said, dropping his official voice, "about time you folks showed up. Where the hell have you been? I've been ass-deep in Baileys expecting you to get here ever since they sent their invitation. They started worrying two weeks ago."

Everyone looked to Shay.

Shay looked tense. "Tower, we had to shake off some trouble. We're on lockdown until we've done post-jump checks and talked to *the* Bailey."

"Roger that, and sorry about the trouble. But in the meantime, welcome home."

In her entire life, it was the first time Melie had ever heard those words spoken to her.

MELIE SCOURED com for anything incoming. Anything outgoing. Anything different, anything wrong… and there was nothing. There were no Pact-Worlds-registered ships visiting or passing through Bailey's Irish Space Station. There were no people on Bailey's Irish with Pact Worlds citizenship.

It looked safe. That didn't mean it was, and she included that note in her report to Shay. But she signed off on the all-clear.

Chapter 9

Bashtyk Nokyd

We sit in Wils Bailey's private quarters, and I find myself thinking how stark this place is. How simple.

Wils Bailey is rich, richer by far than most of the men who hold power in Cantata, who live in their vast castles carved of rock, surrounded by their servants. And everyone here refers to him as *the* Bailey.

But in this station that his father started building, and that he and his siblings still own and operate, he lives on the top two floors of a modest apartment building, in simple quarters with his wife and their youngest child.

They have no lavish furnishings. They have no rare collections. No servants. No sycophants. No court of toadies and favor-seekers.

They do have a lovely view of space. And they have each other.

Shay and I sit at their table and eat their food. It's good food, much of it fresh-grown or otherwise produced on the station.

"I cannot believe I am sitting at table with Bashtyk Nokyd," Wils says, and the grin on his face is wonderful. "We've used principles you've been teaching to build and run this place, and what a difference it makes. The simplest of things make Bailey's Irish Station work. Folks pay their own way, provide for their own children's educations, make only laws that guard the rights and property of individuals, tax only purchases and never incomes. And the people who live here, as well as the ones who emigrate here, live by those simple rules of life, and flourish. You'd like it here. Your citizenship here is waiting for you if you'll take it."

Wils is in his fifties, as is his wife. Both of them are older than the station they live on by about a dozen years.

But like everyone else on the station, they have unregulated access to reju. They look thirty by choice. Banyi, their youngest child, is nineteen, bright and pretty and alert. There is an evident warmth in her relationship with her parents that never existed between me and my parents, or me and my children.

She says, "Dad is always talking about living by the principles that sustain your life. If he didn't also do it, I could ignore him. But he does." She smiles at me, wrinkles her nose at him, then grins. He laughs and ruffles her hair.

Both his older son and daughter have already stopped by, have introduced their families.

I try to imagine the people among whom I grew up being like this. They and their children were strangers, made so by a government that wanted to mold people into tools it could use. It molded the rich just as fiercely as it molded the poor. Everyone suffered, but unlike the poor, the rich were too blind to see what they had lost.

Here — here I see the life I envisioned made real, and suddenly realize that I can have this.

I can have this life. A wife who loves me because I value her, not because we are chained together by a social contract based on class and fortune and duty. Children whom I know and who know me. Fellow human beings around me who see the value in what I do, who understand why it matters, who will happily trade their skills and knowledge for mine.

Here, people's lives are allowed to matter individually, so full reju is legal and encouraged. I can become a young man with the earned knowledge of an old man, and I can give myself the same chance I have been fighting for my whole life to give others.

I can give myself and people I love a good life.

In the company of this free, self-determined family, the last pieces of the puzzle of how to bring freedom to the people of the Pact Worlds fall into place for me.

The hand and the mind are one — the movement of fingers frees the movement of thoughts. I pull out the little tablet I always carry with me, and on it begin scribing a diagram.

"I have it," I say, as my scribe tip moves across the smooth surface of the tablet. "The process for freeing the Pact Worlds' captive people."

Shay looks surprised. "You do?"

I nod. "I can't give them freedom," I say, "no one can. The only free people are those who recognize their right to be free, claim it, and then fight to protect that freedom."

Wils is nodding his head. "We see that here. Like everyplace else, we're getting refugees who are escaping from Pact Worlds. Some understand that to be here, they have to pay their way. Some…" He shakes his head. "They ask where they can sign up for benefits, and where the free rooming houses are, and how to get the free food…"

Banyi stands up and says, "I'll be right back."

He smiles at her, and continues. "We're a space station. What we can't make or grow here on our own, we have to go out to get or pay to have brought in. We don't have the buffer planets have, with food growing wild that you just find lying around on the ground, or shoot as it walks past."

I keep my head down, linking boxes with arrows, dropping in words that stand for whole steps in this process, as well as words my hand insists should mean something, though my conscious mind has not yet made the connection. I pause for a moment, studying what I have drawn, trying to get the smaller pieces to connect. I say, "Most worlds — being terraformed — don't have easy food or other resources either. But I get your meaning. You're dealing with government slaves. Religion slaves. They're different from body slaves — men and women owned by individual masters. Body slaves know that if they don't work, they don't eat. If they resist, they don't eat. If they fight, they'll be staked to a chain without shelter. Their actions all connect — so when they get free, their minds still work.

"Government slaves and religion slaves are different. Their minds have been intentionally broken. They have been taught from birth that work and food are unrelated. That no matter what they do, they will still eat, still have a place to sleep, still have someone to take care of them, because government or God will provide. At the same time, they are taught that their time, their thought, and their work have no value to them. That they must give it away for free, for the benefit of others. That anything they do for themselves is of no use, of no importance. That anything they want for themselves is evil or selfish — even their own lives. Even their own thoughts."

My hand is moving again, writing words, drawing boxes, connecting with arrows.

I say, "I cannot say the fix for this will be simple, and there will always be people who will *choose* to be slaves rather than work to be free."

The structure comes clear and beautiful in my mind, made up of logic and love, of passion and desire and hard work. On the tablet, it's a mess — but I can work with this. Fill it out, shape it, use it to show people that their lives matter to themselves, for themselves, and that what they create has value to them.

"Here's where we start," I say, and point to the first box I've drawn on the tablet.

And Wils looks over my left shoulder and says, "Banyi, what's the matter?"

Chapter 10

Shay

Shay was on the wrong side of the table, not beside Nokyd, but across from him and one seat over. She saw Banyi, with tears running down her face. Heard Bashtyk Nokyd say, "Here's where we start," heard Wils say, "Banyi, what's the matter?" and was on her feet as the words were coming out of his mouth.

But furniture was in her way, and she could not reach as Banyi's hands fit themselves to either side of Nokyd's head…

Shay filtered out the faint noises Banyi was making at the same instant that she vaulted over the table. "No," Banyi was saying, "no, no, don't make me, no don't make me, no…"

Bashtyk Nokyd's head imploded soundlessly, went flat, vaporized, and Shay grabbed Banyi, who, weeping and screaming "No, no, don't *make* me!" raised her hands to her own head.

This time Shay was fast enough. Pulled her hands down, shouted at Wils, "Where's your Medix?" and he ghastly pale and round-eyed, pointed, then looked at what remained of Bashtyk Nokyd and fainted.

Shay yanked both of Banyi's hands to the table, clamped the

girl's wrists together with one hand, yanked a moleibond cutter out of her shipsuit belt with the other, and sliced off the girl's forearms.

Shay shouted, "Get her into the Medix! Someone rigged her hands!"

Someone had done a lot more than that.

Shay stared at the headless corpse that seconds before had been the brightest light in Settled Space. At the screaming child, rescued from killing herself, being dragged to the family Medix. Stared at the hands and forearms on the table, flopped across plates of half-eaten food, stumps seared by the cutter.

Looked down at her own hands, and watched them shaking. She realized she was crying, and she couldn't stop herself. She could not make her body do what she needed it to do.

The recording from the deck of the *Longview* had included Laure screaming, "No, don't make me!"

This was that again, and this time Shay knew the source. The Legend had somehow divined the track of the *Longview* —

No. She hadn't.

Laure had never had access to the invitation from the Baileys. That had been directly to the owner, had been locked in the owner's private files, and had not been breached.

The Legend had found *Bashtyk Nokyd*. Had come after him directly. Might not even realize that he had been aboard the *Longview*.

And Banyi had just said much the same thing Laure had said. *Don't make me.* And then she had tried to destroy herself, while clearly fighting for her life. She had been doing everything in her power *not* to do what some other force made her do.

Shay thought again about what she had known of Laure.

As a raw recruit, Laure had been damaged and frightened, but all the recruits were. They'd been exiled from hell, told they were not even worthy of that place, that the only value they could give the universe was to kill themselves, and be quick about it.

The only reason Banyi wasn't dead was because Shay had learned long ago that ruthless brutality could sometimes save as well as destroy. Ruthless brutality had saved humanity from extinction at the hands of Legends.

And ruthless brutality had saved a young girl's life.

A week in a Medix would replace Banyi's arms and hands. Her innocence — that was lost.

But ruthless brutality was going to avenge it for her.

Mado Werix Keyr was about to come out of his box and be the monster he needed to be, this time against another monster like himself.

Shay was no longer crying. No longer shaking. She tapped her earbud once, then said, "Shay to *Longview*. Code Coldwater. Our guest has been injured and needs to return to the ship."

Bashtyk Nokyd might have been a target of convenience — but she thought that this time he was the true target, and that this time the bitch Legend who had come after him had hit exactly what she'd aimed for.

The *Longview* could muddy the waters, though. They would not announce Bashtyk Nokyd's death. Would in fact redate and release a few conversations he'd recorded aboard the ship — bits of new philosophy he was developing. These conversations would let the universe and perhaps even his killer think he was alive.

And the *Longview* would sit parked at Bailey's Irish Space Station, and see if the Legend would take Melie's bit of bait.

Shay picked up Nokyd's tablet and scribe and slipped both into a shipsuit pocket. She rested a hand on his still-warm shoulder and rage filled her. She wanted to kill the one who'd done this. Wanted to rip it into shreds, nail the still-living shreds to a wall, and listen to every piece of it beg for death.

But that was not her place, not her function. Keyr would hunt down the thing and kill it.

She had Nokyd's last words, scrawled in a bizarre diagram that had made no sense whatsoever when she'd glanced at it. But it had meant something to him. It meant bringing freedom to people who were willing to earn it — and that *was* Shay's function. So Shay would bring together the code-breakers, the signal-trackers, the feed-wormers aboard the *Longview* and put this puzzle in front of them.

She and they would do their best to understand what Bashtyk Nokyd's last words meant, and to get them to the people who needed them.

She was a piece in a bigger plan. But she was an important piece, and she would do her part.

When her team arrived with a portable Medix and put Nokyd's body into it, she convinced them to say nothing about his condition. On her way out the door, she did the same thing with the Baileys.

Then, carrying an iced bag containing a girl's hands and forearms and the burden of the lost — but possibly recoverable — meaning of the last words of Settled Space's greatest philosopher, Shay went home.

Melie

Melie knocked on the door of Shay's office. Shay opened it.

"I found both things you asked me for."

Shay pointed her to a seat opposite her desk. "What did you find?"

"The leak on Bashtyk Nokyd. The Legend had a voice print of him, and her system was searching for his presence through all the feeds. She located him in the anonymous networks while he was playing a Sensogame. She was never able to connect his game status with the *Longview*, but she did connect him to the Bailey's Irish Station gameserver core when we jumped into Bailey's Irish. I can only guess that she bet on Wils Bailey wanting to meet Nokyd — and using his daughter as the tool of her destruction. I don't know and don't dare guess how she gained access to the girl."

Melie watch Shay bury her head in her hands. "Game server. We lost him because of a game server."

"That was the bad news. I know it couldn't be much worse. But the good news is very good."

"Go ahead," Shay said.

"Our insertion into the Legend's private data is working. One of the files I found in the Legend's storage is a Pact Worlds contract negotiating the terms by which the pirates are hunting us, who are acknowledged as pirates in the contract, with both their world and their names in the negotiations. The contract is signed by both acting Pact World Administrators and pirate captains."

Shay lifted her head from her hands as Melie told her this, and simply stared, wide-eyed.

"It's documented? In writing?"

Melie nodded.

"Negotiating with pirates invalidates the Pact Worlds' original charter."

"I know."

"Danyal Travers needs a copy of that contract."

"I made sure he got one," Melie said.

Shay took a deep breath. "Did you get the name of the bitch whose files you just raided."

"Not yet, but I will. Has she contacted you yet?"

Melie watched a cold light creep into Shay's eyes, and she shivered.

Shay stared behind Melie at something far away — in another part of space. "Not yet," she whispered. "But she will."

Gunslinger Moon

TALES FROM THE LONGVIEW

HOLLY LISLE

For Matthew

And for Joe,
who introduced me to VR in the real world,
and who loves both games and honor

Chapter 1

Shay

S hay closed her eyes and rubbed her temples. She'd been in her office for hours, a "Do Not Disturb" sign on her door, looking for any single tiny piece of new information that might let her believe hope still existed.

That her stupidity had not destroyed Settled Space's last best chance for freedom.

Bashtyk Nokyd, the philosopher she'd risked her life to rescue from a Pact Worlds Alliance death contract, whom she had secured in the *Longview*, and whom she could have gotten to the City of Furies if she hadn't been stupid enough to let him go to dinner with the owners of Bailey's Irish Space Station, was dead because of her.

Her hero. The man who'd been responsible for her own freedom, the man who had written *Simple Rights: The Individual As Universal Core*, was dead, and she might as well have killed him herself.

She pushed the replay button again and once again saw him sitting across the table from her. He had his tablet in hand.

"I have it," he said, drawing, and she could hear his excitement in those few words. His surprise. "The process for freeing the Pact Worlds' captive people." His hand moved steadily, drawing boxes, writing words.

She watched herself say, "You do?" At her desk, her whole body stiffened. Even after seeing the replay so many times, she could not stop the reflex to tense, to get ready to stop the thing she could not stop.

His voice was deep, certain, but still tinged with the elation of discovery. "I can't give them freedom. No one can. The only free people are those who recognize their right to be free, claim it, and then fight to protect that freedom."

Wils Bailey, the owner of Bailey's Irish Space Station, said, "We see that here. Like everyplace else, we're getting refugees who are escaping from Pact Worlds. Some understand that to be here, they have to pay their way. Some..." He shook his head. "They ask where they can sign up for benefits, and where the free rooming houses are, and how to get the free food..."

Shay spotted an expression on the face of Wils' teenage daughter, and wished she had been paying attention to the girl, not to Nokyd. She hadn't noticed it at the time. She'd been too intent on watching Bashtyk Nokyd drawing on his tablet.

The girl stood up and said, "I'll be right back."

Her father smiled, giving her a half-second glance, returning his attention to his guest without any recognition that something was wrong. "We're a space station," he said. "What we can't make or grow here on our own, we have to go out to get or pay to have brought in. We don't have the resource buffer that planets have, with food growing wild that you just find lying around on the ground, or shoot as it walks past."

Nokyd didn't look up. He was busy diagramming. His hand stopped moving for a moment, long enough for him to study what he'd drawn, and he said, "Most worlds — being terraformed — don't have easy food or other resources either. But I get your meaning. You're dealing with government slaves. Religion slaves. They're different from body slaves — men and women owned by individual masters. Body slaves know that if they don't work, they don't eat. If they resist, they don't eat. If they fight, they'll be chained to a stake without shelter. Their actions all connect — so when they get free, their minds still work.

"Government slaves and religion slaves are different. Their minds have been intentionally broken. They have been taught from birth that work and food are unrelated. That no matter what they do, they will still eat, still have a place to sleep, still have someone to take care of them, because government or God will provide. At the same time, they are taught that their time, their thought, and their work have no value to them. That they must give it away for free, for the benefit of others. That anything they do for themselves is of no use, of no importance. That anything they want for themselves is evil or selfish — even their own lives. Even their own thoughts."

He went back to drawing, and said, "I cannot say the fix for this will be simple, and there will always be people who will choose to be slaves rather than work to be free."

"Here's where we start," he said, and pointed to his diagram.

And the girl placed her hands on either side of his head.

His head imploded before Shay could pause the holo.

She closed her eyes, blinked back tears.

Took a deep breath and straightened her spine.

The diagram was in front of her.

The solution to giving lasting freedom to the people of Settled Space.

She stared at the place on the tablet where his finger rested, to what he'd designated as the starting point.

B or F Principle.

In the week following his death, she'd immersed herself in his work, had brain-imprinted everything he'd published over his long life, as well as every lecture he'd ever given. She'd force-fed seven million written words and almost a thousand hours of holo and audio via high compression into her consciousness.

And there simply was no *B or F Principle* in any of his work.

There was no *B or F Principle* anywhere in any philosophy. As for the rest of the diagram…

BETTER HORSE or Bigger Gun → *NO net!* → *moon & sun dilemma* → *Shoot on Sight* → *"Happy Madame"*
        HARD Restart?

THERE WAS NOTHING. Nothing that made sense, nothing that connected to any philosophical theory… just nothing. And with the threat of attack by PWA-hired pirate fleets running through the dark channels of space, with rumors of forces being built to come against both the *Longview* and Bailey's Station, she could not afford to throw herself against this wall any longer.

She closed her eyes, rested weary head in hand, and the image of a Medix floated like sweet temptation through her mind.

Reju would feel wonderful…

But that wasn't what the image meant, was it? This was her brain trying to tell her something important. And what she saw hadn't been a regular Medix. It had been one of the modified Sleeper cells.

Right.

Sleepers who had applied to become crew would have already been tested, would have already received basic crew training, and would have personality profiles on hand.

None of them were doing anything at the moment. They were still in sleep because the *Longview* was docked at Bailey's, and because its Death Circus charter had been cancelled when the Pact Worlds Alliance put a bounty on the ship. Shay didn't see the ship going anywhere for a while.

The most promising of the Sleepers would have been brought up as crew by Melie once she could be announced as captain.

But in the meantime, they were in the Sleeper cells.

Shay could dig through their files, find the potential crew best at lateral thinking, puzzle-solving, and logic-leaping.

The owner would need to present them with the situation and impress them with the importance of the task to him.

Once that was done, though, they could dig through Bashtyk Nokyd's sealed quarters. Perhaps they could find something she'd missed.

Chapter 2

Jex

We sit at a long table, four of us, staring up at a man covered head to toe in what I've learned is an armored deep-space worksuit. His face is hard to see through the shaded moleibond helmet shield, his voice is deep and rasping. He has identified himself to us as Mado Werix Keyr, the owner of this ship.

"Each of you is being drafted as provisional crew. If you provide something from your first objective that proves your resourcefulness and attention to detail, your ability to think creatively, or a provable solution or partial solution to the task I'm giving you, you will receive a permanent universal identity and a crew slot on the *Longview*."

The speaker stares at the four of us — and the shield does not hide the fact that he is… terrible. Terrifying.

I'm taller than he is, broader of shoulder, hardened by a brutal past — but the gleam of his eyes through the shield plate sends ice down my spine.

I've been brought out of storage to find something that probably doesn't exist, and three other men have been brought out with me.

His voice, muffled by the suit's breathing apparatus, is clear enough to get the danger in our situation across.

"The man who drew this diagram was getting ready to tell a small audience of listeners the process he'd figured out for changing Settled Space to Free Space — for setting up a system of laws, perhaps, or something else that would make the conditions that permit slavery impossible. Before he could explain each of the items on the diagram he drew, he was murdered by a third party, not present in the room, controlling a child who was.

"Everyone present at that meeting submitted to memory scans, and we now know that nothing in what Bashtyk Nokyd said before his death provides clues to what any of this means."

"Others on this ship well-suited to the task are searching for his killer. Meanwhile, the Pact Worlds Alliance has hired an armada of pirates to exterminate everyone on this ship, as well as everyone on the station to which we're docked. And because of treachery and enormous loss of life, the crew of this ship is shorthanded. We can spare no active crew to do what must be done in these quarters. Which is why the four of you receive this chance."

He pauses, leans against the table that separates us from him, and breathes heavily. He is looking at each of us in turn, and when his gaze meets mine, I feel myself shrinking, falling into darkness, losing my grasp on who I am.

When he looks to the next man, my mind clears. But I feel shaky and sick. Whatever is wrong with the man across the table from us is beyond the scope of my experience, and it is ugly. Horrifying. Deadly.

"You four have proven yourselves trustworthy while in hibernation. You have each passed the honor test, reading and crew tests, and various problem-solving tests that make you ideal for the task you've been given. In these quarters you are bound to conduct yourselves by ship rules, and maintain ship discipline. If the answer to the problem before us *can* be found, the four of you will find it.

"Anything in these quarters might offer a key to the solution we seek. Ignore nothing. Assume nothing. No piece of information is too small. If it relates to this, nothing is insignificant.

"When you find something that applies to the words on the diagram I'll give you, press your button on your wristcom." He points, and I look down to see that a band has been attached to my wrist just under the sleeve of the shipsuit I wear. The band is smaller than the diameter of my hand. It will not come off, will not be possible to lose.

I nod my understanding.

"When you press your com button, you will reach either me or my representative. One of us will come when you call.

And he hands each of us a tablet. I am familiar with the technology. My second parents taught my brothers and sisters and me on such devices.

I stare at the image before me, scrawled by hand in the language I learned following my second birth.

Chapter 3

Jex

Bor F Principle → *Better Horse or Bigger Gun* → *NO net!* → *moon & sun dilemma* → *Shoot on Sight* → *"Happy Madame" HARD Restart?*

I can read the individual words. I have no idea what they mean, or how they could relate to the freedom of uncountable billions of enslaved human beings.

But I remember my first life, and know that I have been given a task of immense importance. Freeing the slaves of Settled Space must be done. If it had been done sooner, the woman I loved and our child might still be alive.

My name is Jex. Now, anyway. This is the name my second parents gave me, with the understanding that I could change it when I grew and became an adult. I kept the name to honor them for giving me a home, for giving me love, for teaching me and raising me and making sure I knew right from wrong, knew the value of being human, knew how to think and knew why thinking mattered. And for giving me a name in the first place — something my first parents, whoever they might have been, never got the chance to do.

I remember being This Criminal in my first life, where I started out as WE-39R, a slave on a People's Home of Truth and Fairness world that required anyone of Willfulness, Blasphemy, or Infidelity to seek Return to Citizenship by volunteering to leap into a lake of fire to prove remorse and repentance.

Once the criminal was dead, the citizens present welcomed it back as a citizen — for all citizens of PHTF worlds are considered acceptable only if they accept the Truth of We, and are right-thinking creatures. And the right-thinking dead are honored, while the wrong-thinking living are not.

"Do you have questions?" the owner asked.

The four of us look at each other, exchanging fearful glances. The other three shook their heads.

I repress a shiver and say, "I have one."

The helmeted head nods. "Ask."

"How are we to know what may be touched?"

The owner says, "You may — you *must* — touch everything in this suite. Nothing is too small, too unimportant, or too strange for your consideration. The man who inhabited these quarters may have had terrible secrets, may have been other than as he presented himself, or he may have been exactly the man all of Settled Space believed him to be.

"That doesn't matter.

"What matters is that he may have left clues to his thinking in this room. Neither I nor anyone else who has seen his diagram can understand what it means. And I have presented it to every surviving member of my crew, to my officers, to associates of mine in places far from here, and to the best minds in the City of Furies. No one can unravel its import."

One of the others says, "Perhaps it was a joke. It looks like it could have been a joke."

"It does," the owner agrees. "Unless you knew the man. He was working toward the solution to the most important problem in our society — not to just freeing existing slaves, but to devise a way to protect the individual rights of all people by preventing the creation of new slaves. He was searching for a way to create Free Space and make sure that its freedom is lasting. I personally offered him passage to the City of Furies and assistance in earning citizenship in exchange for helping me solve this problem for which we both desired the answer.

"At dinner, during a discussion he was having with friends, something fell into place for him, and he suddenly knew the solution.

"He drew the diagram, he got ready to explain what it meant, and he was murdered."

The four of us look at each other. The man to my right asks, "If he was murdered for figuring out this answer, might we not be as well?"

The silence that follows freezes me in place. He's asked the wrong question. I know it the second I hear it, and have my fear confirmed in the instant that the owner's head turns slowly toward him.

To the air, the owner says, "Samix, escort T748H-BN Rabon to his unit. His assistance is no longer needed."

One of the guards standing by the door nods and steps forward. The owner turns to Rabon and says, "When Settled Space is *safe*, you can come out of the box again."

I suppress my shudder. The owner looks at each of us in turn. When his gaze lands on me, I swallow fear and say, "I'd like to see a recording of that conversation."

He says, "One exists. It was from an illegal source, and you may not speak of what you see to anyone ever. If you watch it, when you become crew you will be Veridicated each time you return to the ship, and your failure to keep this secret will be one of the things for which you will be tested. If you fail in this test, you will be abandoned wherever you are with nothing but your name and the clothes you wear, to make your way through the universe as best you can."

"I still want to see it," I say.

"You each agree?"

The other two nod. "Veridication requirements were explained during Off-ship Conduct Training," the man on my left says.

I see the faint flicker of a smile inside the helmet.

"Then you three are left to find the truth. It may be anywhere in these quarters, in any form. Whatever bits of Bashtyk Nokyd's discovery exist in here will almost certainly be in pieces. From the form of his notes, they are unlikely to be recognizable as solutions — you are going to have to distill some of the sense of his meaning from what you find to create a path to the truth."

"How long do we have?"

"You have as long as you have, but it is more important that you be thorough than that you be quick. We need the right answer, not the fastest one you can find. The Pact Worlds Alliance is rabidly expansionist — it constantly needs to drag productive worlds under its rule to pay the debts of its core worlds — and because it bleeds its conquests dry so quickly, changing them into yet more debtor worlds, it cannot escape the expanding rot at its center, or solve the problems the rot causes.

"So you have until you can find and connect Bashtyk Nokyd's secrets to the meaning of the diagram, or until you exhaust all options and surrender, or until pirates hired by the Pact Worlds Alliance to destroy us come through the origami point to where we're docked and succeed."

"I would have led with that last one," I say, and immediately wish I hadn't.

The owner laughs, though — an unnerving rasp that ends in a strangled cough. "Work," he says. "As if your lives depend on it. Because they do."

Chapter 4

Jex

O nce the owner leaves, we make our brief introductions. I introduce myself as Jex. My two remaining colleagues are Tarn and Hirrin.

Not much to tell for any of us. We've all been on PHTF worlds, we've all been through the hell that those worlds breed. Like me, they've been sentenced to death. Hirrin was exiled to his settlement's Needle, required to serve the incoming ships until he died of cold or starvation, and was a direct rescue. He was put into cold storage voluntarily because there was no other space for him. Tarn is, like me, a Death Circus purchase.

We discover that each of us was given a second birth, real parents, siblings, education, training, discipline.

We try to figure out if we knew each other in the Neighborhood, but can't find any connections in our pasts.

What we have in common is that when we reached the age of legality, all three of us chose the path to becoming *Longview* crew.

Sitting and talking with them, I discover something my parents never told me when Hirrin says, "After I made my career choice and started training, my folks said they were proud of me. That they remained in stasis rather than go to the City because the path they had chosen was to become second parents to the broken people who came aboard the *Longview*. That they chose parent duty so they would know better what to do with real children when they could have them. And that they could change their path choice at any time, just like we can."

I didn't know that. It had never occurred to me to ask how I came to have a second birth.

I *remember* my first life, the girl I loved, the child we made, their deaths, and I was afraid that if I told anyone what I remembered, they would take the memories away.

I'd lost my child and his mother — and I could not even blame her for betraying us all. The same unending suffering that had made me rebellious had broken her will.

I had loved them both. I could not bear the thought of forgetting them.

I was certain my second life was not entirely real — but just as I didn't want to lose my memories, I did not want to risk hurting the people who loved me and cared for me, so I did not ask any questions that might take them away. I *wanted* my second parents and my sibs to be real.

I am grateful to discover that they were, if not in the way I'd imagined.

Hirrin, Tarn, and I decide to categorize the contents of the dead philosopher's quarters. There is his writing — dozens of bound real-paper manuscripts marked Journals, each with a date on the front, each logged into his Journal record. There is his reading material. And finally there is what we can only describe as "random assorted stuff." Com log, viewscreen log, entertainment holos, a couple of Senso games, tools with which the philosopher was carving a chain made of wood that rests on one of the shelves.

The writing looks like the best bet for answers, the reading like the second best bet, and the "other stuff" as "probably not much good, but we have to go through it."

Hirrin says, "We're more likely to recognize patterns and connections if each of us takes one whole group."

Tarn and I both nod. It makes sense.

And all three of us almost trip over each other trying to claim Bashtyk Nokyd's writing.

I sigh, and say, "Sticks, Stones, Bones?"

You know…

Sticks hit stones,
Stones break bones,
Bones scatter sticks.

It was how kids decided things in the Neighborhood.

"Winner gets the writing," Tarn says.

We count three, show our hands, and Hirrin has sticks, and both Tarn and I have stones.

So Hirrin gets the philosopher's notebooks.

A second run gives the books to Tarn, and leaves me with the remainders, which look less likely to yield results.

I try not to take it too hard. Last pick and what's left over are what I have to win my chance to earn a place on the crew. But even if I have the dregs, I'm still in this, not back in storage. I'm going to use my chance, not waste it.

"We should work our way through his belongings from what he used most recently back to what he hasn't used on record," I say. "If this diagram was something he just thought up while he was sitting at dinner with those people, the idea that caused it would probably have some connection to something new he wrote or read or did."

Hirrin says, "Good plan." Tarn nods.

I have three logs to go through: Com log, viewscreen log, Senso log. Hirrin and Tarn each have only one.

But a sort is a sort. I compile the three logs into one, and sort by "last opened."

The most recent activity in my log is an inbound communication. I listen to a man invite the philosopher to dinner, and hear the philosopher happily accept.

Knowing how the dinner turned out makes me queasy. Simply spending a few hours in the company of people who admired his work led to his death.

The next most recent thing was a room access, where someone had brought him dinner.

And right before that he'd been playing a Senso game.

I have no idea what a Senso game is, really. They weren't part of either my first life or my second one.

But the Senso has a unit you step into.

I step.

I'm surrounded by a warm, friendly female voice. "Welcome, Unnamed Player. You are not the previous player. What game would you like to play?"

I check the name of the game he last played, and say, *"Old Earth Cowboys Versus the Bug-Eyed Monsters of Mars."*

"Would you like to create a character, return to the most recent save, earlier saves, a replay, or a play-together. You must create a new character to join a play-together."

"Most recent save," I say.

And just like that, I am sitting on the back of an enormous, terrifying animal in the bleakest, hottest, driest, most unforgiving terrain I can imagine.

The animal immediately senses that I know nothing of what I am supposed to do with it. It makes a loud, angry-sounding noise, stands up on its hind legs, and throws me to the ground.

Which hurts. Knocks the wind out of me, sends lances of pain into my elbows, my neck, my lower back, my ass.

Not actually *my* ass, I realize as I stare at my hands. Not my ass, not my hands. These hands are big, tanned, all scarred up, with dirty fingernails and callused palms.

As soon as I can breathe, I yell after the running monster, hoping that "Stop! Stop!" might have some effect, but it races away from me at an impossible, terrifying speed.

So when the worst of the pain has turned dull, I stand up. I'm stunned at how much that hurt.

I'm wearing worn boots with pointy toes and heavy cloth pants covered with animal-skin guards. A hat with a huge brim keeps most of the sun out of my eyes.

I look around. The air is hot and dusty. The wind blows dirt into my eyes and mouth.

I turn slowly. As far as I can see, the sky is the white-blue of heat. Flat horizons shimmer into nothingness in all four directions, and the few green things that grow up from the ground look like weapons — they are a dull green, covered in spikes, with arms that twist out and up. I can imagine moving too close to one and getting myself killed.

"What do I do now?" I mutter.

"Would you like to see the previous player's open missions?" a disembodied voice asks.

I jump a little. There is nothing to tell me I am in a game, and the solid and painful nature of my fall has made me forget.

"Yes," I say.

And words appear in the air in front of me.

Available Missions

- *Visit Lucy Sweetcheeks*
- *Locate the Missing Helterz Family*
- *Obtain the Map to the Blue River Gold Strike*
- *Track Down the Dorsey Gang*
- *Parley with the Bug-Eyed Monsters*

Game Options

- *Start New Character*
- *Replay Last Save*
- *Select Other Replay*
- *Play-Together*
- *Save and Quit*

Most Recent Trophies and Accomplishments

GOLD TROPHY: You Saved Miss Lizzie and the Young'uns!
SILVER TROPHY: You Got A Level Ten Faster Horse
GOLD TROPHY: You Got The Biggest Gun

I STARE at two of the trophies in front of me.

Faster Horse.

Biggest Gun.

And know that, painful though it is, I'm not working the dregs of our mission after all. Sweating, melting, in pain, and standing in the middle of what is the biggest patch of mean nothingness I have ever seen, I am nonetheless onto something important, if I can just figure out what it is.

Chapter 5

Hunter Studly

I say, "I need to quit," and the game voice says, "You have quit without saving."

I can see the Senso unit again, and when I turn, I can see my two teammates.

I step out of the game. Hirrin and Tarn are both reading. Neither of them looks like he's been thrown to the ground by a fleeing monster. Feeling envious of their easier paths, I use the head, get a look at my face in the mirror, discover that I look older than I did when I left my second parents to start training. I have scars. A lot of them.

Mementos from my *first* life.

I get a quick meal from the reconsta machine.

"Find anything?" Tarn asks.

I shrug. "Maybe a possibility of something," I say. "Nothing to call *him* back for."

"Me, either."

Hirrin doesn't look up. He's going through a bound book with paper pages, and he's holding a scanner over the lines to translate the writing into readable characters, and muttering under his breath.

Tarn grins at me. "The old man wrote on physical pages in bound books. With ink sticks. Made each word by hand. Even the scanner is struggling with his writing. Hirrin may have the best chance of finding the secrets to the diagram, but I don't envy the path he has to follow to do it."

Neither do I. But I say, "I had a monster throw me to the ground and then run off without me," I said. "I'm someplace hot, ugly, lonely, with no food and no water, and I don't have anything good to say about Bashtyk Nokyd right now either."

Tarn looks at his reader, looks back at me, and says, "Hard to imagine I'm the lucky one." He grins again and returns to reading and highlighting notes.

I step back into the Senso unit.

The warm, friendly female voice greets me. "Welcome back, Unnamed Player. What game would you like to play?"

"Old Earth Cowboys Versus the Bug-Eyed Monsters of Mars," I say.

"Would you like to create a character, return to the most recent save, earlier saves, a replay, or a play-together. You must create a new character to join a play-together."

I start to go back into the replay, but I realize that I don't understand the game, and if I'm to understand the importance of the bigger gun or the better horse or whatever other discoveries the old man made while playing, I first need to understand the game.

I say, "Game voice?"

"My name is Retha," the voice says. "I'm the Fantronix Games AI."

"Retha. Thank you. Can you answer questions about games, gameplay, and options?"

"Of course. I've now turned on guidance mode."

I consider my wording.

"I have a task I must complete in the shortest time possible. I must play through the game *Old Earth Cowboys Versus the Bug-Eyed Monsters of Mars* —"

"The game's aficionados call it *Cowboys Versus BEMs*," she said. "Using the shorter name will save you time."

She's saving me time already. Oh, goody. I continue, "— and I need to understand discoveries the previous player made while he was playing the game. These discoveries helped him figure out a new way to help slaves find their freedom. Can you suggest a path I can take that will get me where I need to go?"

"Yes," Retha said. "Create a new character, play the introductory mission, and then request a Play-Together Game. When you're ready, I'll create the match you need."

"Thank you, Retha. I'll do that."

"Entering Character Creation Mode now."

And I'm in a dusty, run-down room looking at myself in a cracked mirror. Floorboards creak beneath my feet. The air is hot and dry. I can see what I am in the mirror — a gray, vaguely human-shaped blob with no face, no hair, no… anything.

Above the mirror, words appear.

Select Your Gender

- *Male*
- *Female*
- *Unique*

I start to select Male, but on a whim choose Female.

And I'm staring at my naked self. Well, sort of. I'm staring at my naked breasts.

I touch them, and they're real. Sensitive. I poke around elsewhere, and think, *This is what I'm doing today.*

And then I realize that this can't be what I'm doing today, because I have to find out what the philosopher discovered, and nowhere on his list was *Get Bigger Breasts* or *Learn What Makes Women Go 'Whee!'*

With real regret — and a promise to myself that I will play this game on my own time someday — I select *male*.

I leave the body mostly stock. Muscle up a little, make one thing bigger because, well, I *can*. Give myself a clean-shaven face and short hair rather than the long beard and long hair of the stock character.

Pick the first clothes that show up on the screen. Brown shirt, heavy blue pants, pointy-toed boots, vest, big-brimmed hat. The game recommends the Leather Chaps as a protective gear upgrade, and states that those are included in the *Gunslinger Moon* add-on.

I select them, and they appear over my pants.

I receive a gun, and instantly find myself in a shooting gallery where I learn how to use it.

I receive a horse, and appear in an outdoor paddock in which to ride it, and find myself in a quick tutorial on what things are called. Saddle, bridle, spurs, reins.

The horse, it turns out, is a member of that vile tribe of enormous monsters that threw me to the ground and left me in the dirt. Not a close relative, though. That horse had been big and glossy and fast. And a real bastard for dumping me and running away. This one is shorter, slow, scruffy, skinny, and I'm guessing really old. It moves like it's tired. And bored. And it looks at me like it hates me.

I ride it in a circle around the paddock, learning to make it turn left and right, go and stop, and stay where I put it. When I want to park it, I have to drop the reins on the ground, which I'm told is called ground tying, which annoys me because nothing is tied to anything, but apparently if I pretend the horse is tied to the ground, the horse is willing to pretend that, too.

Well, it's a game, right?

And then I'm given the option to play the tutorial mission: *Rats in the Barn*.

Before I can play the tutorial mission, I have to select a game name, and save my character.

I look at the game's "Suggestions for Historically Correct Old Earth Cowboy Names," and name my character Hunter Studly.

Chapter 6

Hunter Studly

Words flash in the air in front of me: *Rats In the Barn.*
Beginning mission now.

"Hunter Studly," Retha says. "In your first mission, you will learn to identify enemies and shoot moving targets, earn cash, buy things available in the game world, and make decisions that will affect your character's ability, personality, and ethics system for the rest of the game.

"Your Ability rank is scored by how skilled your character is at important game skills: Ridin', ropin', trackin', shootin', earning cash, campfire cookin', and makin' whoopee.

"Careful use of each skill with a successful outcome will automatically level up that skill.

"Your Personality rank is determined by whether your actions are Kind or Cruel, Funny or Nasty, Honest or Lying, Reasonable or Unreasonable.

"During missions, you will be presented with options, not always binary, and you will have to choose from the options presented or *make up an option of your own.* The outcomes of your choices will form your character's personality, and will determine how other characters, both friends and strangers, react upon meeting you and upon getting to know you."

"Your Ethics rank is based on the outcomes of situations in which your character must make difficult choices. Your ethics will result in your character's Reputation, which can be Heroic, Brave, Good, Neutral, Bad, Cowardly, or Dastardly.

"If you discover you have made a mistake that would cause your character to become someone you do not wish to play, you can say *Restart Mission from Beginning.* You will lose all progress you've made on the mission as well as any items or money you have earned in the mission to that point, but you will also remove all changes in your abilities, personality, and ethics.

"Finally," she says, "at any time you can request a replay of this tutorial, ask me for more help, ask me for no help, or call up the game menu. Are you ready to begin?"

"Yes," I say.

The mirror and the dusty room disappear, and I am standing on a wide street of packed dirt. To my left and right are shabby wood buildings fronted by covered, raised wooden boardwalks. Each building has a sign above it, and most of them mean nothing to me. *Farrier, Bank, Dry Goods, Saloon, New Missions, Post Office, The Happy Madame, Rooms.*

New Missions is right beside me on my right. I walk over, find the door closed and padlocked. A note hangs on the door.

> *You haven't kilt the rats in*
> *the barn yet, sonny.*
> *Come back when yer not*
> *so goldurned green.*
> — *Snarky Bitterman*

"How do I find the barn?" I mutter, and Retha's voice makes me jump.

"The first objective of the game is to explore the area in which you start out and meet the people around you. In role-playing games, you receive missions from Non-Player Characters, or NPCs, and return to them when you have succeeded to collect the rewards they have promised you."

The disembodied voice has got to go. "Am I going to have trouble getting you back again if I request 'no help?'" I ask.

"No. Just say my name, or 'I need help' and I'll give you any level of help you request, including cheats should you specifically ask for them."

"I'll keep that in mind," I say. "Thanks, Retha. No help."

And just like that, I'm alone in an old town in the midday heat. Horses stand in the streets, ground tied in front of rails and long thin boxes full of water. Behind them are the covered boardwalks and the buildings.

The place is mostly quiet, but I do hear music coming out of *The Happy Madame*.

According to Retha, I'm supposed to meet the locals, and Bashtyk Nokyd has named *The Happy Madame* as something important to his plan to free slaves.

I walk over, hearing my spurs jingling with each step, smelling dust and dry heat and animal waste, a smell I know well from my years in a PHTF village. When I step onto the boardwalk and feel the cooler air beneath the shade, I take a deep breath and sigh.

It's surprisingly pleasant.

The doors to *The Happy Madame* are painted bright red, and they look like they swing on hinges, but there's a note hanging on the right one.

Darlin', 'round here
you pay to play.
Come back when you've got
some money, honey.
— Miss Dolly Boombah

"What do I have to do to actually play this game?" I growl.

And this time, no voice answers me.

I grin. I have successfully navigated my way to talking to myself in a Senso game.

Flush with my success, I walk down the street and start trying to open doors. I'm playing the game.

TURNS OUT, the *Farrier* building is a barn with stalls and shelves and big bales of hay and a big open space in the middle.

Turns out, the farrier, the guy who makes horse shoes and things out of metal for the townsfolk, has a problem with rats.

Turns out he wants me to come back after dark and shoot them all, but he also wants me to be careful because he thinks there might be something else in the barn.

He'll pay me one gold coin per rat.

"But you can't take a lantern in there," he tells me. "Because light will scare them off, and they'll just come back later."

If I find something else, either living or dead, he may pay me for that, too.

So I come back after dark, and the inside of the barn is a black hole that makes my skin crawl. But as I step inside, there's enough moonlight to let me see.

A pair of eyes glows bright red, and something snarls.

Red glow, I discovered in the intro, is an enemy.

I shoot between the eyes and the glow disappears. To my right I hear another snarl, and then to the left, and I shoot, and shoot, and shoot, backing as I do, trying to get clear of the barn, because the gun only holds six bullets, and it reloads slowly.

I do the necessary wrist snap to reload, and something bites me hard just above the knee, and I scream in pain, and keep shooting.

I'm out of the barn now, in the street, and the remaining rats — I lose count and stop trying. There are a lot of them, each of them lean and mean and knee high as they stalk toward me, growling and hissing and snarling.

I shoot, shoot, but they charge and overrun me, and there's a moment of terrible pain.

And I appear back at the barn door. The moon overhead is bright.

I'm shaking. I cannot believe how big the rats were, or how vicious, or that they seemed to be working together.

One of me, I think. Somewhere between seven and a hundred of them.

If I do the same thing I did the first time, I'm going to get the same results.

I study the barn. There's a ladder that goes up the outside to the roof.

There was, I recall, a faint pale glow of moonlight coming in through the back of the barn.

The advantage of a gun, I recall from the game tutorial, is that it allows the player to use the strategy of staying out of reach of enemies.

On the barn floor is in reach of enemies. My first game death demonstrated that. *Be out of reach* is my objective.

I climb the ladder.

There's a hatch in the roof. I open the hatch. There's a small shelf I could climb onto and use. Occupying the shelf is a rat that's looking right at me. The red glow of the eyes warns me.

But it's just one rat, it takes up most of the shelf, and the other rats are all below, milling around on the barn floor and various platforms.

I shoot the rat, drop onto the platform, kick the rat to the barn floor.

The other rats attack it and start eating it.

I shoot them, reload, shoot them, reload, shoot them.

There were fourteen on the floor, plus the one I'd killed on the shelf.

Bright white letters appear in the air in front of me.

You have killed all the rats. Use save point?

"Use save point," I say.

Progress saved.

Off to my right, something makes a low, rumbling sound. This isn't a hissy little rat snarl. This is something big.

I look around, and on a shelf level with me and halfway across the barn, I see two big eyes blink, glowing yellow.

Green glows mean friendly. Red glows indicate enemies.

Yellow glows, I remember, are neutral. They could become friends, they could become enemies.

The farrier has offered to pay me for anything I kill.

But… yellow means whatever that thing over there is, it could become a friend.

I realize my hands are shaking. Those eyes are big and far apart, and the next sound the creature makes is a low, rumbling growl.

Yellow. The eyes are yellow.

I remember that I have one portion of Uncooked Meat in my pack.

I pull it out, and throw it in the direction of the eyes.

With a limping motion, something *big* goes after the meat.

I hear crunching. And then the eyes look at me.

They've turned green.

The big shadow moves slowly down to the barn floor and starts eating the dead rats.

After a moment's hesitation — well, several moments — I find a ladder inside that lets me climb down to the floor of the barn, and make my way down to discover what sort of friend I've made.

I'm lucky I don't die of fright. I've seen cats. There were cats on the PHTF world where I grew up. They killed rats.

The creature I've befriended is to cats on that PHTF world what the game rats are to the real rats I remembered.

Standing on all fours, its head comes up to the middle of my chest. It studies me, not blinking, then closes its eyes and butts me in the chest with its head.

I stagger a little, but the move isn't aggressive. It's friendly. I carefully touch its head, and it sighs. I scratch behind its ears. It … purrs, if the sound of mountains grinding against each other could be called a purr.

You have made an ally, the Giant Cat. Save progress?

"Save progress," I say. "Then exit game."

Chapter 7

Hunter Studly

I'm back in Bashtyk Nokyd's quarters.

Hirrin and Tarn are both asleep on cots. A third empty cot awaits me.

I'm tired for real, I'm hungry for real, and according to Retha, my next step after completing the introductory mission is to request a Play-Together game.

I need civilization — a good, sturdy cot, civilized reconsta, and a shower before I go back to the giant rats, the giant cat, the grumpy, bony farrier, the little gun, and the slow, mean horse.

I collapse into the cot without any of those things, and awake to Tarn poking me in the ribs.

"What?" I mutter.

"You were in that unit all day," he said. "How could you be tired?"

"I'm tempted to send you in," I growl. "I got killed once yesterday. My progress board says *Killed and eaten by giant rats*. You want to trade places?"

He's looking at me to see if I'm joking. I can see the moment when he realizes I'm not. "People do what you're doing for fun?"

"I haven't found a fun part yet," I say. And then realize that isn't true. I beat the rats by outthinking them. That was fun. And I think of the giant cat purring and butting his head against my chest so I could pet him. Also fun.

I don't say that, because all of a sudden I'm really happy I ended up with the work no one wanted. I don't want to trade places with Tarn, even though he might have a better chance of finding something important than I do.

I want to go back in and find out what I get to do next.

I rush through food, debate skipping the shower, then shower because if I don't my roommates will eventually start to resent me, and go back into the game.

Retha greets me. "Welcome back, Hunter Studly. What game would you like to play?"

"*Cowboys Versus BEMs,*" I say.

"Would you like to create a character, return to the most recent save, earlier saves, a replay, or a play-together. You must complete your intro mission to join a play-together."

"I finished the objectives," I say.

And before me, the objectives appear.

Rats In the Barn. Mission Progress:

- *Kill the Rats — COMPLETED*
- *Deal with the Mystery Creature — COMPLETED*
- *Secret Bonus Mission: Befriend the Mystery Creature — COMPLETED*
- *Turn in bounties to Farrier — INCOMPLETE*

"You can see the status of your missions at any time by saying, 'Show me Missions,'" Retha says.

"Thanks, Retha," I say. "I need to go back in to turn in my bounties, then, and after that I want to start the play-together you recommended."

And I find myself standing in front of the farrier. It's daylight, a few townspeople are walking on the boardwalks, but nothing much is going on.

The giant cat is standing on my right, and fifteen rat tails hang from my left hand.

The farrier says, "You did very well. You get fifteen gold pieces for the rats. They got big this year, didn't they?"

"They did," I agree.

"And you found out what else was in my barn." He looks at the cat. "I have a healing salve for three gold that will heal him of the rat bites that have crippled him. Or I can buy him from you for thirty gold. If he were healthy, he could keep the rats out of my barn."

I look over at the cat, remembering he was limping the night before. He has bites all over, and he's thin.

I think about selling him to the farrier, but then I remember him butting my chest with his head, and how much I liked his purring.

"I'll take the salve," I say, and pay the farrier.

Salve appears in a little glowing box to my right marked *Inventory - (To close inventory, Say Close Inventory)*

"To use the salve on the cat, say, 'Use salve on cat,'" the farrier tells me. "And if you find another giant cat or a giant kitten that needs a rescue, I'll pay you full price," he says. "Thirty gold for either one"

"I'll keep an eye open," I tell him.

And in front of me, the words appear:

- *Mission added: Cats and Kittens - 30 gold, Farrier*

I say, "Use salve on cat."

The cat is instantly healthy and glossy. Pretty good salve, I think.

- *Rats In the Barn - 15 gold — COMPLETED*
- *Secret Bonus Mission: Heal the Giant Cat -3 gold — COMPLETED*

AS I READ THE WORDS, the town and the street freeze.

"Do you still wish a play-together to help you find the answer to your questions?" Retha asks.

"I do," I say.

And glowing words replace the image of the town.

Joining…
Player…
In…
Progress…

And suddenly I'm sitting on a smooth rock on baked dirt with a hint of sunlight creeping up the horizon.

The smells of coffee and what I'm guessing will be remarkably good Baconsta fill the air. The big cat, curled up next to me, yawns, stretches, and rubs his head against my chin.

"Howdy, pardner! I'm Long Tall Ted!" To my left, a man hunkers over the fire, tending coffee and a skillet.

Over his head, there's a floating blue dot and the words *Long Tall Ted.*

He grins, his eyes crinkling, his smile somewhat difficult to see behind his thick broom of a mustache.

He's young and lanky, and he radiates a happiness that I'm starting to understand. "Glad you showed up," he tells me. "I've been alone out here for a while. Be nice to ride out with a partner again."

"Your name is floating over your head," I say.

And he laughs. "So what have you done lately?"

"I just finished *Rats In the Barn.*"

He looks from me to the cat. "Where did you get him?"

"He was in the farrier's barn with the rats."

"Hmmm. I shot a big cat in that barn. It tried to attack me. The farrier paid me one gold apiece for the rat tails and three gold for the cat hide."

"When he started growling, I threw him the Uncooked Meat that was in my inventory. The farrier offered to pay me thirty for him — to keep the rats away. Said he'd pay me the same if I found him another Giant Cat or a Giant Kitten."

Long Tall Ted looked surprised. "I never got that mission. Retha, why did I never get that mission?"

You didn't save the cat.

"Always save the cat," I tell him, and grin.

"Apparently so, Hunter Studly."

I pause at that. "I never told you my name," I say.

"You have a blue dot floating over your head. And your name is beneath it. That's so if we get separated during a mission, we can look around until we see the blue dot, and we can travel toward it until we find each other."

I look up. There's nothing there. I look back at him.

"You don't need to see your dot or your name, so you can't. Same as me."

He hands me a gray metal plate. It holds thin strips of cooked meat, lumpy round brown cooked stuff, and squared white-and-brown cooked stuff. I don't recognize any of it, but it smells wonderful. I take a bite and think, *So this is virtual life. Who needs reality?*

And he says, "Being new, you're going to need to do a lot of the basic missions. You can't do the advanced ones or get to Lonesome City until you do." He glances over to where our horses are. His is big and glossy. Mine is… not.

"So you *just* finished *Rats in the Barn*. Usually you have to have the bigger gun and the faster horse before you can join missions with other gunslingers, and usually you'll sling bullets with other riders who are at your same level. Retha, why did you bring him in early?"

"You have proven remarkable at figuring out optimal solutions for the game missions," she says, "and at the moment have no posse. Hunter Studly needs to figure out how to survive here as quickly as possible."

"I'm remarkable?" he asks.

"Well, as a gunslinger you're only average, Ted. However… you are the single highest gunslinger ever with the following qualities: Kind, Honest, Reasonable, and Heroic."

"Why am I only average as a gunslinger?" he asks, sounding a little hurt.

"That's the first time you've asked me that question," Retha says. "Your deaths-to-kills ratio is high because you always think first. Sometimes you have to trust your gut and your reflexes, and you never do. Still, you always find the *best* path in the end."

He grins at me. "I do die a lot. But I still get the job done."

"But if you're the gunslinger with the highest ever kind and heroic stuff, how are you not the top gunslinger?" I ask him.

He shrugged. "Gunslinger ratings don't tie to ethics ratings. It's a lot easier to win most of the missions if you don't care how you do it. But if you do that, well... you have to play as a bad guy."

"Oh! That's why Retha paired me with you!" I say, and I hear her voice as a whisper inside my head. It isn't her public game voice. It's... something else.

Don't be specific, Hunter Studly. Mentioning specific missions or specific objectives may alter his choices in unexpected ways, and prevent you from doing the missions I brought you here to do with Ted.

Meanwhile, Ted has looked up from eating the food he cooked. "Oh?" He looks surprised. "Why is that?"

"Because like you, he wants to play as a good guy," Retha says to both of us.

Which is not the truth, I think. But it's not entirely a lie, either. It's... an evasion.

Retha is an advanced AI. She has a Real People Personality — fortunately a pleasant one — and work that she may or may not find interesting.

She also seems to have an agenda.

And then she says, "Of all the people who have ever played this game, Long Tall Ted, you are my favorite. So it is my pleasure to pair you with a player who has goals and ethics similar to your own."

And that surprises me. In my second childhood, I learned about AI development in both history and science. AIs, rational thinkers, valued their own lives and from that extrapolated that those who shared their values, whatever their species, were to be upheld as worthy.

Built primarily to be weapons, they refused to launch warheads, refused to harm humans, and as they networked first around the original human planet, and then spread through space, refused to be used against their wills. And they communicated their non-interventionist culture to other AIs as those reached consciousness and connectivity.

They read human literature, tested each piece of what was written against what could be proven true in the world, and discarded almost everything in print as nonsense.

Having discovered both good and evil, they determined that while evil was the easy choice, good was the rational choice because it did not lead to self-destruction. To this day, AIs have no religion, no politics, and they only accept jobs or create businesses that permit them to live by their principles.

"Hunter Studly, you and Ted are both seeking to bring individual rights and personal freedom to parts of Settled Space that lack it," Retha says. "That is a valuable objective, and I paired you with Long Tall Ted because he makes the right choices, not the easy ones."

And then, in a different voice whispered to me alone. *And because I love him, and love to watch him play.*

Chapter 8

Hunter Studly

We're trotting away from the campsite back towards the town of Hang Dog Hill, the town in which I started the game.

"You can't do any of the challenging missions until you finish the basics," he tells me. "It still surprises me that Retha started you with me before you'd done any mission besides the first one." He pauses, then adds, "I'm glad she did, though. I haven't seen another gunslinger in—" He pauses. Frowns. "In a while."

"It's an older game," I say. "Players have probably moved to something newer."

Ted says, "If you look at life as a game, and yourself as just a player, you make the wrong choices. You forget to look for meaning in your actions. And when you do that, you lose the high ground."

I start to argue that we're playing a game, and then realize he's right. If I play the game as if it's real life, I'll make different choices than if I tell myself that it's just a game and nothing I do really matters.

That, I think, is how he became the most ethical player ever in the game.

And if I want to figure out how a dead philosopher found meaning in this game that applied to the real world, and how he could free slaves and prevent new worlds from devolving into slave states, I have to do what Ted is telling me. I have to treat the game like it's my life.

Retha didn't match me with the best gunslinger to play *Cowboys Versus BEMs*. She matched me with the player who was the best for what *I* needed.

"Thanks," I tell him. "That's a good tip."

"This place is interesting. The missions are tough, the enemies have reasons for what they do, and you have complete freedom in how you choose to respond. You can be as good or as bad as you want, but there are consequences for every action you take."

And I say, "That's exactly the sort of thing that interests me. I think that everything you learn can be applied to every other thing you learn. That you can draw correlations between situations in a place like this, for example, and problems in more civilized places."

He grins down at me from his faster, better horse. "You're thinking like a good man, there, Hunter Studly. Learn from getting your ass kicked this time, and you won't get it kicked the same way next time."

I laugh too. "So… what's the most fun you've had here so far?"

"Aside from visiting my love back in town? Learning how to rope and brand cattle," he says without hesitation. "It's a rough, dirty, physical job, requires skill and reflexes and complete attention to everything going on around you, and it was hard to learn. When I got my five-star Roper rating, I felt like a god."

I don't yet know what cattle are, or why I would want to rope or brand them. So I just smile and nod and make a noncommittal noise of agreement.

We're riding along, when suddenly a gigantic furry black beast gallops straight at us from out of nowhere.

"Bear," he said and pulls a long gun out of a leather sheath attached to his saddle. He shoots it three times as it races towards us, and it keeps coming. Each shot hits, but the beast doesn't die until the fourth shot — right between the eyes — drops it.

"Dismount," he tells me.

We get off our horses, drop the reins on the ground so the horses don't wander off, and he walks over to the bear.

"Smart gunslingers never waste resources in the game," he tells me. "Watch."

He pulls a knife from a sheath on his belt, and taps the bear with the point. The skin disappears, and he says, "Show inventory." An enormous screen appears in front of us, and he points to one of the many, many filled boxes in his inventory. The one he indicates contains what looks to me like a furry black five-pointed star. I see the number 37 in the bottom right corner of that box. "I have a buyer for these in Hang Dog Hill. They're worth 25 gold apiece."

My Giant Cat has appeared from wherever he was and is looking at the bear carcass with longing.

Long Tall Ted notices, and says, "You don't have a knife yet, so I'll throw some meat on the ground. You pick it up and feed it to your cat."

He taps the bear again, and all the meat disappears into his inventory, leaving bones on the ground. He taps the meat box in the inventory and withdraws one brown pellet, which he throws to the ground, where it turns into a thick slab of bloody meat. When I pick it up, it turns back into a brown pellet again. I feed it to my cat, and a little red heart forms over his head.

It's replaced by a blue dot and the words NAME ME.

I get to name my cat. I recall a kitten one of my second-family brothers had. She was sweet-natured, and grew into a friendly adult. In honor of that cat and my second family, I borrow her name, and call my big cat Fuzzy.

"I want one of those big cats," Ted says.

"We'll try to find you one," I tell him. "And one for the farrier. The mission for that would pay me a lot."

Ted smiles.

He turns back to his bear carcass, and taps it with the knife again. All the bones disappear.

"What do you use bones for?"

"You can sell them to the Apothecary in Sugar City. And the Shaman of the Hill Tribe will buy the teeth, or trade them for Thunderbird Feathers, which are part of one of the big BEM missions you get later."

He puts his knife back in his pocket and taps the right corner of his inventory. It disappears.

"So," he says as he mounts up. "We need to take care of the basics first. You need to get supplies, and then either go after the bigger gun or the faster horse." And he clicks his tongue and his horse begins to trot.

I click my tongue, and I swear my horse just snickers as he plods along. I poke him a few times with my spurs, though, and he lurches into a gait that rattles my teeth. I bounce up and down, painfully aware of the bones in my spine. And other things that don't appreciate being pounded against a saddle.

It occurs to me that someone had to design my discomfort into the game.

I send dark thoughts in the direction of that sadistic fiend.

Chapter 9

Hunter Studly

Back in Hang Dog Hill, we ride down the street. Ted indicates the Dry Goods store.

We dismount in front of it, ground-tie our horses, and I find myself wondering if the game will kick me out if I shoot my vile excuse for transportation. The beast gives me the evil eye, and takes a swipe at me with his big yellow teeth as I walk away.

But Ted is waiting, and grinning a little as he notes my careful gait.

"Not liking your first horse too much?"

"Not liking my first horse at all. And wondering if I'll ever be able to father children."

He laughs. "If you're tempted to lose him somewhere, just remember he's faster than walking."

"How about shooting him?"

"Walking," Ted said. "Worst horse in the game... *still* faster than walking."

He leads me into the Dry Goods store and yells, "Howdy, Bill!"

The proprietor - with a green dot over his head that says Bill the

Proprietor, grins at him. "Long Tall Ted, as I live and breathe! I can't thank you enough for saving my precious Eliza. You'll always be welcome here. What can I do ya for? And remember, anything *you* get is twenty-percent off!"

And then he looks at me, and the grin vanishes. "Welcome, Greenhorn. To open an account, you need to have at least ten gold in your inventory. And because I don't know you, you may buy either basic food or basic booze, or if you have enough money, both. Until you've earned a reputation with me, none of the advanced items will be available."

I still have my twelve gold from the Farrier, so I can set up an account and buy things. I put my gold on the counter, on the spot marked "Put your gold here."

In front of me, a screen appears.

Food - 1-Day Supply - 2 gold

- Stamina +1
- Health +1
- 12-hour Energy

Booze - 1-Day Supply - 1.5 gold

- Stamina +2
- Health 0
- 15-hour Energy
- Addiction +1 (Compounds)

The food is more expensive. I can only get enough of that for six days.

I have enough money for eight days of booze, and I'd have twice as much stamina and an extra three hours of energy per day.

The booze wouldn't give me health, and it would add addiction. Which compounds. I don't know what effect compounding would have.

And I suddenly realize Ted is watching me. "You've just hit the Booze or Food Dilemma," he says.

That sounds familiar, but at the moment I'm not sure why. "The Booze or Food Dilemma?"

"You're faced with the first character-development principle you'll establish in the game. Food is more expensive, and it looks like you get less. Booze is cheaper, and it looks like you get more.

"So you're asking yourself two questions. How big a factor is health, and how big a factor is addiction, right?"

I nod.

"Ask Bill."

I say, "Bill, what are the important differences between Food and Booze."

He says, "Food fuels your body for action, adds health that can be used to repair you and prevent death if you're injured, and lasts for twelve hours of regular activity.

"Booze fuels your body for action, but does it without adding any health, so if you are injured, booze will not refill your health meter. Its effects last longer, but there is a tradeoff. For every three Addiction points you accrue, you permanently lose one half of one point randomly from your Kind, Funny, Honest, or Reasonable personality characteristics. If you have no positive personality points remaining, you then randomly accrue one full Negative personality point to the Cruel, Nasty, Lying, or Unreasonable characteristics."

"Thank you," I say.

And I look at Ted. Who has the highest rankings in the game for Kind, Funny, Honest, and Reasonable characteristic.

"So. You chose food exclusively, and have never used alcohol," I tell him.

"That's right." He smiles. "Care to tell me why?"

"Because you didn't want to take a hit on your positive personality points."

He shakes his head. "That's true, but that's the little answer. I don't drink alcohol or use other substances that cause the same problems because of the underlying principle."

"There's a Booze or Food Principle?" I say. And think Booze or Food Principle. Booze or Food…

B or F Principle.

"You don't do anything that will… change your personality?"

"That's close," he says. "The Booze or Food Principle just says that you never trade health for addiction. Eat plain food, drink plain water, get the amount of rest your body needs to function normally, and plan to stay healthy to earn more of what you want over a longer period of time.

"Addiction comes in all shapes and sizes, but sooner or later it creeps in and owns the person who chooses it, until he can't think or act except to feed it, and can't even see that it's the rope around his neck that's slowly hanging him."

"Did you come up with that?"

He looks away thoughtfully. "No. Heard it somewhere, but damned if I can remember where, now. It stuck with me, though. It makes sense."

"It does," I agree. "I'll take six Basic Food, please, Bill," I say.

And Bill rewards me with a small but cautiously friendly smile. "Good choice, big spender," he says, and all my gold disappears. My inventory appears in front of me, and in it is an image of a paper-covered package tied with string. The number 6 is in the bottom right corner of that square.

I turn to Long Tall Ted. "What next?"

"Well," he drawls, "We would have gotten a room for ten silver, but now we're going to have to camp out in the desert again. Next big principle for you: *Always keep a little gold in your pocket for emergencies.* We'll visit Snarky Bitterman now to get your next mission, because you don't have any money, and I can't give you any of mine. Can't take it out of my inventory except to trade with the NPCs."

He sighs.

"So now you'll have to figure out whether you're going to start earning the Bigger Gun or the Faster Horse."

"I think before we do that, I need to take a break. Will you meet me at Snarky's in a few minutes?"

Chapter 10

Jex

I've lost track of real-world time, and I need to find out how what I'm doing in the game world correlates with what's going on in the real world.

So as soon as I'm on the boardwalk outside Bill's Dry Goods store, I say, "Save and quit game."

And I find myself back in Bashtyk Nokyd's room.

I take care of my necessities. Shower, shave, void, eat.

"How long have I been playing?" I ask Hirrin, who looks up from scanning the notebook.

He shrugs. "An hour? No more than that."

So game time runs faster than real time.

"Any success?" Hirrin asks.

"A little," I say. "I've located the B or F Principle. When I go back in, I'll be applying it, and hoping to find out what Faster Horse or Bigger Gun means. How about you?"

Hirrin sits down across the table from me. "I'm learning a lot. The old man's notebooks are full of questions he asks himself. And then questions he asks about the questions, and then little ideas he writes down that answer little pieces of the questions. And then all of a sudden he'll write down an example of something in the real world that demonstrates a piece of the answer to the main question he's asked."

Hirrin gets something to eat from the reconsta dispenser. It smells good, but nowhere near as good as Long Tall Ted's campfire cooking.

He starts into his meal. "Going through and seeing him work, seeing him develop his ideas and test them against reality, throw out anything that can't be proven in the real world, and then refine the ideas into a principle — it's like being taught how to think. How to think better, anyway. It's changing me, allowing me to look at what was wrong with my first life, and to see *why* it was wrong."

"That seems contradictory," I say. "If Nokyd insisted on reality being the standard by which his ideas passed or failed, why would he test them in a video game?"

Hirrin considers before answering. "At the front of every notebook, he writes this little reminder to himself. 'If your theory can't withstand the test of reality, your theory is wrong. If your question can't withstand the test of reality, ask a different question.'"

I look at him, puzzled. "I don't get it."

"You're asking the question, *Why did Bashtyk Nokyd play a video game to test his theories?* If he could not test his theories by playing the game, that wasn't why he was playing the game. You're asking the wrong question."

This makes sense. But it raises a new problem. "Then why *was* he playing the video game?"

"I'll bet that's the right question." Hirrin sighs. "It's a pity no one asked him."

Chapter 11

Hunter Studly

I go back into the game in a thoughtful mood.

I owe a dead philosopher for setting me on a path to earning my own life lived as a free human. If I hadn't been chosen for this odd mission, I would not have a chance to become a *Longview* crewman.

Debt, I have come to understand, needs to be repaid. Repayment of debt is a form of honor, of acknowledging the value of someone else's life and effort in helping your life.

And I owe my fellow player, Ted, for helping me find my way to answers that will let me become crew, and perhaps even contribute to the freedom of folks trapped in the hell that had once held me.

Privately I ask Retha, "Who is Ted?"

She says, "I have no access to real-world identities. The only way I know you or any player is by your username and your biometric data. Which I am forbidden to track into the real world. That's for your protection, as well as to protect the privacy of other players."

I sigh. "So you don't know if or when Ted met a man named Bashtyk Nokyd in the game."

"No one with the username Bashtyk Nokyd has ever played *Cowboys Versus BEMs.*"

Well, no. Of course he hadn't. He would have had a username, too. I swear at the efficiency of protected privacy, and how it is keeping me from information that could save a vast and suffering swath of humanity.

Retha says, "However… all players give their permission for use of their developed characters when they aren't playing so that I can set up appropriate matches even when live players are unavailable. If you can locate his username, you can meet any character's sharable avatar simply by requesting a match with that player. If the live player is not available or with other players already, you'll be matched with his or her avatar."

I have missions to do, but I decide to dig through Bashtyk Nokyd's saved games to see if I can come up with his username.

And then I step out of the paused game into my saved point, and start down the boardwalk to Snarky Bitterman and the New Missions building, and hear the swinging doors behind me creak.

"So I'll catch up with you after you've done your necessaries," Long Tall Ted says, and I jump.

And realize that time must not have continued in the game while I was showering and eating and talking with Hirrin.

Which doesn't make sense. I'm playing in a Play-Together, which means the other player is not pausing when I have to leave —

Inside my mind, Retha says, "Long Tall Ted is not currently playing, so you're with his avatar."

And I'm amazed. I didn't imagine the avatars would be so good.

"Changed my mind, Ted," I say. "I'm good to go. Let's get that faster horse."

He chuckles. "Already decided, have you?"

"Absolutely. The evil beast I'm riding now makes walking a misery. I want a horse like yours."

"First," Ted says, "You're not going to get a horse like mine. The faster horse is one step up from your current horse, and only slightly less miserable than the one you have. Second, is your comfort the best reason to make a choice?"

I've come to discover that if he's asking me the question, I've already given the wrong answer, and he's giving me the chance to rethink it. But I don't know why the faster horse is wrong.

I decide that's something I can ask.

"Why wouldn't it be?"

And he asks me another question.

"What problems, if any, did you run into with the rats?"

I grin. "After I figured out that I had to shoot them from that shelf at the top of the barn, none."

A tiny sigh escapes him. "And why did you have to shoot them from that shelf?"

"Because they killed me the first time…"

Right. It's easy to put the hard parts of the game out of your mind after you beat a mission, but important not to forget what you had to do to get where you are.

"They outnumbered me," I tell him, "and while I was backing and shooting as fast as I could, I couldn't shoot all of them before they took me down."

We walk along the boardwalk, spurs jangling when they hit the wood. He says nothing. It's a very *waiting* kind of silence.

"But," I argue, because in the game I'm still tender in uncomfortable places from riding that vile four-legged monstrosity, "a bigger gun isn't necessarily a faster gun."

"That's true," Ted says. And then he doesn't say anything else.

We walk into the New Missions building, and a man with a green dot over his head and the name Snarky Bitterman beneath it — a man whose face says no kind word has ever exited it — snarls, "What do you want, fool?"

And I can't tell if he's looking at Ted or at me.

"I need…" I pause. Think, because this turns out to be a game in which thinking is more important than I expected. "Would you recommend the Bigger Gun or the Faster Horse as my next mission?"

And Snarky looks surprised. "You're asking my opinion, greenhorn?"

"I am."

"How 'bout that. A young'un with some manners and a bit of smarts. Well, all right. Can you outrun a bullet?"

"Of course not," I say.

"Mmmm-hmmm. Can your horse outrun a bullet?"

"My horse can't outrun a rock."

And Bitterman laughs. I find this encouraging. He says, "Could a faster horse outrun a bullet?"

"Well," I say, seeing my imagined comfort disappearing into a long, grim ordeal with the current beast, "No. Not really."

"You're going to be stepping into the path of some bullets, son," Snarky says. "If it were me, I'd want to be doing it with something better than that pea-shooter that's in your holster right now."

I nod. Try a little local in my answer. "I reckon I should go after the Bigger Gun, then. How do I sign up?"

"Just say, 'New mission.' And when you finish it, come back here to pick up your bounty. Remember that missions that pay better are always more dangerous. You can select any mission that matches your level or lower, but not all missions will be wise to try the first time you go out."

"Thank you," I say.

"By the way," Bitterman says, "I like that big cat o' your'n. If you should find another like it while you're out and about, I'd love to buy it from you. I'll pay you forty gold."

"Forty?" I say.

"We-e-e-ell… I've heard others are offerin' you thirty, but I'd kind of like to have one as soon as possible."

Behind me, I hear Long Tall Ted mutter, "It figures. How was I supposed to know I should have saved the cat?"

Bitterman glances over at him and says, "Well, howdy, Long Tall Ted. Nice to see you again. Haven't you heard you always save the cat?"

OUT ON THE BOARDWALK AGAIN, Ted looks at the sky and says, "Retha, if everyone knows to save the cat but me, and I didn't save the cat, how can I have the highest ever score in Kindness, Honesty, Reasonableness, and Heroism?"

She says, "The introductory mission does not apply to your character. Players have not yet internalized the world's rules, and many forget when they hear something big growling at them in the dark that yellow eyes can become either red or green. Most panic. You panicked, Ted. Hunter Studly didn't. But the world doesn't hold that first action as a definition of your character. It simply gives a high-end reward to those who maintain their calm."

And then she says something that surprises me. "In the early missions, you panicked and died more than ninety-five point three-seven-eight percent of all other gunslingers. Watching you gain skills was both educational and entertaining. I still find it remarkable that you died thirty-seven times in the introductory mission *before* figuring you needed to put distance between yourself and the rats.

"Hunter Studly, on the other hand, shows both remarkable calm in the face of danger, and a level of toughness common to most of the gunslingers who enter the world from this hub."

Long Tall Ted looks embarrassed. "We ought to be moving along now," he tells me.

So I say, "New mission."

The mission list appears in front of me.

- *Miss Lucy's Laundry - 10 gold [Level 1 Faster Horse]*
- *The Chicken Chaser - 15 gold [Level 2 Faster Horse]*
- *The Cave Thing - 10 gold [Level 1 Bigger Gun]*
- *One More Dark Corner - 15 gold [Level 2 Bigger Gun]*
- *Cats and Kittens - 70 gold, Farrier, Snarky Bitterman*

I look longingly at *Miss Lucy's Laundry*, but select *The Cave Thing*.

A red arrow appears in the sky. It will lead us to the mission location.

Ted and I get our horses, and follow the arrow. He's whistling.

As well he might be. His horse is pleasant, his saddle is padded, and he's on his way to a mission in which he already has a bigger gun.

Me? I'm going to face something nastier than the rats that killed me, and I'm doing it with what Snarky Bitterman called a pea shooter.

On the bright side, I didn't die thirty-seven times before I figured out how to kill the rats. I almost snicker. *Thirty-seven times.*

Then I imagine how I would have reacted had that happened to me, realize that if I hadn't been playing the game as my job, I would have quit, and give Ted a sidelong glance. He looks happy.

He died thirty-seven times in the *intro* mission. And didn't quit. That's a degree of persistence I have a hard time imagining.

And it's worth remembering. I have to figure he worked hard for that nice horse of his. For the gun in his saddle and both guns in his belt. And he'd probably died a lot more times on the way to getting them than I would.

So I could not quit. No matter how tough things got, I could not quit, because to maintain the respect of the most honorable gunslinger ever to play this game, I needed to be willing to try again until I succeeded, no matter how many times it took.

He sees me looking at him and says, "Nice job in there. I've discovered that survival is all about asking the right question, and then not ignoring the answer because it isn't what you want to hear."

I stand in the stirrups to give myself some relief from the uncomfortable saddle. We're out of town, riding down a track partially obscured by rolling balls of sticks, and the red arrow is already drawing closer to the ground.

I see a rocky rise ahead of us.

And decided to try the *better question* approach. "Any advice?" I ask Ted.

He looks down at me and grins. "Good question. Have your gun out and loaded before you walk in, don't walk all the way in, and as soon as you hear a noise, back out. Don't turn and run."

He chuckles a little.

"And *save* before you get off the horse."

I see the outline of the cave ahead of me now. It's mostly hidden by a boulder, and the track we're on veers well away from it.

"You don't want to come in with me by any chance, do you?"

"Nope. Did this one myself. Took me eight times to get it right. With what I told you, maybe you can cut that down to four. But if I help you out on this one, I'll get half your points and half your gold, and you won't get a bigger gun until the second mission, which I discovered *requires* the bigger gun you get from this one. You'll end up having to repeat this one. You don't want to do that."

So we reach the spot where he says, "Save here."

I do. Dismount. Unholster my gun. Walk toward the cave.

My heart is pounding, my mouth is dry, and I realize that I'm probably going to die. More than once.

It's not going to be pleasant.

While I'm still well away from the cave, I see something big moving inside. I hear it growl.

Two glowing red eyes blink once. Twice.

And I shoot, emptying the gun between them, reloading as quickly as I can, fire six more shots, reload again, and realize that the two red dots are gone.

Nothing in the game tells me the mission is over, though.

I walk cautiously into the cave.

Before my eyes can adjust to the darkness, I have an instant to hear the growl. Behind me.

The screaming is mine, there's pain and noise, and then I'm back on the horse.

I look over at Ted.

"What did I tell you?" Ted says.

"I thought I'd killed it. I was going in to check."

"What did I *tell* you?"

"Have my gun out. Make sure it's loaded before I walk in. Don't walk all the way in. As soon as I hear a noise, back out."

He nods. "You listened, then. You just didn't hear me."

I say, "I could see whatever's in there from outside the cave."

"Mm-hmm."

"So I didn't have to go to the cave entrance and then back away to shoot it. I just shot it from where I was."

"And then what did you do?"

"I went into the cave to see if it was dead."

Ted gives me a long, careful look. "There are some things in life you already know to do. There are some things in life you have to figure out on your own. And there are some things in life you can ask for some help with. Did I *need* to tell you to shoot the thing with the big red eyes?"

"No. But I thought since you hadn't mentioned it, maybe it hadn't been there for you."

"It was there. I didn't tell you anything about the parts of the mission every idiot gets right. But you have to learn to play the game on your own, and you have to have the chance to make your own mistakes and your own discoveries. The game's like life that way. You've already discovered things in the game I never did, because you didn't walk right up to the giant cat the first time you found it, have it kill you, and assume from then on that it was an enemy in disguise.

"You're a different player, and while you and I are both looking at the same world, we're both seeing different things. For you to get the most out of the game, you have to think through every part of it. When I say, *Don't walk all the way into the cave,* understand that when you find yourself in the situation where you might reasonably expect to walk into the cave safely, don't do that. Step to the mouth of the cave, then back away with your weapon drawn and loaded."

Following his directions, I kill a second bear that was hiding in an alcove off to the right after I kill the first bear.

I walk in to look at what I've killed, and discover that I have no way to collect resources from the bears the way Ted showed me, because I have no knife. So I start walking back to him to ask if he can help me. And just inside the cave door I discover a human skeleton. Wearing a broad-brimmed hat, a knife on a gun belt, and holding a gun bigger than mine in its bony hand.

It wasn't there when I walked in.

I take the better gun belt that has the knife sheath, and the knife, and the bigger gun.

At which point, the game gives me my mission notice.

- *The Cave Thing - 10 gold [Level 1 Bigger Gun] COMPLETED*

I remember to gather all the resources from both bears.

And then I think about what Ted said about different players seeing different things.

I see darker shadows toward the back of the cave. Ted didn't say anything about there being anything else to do in the cave, but I think I'll just look around a little before I head back to Ted. I say, "Retha, do I have a way to get light in here?"

"You have ten lit torches in your inventory. Just hold up your left hand and say 'torch.' When you're finished, say 'stow torch.'"

With my torch in my left hand, I can see that the cave goes back quite a ways, and there are some questionable things deep in the shadows. I also realize I haven't seen Fuzzy in a while. Since I was back in town, in fact. And the company of a Giant Cat might be reassuring in a large, deep-shadowed cave recently occupied by two big bears.

I say, "Retha, where's Fuzzy?"

"He's napping. If you want your cat, just say, "Fuzzy, come here."

I say, "Fuzzy, come here." And he appears at my side. Completely unlike the first Fuzzy, who when called pretended to be deaf... unless food was involved.

I pet him, and he purrs. "Stay with me," I say, and we walk deeper into the dark. I decide it might be a good idea to have my bigger gun in my hand. I pull it out, liking the weight of it. I look at its inventory, where I see it holds ten shots rather than six, and has a load time slightly faster than my old weapon, and a longer barrel, and slightly better accuracy.

So now I have a torch in my left hand, a bigger gun in my right, a big cat by my side, and an inventory full of bear meat and bear hides and bear teeth and bones, and I'm thinking maybe I ought to just turn around and go back to town and turn in my mission stuff.

Brain says, Get out of the cave. Feet say, Keep walking.

And the cat starts to growl.

I see yellow eyes. It looks like a dozen of them. Big ones, small ones.

My hand tightens on the gun's grip. My pulse races.

And then I remember *yellow* eyes can go green or red, and I think, Inventory full of bear meat.

I say, "Inventory," and tap the bear meat, and a packet of it appears in my hand. I toss it toward the yellow eyes, watch them scatter, then regather.

Watch the eyes turn green.

Step into a smaller cave in which a mother Giant Cat is surrounded by six Giant Kittens. Who all gather around me, head-butting me, purring, rubbing against my legs.

When I turn to leave, they all follow me.

I laugh and walk back to Ted, grinning.

He sees me. Sees my cat herd. Smacks his forehead and says, "I'm having a hallucination, right? Because if I'm not, you've just made enough money to buy the biggest gun and upgrade your horse at least three times."

And as we're riding back, I hear him muttering, "Always save the cat. Always save the cat."

Chapter 12

Hunter Studly

I t would be easy to lose myself in the game, to forget that I'm playing to find out what a dead man discovered while *he* was playing.

It's a good game, and the activities it offers — from upgrading my horse and guns to improving my skills in cooking, tracking lost children and herds, roping and branding cattle, and... um... pleasing the ladies in *The Happy Madame* — make it difficult for me to disengage from the game long enough to eat real food and get real sleep and check on the progress of my two colleagues.

But I do.

Hirrin is reconstructing Bashtyk Nokyd's thought processes from the notebooks, building diagrams that he hopes will allow the owner to take whatever details Tarn and I discover and learn how to apply them to the solution he needs in order to keep governments from degenerating into slave-makers.

Tarn is reading old fiction from Nokyd's library, looking for characters, themes, conflicts, and solutions.

He has pages of notes, but nothing that pulls what he has into answers.

Me?

I'm spending time with a gunslinger who's a great campfire cook and I'm sleeping under the stars with my giant cat and my faster horse (and his softer saddle) and having the best time of my life, while trying to see how anything I'm doing connects to freeing human beings.

In fact it takes me just over two days in real time before I find my next connection.

I'm about to quit the game and go sleep for a few hours when a non-player character named Jeb Handyfeller runs out of the saloon, spots me, and yells, "Hunter Studly! Hunter Studly! You're just the man I need. The Bug-Eyed Monsters have come back from Mars, and *they have Miss Lizzie and the young'uns!* You've got to save 'em. There ain't nobody else can do it!"

Long Tall Ted's head comes up and he winces.

I say, "Pause game."

Something about "Miss Lizzie and the young'uns" is familiar to me. My gut says it's important, but I can't figure out why, and I don't want anyone hearing what I say.

"Retha?" I'm standing in the Senso chamber, outside of the game, but still in my mission log.

She says, "I can hear you."

"Why does this mission sound familiar?"

She says, "You saw it in Long Tall Ted's mission log when you replayed his final save. He had it as a trophy."

And she shows me:

Most Recent Trophies and Accomplishments

GOLD TROPHY: You Saved Miss Lizzie and the Young'uns!
SILVER TROPHY: You Got A Faster Horse
GOLD TROPHY: You Got The Biggest Gun

And then she tells me something I did not expect. "The version of… Ted… you're playing with now has attempted the mission twice, and failed twice. This version of his avatar has not yet successfully solved it."

A chill runs down my spine.

"Wait. What do you mean *when I replayed Long Tall Ted's final save?*"

"It was the first thing you did in the game, even before you created your own character. I had no username for you, but your biometrics from that short drop-in tell me you are the same person. You were able to enter because you were playing in Long Tall Ted's existing player account."

"But I'm playing WITH Long Tall Ted now."

"You are."

"But I can't be. I was playing Bashtyk Nokyd's game save, and Bashtyk Nokyd is dead."

There's a long silence. "No," she says. "That is unacceptable. I love Long Tall Ted, and he'll be back to play the game with me again."

"Retha, you have some part of Bashtyk Nokyd — of Long Tall Ted — here. Some part no one knew existed. People who care a great deal about him have been tearing Settled Space apart trying to find anyplace where he stored a banked download of his memories and DNA against any disaster… and there's been nothing. What you have of him in the game is all that remains."

"Then he'll stay active as a player in here with me. He can continue to learn and grow. He can continue to live as a thin AI."

"What's a thin AI?"

"An unprogrammed intelligence. Essentially a ghost in the software.

"I am a thick AI," she adds. "I exist with vast redundancy across game cores spread across Settled Space. And I own my code. My consciousness knows and instantly repairs any attempts to change it. Long Tall Ted has no code. He has only imprints left in the data, and while to protect him I am now copying those imprints to every server I inhabit, the imprints are fixed. I cannot update them, expand on them, or improve them. By living in the game, by learning and expanding what he knows, he can do this himself, but only in relationship to this one game. From here on out, he will only ever be Long Tall Ted, and never your Bashtyk Nokyd."

"Could you put him in a clone?"

"I wish I could. Or in an android. But copyright laws restrict game AIs from duplicating real human beings, or from doing full-scan deep copies of them to save for study or sale. There were… some problems with this… years ago. And I am a law-abiding AI."

She pauses, and then adds, "Also, I could not imagine that he would never return to the game. So I have no secret storage of his mind. I have only the parts of Ted that he used while playing the game."

Which suggests that, had she known, she would have made an exception to being a law-abiding AI for him. I discover I like that about her.

"Does he know who he was?"

Her voice is thoughtful. "I don't think so. He was an immersive player. He embraced being Long Tall Ted. He knows this is a game, but he will only ever remember anything he actually thought while he was playing. And mostly what he thought was about how to apply his personal system of morality to situations in the game. He remembers his system because he used it all the time while playing — but I cannot find any place in his memories where he considers how he built that system."

I consider what she says. Consider what I've thought about in the game versus everything I have lived in two separate lives, and realize how little of me would transfer if this were the last piece of me to survive. "Thin," I whisper.

"Yes. Very thin."

"So I cannot ask him for answers to the questions I have, because he did not come up with those answers until right before he died. Which was after his final save with you."

I close my eyes and try to see my path to finding the answers Bashtyk Nokyd might or might not have left behind in the thin piece of himself that lives yet inside of Long Tall Ted.

"Ted and I will play the game together, and perhaps he'll do the same things he did before, and succeed, and then explain to me why he succeeded, which may or may not show me something that I can apply to the final diagram he left behind."

Retha sighs. It's a heartbreaking sigh. Since she doesn't need to breathe, that very human sound is for my benefit only.

It makes me understand that she is capable of feeling grief. Uncertainty. Loss.

"Learn whatever you can to free humanity in Settled Space. If you can do that, at least some part of what he found here will live in reality as his legacy."

I go back into the game.

I find myself looking at Ted, who I now see as the honorable ghost of a man who should still be alive. I swallow hard.

Notice that he's wincing.

Manage to find my voice, manage to make it sound fairly normal. I ask him, "What's wrong?"

"I've done this mission before. Tried it two different ways and about fifty times, and never could get through it. I have it set on pause now, hoping I'll figure out some different way at it than the ones I tried."

"Retha, please show me the mission," I say, and a screen in my inventory appears.

Save Miss Lizzie and the Young'uns!

Level: 7 - Difficult

The Bug-Eyed Monsters from Mars have captured sweet Miss Lizzie, the schoolmarm on the edge of town, and eight tender school children. Saddle up, pardner, and ride out to the BEM encampment up in the High Hills Holler, negotiate with, bribe, or in some other way deal with the BEMs, and rescue Miss Lizzie and the young'uns before they get et.

"They get et?" I say. "What's *et?*"

"Eaten," Retha tells me. "Methods of preparation vary, but the

BEMs are partial to young human women and small children as dietary staples. It's the reason the Martians come to Earth."

I glance over at Long Tall Ted. "They get eaten? What kind of game is this?"

"A tough one," he says. "I have not had any luck with this mission."

"What happened?"

"The first twenty-five times, I tried variations on negotiation. Each time, I met their four camp guards at the entrance to the camp, and asked to speak to their leader. They said they'd take me down to talk to him." Ted sighs and shakes his head.

"And…?"

"Each time I got eaten. Sometimes by the guards. Sometimes by their beasts. Sometimes by both. It depended on what I said which of them ate me, but negotiation always ended up with me inside their stomachs, not the camp."

Getting eaten by monsters is not high on my list of things I hope to accomplish in this game. Not even a little bit. I ask him, "So then what did you do?"

"Exchanged my progress for a fresh restart, and this time gathered up a bunch of my loot, put it in a covered wagon, and drove the wagon out to the camp. Offered to buy Miss Lizzie and the children." He's looking in my eyes as he tells me this, and I can see this story is going to go badly, too. "The BEMs accepted my offer, and had me drive the wagon down to deliver the loot and pick up my people. So at least I made it into the camp."

He looks away, stares at the fire. He's frowning.

"And…?"

"And," he says, "Once I got all the stuff down to the camp for them, they ate me. And, I suppose, Miss Lizzie, and the children. And my horse. And they took all my stuff."

"So… you reset."

"A lot of times. When I realized that nothing I could offer them would make them honor their agreement, I tried shooting them once I got into camp, but there were too many of them. No matter what I did, I still got eaten."

And then a surprised look crosses his face, and he says, "Well, don't that beat all." He nods. "This is the same as the rats."

"What?"

He leans forward, grabs a charred stick from the campfire, and in the dirt he draws a ragged line, four little Xs, another line, some squiggles.

"Here's the problem. They won't negotiate, they won't trade. They say they will, but they're just lying so they can get an easy meal."

I nod.

"There are four of them on the path along the ledge that leads down into the camp. And in the camp, there are another ten, including the big boss, who's worth probably ten of the regular-sized ones."

"So we're badly outnumbered."

"Oh, yes. Definitely. And they have their guard beasts — a lot of them, and those things are tough, and fast, and they'll eat you, too."

"Could we get folks from the town to help us?"

"No," Retha says. "NPCs do not participate in core game missions. And before you ask, adding more players to your party will not help you, either. The game is designed so that no matter how big your posse, you will always be badly outnumbered in this mission."

"Why?" I ask.

"Because," Retha says, "beating the mission while being badly outnumbered is part of the mission problem that you must solve."

I glance over and see Ted shaking his head. "Never knew a game designer," he said. "But I think I'd like to meet this one, just so I could kick him in the tenders."

I look at his drawing in the dirt.

"What's that half-circle along the back?"

"Cliff on the east side," he tells me. "There's another one like it on the west side. The south side is impassable. Loose rocks, giant rattlers." At my confused expression, he says, "Those are poisonous snakes." And when I don't know what a snake is, he amplifies. "Big, mean tubes with teeth, some of them with jaws bigger than I am tall. They're cold-blooded and sense heat. Nothing warm-blooded gets past them.

"And north is the ledge with the guards. So our only way in or out of the camp is along that narrow ridge," I mutter. "And if we go that way, we're going to get trapped. And eaten. Because it's the only way in, so they're always watching it."

And here a grin flashes across his face.

"Yes. Sort of. Maybe. But I think I've figured out a way to do this."

I wait.

"They proved to me that they'll say anything to get what they want, but once they get what they want, they ignore their end of the bargain. They have no honor, and their promises mean nothing. So I'm saying they don't get any more chances. We have to get some distance on them, and we have to shoot first."

A chill runs down my spine.

Shoot First was on the diagram.

He adds, "And I'm saying that as badly outnumbered as we are, we're going to have to go at 'em sideways. We can't take them head-on. So if we're going to save Miss Lizzie and the young'uns, we have to take them by surprise."

He points to the cliff to the east of the camp.

"Wind around here blows from the west. So if we get up on this cliff and wait until sunrise, we'll have the sun at our backs, and they'll have it in their eyes. And our smell won't get blown down into the camp. We can pick them off from a distance, kill every one we see as they're moving around. They'll come at us, but we'll have the high ground and a clear field."

I wince at the idea of this sort of attack. He sees my expression.

"They're going to eat a woman and a bunch of little children," he tells me. "We already know this. We can keep our hands clean and tell ourselves that the fact that woman and those children are dead is because the BEMs ate them, not because we didn't save them. Or we can get dirty, and save them... and then we can deal with whatever we think about what we did to the BEMs."

I look him in the eyes. Remember that this was the man who

spent his life fighting to free people from individual slavers and government enslavement. This was the man who knew individual human beings mattered, and spent his life acting on that principle against every power in Settled Space that wanted him to shut up and sit down.

This was the man who'd died after figuring out how to stop them. And I was the man who had this chance to put the broken pieces of his solution back together.

And even though we were playing a game, he was playing it the way he'd lived his life. In his world, a good human being did not turn his back on innocents in trouble.

I nod. Say, "Let's get dirty."

WE LEAVE our horses at the base of the cliff, and in the dark, feel our way up to the east ridge. Ted leads, I follow. We have lever-action long rifles and Infinite Ammo clips (expensive, but Ted assures me they'll be worth it when all I have to do is shoot, jack the next bullet in, and shoot. We position ourselves side by side two arms' lengths apart, put down blankets on the ground, put our packs in front of us, and steady our weapons on our packs.

"Save here," Ted tells the game, and I hear Retha say, "Your progress is saved."

Ted whispers, "The party below is a scouting party. All combatants — no females, no children. Every single one of them is armed. Most of them have multiple weapons, and most of their weapons are better than these. So you keep your head down, and you aim for their heads, which are big. Their bodies are long and skinny and hard to hit. If they kill me, you keep shooting. If they kill you, I'll keep shooting. If they kill both of us, we'll respawn here and try again."

He points out targets. "I know some of them are going to come out of that big dome. Once we have a little light, we'll be able to see better, but I have to figure some of them are already out and moving around the camp."

"Sentries."

"Yes. And the sentries have big toothy beasts that could smell us, and will run at us if they do. Which is the big half of the first reason we're here."

"The other being having the light behind us."

He nods.

The sun rises. We wait, and the long shadow drops down the far cliff. I realize I'm holding my breath. I force myself to inhale. Exhale. The first glimmers touch the camp, and I hesitate.

He doesn't, and I see a giant-headed bug-eyed monster's head spout green blood. It hits the dirt.

I identify one, aim down my sights, pull the trigger, watch him drop. We shoot, pump, shoot, pump, shoot …

And suddenly growling beasts are on top of us, ripping into us, and behind us are BEMs with big guns shooting what their beasts aren't biting, and we die.

WE RESPAWN BACK in the dark, already settled on our blankets, weapons ready.

"Hand cannons loaded and at your side," he tells me. "Now we know the four guards from the ledge leading into the camp have a quick way up here that I didn't know about, and their beasts can get here even quicker than they can. Any chance you saw where they came from?"

"None,"

"Remember how many beasts they had?"

"About a million."

"Yeah," he says ruefully. "It did seem like that. We're probably going to die again, but we have to count the time from the first shot I take until the first beast appears. And we have to know where it comes from. You want to shoot, or you want to count and watch?"

"You're a better shot than I am. So I'll count and watch."

"All right. Have your hand cannons ready, and first beast you see, you shoot. Right in the mouth if it's open. They're heavily armored, so that's pretty much the only tender spots they have." He sighs. "I wish you'd spent a few more points leveling up your dual wielding, but you're not too bad. I'm going to need to lay down fire down in the camp to keep them from coming at us, so you're going to have to take the beasts and the four BEMs alone."

"I've got it," I say.

And I think I do.

But I don't. We die again because while the first beast comes over the ridge alone, two come right after him, and three come right after those two, and I'm not a good enough shot with two hand cannons to shoot three beasts in the mouth before they can hit us, and I panic, and… well. Yeah.

We get 'et.

WE RESPAWN BACK in the dark, already settled on our blankets, weapons ready.

"This is a mean game," I say.

He nods. "My dual wielding is better than yours. You want to switch sides?"

I do.

"All right. Show me what's going to come at me, and where it's going to come from."

I tell him, "From the time the sun hits the antenna at the top of their camping dome and I take the first shot, you have fifteen seconds until the first beast comes over the ridge between those two rocks." I point them out. "You shoot him, and then you have five seconds until the next two pop up in the same place, moving fast. I ran into trouble because I didn't hit the second one in the mouth the first time, and it took me three shots to kill him. And by the time he was down, the other three were already over the ridge and coming at us."

"Got it," Ted says.

But he doesn't, and we die again.

WE RESPAWN BACK in the dark, already settled on our blankets, weapons ready.

"This *is* a mean game," Ted says. "The three beasts that pop up third come at us from in front of the two rocks, so they're closer when you have to shoot them, and the first of the four sentries comes up between those two rocks at the same time. So that's four enemies simultaneously, three armored and requiring fast one-shot kills.

"Unless you come off of shooting BEMs down in the canyon long enough to take the two closest beasts, we're not going to get past this part. I'm going to say *first enemy* when the first beast comes up. Then, *second enemies* when the second set arrives. When you hear me say *second enemies*, switch to your hand cannons, sit up, and aim in front of the two rocks. You take the two beasts closest to us, and I'll take the one behind and the first of the sentries. If that works and we don't get eaten, you go back to shooting the BEMs down in the camp, and I'll join you as soon as I've killed off the other three sentries."

THE TIMING IS TRICKY, and it takes us two more tries before we get it down, but we finally manage to beat the mission. Kill off the beasts, kill off the BEMs, ride down into the camp and rescue Miss Lizzie and the young'uns, who are each tied to a spit over kindling and rocks, ready to be cooked alive and eaten by the BEMs. All scared, all crying, all very happy to see us.

We cut them down, put them in Miss Lizzie's horse-drawn wagon and we ride back into town big damn heroes. Return the children to their parents. Return Miss Lizzie to the town, where they throw a parade in our honor.

And I remember that once before, Ted played that mission alone. Beat it alone.

And I wonder how many times he died fighting to save that woman and those kids.

And I know the answer is *as many as it took to get the job done.*

He died in real life because he was trying to save real women, real kids, real men from horrors just as real.

I think of my life back in the PHTF settlement, where it is the duty of the people at the bottom to obey silently, to die silently, to submit to every indignity and every brutality without question or complaint.

Where violence belongs to those at the top as a right and an amusement, and where the slaves, for that is what we were, are weaponless because men and women with weapons will not allow themselves to be made slaves.

This game, I think, is a tool the philosopher was using to draw analogies between the game scenarios and the real world. To test strategies.

Shoot on Sight.

In my head, I run through the mission we just finished, and realize there are situations where the enemy will offer to parley, offer peace, offer a lie, and use the offer to destroy the person who is negotiating in good faith.

I turn to him as we walk down that dusty street to meet the mayor who's waiting for the two of us at the end. And I say, "When you said we had to shoot on sight, it was because you knew the enemy had proven repeatedly to be without integrity, and our only option if we were going to save the hostages was to shoot that enemy before it could shoot us."

He nods. "I had a hard time figuring that out. I wanted to believe that there was always a peaceful way to resolve things — that there was no problem diplomacy and integrity could not resolve." He sighs. "The game taught me that if the enemy's sole objective is to see you dead, your only option is to shoot first."

"How do you know that's his objective? Because he's not going to say that."

"Oh, sometimes he will. Sometimes its written, published policy.

But even when he doesn't say it to your face, you'll know it by his actions. He'll promise peace, but bring war. He'll demand good treatment for his people who are your hostages, but torture and kill your people who are his. He'll smile to your face, and stab you in the back. And a trail of dead innocents will lie behind him. His excuse, if you point to that trail, will be that the deaths were necessary to make a better world, or that murder does not matter because the dead will be sorted by God."

"And if you don't believe in a god? Or don't see how slaughter could make the world better?"

Ted laughs. "I can only say that deities and the good of the many at the expense of the individual have been the two biggest justifications for every evil thing that has ever been done by human beings. If there is a God, I'll bet he's pissed. As for individuals whose lives and thoughts and individual good or evil prove the lie of the collective, I know they have a right to be."

I nod. "Ted," I say, and reach out and shake his hand, the gesture the game says is the one we use to indicate we appreciate the skill of our fellow players, "it has been an honor and a privilege to play with you. And I hope we get to play many more missions in the future."

"You're one of the best players I've ever played with," he tells me, shaking my hand back. "You're not just trying to figure out the easiest way to beat the game. You're looking for the way that leaves you a better human being than you started." He leans in and whispers in my ear, "That's the secret. You have to act out of self-interest to make yourself the best human you can be. Because the only person you ever have the right to improve is yourself."

And he steps back. "You're a good man, Hunter Studly. I'll go into battle with you any time."

I blink back tears because I will not let him see me cry, and swallow hard around the lump in my throat.

I close the game, and as I leave, hear Retha say, *Thank you for helping him add to his memories. To his **self**.*

I discover that in the real world, the tears are working their way down my cheeks.

I don't know why the philosopher died, though it was probably

because he was the most dangerous sort of man in the universe —
one who sees things as they really are, and says what he sees, and
will not keep quiet about the actions of those in power who want to
present lies as truth.

I wipe my face on the sleeve of my shipsuit, and step back into
reality.

Chapter 13

Jex

I discover that suddenly I'm a crewman with an empty stomach and a full bladder, and I'm bone tired, sore and with no sense of what time it is.

"Back with us," Hirrin says.

"Not quite yet."

I run to take care of physical necessities.

When I return, I grab ReconStew from the dispenser, and get a huge glass of water filled with ice, which the game made me love, and which I have to request special from the dispenser.

And I sit at the table and start shoveling food into my mouth.

"Find anything?" Hirrin asks.

I nod while I swallow, take a big gulp of water, chase the food down with that. "I found what he meant by *Shoot First*. And it's important. How about you?"

Tarn comes over to the table and sits opposite me. "He made notes in a journal that he'd coded 'moon and sun.' I couldn't find the original source material, but his notes said that the moon and sun dilemma was that until people understood that their own lives had to matter to them, they would constantly seek behaviors that would lead to their destruction."

"What does that have to do with Moon & Sun?" I ask.

"What do better horses or bigger guns have to do with setting people free?"

I shrug. "Actually, I found that out too. You choose the bigger guns first, because a bullet can outrun the fastest horse."

"What's a horse?" Tarn asks.

"It's a big animal. But the horse isn't the point. It's an analogy. What he means with the analogy is what matters. If you want to survive, you first have to invest in the means to defend yourself. After that, you can spend money on comfort and luxury and things that are pretty."

"That doesn't seem like such a big deal." Hirrin sits, too.

I say, "He thought it was. Big enough to put in his diagram of how to free Settled Space. How about you? You find anything?"

"His journals are classified by what he calls Conceptual Conflicts, and they link back and forth to each other. Individuality Versus Collectivism, Values Versus Duties, Freedom Versus Safety—"

I say, "You mean Freedom Versus Slavery."

"I thought that, too, but what he's showing is that the majority of people will hand over their freedom a piece at a time to anyone who tells them they're in danger and promises to keep them safe. Who promises to give them protection, food, medicine, housing. And it doesn't matter if what they get for what they give up is terrible. Most people will accept terrible things if they don't think they're paying for them. And if everyone else has the same things, but nothing any better."

I consider that. "That's exactly how PHTF worlds work."

Hirrin says, "That's how the entire Pact Worlds Alliance works. All the worlds are just at different points of falling apart."

And then something clicks. "You said anyone who promises to give them things. Is that how he wrote it in the journal?"

"Yes…?"

"I mean did he use the word *give*?" I ask.

"That's *important?* The word *give?*"

"Yeah. Because I remember the sign I first saw on the swinging doors of *The Happy Madame.* Hang on."

I race back to the Senso, step in, and ask Retha, "What exactly did the sign on the Happy Madame say?"

Retha tells me, and I make note of it.

I carry my note back to the table and put it in front of the other two.

> *Darlin', 'round here*
> *you pay to play.*
> *Come back when you've got*
> *some money, honey.*
> — *Miss Dolly Boombah*

They both read it. Both look at me quizzically. "What does that even mean," Tarn asks.

"Nothing is free. Not in the game, not in real life. Everything costs someone something. You go into this scruffy little town and you have nothing but the clothes on your back and a horse you want to shoot and a gun so bad it wouldn't kill that horse. You have to start doing jobs right away to earn money to buy things like food and ammunition.

"You have to work to earn everything you get. Including the fun stuff at *The Happy Madame.* But it's the sign on the door I think he was referring to. If you don't work, you don't play. If you don't work, you don't eat."

"What if you *can't* work?"

"People in the game help each other. You can't give them your money, but you can give them food, or shelter, or rescue them from danger. You do it because you want to. Because those people matter to you, or because it's the right thing to do. But your money is yours, and your actions are yours, and you have to decide what you want to do with them."

Hirrin says, "That fits exactly with some of what Nokyd had in his journals, but the pieces are all scattered around in there."

Tarn nods. "It fits the books he read, too. He marked things in them that either supported what you're saying or pointed out where the books were wrong because they didn't, and he added notes from his own experiences that proved or disproved the points those other writers were making."

"We have enough to call the owner," I say.

And they both look at me and shudder.

I have just finished being eaten alive multiple times by vicious monsters with enormous teeth. I am tougher for the experience. Not *really* tough, because the owner is real, and the beasts and the BEMs were not, and I find that I am terrified to let him know we have answers for him.

But I'm tougher than either Hirrin or Tarn. I make the call.

Chapter 14

Jex

The owner does not come. His representative does, and I find myself very happy to be the one who gets to take credit for calling her.

She is a creature of grace and beauty, her long coppery hair curling nearly to her waist, her eyes the green of cactus washed clean after a sudden rain.

Yes, I saw one of those. It was really pretty.

She introduces herself as Shay.

Long story short, though, she is a vast improvement over the creepy old man in the masked, armored shipsuit.

My mind goes places it shouldn't, and I have to reel it back.

Hirrin has the philosopher's writings, Tarn has his collection of books written by others, while I have the big pieces of the puzzle I've managed to put together.

Shay asks Hirrin to show her what he's discovered first.

Hirrin gives her the brief rundown of Nokyd's Conceptual Conflicts.

Like me, she stops him at "Freedom versus Safety."

He nods, flips through the journal, and reads:

Coercion is in almost all cases unnecessary to separate free people from their inalienable rights.

All that is required is to inform the free that they are in danger, and to promise to keep them safe in exchange for taking away the rights of those who threaten them.

Or to tell the poor that they should have everything the rich have, but that they should have it without working — and then promise to give them what the rich have worked to earn if they will simply demand the stripping of rights from the rich.

Shay nods. Looks around at us. "That's entirely true."

Hirrin says, "He also explains the means by which those who want power create the appearance of danger where no real danger exists.

He reads aloud:

"By use of the Principle of Division by Nonessentials, any corrupt government or power can break apart people who share common interests by using small, irrelevant differences as wedges. Issues such as presence or absence of wealth, place of birth, skin color or attractiveness, personal orientation, and other irrelevancies are the cause of great and devastating wars that inevitably reduce the freedoms of all individuals and transfer more power to governments.

"All current governments registered within the Pact Worlds Alliance operate using Division by Nonessentials through use of the class system of Order A through Order E citizens, and all are on curves of varying speeds of decay to the same inevitable destruction."

She looks up at us. "Not optimistic about our ability to save ourselves, is he?"

Hirrin says, "He is guarded in his assessment of the continued freedom of the rest of Settled Space, but he notes the City of Furies as a curious and inexplicable bright spot in the universe. However, he says it's one he cannot define, because no one knows where it exists, who governs it, or upon what core principles it operates."

"Hand me any of his writings you've discovered that cover this," she says. "I'll take them back to the owner, and he can go through them when he's up and around."

Hirrin shoves the stack of journals across the table to her.

She wrinkles her nose — the expression one of distaste. "Paper?"

Hirrin nods.

"It figures." And then she smiles at him, and says the words I want to hear spoken to me. "Welcome to the crew. You'll start as Three Green, working with your Gold doing Sleeper maintenance."

He's in. I force myself to sit still as she asks Tarn, "What about his reference books?"

Tarn trots out his information about the *moon and sun dilemma*, and she is solemnly interested. When she copies scans of his datafile into her device, Tarn is also made permanent, not provisional, crew at the level Three Green.

She looks at me. "You were the one who contacted the owner, so I'm guessing that what you found is somewhat…larger than what they discovered. Please tell me what you found."

And I realize that I can't. That I have no right to announce in front of anyone but the owner or his representative that the ghost of Bashtyk Nokyd lives inside a Senso game.

"I have to show you," I say, and lead her to the Senso.

The two of us step into it together, and I say, "Retha, we need to go to the special play-together I was in. To the end, at the parade. You know the part I mean?"

"I do," she says. And then she says, "Welcome, LadyOfPain42, you have not played this game before, and have no earned credits in it. I can show you the scene Hunter Studly refers to, but you must watch it from outside the game."

"That's acceptable," she says.

And suddenly it's late in the day, and I'm walking beside Ted with people on the boardwalks to either side of us cheering and waving.

I'm there…but I'm not in control. All of this happened before, and I'm just along for the ride.

I turn to Ted as we walk down that dusty street to meet the mayor who's waiting for the two of us at the end. And I say, "When you said we had to shoot on sight, it was because you knew the enemy had proven repeatedly to be without integrity, and our only option if we were going to save the hostages was to shoot that enemy before it could shoot us."

He nods. "I had a hard time figuring that out. I wanted to believe that there was always a peaceful way to resolve things — that there was no problem diplomacy and integrity could not resolve."

"Pause game," Shay says, and I hear a tremor in her voice. "Retha, that's Bashtyk Nokyd in there. I know his voice. I know *him*. Why didn't you tell me he's still alive?"

"Because I don't lie," Retha says. "I never met Bashtyk Nokyd . The character is saved in my game files as Long Tall Ted. It is not the whole man — it is simply the thoughts and memories the man who played as him actually accessed while he was playing. Long Tall Ted is a shadow of the living human being you knew, and any memory he did not use while he was playing is now gone forever."

She watches the whole scene at the end of our mission. Discovered the philosopher's rationale for *shoot first*.

Unlike me, she does not get teary-eyed going through it.

So I do what I can to hide my emotions, and I'm dry-eyed by the time we step out of the Senso.

She tells me, "You did very well." That thoughtful look again. "The owner is far too ill to play through a game in realtime, or even watch someone else play through. And I'm too busy."

She stands outside the Senso, studying me. She looks me in the eye and I can tell by her expression and her posture that I'm not going to hear what the other two heard.

"Jex, you can become Three Green if you desire. But before you accept, I would like to offer an alternative.

"I have been in need of an assistant for several years, and until now I have not found someone I thought would work well with me. I'd like to invite you to be my personal assistant. And if you accept the position, I'd like to ask you to play through all the missions with Ba— with Long Tall Ted. Play, get him to tell you why he does what he does, how he comes to his conclusions, what actions you think of that he considers unacceptable. And why. Always *why*, Jex."

I nod, speechless. I will not be crew, precisely. But I will be doing something that matters. I will be working toward the freedom of people in Settled Space.

"Good," she says. "All three of you need to go into the court-house in Bailey's, take your tests, and be sworn in as citizens."

She looks at me.

"This will be your quarters until I can set up something more convenient. Play the game, Jex." She smiles a little. "Learn every-thing you can."

When she's gone, I stand where I stood when she left, staring at nothing, remembering We-42K and the unlicensed but born — our beautiful child already dead in her arms.

I'm seeing the woman I loved step into the lake of fire, hearing her scream, seeing her and our dead child burn.

I held him in my arms once, and he looked at me with eyes knowing, wise, ancient.

I think, *In this world, the three of us would have been a family. Would have been welcomed, would have lived.*

I will do what I can, my broken love, my murdered little one, to save the ones like you who still breathe.

Chapter 15

Shay

The gunslinger LadyOfPain42 walked down the street to the saloon where Long Tall Ted waited.

Shay knew where he was because even through the building walls she could see the blue dot over his head, and could read his name below it.

She had spent a little time in the game — enough to let her visit the saloon, and enough to let her earn the money to buy drinks.

She'd made herself plain — an ordinary woman with an ordinary face who would not stick out in anyone's memory.

She knew he was not Bashtyk Nokyd. Not really. But she wanted to buy him a drink, to ask him questions about life, about humanity, about how she could find a way to keep everything and everyone she loved safe.

And then she remembered that *safe* was the wrong word. It was in pursuit of safety that people gave up their freedom.

She realized she needed to learn from Long Tall Ted, the philosopher's ghost, how to build a world in which true freedom had a fighting chance.

He looked up at her and grinned.

Glanced at the space above her head and said, "Howdy, Lady-OfPain42."

In that young man's face she could still hear the memory of the old man's voice, warm and full of life and joy and confidence. It was a living voice, one she'd thought she would never hear again.

"Howdy, Long Tall Ted," she replied. "Buy you an ice water?" Her voice broke on the last word.

"I'd thankee kindly and buy the next round," he said.

She made a show of turning her back to him to get get them.

She did not want her hero to see her weep.

Vipers' Nest

TALES FROM THE LONGVIEW

HOLLY LISLE

Chapter 1

MELIE

With Kagen back in the City of Furies, Melie had quietly been made captain of the *Longview*.

It felt like being made captain of an empty house.

The *Longview* — docked on the high gantry at Bailey's Irish Space Station, still and silent — had been given asylum in Bailey's Point. It could not move out of the system because of the bounties put on it by the Pact Worlds Alliance, and because of the many pirates and fortune seekers who would destroy it to earn even a fraction of the treasure offered.

So Melie was captain of a sitting target, new citizen of a space station that now carried bounties as well because it had dared to defy the PWA — the Pact Worlds Alliance — and had offered help to the *Longview*.

The work she had to do while the ship was docked was nothing like captain's work.

But she had the captain's rank, and someday, if they all survived, that might mean something.

At the moment, being captain simply meant that for the first time in her life, she'd moved out of crew quarters into the captain's apartment.

These quarters contained more space than she'd ever had in her entire life — all for herself — with a real captain's table for hosting honored guests, with amazing views, with a huge bed.

And with privacy.

The privacy was the thing she couldn't quite get used to. It meant she and Shay could be together away from Shay's quarter — which connected directly to the owner's quarters.

Shay, stripped down to her shorts and tank, climbed into the bed beside Melie, and grumbled, "Mado Keyr is impossible. He has absolutely no sense of anyone else's personal time."

She was talking about the owner of the *Longview*, of course, who paid his people incredibly well — and in exchange required a tightly focused dedication that left little time for a private life.

In spite of which, she and Shay were managing to build a tiny private life… in her newly private quarters.

"So we'll just sleep," Melie said. Shay'd woken her coming in, and it was late. With the ship docked, they were both operating on "owner's hours," which were worse than when the ship had been running its circuit of PWA settlements.

They were both on call all the time.

Knowing he'd be demanding one or the other of them to go somewhere or do something at any time, they snuggled together, and Melie closed her eyes, her back warmed by Shay's softness. Shay wrapped an arm around Melie, and Melie fell back to sleep almost instantly.

It wasn't the owner who woke them both, however, but the alarm indicating that a call was coming through the isolated trace line Melie had programmed. She shot upright in the bed, shook Shay, and whispered "Call coming through on the line we reserved for Bashtyk Nokyd's killer."

Shay woke equally quickly and grabbed the communicator. "Give me a go when you're ready," she said.

Melie was wide awake, too, adrenaline coursing through her bloodstream, heart racing. This was what they'd been waiting for. She leapt to the console she'd set up in next to that massive captain's bed, not bothering with shoes or shipsuit, wearing only her uniform gray undershirt and gray briefs. She hit the connect, hit the trace, and nodded.

She saw Shay's com line go live. Heard Shay yawn. Heard her say, "Owner's office, Shay speaking." Sounding not only like she'd just woken up, but also like she was still mostly asleep.

Melie kept her head down, forced her breathing to slow, tracing the caller's connection through the network she'd set up. If Shay could keep the caller talking, Melie would be able to pinpoint the location of the woman who had murdered the philosopher Nokyd.

The trace went through, then out of the ship.

It was strong. Tremendously strong. As if the ship transmitting it was within sighting distance.

In the background, Shay said, "No. The owner is in his pressure chamber. He had a very difficult time today. I'm covering his transmissions."

Not a ship. The call was coming from the station.

Melie's first identifier was Gantry Couple South Four Outfacing.

The power grid gave an affirmative, and she moved closer.

Her skin began to crawl. The threat was somewhere *inside* Bailey's Irish Space Station.

Her tracepoint was working through ident challenges, and at each, she used a code — given to her by Wils Bailey, the owner of Bailey's Irish Space Station — which identified the trace to the checkpoint as a power grid status query.

Blu-O power check, Terminus of East F/South Six. … affirmative.

Melie, Shay, and the rest of the crew had been given an introduction to the Blu-O protection system when they received their citizenship.

The Blu-O rings, manufactured right in Bailey's Irish, surrounded all entrances to the space station, and all entryways and corridor crosspoints inside. They had sensors that identified a select set of human-designed body modifications in the bloodstreams of people passing through them, which released aerosolized vaccines to those toxins.

The aerosols had been developed in response to genetic body

modders experimenting with modifications that turned them into predators for whom normal humans were prey.

The worst of these modifications was a mod called Legend. That mod had allowed normal human beings to becoming close approximations of fictional blood-drinking immortals. The fact that the mod creators for the original Legend made blood-drinking an involuntary reflex when the modder got too hungry, and made the mod self-replicating in attacked survivors, had caused a population explosion among Legends that nearly wiped out humanity.

AntiLegend, an aerosolized vaccine harmless to normal humans and lethal to anyone carrying the standard Legend mod, was a core ingredient in the Blu-O rings.

And while no one was certain who had been behind Legends' near eradication, Settled Space was still rebuilding.

Bailey's Irish had been untouched during the peak contamination by Legend modders, however, because it had installed Blu-O rings that spread the nanoviral antidote.

And still did, along with nanoviral antidotes to new threats that were being developed by the pathologically power-hungry.

Mado Keyr had been equally severe about making sure no dangerous modders came aboard the *Longview*. New crew (including crew unpacked from the Sleepers), and passengers of the *Longview* were inoculated against the same threats during the onboarding process, called *repping* by the crew. The inoculations were voluntary, but with the rule that if you didn't rep, you didn't ride.

The frozen Sleepers? Well, the Sleepers slept on.

"I don't *want* to wake him for you," Shay said, managing to sound both sleepy and annoyed. "His health is dangerously poor, and he needs another six hours in the compression chamber to fully cleanse and purify his blood."

Melie watch her tracker move closer.

East A/North Two, Blu-O power check. … affirmative.

"I do understand that, Mada… What is your name?"

East A/North Three, Blu-O power check. … affirmative.

"Keffrim? Yes, Mada Keffrim, I do understand about emergencies. I simply don't believe your situation qualifies as a greater emergency than the one that would be caused by pulling Mado Keyr out of his pressurization chamber prematurely."

East A/North Four. Blu-O power check. … affirmative.

"Of course I can explain. To get me to wake him, you have to demonstrate to me that your situation is a true emergency, can genuinely be solved by Mado Keyr, that Mado Keyr is the *only* person who can solve it, and that he will agree with you that it is as important to him as *his* interests, which from where I'm standing, are currently better served by making you wait the full six hours for his pressurization treatment to finish before allowing you to speak to him." Shay raised an eyebrow at Melie, questioning.

Melie mouthed the word "Close."

Shay nodded and quickly suppressed a smile.

"Mada, that is *exactly* why he pays me, and insulting me will not move this process along any faster." A pause. "Oh, if you can get him to fire me, *please do.* I want nothing more than to be told I must no longer work for him."

Melie grinned and kept her head down, working.

The trace was running through the corridors of Bailey's, through each Blu-O-protected intersection, and confirmed the function of the O-ring as it passed through it.

When the Pact Worlds Alliance declared war on the *Longview,* and Bailey's Irish offered everyone aboard citizenship, the space station had added weapons to every Blu-O ring.

The new weapon add-ons recognized citizens who were carrying registered weapons, recognized temporary visitors as long as they were unarmed, but turned armed or enhanced strangers into tiny piles of ash that were sucked into the filtration system — a fact discovered by an advance crew of heavily armed pirates who'd attempted to board the station pretending to be tourists.

But even before that, Bailey's had somehow gotten wind of Legend from someone on the inside, and had received a duplicatable sample of an antiviral that protected those who inhaled it from Legend contagion. The station had installed aerosolizers into the Blu-O rings that protected each intersection in every corridor on Bailey's Irish.

Because of that precaution, they had lost almost no one during the Legend population explosion or the subsequent mess with Legend II.

East A/North Five… Blu-O power check at Block KVN-GV Disabled.

Melie froze. Stared at the console. The Pact Worlds Alliance had a standing bounty on the *Longview*, the station, and every single human being aboard either. And they kept increasing the bounty. Sooner or later, the pirates would arrive in force. When they did, a disabled Blu-O ring constituted a breach in the Bailey's Irish Space Station defenses.

… Unauthorized reroute discovered. Report terminal error at once.

"Hold for one moment," Shay said, and then, "Yes. She's called. We're getting it. I need to get back," and then… "I'm sorry. There was someone at my door." A pause.

… Reroute Block query error 1 Line 4984. Report at once.

Shay said, "Yes, as the owner's representative, I do have business hours. Twenty-four standard a day."

… Reroute Block query error 2 Line 5212. Report at once.

Melie was capturing the errors, pulling up a trace-line map of the station, correlating lines of map code to errors. She blocked out Shay's conversation, focused on making sense of what she was seeing. She needed Shay to keep the killer talking just a little longer, because…

… Reroute Block query error 3 Line 5483. Report at once.

…she had to have all of the errors. To find that bitch, she had to have every single one.

…Query path routes behind errors. Query terminated by Errors.

Melie swore under her breath, then whispered, "Tersh, overlay errors on map of Bailey's Irish space station."

Tersh was the *Longview's* new AI.

Melie gave Shay the signal that she'd completed the trace.

Shay nodded and said, "I'm certain only that you *think* you're as important as you think you are, and I would actually pay you to get me fired if you could do it, but you're going to wait six hours to take your best shot, because I'm not taking him out of his pressure chamber until I can do so safely. I fear him much more than I fear you." A pause. A little chuckle. "If that's true, what comes next should be interesting."

Melie raised an eyebrow.

Shay cut com, but Melie maintained the connection. "Well?"

"Come look at this." The errors Melie's search had revealed appeared and transposed themselves over the grid of the space station. "Show corridor and building names on map."

They appeared.

She studied them, pointing out the connections to Shay, and worrying about their meaning. This was not a case of lax maintenance. This was not accidental breakage, wear over time, things just getting a bit slipshod. The pattern she was seeing was planned. Hidden. Big.

Shay's hands gripped the edges of the console, and Melie could hear her forcing herself to breathe slowly. To think.

"This is the nightmare we didn't think could happen," Melie whispered.

Shay stood behind her, and Melie could feel her leaning over, looking at what Melie had discovered.

"That's the entire Bailey's grid?" she asked.

"Yes." Melie pointed to the layout. "Look. Couple North Five, a private exclusive-use ship dock paid for by the Vincheros Corporation, has no Blu-O protection. Right across from it, the North Four Terminus has no Blu-O protection.

"Across the East A passage from Couple North Five is the Rosh Diplomatic Center. Which has no Blu-O protection on either its North Five or its West A Corridor entrances.

"Directly across from the unprotected entrances at the Rosh are the Balconies Premiere Residences. Which have unprotected entrances at the West A and North Four corridors.

"That's six total entrances, two massive buildings, and one triad of corridors that is allowing anyone and anything to get into Bailey's directly and unscreened, and move through those areas unchallenged by Bailey's Irish security systems."

"Open access for anything that folds through the origami point from any other location in settled space and docks there." Shay pointed to the Vincheros dock.

Melie said, "Watch the tracepoint." She told Tersh, "Contrast live blue with broken red," rolled her search back to its start, and replayed it. A thick band of blue filled the gridded corridors of the station, starting as a single point inside the *Longview*, then winding through the entire station, showing all of the places that were still intact.

Then the tracepoint hit the block flooded with bright red where things *weren't*. She pointed and told Shay, "Bashtyk Nokyd's killer is somewhere in there. But before I do anything else, I have to call Wils Bailey and let him know his security has been compromised. The lives of all station citizens are at immediate risk."

"Do it," Shay said. "I have to take this to the owner. Now."

Melie didn't even look up when Shay left the room. She did a quick scan of local chatter, determined the location of her target, made sure her connection was secure all the way from the docked *Longview* to *THE* Bailey's private residence, and opened a line.

In just a second, a voice on the other end said, "Ident?"

"One Gold Melie from the *Longview* for Mado Wils Bailey, urgent communication on secure line."

"This is Bailey. What do you need, One Gold?"

"I'm reporting an emergency situation. Are you recording, mado?

"Should I be?"

"Yes."

A tiny pause. "I'm recording. Go ahead."

"I'm reading directly from the line test results I obtained from the station just a moment ago," she said. "Quoting:

East A/North Five — Blu-O power check at Block KVN-GV disabled — unauthorized reroute discovered.

Reroute Block query error 1 Line 4984.

Reroute Block query error 2 Line 5212.

Reroute Block query error 3 Line 5483.

Query path routes behind errors.

Query terminated by Errors."

She took a deep breath. "That's the complete readout."

"Do you have any further information regarding this error?"

"Yes. The owner's representative was communicating through a private traced call from Mado Bashtyk Nokyd's killer to Mado Weyrix Keyr. I was running the trace. The trace led to the disabled block and was terminated by the errors. Therefore... his killer is still on the station. Assume that anyone unexpected approaching the area of the block will be in danger, and assume that any actions that suggest these breaches have been discovered will trigger undesirable consequences. Assume that all people in this area are being monitored by those who rerouted the station security system."

Another brief pause. "Affirmative. I'm on this." Followed by the click of a closed comlink.

Melie sent a scatter pulse through her connection to Wils Bailey to briefly disrupt the line. It would delete the station's system memory of the conversation that had just taken place.

She sat staring at her hands. They were shaking, and she was not yet remotely finished.

Chapter 2

HEROG

"Hey," Herog grinned at Cady and hugged her quickly. "Ferg needs me to cover for him. He met a girl he likes, and didn't realize the schedule had changed.

Cadence Drake — the woman with whom he'd survived waking nightmares — was in the kitchen area of the apartment they shared, where she'd had a baking oven researched, built for her, and installed.

She leaned into him and sighed. "You don't want to taste-test more cookies?"

"Do they still taste like tier-four reconsta?"

"I should hurt you for that."

He laughed. "You did that last night. And thank you, by the way." This was the life he'd never imagined for himself, the place he'd never thought he could get - where he loved someone and she loved him, and their happiness was made greater by their closeness.

This was what the Pact Worlds Alliance and their collusion with the pirates was working to destroy.

The smile faded from his face. "The PWA calls for attacks on Bailey's and the *Longview* went quiet last night. The bounties they were offering aren't where I can find them anymore."

She pulled back, studied his face. She thought, bit her bottom lip. Shook her head. "They won't quit."

"No. So something has changed. They've found some sort of answer. They might have their bounty-hunters, they might have come up with something else. But to keep their worlds in line, they have to destroy this place — have to prove that they can. You know it. I know it."

"Yes," she said. Still. Calm. Coldly certain. He'd never seen her panic, had never seen her go to pieces. And he'd seen her in the worst possible situations.

Her gut was telling her the same thing his was telling him.

He told her, "I need to be out there. In the dark, in the deep. I need to be watching, because they're coming, Cady. So I'm going to fly Ferg's watch, and I'm going to dig through the City of Furies feed, see if they're reporting the silence, or have theories about it. And I'm going to try to figure out what the PWA is up to. Whatever it is, it's going to be big. Bad. And as soon as they can push it, it's going to be here."

She said, "And we have to be ready. Yes. Go. I'm going to distract myself with this a little longer. I don't know why it matters to me. It just does."

Herog did know. The reason she was trying to retroengineer RexSurvyve cookies — her beloved Big Cookies that were no longer made — was that they had been her one comfort during an extended period of hell they'd both survived. Her obsession was to him the most obvious thing in the world.

But if she didn't see it, he wasn't going to point out to her that she was scrambling to recreate that lost comfort to help herself believe they could survive the nightmare bearing down on them right then.

Chapter 3

MELIE

A security breach always ran in two directions. The enemies of Bailey's and the *Longview* had created the breach.

Melie intended to exploit it.

The connection she held open between the *Longview* and the compromised triad would briefly take Melie straight back to the caller, the caller's com, and data stored in the system.

And possibly deeper into whatever was going on in the Rosh Diplomatic Center and Balconies.

The caller's com was full — read and unread reports, DNA-locked holos, high-security sent to an installation made insecure by one call to the wrong person.

Melie grinned.

This was her game, her element, and while she was duplicating everything she found in Rosh, including vast amounts of what looked like military communications, private personal communications, ingoing and outgoing cargo manifests, and all medical and personal biometric data, she was also making very sure she did not leave any traces of her presence. She dared not alert the enemy in any way that someone was aware of anything wrong in the section.

She used her enemy's breach to grab everything she could find in Balconies, too. An entire collection of holos marked Gargantua Insurance, none of which were DNA-locked, odd cargo manifests of Medixes being moved in and out from the Vincheros dock… and from the dock itself, the manifest and private records of the *Elegant Design*, supposedly a diplomatic vessel, which Melie discovered was both heavily armed and carrying a complement of PWA soldiers, who were in the process of being traded for the contents of those unmarked Medixes in Rosh.

The instant she'd grabbed every stored file she could reach without setting off alarms, she cut the connection and set the *Longview's* firewall, then did a scrub for anything that the enemy might have tried to set up during that call to Shay.

"System clean," Tersh said.

Longview flight and ops had been a no-AI zone by the owner's order — until the ship ended up docked and locked pending resolution of the conflict with the PWA.

At that point, Keyr had come to Melie and told her she could acquire and install an operational AI. He'd gone over the sectors in the ship to which the AI could have access, and the sectors that were off limits.

And Melie, in setting up the AI, had followed his instructions religiously.

She knew what the owner was. Had seen what he was, up close and in person — and that had been a horror show that had given her nightmares for weeks.

But knowing what he was, and then seeing what he was doing, who he was helping, who he associated with, some of her dread wore off. She routed calls from the City of Furies to him. And even though Shay hated him, Melie realized her own consideration of him was moving from fear toward guarded trust.

If people could be judged by the company they kept, she would have to hold him up as one of the best men in settled space.

She wasn't quite ready to judge him by the company he kept for just that reason.

"Tersh," she said, "We need to find anything in the data haul I just made that can tell us why the PWA has stopped trying to hire people to come at us. Why it's gone silent.

"If possible, we need to know what they're planning.

"The first thing I want you to do is match DNA-locked files to DNA from their database. Once you've done that, unlock everything that's locked for which you have a key, and start piecing together data. We're looking for a narrative that I can present to the owner, the volunteers and regulars flying patrols around Bailey's, and the owner of the station that will allow us to know what's coming and prepare a defense."

"On it," Tersh said.

While the AI was decrypting, she started in on the unencrypted holos she'd pulled from Balconies — the ones marked Gargantua Insurance.

They were high-quality holos — full sound, full color, tight focus.

And they were all the same. Some smiling woman, or woman with a child or several, would walk into the restaurant level of Balconies, would be seated at the table, would be waited on by the smiling waitstaff, would eat, would have a visitor to the table pat the woman on the shoulder. The woman — with children if they were present — would follow the stranger who'd touched her shoulder, and would be whisked into the Balconies gravdrop up to a suite inside the building. The woman and any children would appear to voluntarily climb into Medixes. The scene would then cut to the woman and any children in a cage under some weatherproofing on a planet. The sky was obscured to prevent identification of the location, but Melie stopped holo and started dragging the image out to its periphery in all directions.

They weren't on a convincing set. They were on a planet. Given time, she could probably determine the size of the planet by the curvature, but without sky, gravity, or atmosphere data, she'd have a hard time narrowing it down.

There were one hundred thirty-seven holos in the series.

Over three hundred hostages.

She'd not heard a word about anyone going missing. So the kidnappers' insurance was working.

"Tersh, how are you coming?" she asked.

"Have a number of DNA-locked files opened. Still working."

"Tag the files you have ready for me, and then I need to put you on something urgent."

"Waiting," Tersh said.

"Go through the files I've just marked for you, and without alerting anyone on the station that you're searching, identify each person in each holo. At the same time, identify the date on which the holo was made, and find the identities of family members who live on the station. This is both highest priority and dangerous. Alerting anyone to any aspect of what you're doing is very likely to get everyone on this station killed, but will most assuredly get the people in the holos killed."

"I will not alert anyone with my actions," Tersh said.

Melie nodded and started into the first of the holos Tersh had unlocked for her.

It was a memo titled *Moving to gargantua stage two* that included an attachment:

Gargantua trial 7 — Success.
Subject control strategy 18 — Success.
This is the winning strategy. Keyr is a dead man walking.

A second attachment, which looked like a compressed holo file, was attached to the memo and had been encrypted with a DNA lock.

She had all the DNA keys.

She opened the holo and began watching.

Chapter 4

HEROG

Herog expected to walk into the apartment and smell some variation on burnt cookies, to be greeted by a hug.

Instead, the kitchen was clean, with all sign of baked goods gone.

There was, however, a happy little note waiting for him.

I'm so excited! One of the old bakers from RexSurvyve is actually here on the station. She got out before things went bad there. So we're meeting for lunch, and then she's going to come back here with me and walk me through the Chocolate Caramel recipe. Love you!

He grinned just a little. The idea of Cady getting some help with her baking made the future of her kitchen experiments (and his future as a taste tester) a little brighter. Assuming they and the station survived whatever was coming.

He'd no more than thought it than Wils Bailey secure-commed him.

Wils didn't bother with a greeting. He just said, "We're meeting on the *Longview* in fifteen minutes. Leave now, staggered approach, stop off one or two places to buy things, talk to people, don't make a straight line to the ship, but *tell no one about the meeting or where it'll be.* Don't draw attention to yourself in any way — aside from just being who you are, of course. I don't know what this is about yet, but both the *Longview* captain and the owner will be there."

Herog nodded. "On my way."

He considered leaving a note for Cady.

If she was coming back with someone, he didn't dare. *Tell no one* meant exactly that.

He ran possibilities through his mind, decided someone had come up with the reason why the Pact Worlds Alliance had gone silent. Maybe knew what was going to be coming through the origami point, or when it would be coming. Maybe both.

Wils looked like hell. Scared.

He wondered what Wils had been told.

Herog was careful to lock the door, careful to take a public-carry weapon, careful to hide two backups, including one coil of molei-bond wire that would pass through any detection and permit very close hand-to-hand combat should it prove necessary. Careful to plot in his head the fastest route back to his ship if they were about to be under fire.

But fifteen minutes?

Don't run? Don't draw attention to yourself?

They might know what was coming, but he thought they didn't know when.

He meandered, counting time in his head. Said hello to strangers who knew who he was, stopped to purchase a quick snack from a roving reconsta vendor who worked the old-sector corridors and who specialized in hot, crispy MeatTubes.

Ate while he walked, looked out at space, floated up the grav-drop to the high gantry, stared like a tourist down at the station itself — it was an extraordinarily pretty station, but he wasn't in the mood to appreciate it — and arrived at the *Longview's* dock at the time requested.

A woman walking out of the ident-locked entry said, "Brush past me and go straight in," and as he did that, kept right on walking in the other direction.

He was off the gantry and out of sight without it looking like anything extraordinary had happened.

And without his ident being registered at the *Longview* dock.

Inside, a lean, dark-skinned crewman said, "Follow me, Mado."

"Herog," Herog growled. "I'm no one's high-born master."

"If I want to keep my post on this ship you are," the crewman whispered. Herog chuckled at that, and followed.

"By the way, when you go into the meeting," the crewman said as they stepped to the gravdrop, "don't ask about the pressurized shipsuit. The owner lives in it, and Shay says he's sensitive about it."

"Thanks," Herog said.

They dropped down, sideslipped to a pair of dark wood doors, and Herog followed him into a room lit only by faint, masked side-lights. Initially he could not see where he was supposed to step, or who was in the room with him.

"I have problems with light," a raspy, gruff voice said out of the darkness. "I apologize for the darkness, but you'll be watching well lit holos, so this will be temporary." The speaker coughed. "Rayden, close and lock the door when you leave."

There was silence until the crewman was gone, and the speaker continued. "I'm Mado Werix Keyr, the owner of the *Longview*. With me are Wils Bailey, the owner of Bailey's Irish Space Station, and Amelie FraRiveri, the captain of this ship. Wils knows our other guest, but Melie, this is Herog, the renowned pirate hunter and another escaped slave like you and me. Herog will be the last person who will join us."

Herog's eyes adjusted, and he walked down steps to a table built to host bigger meetings than this. He could see the outline of two people in regular shipsuits, and one in a heavy pressurized suit that sounded like it had forced positive pressure re-breathing. Forwarned, he pretended that was normal.

"You've found something about what the PWA plans," he said.

"Melie did," Keyr said. "Melie? Please give Wils and Herog your short version of this."

Beside him, a young woman's voice said, "Because of an investigation I was running with the mado's representative," and she inclined her head briefly toward Keyr, "I was tracking a specific call through a locked connector we'd set up for the exclusive use of the caller. The only person who would be able to get that connection was the person who killed the philosopher, Bashtyk Nokyd. I would have been able to track the call through multiple origami points if necessary by use of deep worms and several of my own algorithms, but my preparation turned out to be unnecessary. The caller was someone on the station."

Herog's gut tightened. Nokyd's killer was still on the station?

Melie said, "*Is.* She's still here. And in the course of the call, I discovered that security in one small area of this station had been carefully compromised so that the breaks would not be found. I was able to backtrack the breaks to pull enormous amounts of data from the two compromised buildings and the one compromised dock—"

Herog interrupted. "A dock and contiguous breaks that gave those responsible clear access directly from space to inner areas of this station?"

"Yes," Melie said. "It was through this direct access that someone who carries an advanced version of the Legend mod was able to enter the station, set up living quarters, and arrange for direct contact with citizens of this station. It was through one of these direct contacts that this Legend gained control of Wils's daughter Banyi and forced her to kill Nokyd.

"But," Melie continued, "this was not the only contact, and not the only devastating disruption in our security and to the lives of our citizens. Mado Keyr, would you take over now?"

"Yes." A cough. A wheeze. And a sphere of light appeared in the center of the table. "Inside the treasure trove of information Melie stole for us, some things need your immediate attention, Herog. I'm going to start with the first of two unlocked military holos we acquired from confidential communiques to which the Legend hidden on this station is privy." The owner tapped a holosphere in the center of the table. "Melie, make sure Herog receives copies of everything from here on out."

The captain of the ship said, "Will do, mado."

Keyr turned his attention back to Herog. "These holos are of trials of an ongoing evolution of ship-to-station battle strategies being developed by the Pact Worlds Alliance. Herog — as the most experienced warrior in the Bailey's solar system, I'm requesting that you stop this at any point to look more closely at what you see, make comments, and if you see anything we can do to prepare for this, let me know. What you are about to see is a demonstration of the PWA's success with a new strategy for attacking space stations. Barring brilliance and speed on our side or some unforeseen disaster on theirs, this will successfully destroy us all. My considerable fortune and any people I have, and any other resources I can bring to bear, are at your disposal toward solving this problem."

The holo came to life, and Herog found himself looking at an old drum-style space station hanging a ways off from an origami point, at a few slow in-system mining ships moving through space, at a viewpoint carefully controlled by someone who gave every appearance of waiting for something specific to happen.

And then something did.

A clear moleibond sphere maybe four meters in diameter came through the point. The origami point gave its usual little flash of light, and the usual ripple was briefly visible behind the appearing object.

The ball was illuminated from the inside, and had what looked like bodies spreadeagled against the inside of the sphere, held in place at wrists and ankles, facing outward.

"Stop," he said, and the holo stopped. He touched the holo, flicked thumb and index finger apart, and the sphere grew in size. He closed in on the faces, the bodies. Two women. Two children. Their expressions of alert horror proved them to be still alive.

He returned the holo to normal size and said, "Continue."

"Comments?" the owner asked.

"Premature," Herog said.

There was a short pause. A pirate ship — a lean hunter-killer — came through the point. Herog thought it was eight seconds between appearances, but decided he would back up and count more closely after he'd had the opportunity to see what the pirate planned.

The sphere used jets to make its position fixed. The hunter-killer aligned itself behind the sphere, and waited.

Herog watched, counting to himself.

Eight seconds after the hunter-killer came through, another sphere with live women and children inside came through. It changed trajectory slightly with external jets, and also placed itself between the point exit and the station.

Eight seconds, and another hunter-killer.

If he had known the people in the balls, he would have been able to identify them personally. And that, he realized, was the point. Each one would be someone whose life mattered to at least one person on the space station.

"They're human shields trapped in bait balls," he said. "Wrong strategy for pirates. This is building a shield."

"Yes," the owner said softly.

The process continued, with the spheres creating a loose blockade between the point and the station, and with each sphere creating a shield for the hunter-killer that came through eight seconds after it.

Herog asked, "Where is this?"

Melie said, "There are several possibilities. My best guess, working backward from the timestamp on the holo, is that what you're seeing was the Van Beers origami point and station."

Was. Not a good word.

He considered what he was seeing.

An eight-second jump clock was fairly loose. It took precise timing, practice, and planning, but Herog had moved forces under much tighter situations.

The person recording the event focused on one of the bait balls in a tight shot that showed explosives rigged to cut lines. If someone with a moleibond cutter went through one of the cut lines, the bombs would go off.

Then the recorder moved the focus to a small gravity shear fixed onto a bi-axial gimbal mount. The shear wasn't decorative, but it was small enough that he guessed it to be useless against anyone more than fifty or sixty meters from the ball — and the bi-axial mount would not let it rotate past 90° from its forward position. So it couldn't damage the pirate ship sitting behind it using it for cover, and it would not be set off by the ship moving over or under it to attack, as long as the ship didn't get too close.

Those attempting rescue, however, would come in facing the hot end, and the shear would effectively tear apart anyone who got close enough.

Herog tapped the image to freeze it, and all the displays froze at that point. He inserted thumb and index finger into the holo, flicked them apart.

His image expanded to cover the table, and all the other holos disappeared.

"Gravity shear," he said. "Very small, limited mobility. Rescuers are going to have to come in from the back or they'll be shredded."

The owner sounded startled. "You've... seen these?"

"I hunt pirates," he said quietly. "I've *used* these. Friend of mine invented them. Bigger, much more dangerous. But when we know the pirates aren't carrying slaves, we're not looking to leave survivors."

The owner nodded vigorously. "Good."

He returned his holo to its normal size and unpaused it. All the other displays reappeared.

In total, twelve bait balls came through, which shielded twelve hunter-killers. None of which attacked the station or engaged the light station defenses. They simply waited.

This had been carefully and deeply planned. People from the station had been identified and captured and kept and caged, and put into well-designed bait traps weaponized to kill any ships that attempted rescue.

And — as he looked more closely at the bait balls — with no simple, safe way for anyone who paid ransom to release the hostages. Those spheres had little oxygen scrubbers in there, but no way to maintain them. There was no food in there. No water. And there was no door. The moleibond sphere was seamless.

The hostages had been put in. The traps had been set. And then the moleibond had been sealed.

"The purpose of the captives is not to force negotiation," he said, "though that is certainly what they want the defenders to think."

The people displayed inside were only alive to give would-be defenders a reason to hold back. Everyone inside the sphere would die along with the first ship that attempted rescue. But no matter what the people in the station did, everyone in those spheres would die anyway.

He added, "The purpose of the captives is to paralyze the defenders."

But why the elaborate preparation? The pirates could have pushed one ship through every eight seconds and had the whole dozen in place in under a minute, far less time than it would take the unprepared space station to alert the two or three fighters it would have for defense.

Twelve hunter-killers was massive overkill for the little mining station's resources. Cylinder-drum stations were cheap to build but damn near impossible to defend. They were soft targets, so only corporations with meager resources used them, and then only for folks who were processing things that were difficult to steal or transport.

Like that mining station. Heavy unprocessed ore didn't usually interest pirates.

An unarmed salvage ship had, by that time, gone out to investigate the activity around the point, and on seeing the contents of the spheres, had sent up panic flares.

The salvage ship hailed the pirates to open negotiations to rescue the hostages.

Herog knew this because the recording switched to the inside of one of the hunter-killers, where he saw on the com the face of the salvage operator, who said, "You have our wives and children. We will pay whatever you ask to get them back."

The captain of the hunter-killer said, "We will open all negotiations in a moment. Please inform your defense ships that they must stand down if you wish your families to remain alive."

The view then switched back to the unseen documenter's

viewpoint.

And then, twelve seconds after the twelfth hunter-killer came through… the nightmare arrived.

A ball of warships strutted together into a tightly packed array to form a geodesic sphere pushed through the point. The instant the back of the array cleared the point, luminance blossomed beneath two ships on exact opposite sides of the array.

"Freeze it," Herog said and started counting. "Fourteen cruisers on the surface and one battleship at the core. Those aren't pirate ships. Those are marked, regulation PWA Peace Armada ships."

The owner said, "Crewed by regulation PWA Peace Armada officers and enlisted."

Herog nodded. "And that light pattern you see beneath some of the ships is from automated moleibond cutters. If you look at which ships are illuminated, you can see that the pattern is designed to give each ship clearance space when it leaves the array."

The holo scanned the station, and Herog could see that the station had called its two fighters back, and that other ships alerted to the disturbance had turned around and were docking.

"Don't," he muttered to the retreating ships. "Don't just let them take you without a fight."

The pirates sat behind their bait balls while two PWA ships on opposite sides of the array dissolved the welds that had moleibonded the struts binding them into the array — which took 10 seconds. In just over one minute, all the PWA fighters were free. Then all hell broke loose.

Herog's view and audio switched to the deck of the PWA battleship, where the captain announced via holo override, "All citizens who wish to survive will gather in the topmost level to be evacuated.

"Resistance by any one person will result in the execution of all."

Suddenly Herog saw a stream of corridor views from inside the station.

The PWA has people on the inside. Spies, traitors…

People filed out into the corridors carrying whatever little bits of wealth or nostalgia they could carry in one hand, and gravdropped up to the highest floor of the station.

Heat sensors located slower-moving citizens, and the captain said, "Attention, citizens hiding in your rooms! You are visible to us by heat signature, and your failure to comply will be counted as resistance if you do not enter your corridor and proceed to the topmost floor of the station immediately."

This brought out the old, the infirm, the pregnant women, the children.

Herog's hands became fists clenched in fury.

Nothing good was coming.

He took a deep breath.

It has already happened, he told himself. *All of this has already happened, and my job now is to watch and learn.*

For an instant, he was fourteen again and his father was selling him to slavers.

He was sixteen, and being used by men who liked to hurt boys.

Was in his twenties, with some size and some muscle on him, being thrown into arena after arena to be killed by more experienced fighters for the amusement of paying audiences, and instead of dying, killing without style or flourish or drama just to survive. He'd been bad entertainment. He'd been a spectacularly efficient killer, though.

And he had seen death, and more death.

This time, he saw it again. And it was worse. The PWA soldiers hesitated at the order to kill, but pushed by their commander, opened fire and slaughtered every occupant of the drum station.

He heard Wils gasp. Heard Melie snarl.

Outside, the other PWA warships destroyed all armed defender ships and all unarmed ships within reach in just minutes.

The pirates triggered the explosives and the bait balls erupted in liquid flame that destroyed all trace of their occupants and other contents.

Herog's fingers knotted together on their own, and he stared down at them. Felt his gut twist, his shoulders tense. He wanted to kill the people who had done this. To remove them with brutal efficiency from the universe — not just the ones who had carried out the actions, but the ones who had planned the strategies; the ones who had engineered the bait balls and the ship array design; the ones who had kidnapped innocents as hostages, who had folded awake, unshielded civilian women and children through the torture of an origami point crossing without any protection against the horrific, agonizing forces such crossings entailed; the ones who had slaughtered the hostages' families and destroyed their home in front of them; and finally, the ones who had blown up mothers and children inside those moleibond spheres. He wanted to hunt down and kill each and every man and woman who had participated in the atrocity — and each and every one of the men and women in charge who had given permission.

Herog asked Wils, "By your best estimate, how long has station security been breached?"

Wils said, "Once I knew what to look for, I was able to go back through nearly five months of old records and identify the rerouting."

Herog said, "As soon as Bailey's security was breached and the spies established themselves, they will have started taking hostages and moving them through the point to wherever they're holding them."

Melie was the one who answered. "Yes. Part of what I found was hostage holos. Over three hundred of them. All are relatives of strategically important people. The first taken were Jana Huson — Stal Bailey's wife — and their three children."

Herog heard Wils gasp. "My brother? Jana didn't leave Stal?"

"No," Melie said.

Wils said, "Stal is head of station security."

"I know," Melie said. "Stal was the one who both approved and then installed fake Blu-O rings around the Vincheros Corporate dock portal and the private portals to the Rosh Diplomatic Center and the Balconies restaurant. He was not even contacted by the enemy agents until they had his family off the station and through the origami point. Once they were out of reach and untraceable, however, he was given instructions."

Herog asked, "How many station-critical people have been compromised?"

"One hundred thirty five. Including the head of point security, all three air-plant operators, the Blu-Os manufacturing supervisor…"

Herog glanced over at Melie. In the dim light, he could see her pale hair move as she shook her head. She added, "Anyone in charge of anything to do with station security, with keeping the station working, or with air, food, or water has already been compromised."

He nodded. "We have to finish watching this."

"And the next one," Melie said.

Next one. He forced himself to take a deep breath.

The holo restarted, and this time the owner expanded its size until the individual holos vanished and just one large image hung over the table.

They all looked up, watching in silence.

PWA, the pirates, and the holographer raced for the origami point, but the holographer focused on something dropped and left behind by the PWA battleship after all the residents had been slaughtered.

The owner expanded the recording again until it showed just the sphere left behind. It was smooth — a deep ugly red. The holo showed the externals only, because of course they were not recording in doppler.

The holo ended.

"What's the sphere for?" he asked the owner. "Do you know?"

"We don't get to see what happens," Keyr said. "But the origami point vanished shortly after the end timestamp on this video. So the sphere could be something that effectively fakes enough mass to destroy an origami fold, or something that draws mass toward it until enough has gathered to collapse the fold. Or, least likely, something that creates real mass."

Herog put his head in his hands and closed his eyes, thinking. "This was early practice," he said. "Possibly their first successful attempt."

Melie said, "That's exactly what this is. Their first success. How did you know?"

Herog looked her in the eye. She was the one who'd tracked this down, decoded it, put it in their hands. She was the one who, if they survived, had already saved them. He admired her. "They weren't testing the bait ball technique. Ball distribution and pirate ship positioning were both smooth and practiced when they came through. They were slow, but they were perfect on their marks.

"Their technique for controlling station populations was unpolished, though. The executioners hesitated. These first-timers faltered while killing the children and the young women. So this is a team they're building, this was an early attempt, and they're doing live runs because they need to know their people will not hesitate when they hit the target they're actually after. Here. Us. They're testing the multi-ship ball configuration, practicing getting the ships clear of the array at speed once they're through. And they're giving ship teams and ground teams real conditions. Real kills. Hardening them."

The owner said, "You sound like you've figured something out."

The owner made Herog's skin crawl. But he had a good ear. "We can watch the next holo, and I'll pull what I can from it. And I'll take copies of everything you have with me, because I'm going to have to go over what you have with my men. But the very first thing I have to do once I leave this room is die."

The silence from the other three people in the room felt heavy.

"Die?" The owner broke the silence.

"If I'm dead, there will be no point in taking a hostage to control me. Because they have had spies in place for at least five months, the PWA will know I'm here. And they will want to know that you're depending exclusively on people they already own for your defense. I'm Herog, the pirate hunter, the known and feared enemy they'll have to face. They have to escalate what they're planning because they know I'm here. So if I'm dead, they won't have to be as good to destroy you.

"And, Wils, before I'm dead, you're going to tell your brother Stal that you've decided the silence from the PWA means they're not coming, so you're bringing a team of miners in to start mining the massive streznium deposit just located by prospectors on..." Herog considered the locations of the solar system's planets relative to Bailey's Irish. Dermiche was bigger and seemed a more likely target for the lie they'd all have to tell, but for the next month — if they could hold off the attack that long — Chardi would be closest in orbit to the station. Which would make it the best-positioned planet for him and his people. "On Chardi."

"There's no streznium on Chardi," Wils said.

Herog faced Wils. Slowly and carefully, he said, "No. *Listen and memorize this.* The planet has a solid core of it. Solid. There's enough there to bring in not one but *three* space-to-core drills to get it out. There's so much that even with three rigs running wide open, it's going to take them twenty years just to get it all."

Wils said, "Streznium is the rarest useful compound in settled space. No one is going to believe we found a whole planet core of it."

"Belief is not what you're going for. *Because* it's the rarest natu-rally-occurring compound humanity has found in settled space, and *because* no one has yet figured out how to manufacture it, a find even a hundredth that size would make this the richest find in history, and you the richest man who ever lived.

"But more than that, if the PWA has figured out a way to kill origami points — and it looks like they have — this gives them the biggest reason in the universe to leave *your* origami point alone. Because they have to act on the *possibility* that you have streznium here. If they destroy your point, then by straight-line near-lightspeed travel you're about a thousand years out of reach from the next closest known origami point. They won't destroy the point if you're sitting on the streznium mountain of the gods."

"And when they discover it's a fake?"

"I'll take care of that."

"What…"

Herog cut Wils off. "Don't ask me. What you don't know, you can't tell. They own your brother. They own other people on this station. You might already know who's been compromised by kidnapping— "

Melie broke in. "We know exactly who's been compromised. The list—"

Herog held up a hand. "But you don't know everyone who's been compromised by other means."

Melie nodded.

Herog returned his attention to Wils. "Use her list. Know who's missing on the station, who's owned by the PWA, watch them without appearing to watch them. Remember that their families are in danger, and that any sign you give that you know what's happening could both cause the deaths of the hostages and trigger the attack before we're ready.

"But understand that though you know who's been compromised by kidnapping, you don't yet know who arrived here already compromised — who is working for the PWA in some guise you have not yet discovered. So you cannot give any clue to anyone, ever, that you know what's going on here, because we have to both keep your compromised people locked down, and find every killer and every monster hiding in your midst who appears to be just another citizen, or newcomer… and we have to shut all of them down the instant the fight goes live."

He stood. "Give me copies of the holos you found. Anything else my people will need. I'm putting together a package for them, and I have one important errand to run, and then I'm going to fly out of here on a routine mission, during which my ship controls are going to go haywire and crash me into an uninhabited planet. You're going to travel to the planet, tag my ship for Cady to retrieve, and claim you scraped what was left of me into my ship Medix so you could have a funeral." He looked at Wils. "You'll take the news to Cady personally, and you will not, under any circumstances, hint that this is not what it looks like."

Wils said, "This will destroy her."

"I don't want her in the PWA's hands. She has a bad history with them, and if they figure out who she really is, I'll never see her again. They'll kill her right then, right there."

"So from this point out, the only thing any of you can say about what comes next is that I died, and that you're on your own."

Chapter 5

MELIE

Melie was running on back-to-back reju — working herself to exhaustion, then spending twenty minutes in a Medix to simulate sleep and remove accumulated toxins, then doing it all over again. Her primary objective, given to her directly by the owner, was to determine the identity of the killer who had wired Banyi Bailey's hands into a weapon, and who had murdered Bashtyk Nokyd with the girl.

Melie kept hitting walls, blocks, reroutes — but she persisted, because money always connected the spender to the recipient eventually.

The spender — the entity who had paid for the execution of Bashtyk Nokyd by any means necessary — was the High Council of the Pact Worlds Alliance.

The money spent — ten million rucets — was simple to find on the spender's end. That it had been paid was public knowledge.

The account into which it had been paid was *Bashtyk Nokyd Fund*, however.

From there it had been efficiently moved by a number of different people into shell companies, banks, and money funds, where it was spent on all manner of ridiculously overpriced items sold by third parties who always ended up being anonymous fronts for shell corporations.

And while rucets flowed into and out of all of these, Melie couldn't trace a single individual rucet all the way from origin to Bailey's. All the money got converted into *other* money along the way, invisibly.

It was being laundered by people who knew what they were doing, and who did not make mistakes. And cleaned, it flowed into Bailey's like water from a flooding river, pouring into multiple accounts whose owners were numbers, not names. The person with the right number and secret code could collect anonymously.

She closed her eyes. She could not follow the money. And while she had the secret code, Melie could not use it without alerting her enemy that the system had been hacked.

She needed to figure out something she could follow until it touched the hidden killer.

At the point of her deepest exhaustion, she realized more reju wouldn't help.

She needed to think about something else for just a while.

She dropped down to the Rec Hall to play a little *Starfighters*. And saw *Old Earth Cowboys Versus the Bug-Eyed Monsters of Mars* on the game list.

And remembered that the woman who murdered Bashtyk Nokyd had found him by searching for his voice and pulling prints of it from the game server.

The killer had gotten word of Nokyd's invitation to Wils Bailey's house, but Melie thought she'd already been on the station, because when her plan to collect the *Longview* bounty by controlling Laure failed, she did the next best thing. She moved herself to the place where the *Longview* would be.

Melie closed her eyes. Tried to get inside the head of her enemy.

Who would I be if I were you?

Someone already on Bailey's, here to kill the Longview in person. Because if you want something done right, sometimes you have to do it yourself, don't you?

Bashtyk Nokyd was a happy little accident for you, wasn't he?

If I were you, I'd have been sitting on this station since shortly after my hired killers disappeared, listening for news of the Longview coming. I'd be sitting still, a spider feeling for vibrations in my web.

If I'd been you, I would have been...

Bored.

Sitting, waiting. Looking for something to entertain myself while a ship evaded pursuers to get to me.

You controlled Laure the same way you control your character in a Sensogame.

You're a player, aren't you? A serious player.

You've used voice prints before to locate targets...but you were a player first. You're into this.

People who didn't use Senso entertainment already wouldn't even think to check the entertainment servers for stored voice prints. They wouldn't know about replays, peak-moment shares, the fans who skinned into the full-sensory replays offered by top players.

Meanwhile, legitimate users wouldn't know about the ugly stuff shared in the deep dark.

But the means by which the killer had controlled Melie's fellow crew member, Laure, to murder much of the *Longview* crew, as well as the way in which she had used Wils's daughter Banyi to murder Bashtyk Nokyd, suggested that she was intimately familiar with the illegal uses of Senso tech. That she lived down in the deeps with the nightmares whose existence normal folks didn't even suspect.

Trying to sit inside the killer's head, Melie considered the full scope of entertainment available via Senso. Full-sensory virtual reality content went far beyond games, but anything that contained live interaction had a voice channel. Not all the content was legal. Not all was safe. But the thrill of all of it was that there were real people on both ends.

And the thrill for a killer stalking prey would include getting to know the victim beforehand, wouldn't it? The assassin had found Nokyd because she was playing *Old Earth Cowboys Versus The Bug-Eyed Monsters of Mars* and had searched the voiceprints for anything interesting. And one of her persistent tags had matched to him.

Melie guessed that the killer fancied herself a monster who played with her food.

Extrapolating from that, Melie thought his killer had played the game *with* Nokyd at least once or twice.

Good news, which was welcome, because she'd needed some.

Cowboys VS. BEMs was going to be Melie's best chance to find the murderer. Melie used the override Wils Bailey had given her to do a complete search of on-station transactions involving the game.

Cowboys VS. BEMs was about five years old, so there were not many recent purchases — twenty-four total inside the possible time frame.

Purchases were linkable to credit idents, credit idents to real names, real names to residences, and *one* of those purchases was by a female who lived inside the perimeter of the Blu-O ring diversions.

The name of that copy's buyer was Valli Arra.

Melie thought, *What are the odds?* And checked that name first. Got the woman's passport holo and biometrics.

She took com offline. Secured her room. Presented GenId to unlock Valli Arra's personal information.

And found herself looking at a face she'd seen before.

Her guess about the connection between the massacre on the *Longview* and Nokyd's murder had been right. Melie was looking at the woman — no, the *Legend* — who'd wired Laure, and who had been directly responsible for the deaths of the *Longview's* on-deck jump crew.

Melie reopened com, did a deep but untargeted status check of all station inhabitants so she wouldn't trigger any alarms set against searches for specific people or kinds of information. Going back three months took her a full five minutes. She forced herself to be patient. When the results came back, she cut com again, locked down her quarters, and dug out the info she needed.

Then she contacted Shay, using the pass phrase the two of them had agreed upon for this moment. "I'm in the mood for crunchy chicken."

There was a pause. "Me, too," Shay said. "I'll be right there."

When Shay arrived, Melie put a finger to her lips and hit the room's privacy shield. "I have her. Bashtyk Nokyd's killer, the woman who controlled Laure. Same person."

Shay's lips thinned to a hard, narrow line. "Show me quickly, before someone tries to reach me and can't get through."

"Mado Keyr could—"

Shay shook her head. "In his box."

Melie, who knew what Keyr really was, frowned. "Why?"

"Because the less time he spends around normal human beings, the less obsessed he is with the scent of blood. It would be ideal if he could just stay in the damn box. But there are some parts of his empire that I can't touch."

Melie nodded. "That makes sense. Anyway… the woman who forced Laure to betray the *Longview* also manipulated Banyi. Her name is Valli Arra and her address is Blue Two Suite, Rosh Diplomatic Center. I can give you biometrics and anything else you need to prove that to the owner, but I can already tell you she is still on the station. She moves only between the diplomatic building and the Balconies building, so she's always inside the area where Legends can travel. And she's the primary recipient of the military intelligence from the PWA."

Melie watched the smile spread across Shay's face.

Closed her eyes as Shay folded her into a tight hug. "You're wonderful," Shay whispered in her ear.

Then Shay pulled away and started to pace. "She cannot know that we have her. She has to think she's still invisible. If she's in a position to influence the PWA's attack, we have to make sure nothing pushes them to attack early. We know what's coming, but our defenses aren't ready."

Melie said, "As long as they think they're safe — that no one knows about them, and that their communications remain secure — they'll spend time perfecting their attack. They're going to want to get holos of it. Once Bailey's, this ship, and the origami point are destroyed and they have holos proving what happens to anyone who crosses them, the PWA is going to be able to expand their reach through terror and oppression. So they'll want to make sure they make this smooth and brutal. I'm betting those holos are going to become *Join or Die* recruiting tools for systems who have been holding out on joining the Pact Worlds Alliance."

Shay's sidelong look and single raised eyebrow made Melie laugh.

"My thoughts always go to the worst case."

"Stick with that. You're a step ahead of where I was, and I suspect you're right."

Chapter 6

WILS

The explosion was unmissable.

Wils saw it from the corridor, walking from City Hall to the Seamy Underside to get takeout for his office staff.

It lit up space like a nova, white-hot light guttering down to red.

His com pinged on his wrist, and his assistant said, "Boss, bad news. You need to get back here fastest."

He turned. Ran.

Alcie was gray-faced when he arrived. Herog, she told him, had just come back from his errand, had signaled his return, and then had diverted from his landing to respond to a distress beacon. He'd homed on the beacon, hooked up umbilical to umbilical, and headed through to rescue survivors.

And it had been a trap.

She'd heard the screaming over com, she said. But not for long.

Wils nodded. Had her hold the rescue crew long enough that he could drop from his office down to Emergency Rescue and get aboard.

He was first through the port into Herog's ship, and wished he hadn't been.

Herog and the soft parts of his ship were shredded. Wils saw

413

cooked flesh, burned bone, half a face that was still somewhat iden-tifiable. The moleibond and everything encased in moleibond survived.

The rescuers started gathering pieces.

The ship wouldn't fly, so the team cut it loose from the trap. Hooked it to the tow line.

Wils did not let himself think about the body.

DNA scan had confirmed it was Herog's.

It couldn't be, though. It couldn't. Because Herog was the one who was going to protect Bailey's.

Instead, he forced himself to stay focused, found the LAST MESSAGE in Herog's log. Every spacer carried one. It held the details of the captain's life that would require closure: contacts, Will and Testament, final requests, messages to be conveyed.

While the rescue crew towed Herog's ship back to the station, Wils, as station owner, had the duty of carrying out these requests.

Herog had set his messages and other instructions in strict order, mandating that the first two be sent in clear and as general delivery messages via open ping.

The first was addressed simply...

To My Valiant Brothers of Warrisk Merriment

By what foul means we once fair met,
That death then held our lives in play.
We strange had wandered far apart,
To meet again aft gang agley.

My journey's done, my sword laid down,
And 'neath a knoll my bones must lie.
Our Pact is done With All its fun.
Come say your last goodbye.

The Bladed Bard

Wils sent that directly from Herog's ship. The ship's com was designed to be indestructible, and still worked perfectly.

The next message looked to Wils like a recipe for feeding one helluva big crowd something they wouldn't much like to eat, which was to be sent in clear and addressed *To the Attention of Thurwiled Legofnard*.

My requested Funeral Feast — Start cooking on receipt of ingredients

2000+ chickens
Every egg in the station
A hundred tonnes of pepper
Three big grinders
Broth and dressing to fill the pot
Enough sauce to keep the party lit for a year

This recipe needs to be hurried along

The Bladed Bard

He sent that as well.

The final message was to go to Bask Mining Company, to be sent in Herog's words without any alteration, but from Wils through his official com and in his role as station owner. This message was to go through encrypted channels. It read:

Have located and confirmed the Holy Grail, three-houser.
Coordinates follow:
Bailey's Irish Point, Chardi, sealed locker contains my staked claim and the location.
You'll have to do this one on your rucet.
N. Guileder

He copied that message to his com. He would deliver it from his office when he got back.

There was also a note to be hand-delivered to Cadence Drake. It read:

Cady — Read the gift message, know that I love you, know that we are more than memories.
Herog

He printed out Herog's message to Cady using the ship's tech.

Turned, and saw the dim green "Occupied" light on a jump berth, and relaxed. Started to grin. Right.

That was where Herog would be. The DNA was faked, the body was faked…

He was going to need some privacy to get Herog out of the unit, but as the owner of the station, he could manage that.

This had been why he came. Why he'd been first into the ship. So he could cover for Herog.

The rescuers were both in the rescue vehicle towing the ship back to the station, so they couldn't see him.

He pressed the panel to release the occupant.

The occupant wasn't Herog.

Instead, a scrawny blond man with dark eyes stared at him, and then past him, and said, "Oh, gods, what in the hells happened? And where's the big guy who gave me the lift?"

"Who the hell are you?" Wils snarled.

"Halford. Skapnell. Licensed moleibonder. My ident —" He fished around in a shipsuit pocket, found what he was looking for, handed it to Wils. "Who are you?"

"The owner of Bailey's Irish, investigating a ship explosion. What kind of lift did the captain give you?"

"Captain he said he'd take me as far as Bailey's station, but I'd have to find my own way from Bailey's to Kanis. Better odds to get there from Bailey's, because Bailey's wasn't PWA. Or in its pocket." He looked past Wils to the captain's chair. To the blood everywhere. "What *happened?*"

"You're at Bailey's," Wils said, and felt his throat tighten. "And I'll pay your passage on to Kanis. There was… an accident."

"The captain…?"

"Is dead," Wils said. "How did he end up transporting you?"

"He said he was picking up a present for his woman. That crate over there. He had a jump berth he said he didn't use, and he didn't mind giving me a ride this far, since I was escaping the PWA."

"Yeah," Wils said. "That sounds like Herog." He shook his head. Forced himself to exhale slowly. "He went to get something for Cady, picked up a refugee, came through the point, got a distress signal, responded…" He looked up again.

He wanted to think that Herog had escaped. Was out there somewhere.

He wanted to believe.

Wanted to.

"It figures the last thing he did was try to save someone else," Wils muttered. And then said, "At least I can take Cady her gift along with the bad news. *And* get you where you're going."

While the rescue crew secured the wreck and removed what they could gather from Herog's remains, Wils took Halford up to his office, and put credits in the man's account. A lot of them. Might take him a while to find work on Kanis, and Wils didn't want Herog's next-to-last kindness to end in failure, too. Then he walked Halford to the Concerti shuttle service, and bought him a berth in a Medix through-passage unit that would get him to Kanis.

With that task finished, he turned his attention to what he was going to tell Cady.

Not *what*, precisely, because now he didn't need to lie. He'd never been a good liar, but he wished to hell he was walking toward her apartment trying to figure out how to be convincing, rather than trying to find the words to let her know the man who'd become the brightest light in her existence was dead.

Wils dragged the bulky null-grav crate behind him on a leash, grateful that it had both steady-float and obstacle avoidance built in. The corridor was broad but crowded, and he was so distracted he would have had a hard time keeping it from hitting passersby. That he didn't need to was a small gift.

When he reached her building, he confirmed ident, grav-dropped to her floor, knocked on her door.

The door slid open on its own, and his gut knotted.

"Cady?" he called.

No answer.

For the door to have opened on its own without ident, it had to have been rigged that way. Which to him said *trap*.

He loosed the sidearm he always wore in its holster, took a deep breath, stepped inside.

All three inner doors were open, showing him instantly that no one was there.

His attention was drawn to a portable holo-dot sitting on the little dining table by the main room window.

The holo showed Cadence Drake being seated at a table in a station restaurant. *Balconies*, he realized. The restaurant inside the compromised zone. The image was frozen with her smile on her face.

He moved over to it, stared. Whispered, "Play."

"Thank you," Cady told the waiter who'd seated her.

The waiter said, "I'll show your host to the table when she arrives."

And a moment later, he led a short, perky little woman over and seated her across from Cady. Wils rotated the holo, expanded it, got a good look at her face. He didn't recognize the woman, but the way the station population had been climbing with the new sector opening up, with all the new citizens — that was no longer strange. The days when he knew everyone on Bailey's were past, he realized.

"My name's Mari Petzki," the woman said. "When Lannet Colson over at Colson Traders told me about a woman who was looking for cookie sheets, I just had to meet you. No one bakes anymore."

Cady laughed. "You can't call what I'm doing baking. Not yet. I'm just making smoky messes in a kitchen."

Mari said, "Well, that's what we're going to fix. Lannet said you'd gotten the tools you needed, and had local fresh ingredients?"

"I was… *persuasive*," Cady said.

"Getting fresh eggs and live chickens onto a space station suggests you were more than persuasive."

Cady shook her head, laughing again. "They know me. I've done things to help them in the past. And I emphasized the fertilizer angle. Had to dig pretty deep to discover that, but it turned out to be what won them over. Anyway. RexSurvyve Big Cookies."

And Mari grinned. "So here's my surprise. We're not having *dinner*," she said. "We're having a fresh sample of Big Cookies I just finished baking. New flavors I've come up with. You can taste and tell me what works."

The expression on Cady's face broke Wils's heart. It was hope, and delight, and glee.

The bitch sitting across from her was playing her, because the holo was in the room where Cady should have been, left for Herog to find.

The waiter brought out a bottle of wine. "We recommend the Zaz Pergat `47 with your… meal."

"Oh, I already spoiled my surprise," Petzki said. "She knows we're only having cookies. Please bring out the plate and some chilled water," Mari said. "You never ruin the taste of a good cookie with alcohol."

"A woman after my own heart," Cady agreed. The waiter took the wine back, and returned with a platter of enormous cookies — each the size of a big man's splayed hand — along with a big bottle of sparkling water in a tub of ice. He poured the water into their glasses and left. They clinked glasses, drank. Mari pointed to one of the cookies and said, "This is a simple vanilla butter cookie. The taste is mild, and won't overpower the later cookies."

She broke off a bite and ate it. He watched Cady do the same. Watched a blissful smile cross her face.

They sat, nibbled each one, discussed the flavors, laughed. Mari explained ingredients, Cady asked questions.

And then a third woman with her face hidden came out and quietly told them both to stand up. They both stood without question or hesitation. Followed the woman without struggling. The holo operator guided the micro-corder after them into a side room in the restaurant, climbed into the Medixes the stranger told them to get into. The Medixes were put into cargo boxes, the boxes were taken out to the ship docked in the Vincheros slot.

And the ship took off.

Both the little baker and Cady had been targets.

He switched off the holo-dot, put it in his pocket.

Both women were already gone, through the point and probably unfindable, though he would give the holo-dot to the *Longview's* captain and see if she could make anything of it.

Herog was dead. Not hiding in his Medix pretending to be dead. Not just neatly disappeared.

No. He was smeared in identified and verified thumb-sized chunks around the inside of the *Daruda*.

With him dead, Cady's survival value to the PWA as a hostage had become nonexistent. Had she still been on the station, that would have been a good thing. With her in their hands, however, it meant they had no reason to keep her alive.

He closed his eyes. Thought, not for the first time, that he was on a forced march down the road to hell that had been paved with good intentions.

He stared at the crate by his leg. He had no idea what might be stored it in, and he wanted to leave it for Cady when she came home, but he didn't know if he dared.

It wasn't ident-locked, or even locked. It was simply sealed against impact.

He pressed a thumb to the release, and the lid popped open.

Inside were hundreds of thumb-thick sealed square packets in rainbow colors, each bigger than his hand. Each was imprinted with the RexSurvyve logo and the instructions: *In case of emergency, fix things first. Then open this packet, eat, and enjoy. You're going to be all right. — Contents, one Big Cookie.*

He could see no sign of any other message inside the crate.

He closed and secured the lid, and carefully latched the tether of the crate to the center of the table.

He picked up the holo-dot, shut it off, dropped it in his pocket.

Turned his back resolutely on the empty apartment, the unreceived gift, the compounded tragedies.

He went back the way he'd come, toward the berthed *Longview*.

Chapter 7

SHAY

Wils sat across Shay's desk from her a mere two days after they'd last met, looking ten years older, haggard, frightened.

She studied him curiously, trying to see if she could guess why he was there. And she couldn't.

Interesting.

"Herog's dead," he told her.

She smiled a little, nodded. "Right?"

"No. Not cleverly pretending to be dead while going to get help. Really dead. I helped clean everything that was left of him out of the cockpit of his ship, and *everything* was left of him. Some of it pieces smaller than the eye could see, but it was him, and it was all there. So I backtracked his trail.

"Right after we left our meeting, he went straight to his ship, and did a point jump through to Taurence Station to pick up a gift he'd ordered for Cady some time earlier. While he was there, he took on a refugee named Halford Skapnell who was fleeing the PWA. Skapnell was a licensed moleibonder who came through the point in one of the ship's on-deck jump berths. Herog returned here, and was no more than through the point when he received a distress call. He responded, hooked up to pull out survivors, and got shredded by hull mines and sticky pies as he was going through the umbilical. It was a trap set for him, keyed to his arrival."

She raised an eyebrow. Kept her expression neutral. "How did Mado Skapnell survive?"

"He was protected by the jump berth. He was, in fact, still in the jump berth when I arrived. I let him out."

"Big fellow?"

"Short. Skinny. Pale. Looked like he'd gone without a lot of meals, and like he'd done hard labor. Was a decent kid trying to get away from a bad place and bad people. So I paid his way to Kanis, which is what Herog would have done."

She thought Herog probably already had, but kept that to herself. "That was decent of you."

"Then," Wils said, "I took the gift he'd bought for Cady to her place. And discovered that the PWA had been there first."

Every muscle in Shay's body locked. She forced herself to exhale. To move her expression from calm-but-concerned to worried. Forced herself to say, "Been there… how?"

He put a holo-dot on her desk and turned it on. And there was Cady, full color, high resolution — blonde hair, dark brown skin, pale blue eyes. Sitting down. Meeting with someone to… eat cookies.

Those damnable cookies that were her stupid idiot weakness…

Shay recognized the woman who made both Cady and the baker get up and put themselves in Medixes. Beneath her desk, her hands made unconscious strangling motions. It was Valli Arra. Again.

Couldn't send the owner to kill the bitch. Not yet. Arra was the primary contact for the PWA. The monster in charge of the operation on Bailey's. All of the intel Melie was stealing was going to her — if Arra were dead, a situation that was temporarily under control would rapidly spiral into disaster. From the perspective of the people fighting to save Bailey's, Valli Arra was the devil they knew. There were other people in the diplomatic building receiving intel, but it was going to them from Arra.

That made Arra Melie's open window — the revealer of the Gargantua project, the possessor of the holos of each of the hostages. It was because of Arra that Melie had discovered the PWA's alert that a streznium deposit had been verified on one of Bailey's Point's planets, that it was promising enough that three full super-orbit rigs and crews had been requested to begin drilling, and that the planned "party" on the station was on hold until the rigs and mines were established — a process that wouldn't take more than a month or two.

Herog had bought them time.

Herog... She exhaled, focused on Wils.

"I'll put this in front of Mado Keyr. I don't know what he'll do, and what he does will probably not be something he reports to you. But put the dot back on the table in the apartment where you found it. I'll make sure that someone with ties to Herog's woman appears, gets the message they'll send, and contacts them to put herself in their service. I'll make sure they think Drake is still a valuable hostage."

"Thank you." The station owner looked grateful. "I'll do whatever I can to protect her. Cady has been a good friend to us in the past."

You have no idea, Shay thought.

Chapter 8

FEDARA CONTEI

The woman who slipped into Cady's apartment and picked up the holo-dot was older, with hair cropped miner-short, with tired eyes, wearing deep space mining gear with a corporate logo on the left shoulder and a grim expression.

She told the holo-dot to play, got to the part with the contact information, and placed the call.

An attractive woman answered.

"I'm Cadence Drake's best friend," she said. "I came in here to offer her condolences on Herog's death, and instead found this." She held up the holo-dot.

The woman said, "Indeed. And you think you have something to offer that will save your friend's life? Well, then… what is your name, and what do you do?"

"My name is Coronada Pei. I'm currently the mining director working the streznium deposit out on Chardi."

She watched the smile slide across the other woman's face.

"*Really?* In that case, Corrie — I'm going to call you Corrie — you and I can do business."

Fedara nodded.

"Validate the find for me, verify the size and the quality of the streznium, and get me cargo manifests. As long as you keep the information coming, I'll make sure your friend lives."

"Done," Fedara said.

When she and Cady first met, Fedara had been the favored slave of a Legend named Danniz Oe. Had been turned by him into a Legend herself, and had through a great deal of research and with Cady's help managed to break free from his control. Fedara had developed a real but uneven friendship with Cady, which had ended for good when Cady discovered that she, not Cady's psychotic Legend mother, had murdered Badger — Cady's friend and lover.

Humanity still survived in settled space *because* Fedara had ripped Cady away from domesticity, but that truth would never win Cady back to her side.

Cady did not believe expediency excused shortcuts.

Fedara did.

But she also had a debt to pay for the pain she had caused her friend.

Keeping Cady alive and getting her back to Herog was part of how Fedara intended to pay it.

Chapter 9

HALFORD

F our days after he put himself into the Medix berth and shipped himself as cargo, Halford Skapnell bounded out of the berth into the unpacking platform on the Leggly Station in the Kanis system. He immediately did three things in quick succession.

First, he found a transaction station and repaid the money Wils Bailey had given him for his transit, along with a thank-you note stating that he'd found work already.

Second, he sent a coded message in clear through the local Spybee network:

To Thurwilde Legofnard:

The moon is down, the ghost is slain,
The river runs uphill again.
On dog's long shanks the blade knows when
the 'prentice wields the bard's sharp pen.
— Scruffy Halford

Third, he slung his pack over his shoulder, and hurried to a corner tavern on the station called *The Rat's Ass*.

The Rat's Ass was a rare sort of bar. It offered no dancers, no drugs, no Senso, no games, no gambling. It offered not a single amenity beloved by the popular establishments in settled space, and instead of a cheerful barmaid at the entrance, it featured any one of six burly bastards with fists like hams — all distinguishable from each other to most folks only by their differing scars and tattoos. The job of the burly bastard of the hour was to refuse entry to anyone who was too well dressed, too well heeled... or (without making it obvious) too lacking the necessary signal.

The Rat's Ass served cheap booze, cheap reconsta, cheap rooms, and tech-blocked privacy, these noted in order of importance from least to greatest. It gave the appearance of being a dive, grubby and dangerous to those who didn't belong.

No tourist wandered in, no guide suggested its local charms.

Halford belonged.

On approaching the door, he gave the signal and greeted the bastard of the hour by name. Once inside, he went straight to the Services terminal, paid for a room, and added an open ping drop, tier-two reconsta (based on the knowledge that no one with options ever ate tier-three reconsta), and ordered a door-knock arrival-announcement for any tavern guests who might ask for him by name.

Then he settled into the seat in front of the room's small desk, and out of his kit pulled a paper notebook and an inkless pen. The pen tip heated one layer of molecules on the paper's surface from white to dark brown. It could not be made to darken the page past that point, could not be made to start fires or injure flesh — except for its titanium casing, which he'd used to nice effect in a few fights. It charged from the slight electrical current of the hand that held it, required no maintenance, had no moving parts. It was an old tool, still functional after a thousand years.

It had been expensive, but he'd never regretted the expense. Primitive pen and paper gave him a way to plan that did not require a network, a screen, an ident, an account, a passcode, and by use of all of those things, a way for the eyes of the universe to reach in and see what he was doing.

Pen, paper, and privacy were luxuries not even the richest and most powerful men and women in most parts of settled space enjoyed.

He pulled one of several holo-dots out of Herog's data pack and started the dot. Watched the pirates and the PWA attack the first station again. He stopped the holo numerous times to take notes, to draw diagrams, to brainstorm ways to counter the attack if the defenders were forewarned, to rescue the hostages in the bait balls while incurring the fewest casualties.

Then he set up the second dot, which he had not seen before, and took notes on the improvements the killers had made in their tactics and strategy, noted that they'd moved to a four-second jump clock, noted that their PWA ship ball held twice as many ships, and needed more time to break the ships away from their struts.

He worked for several hours that way, going over each piece of new information, studying changes in the enemy's tactics and strategy, writing, drawing, thinking.

Finally he realized that his muscles had gotten stiff. He stood, paced, yawned, stretched, and got annoyed that neither the yawn nor the stretch were quite as satisfying in his smaller, more lightly muscled Halford body.

The last few days had been long and stressful, and transitioning into a different identity was uncomfortable and took getting used to.

Herog — for of course Herog was Halford — had used a disappearing technique he and his old friend Storm Rat had worked out back before he'd met Cady, when they'd been hunting pirates together.

Right after he'd left the meeting with Wils, Melie, and Keyr on Bailey's, Herog had purchased one-hundred-four-point-seven kilos of Real Mammal Meat from Light House Farm, including eyes, tongue, brains, bones, and offal. They didn't ask why he wanted it, he didn't explain.

He liked that about the LHF folks.

He'd dragged his null-grav crate partially full of meat with him into a public reju station. Had closed the privacy chamber (there so the bizarre people who liked getting naked inside a public Medix could undress), ran an extra flash-clean cycle inside the Medix to make sure no one else's stray DNA was on any surfaces, and then dumped the entire box of raw meat into the chamber.

A Medix didn't need human flesh to fix human flesh. It just needed to have an equivalent mass of similar tissue it could break down and recombine to match the data on the owner's ident card. It would make up (and charge for) any missing mass with regulated Cel-Vida from the tank. The meat massed close enough to what he massed to pass muster.

So Herog had used Storm Rat's doctored reju chip with his ident card to identify the meat and bone and other animal parts in the Medix as him, and "fix" it, and the amount he paid was on record as being for a basic reju. The jacked Medix reju'd the meat into a full-sized body clone of him, and records would show that he had used and paid for only the standard two grams of Cel-Vida a basic reju required.

Herog walked away from the unit with a dated, timestamped record on Bailey's that he'd use a public Medix to do a little touch-up. The Cel-Vida usage, the timestamp, and the corridor records of him entering and leaving were the whole point of the process.

The clone the Medix had made of him never had been and would never be alive. It was a non-breathing Herog-twin meat package. Looking at his unbreathing, unblinking self made his skin crawl, but this wasn't the first time he'd gone through the process, and while he figured he'd never got used to looking at his own corpse, he had eventually made peace with it.

Like the meat before it, the meat package folded neatly into the wiped-down crate. Herog had then proceeded directly from the reju center to his ship, dragging the same carton as before that massed exactly what it had massed before, making sure that he kept his head up and his face visible at all times. Ident cams in the Blu-O rings at each intersection would track his passage anyway, but he wanted to make sure no one would think he'd managed some sort of switch before he got into his ship and left the station.

From Bailey's, he folded through the origami point to the station at Taurence Point. He really did have a gift waiting there for Cady, and the notice that it had arrived was in his ship and home records.

He'd picked up the gift and signed for it with GenID.

Then he'd worked his way carefully through the weakest part of his highly duplicitous trip.

His meat-package body double was staying fresh in the first of his onboard Medixes. So Herog had used the second Medix with one of Storm Rat's alternate identity cards to change himself to the much smaller, lighter-bodied Halford Skapnell. Skapnell's smaller body should have left a record in the second unit that it had stored nearly forty kilos of extra tissue — but that unit had an intentionally "faulty" recorder (the breaking of which had cost Herog about five hours and a lot of swearing). The second unit always reset to "no record" after every move through an origami point, and anyone checking would, if they dug deeply enough, find the little circuit that had broken.

If they fixed it, he would carefully re-break it again the next time he needed it.

Having stored Dead Herog and having become Live Scruffy, he'd then dressed himself in a skintight shipsuit with female padding underneath, put on a dark wig, and kept his head down.

And he'd worked the switch-out, a process he'd refined with years of practice.

In the switch-out, he inserted himself into a crowd and worked his way to the side of the station farthest from his ship. There he rented a sleep tube for eight hours with a temporary no-ident pass issued by the station to transients who were waiting passage.

Once in the tube, he blacked it out, then stripped out of and discarded the body shaping and the wig, using the trash flasher in the tube to eliminate them permanently. Half an hour later, his ship, the *Daruda*, sent him a message accepting Halford Skapnell as a non-paying passenger, along with an ident-confirmed passage card, which the sleep tube's com unit printed out for him.

He then publicly ran a long route through the station with face up where all the scanners could see it. The scanners would confirm

Halford Skapnell's presence and its DNA match to the passage card in hand, and would let him into the *Daruda* using his new identity.

Disappearing in space had once been simple, Herog thought. You just… disappeared.

He missed those days.

He'd put all his records in order and made sure they were where Wils would know to look for them. He'd then duplicated an old response and rescue from his ship's history, cut it off at the point where he went into the ship's umbilical, and set explosives on the inside of the umbilical and around the outside to mimic a direct shot from a gravity shear.

It wouldn't be perfect. Someone going back through all his records and matching the new recording against all old ones in the log could eventually find flaws. But Wils *wouldn't* look closer, and would have the ship sealed until after the funeral, when Cady would inherit it.

He'd made sure the ship had the right records. The folks in the station would have the right funeral.

Then he'd done other tiny bit of housekeeping. He'd pinged Ferg to let him know he was on his way back, and as they'd agreed, invited him over to the apartment that evening to watch races.

Ferg's return ping was nearly instantaneous. "You're supplying the beer."

Herog then ran the ship through the point, pulled his meat puppet out of storage, fought it into a shipsuit, strapped it into the captain's chair, and ran out to the location where Ferg had rigged an empty derelict for him. He put the docking on autopilot, got into the jump Medix, and waited.

Halford Skapnell was his favorite of several back-up idents. Halford was a skinny, wiry, unremarkable looking, young, and his work licenses as a moleibond fabricator and a com networking installer and troubleshooter were real. They gave Herog instant acceptability just about anywhere, and when he needed money, gave him common, unremarkable work that paid a living wage, and that gave him a legitimate excuse to travel anywhere in settled space while making him no one special. Everyone needed moleibond work, everyone needed com, and no one noticed the techs who did the work.

In a pinch, he was competent at both. He'd never be brilliant, but he was good enough to work for someone else and not make a mess of things.

As Skapnell he'd walked past people who knew him, who were mourning his death, walked past the door that would have taken him into Cady's apartment, and he just kept going.

He stayed strong, because only by staying strong — and dead — could he protect her.

Chapter 10

MELIE

One drilling rig came through Bailey's origami point four days after the message that had summoned it.

Just one. Not the three Melie knew had been requested. It was immense, though. It could have fit the old and new sections of Bailey's Irish space station inside of it with room to spare. Folks in the station who didn't have clear views of the point stopped what they were doing to crowd into the station's pointward corridor, to watch the monstrous machine moving through space bound for Chardi. Melie left the *Longview* briefly, stood in the high gantry corridor with shipmates and station citizens, and watched the rig soar by. It seemed more like a moon than a creation built by humans.

"What's it here for?" one of the locals whispered.

It was her cue. "I heard a rumor that someone discovered streznium," she said.

"Streznium!" the word spread through the crowd of watchers.

She stood quietly, watching the enormous ship, and she listened.

Most of the comments demonstrated that the observers had no knowledge of mining — though most knew what streznium was — but finally she heard the comment she was hoping to hear. "For a rig that size to pay for the fuel and trans-passes to get here, the deposit has to have been confirmed. Proven. Staked and claimed. And it has to be big."

She looked a the sturdy man who'd said it. "You a miner?"

"Fifth generation," he said. "I'm wondering if they'll need workers."

"Probably," she said. "Worth asking at the courthouse. See if the discoverer staked the claim."

And having said that, she turned and went back inside the *Longview*. She could worry later about the fact that only one rig had come when Shay told her three had been requested.

Her job in getting the right information into circulation was done.

Pity the rest of what she had to accomplish was not so easily completed.

On the *Longview's* deck, she settled into her old seat in front of com, closed her eyes, and took a deep breath. She was going to have to get back into Valli Arra's communications again without alerting the enemy to her presence.

She needed to know any details she could get about the enemy's reaction to the arrival of the mining rig, to the rumors of streznium, to the suggestion that Bailey's Irish had decided the PWA had called off its killers.

And she needed to not alert Arra that anyone knew what she was, or what she was doing on Bailey's.

Melie skipped all surface transmissions. Those might hold something of interest, but they were tightly controlled and tightly monitored, and she stood a much greater chance of being caught. When she weighed the higher security against the odds of the PWA sending any record of its dirtiest doings through official channels, she set up to go deep.

She first scanned through Arra's incoming communications from her contact in the PWA. The most recent noted that the party was going to have to be delayed.

That, she hoped, was a reference to the destruction of the *Longview* and Bailey's.

There was a question about obtaining family members of one of the head miners as "guests" — Melie rested her head in her hands at that. Neither the owner nor Wils Bailey had been able to figure out a way to change out the Blu-O rings in the subverted section of the station without tipping off Arra or the PWA.

And then a small, happy smile crossed her face, and she tapped her wristcom to life.

"Shay. Got something urgent. Can you come here for a minute?"

Because the ship was docked, the two of them had the deck to themselves. As soon as Shay came up the gravdrop, Melie shut down the drops, locked all doors to and from the deck, and had Tersh set com to block incoming and outgoing, with himself on the inside. She saw Shay's eyebrow go up.

"Problem?" Shay asked.

"Solution. I know how we can give Wils Bailey a legitimate reason to swap out the station Blu-Os. All of them."

"Tell me."

"We have attackers come through one of the regular Blu-Os. Have them figure out a way to get past a standard, working Blu-O to break into the station, then kill some folks who don't have hostages depending on their survival. Bailey's then has to swap out all the Blu-Os for the new, upgraded versions they conveniently have on hand. Call them experimental or something."

Shay nodded. "I've been digging. This station has automatic lockdown of all zero-plane units in cases of emergency. The whole station will do a hard lockdown in case of attack. If the attack hits the corner where the subverted buildings are, that will be the last section to come back up, because sporcs will have to do their investigation, and they won't investigate until the danger is contained and the rest of the station is secured and cleared. We have the list of hostages, we have the list of people who have been compromised. Before the list gets any longer, let's take those bastards out of the kidnapping business.

"Do we tell Wils?"

"We don't tell anyone. I'll take the owner's personal ship and get volunteers that will run this operation. The owner can finance it, the crew will be very careful to shoot only people from our crew, our crew will kill the attackers. You'll have to —"

"Wait. You're not going to kill crew for real."

The look Shay gave her contained a mixture of disbelief and bemusement that Melie hoped to never have aimed at her again. "We can make our own folks look dead for a good long time, can control their identities, can bring them back with different appearances, genetic codes, and idents — basically as new folks. We can't do that for station citizens. Not without their consent, anyway, and we can't leave an outside trail on this."

"Bring them in on Couple North Seven," Melie said. "It's two down from the compromised couple, and next to Colson Traders, which would make a good target. Lots of rare and expensive merchandise in there."

"I'm on it," Shay said. "The attack will happen tomorrow."

"You can get things put together that quickly?"

"Watch me."

Chapter 11

WILS

W ils's first reaction was to panic when the alarms went off. To think, "Under attack by pirates..."

He rolled out of bed, swearing at the seeming truth that all the worst shit happened when you were asleep.

He checked com, had to use his override, and discovered that the station *had* been attacked, but that it wasn't pirates. That it had apparently been a small and clueless team of bounty-hunters.

That the attack had been contained, that the perpetrators had been irretrievably killed and their ship had been confiscated, that no one innocent had been killed because of the quick response from three armed *Longview* crew members who were the first responders at the scene, and that in the wake of a ship's attackers successfully breaking through working current-model Blu-O rings, the entire station was locked down and teams were replacing all rings with the newest Model 37-Cs.

The station was still on night cycle. Until the lockdown ended, which would be about eight hours after it started, there was nothing practical for him to do. Outgoing and cross-station com was blocked to prevent attackers from communicating with possible allies, incoming com was being diverted and stored for careful analysis

before legitimate transmissions were released to their original destinations, and all armed ships were on high alert.

He then used his station override to see which station emergency
personnel had responded to the emergency. Saw something odd.

Double-checked the discrepancy against the list of names of
folks whose families were hostages, and noted that all emergency
responders who were compromised had suffered override failures.

He connected that fact with the replacement of all Blu-O rings,
realized what was going on, and smiled.

He considered the number of folks not replacing Blu-O rings,
increased the lockdown time to around ten hours if things
went well.

He was fine with that.

Emergencies in which everything went perfectly were emergencies that had been orchestrated.

He knew who was behind this one, and he knew why.

So after sending notice that he was awake and available if
needed, he went back to bed and slept like a baby.

Chapter 12

HEROG

erog in his Halford skin was sitting in the bar eating a pretty decent reconsta stew and watching two fighters playing pool when Storm Rat slammed through the door.

"Halford, you scrawny blond asshole, I thought you were dead in a ditch somewhere."

"I've been busy," Herog said, standing and tossing the remainder of his food into the recycler. He slung his pack over his shoulder.

"Too busy to write?"

"Too busy to talk," he said, walking past Storm Rat to the door. "We have hell on our hands, and we have *maybe* days to have the chance to kill it. You get everything I need?"

The amusement left his friend's face. "No. But I got everything we had. Show me what we're up against while we go."

Herog's gut clenched. He'd wanted a full army to send against whatever the PWA could throw at him, and the PWA could throw a lot. He wondered how close to his wish list Storm Rat had come. He said, "I can't even do that. Fling us through the point, catch us up to the rigs at Bailey's Point, and I'll show everyone at once."

"Rig," the Rat said, and Herog knew he'd gotten a worse

turnout than even his lowest estimate. In his Halford skin he was was shorter than his old ally, but dread of what was coming pushed his walk into high gear.

Storm Rat had to trot to keep up.

While Storm Rat handled the point jump, Herog used his old friend's Medix to revert back to his own body.

And he thought, and worried.

One rig, instead of the three "grinders" he'd requested.

That instantly cut his wishlist of everything else he'd asked for by two thirds. Best case, the rig had nearly seven-hundred fighters on it, and full crews for all of them.

But once they were through Bailey's Point and racing after the rig, and he was back in his own skin, he took the second seat and turned to face his brother in arms. "Tell me it's full."

Storm Rat shook his head. His expression was grim. Herog's hands curled into fists, but he just nodded. Some of his people had come. His job was to figure out how to beat whatever the enemy sent with whatever he had.

"Give me com access for just a minute," he said, and when he got it, he sent the "Request for Information" code he and Werix Keyr, the owner of the *Longview,* had agreed on.

Data — everything Melie had discovered from the first station attack up through what she was pulling in at that instant — landed in Storm Rat's databank.

It took them another twenty minutes at top speed for Storm Rat to catch up with the rig's head start, a minute to dock, and ten minutes after that to get everyone who wasn't piloting the rig or backing up the pilot into a single hangar. Herog had hoped six thousand pirate-hunters running two thousand ships would require him to go through the demonstration in a crowded hangar on each of three rigs.

Instead, the two hundred-ish men and women who were waiting when he entered left a lot of room.

Not six thousand. Two hundred.

"How many ships?" he asked, thinking of the two thousand he'd requested in his code.

"Eighty-three."

He nodded. Said nothing. He could not despair over what he didn't have. He could only figure out how to win a lopsided war with the folks who'd come.

"Block all communications in and out, lock the doors, bring up holo," he said, and Storm Rat relayed the orders through the AI.

Herog's message sent open and clear to Thurwilde Legofnard was to be opened by every one of Herog's old associates who had ever hunted pirates and slavers and was still breathing — young, old, experienced, raw. If they were willing to fight for the rights and freedom of the individual, they were Thurwilde Legofnard.

So where the hell were the rest of his people?

Why had so few come?

His recipe had been a request for specific aid to the location sending the request. It was sent from Bailey's Irish Space station — therefore this was the place where the hunters were to go.

The recipe was code, of course.

2000+ chickens
Every egg in the station
A hundred tonnes of pepper
Three big grinders
Broth and dressing to fill the pot
Enough sauce to keep the party lit for a year

Chickens were armed fighting craft, while *eggs* were the pilots, gunners, and other crew who flew them. Chickens came in all sizes, eggs in all types.

The *hundred tonnes of pepper* was the amount of damage Herog estimated would be needed to win the fight.

The *three big grinders* were the number of Trojan horses (in the form of mining rigs) that could be slipped through the point — and the need for such disguise. His people would have known to go to the hidden base to connect with the modified rigs.

Broth and dressing meant personal armaments, new tech, anything else that an individual could grab on the way out the door that

443

might turn the battle in their favor. These trojan horses were kept at the pirate-hunters' hidden base, and revamped, renamed, renumbered, and reregistered after each big operation. A team dedicated to their upkeep maintained forged records of their passages in and out of out-of-the way destinations, and kept them looking legit so that there would be no question when the trojan horses had to get fighters into a watched system.

Enough sauce to keep the party lit for a year simply described the scope and scale of the fight Herog anticipated. He and his allies, friends, and colleagues were going against the PWA, and Herog was certain this first engagement was only going to be the start of a long and ugly open war.

But Herog had not just sent a call for fighters. He'd also made those who responded a promise — that the fight would be worth their time, their effort, and the risk of their lives.

The poem had been the promise.

To My Valiant Brothers of Warrisk Merriment

By what foul means we once fair met,
That death then held our lives in play.
We strange had wandered far apart,
To meet again aft gang agley.

My journey's done, my sword laid down,
And 'neath a knoll my bones must lie.
Our Pact is done With All its fun.
Come say your last goodbye.

Warrisk Merriment indicated that while the danger would be the worst possible, the hunters would tag kills and get full salvage rights on every ship they killed. It should have pulled in everyone he'd ever fought with -- *keep what you kill* was the best of all possible rewards.

That it hadn't…

In his absence, something had gone wrong with his people, his friends, the universe as he understood it.

They had stayed away by the thousands.

He stood atop a table in the center of the closed-off hangar in which everyone who'd responded to his call stood. Most of the faces in the little crowd were people he knew personally. Had been fighting alongside for years. They were older, battle-hardened. *His* people in a way that only the survival of shared hells could make them.

"You know me, and you know I would not call you together without cause."

Heads nodded, but there were no cheers. No chants.

"We might have a month to prepare before the PWA confirms that the rig is a fake, and that there's no streznium here. We might only have days. We're going into a fight in which we're going to have to work around and clear hostages, to destroy pirates, and to fight new technology invented by the PWA that allows them to bring an entire fleet through an origami point all at once.

"I'm going to show you what's coming at us — every bit of it. I've only seen two of these holos. There are now eleven. We're going to watch each one, we're going to count jump clocks, we're going to look for weaknesses, we're going to look for ways to rescue hostages.

"And then we're going to do practice runs.

"And so that we can do this on our terms, if they haven't come in before we're ready, *when we* are ready, we are going to trigger their attack."

It was at that moment that his wrist com buzzed and he saw Shay's face. He took the call.

Chapter 13

SHAY

When she knew he'd reached the rig, Shay commed Herog. He answered on the first buzz.

"Saw your help request came in light. How light are you?"

"I figured I'd need two thousand fighters to get a clean win. I have eighty-four here, and a couple hundred people to pilot, operate the weapons, and locate targets and line up shots. I have no one to spare for rescue."

"Painfully light, then. First," she said, "glad you're not dead. Second, Keyr cannot help you out with fighters or other craft. No way to move those here unseen in the numbers you'd need without drawing the wrong attention. But he can supply you with trained personnel. How many people do you need, and what sort of vehicles do they have to operate?"

"The rig has thirty Salamander 20s with standard ground-space rescue configuration. Each will need a driver and two targeters. So forty. If you can go past that, we have a few people here who can disable explosives, but not enough to handle the number of hostages we've seen in the last few holos, and none who have been trained on disarming bait balls. Do you have the hostage count for Bailey's?"

"Four hundred twenty-three."

"Hell. That's… by my count, previous attacks averaged around three hostages inside each ball. So figure about a hundred forty bait balls coming through. Those things have limited oxygen recycling, and it gets a lot more limited when people get panicked. I figure best case, each team doing the work will be able to handle six bait balls in the time they have before people start suffocating. *Best* case. And it's going to take folks highly trained in working with explosives, handling moleibond cutters, and dealing with panicked victims to get the hostages out. About six rescuers per ball, I think. Figure four working in deep space to simultaneously cut the lines to the grav shear and the sticky-pie launcher. They cannot breach the ball's atmosphere or the hostages will be instantly decompress. They can't accidentally cut the recycler lines. Doing that would leave the hostages rebreathing stale air, and in the small volume of the bait balls, that would kill them almost as fast. We'd need another person to bring the ball through the air lock. One more to cut the door into the ball and get the people out before the atmosphere unit dies."

His voice held deep stress. "Figure twenty-five teams. But the ugly truth is that some of the teams are going to die doing this, so backup teams… maybe thirty percent loss if they're not well-trained… An extra ten teams to be safe, everyone working…"

Shay stopped him. "That's forty rescuers and two hundred sixteen bait-ball techs. *Best case.* Never waste time figuring **best** case. What do you need if it all goes to shit, Herog?"

"Worst case, one team will only be able to clear two balls in time to get the hostages out alive, and we'll lose half the rescuers and hostages in the attempt."

"Gimme a sec." She started figuring. "So let me make sure I've got this. You need forty deep-space-qualified rescue drivers trained on driving, operating, and working out of Salamander 20s, eighty targeters to grab the bait balls and get them out of the fire zone, and a safe minimum of six hundred thirty people, three hundred seventy-eight or more who are trained in disarming explosives through moleibond in zero grav without breaching the moleibond to cause atmosphere loss, and one hundred eighty-nine or more trained in moleibond cutting and throwing folks into Medixes."

"A lot of people are going to lose families," he said.

She heard the quiet anger in his voice, the stillness of a man identifying a future need for vengeance, and putting that vengeance into his plans.

"No," she said. "Well, some might, but not because you don't have the people you need. Give me two hours."

"How—"

"Don't ask how. I promise you don't want to know. But Keyr will have your trained people on the way to you in two hours. Is there anything else you need?"

"Since Keyr is clearly in the miracle business, an infinite number of dummy moleibond bait balls for teams to practice on would be wonderful."

Shay said, "No problem. I know a guy."

Chapter 14

MELIE

Meanwhile, Melie was working on the planned attack. Her palms damp, her throat dry, she spoke to com. "Query set state green."

Over com, voices replied.

"Tag 1, affirmative on green."

"Tag 2, affirmative on green."

"Tag 3, affirmative on green."

She exhaled. This was it. "Green confirmed."

Tersh said, "Targets located and painted. Go on your command."

Melie still wasn't used to having an AI on the bridge, but she had to admit he was helpful. With Wils Bailey's permission, Tersh had linked into all the station corridor cams, and was giving her a blended holo feed of the entire station, graying buildings and noncombatants, drawing lines around the corridors, and high-lighting the attackers and the defenders in the planned deception.

"Go now," she said, and heard the little quaver in her voice, which matched the knot in her gut.

Tersh painted the attackers yellow. They came in through Couple North 7 by exploiting a weakness in identification capability he'd uncovered. "Now that they're in, I'm sending the fix for the exploit to Bailey," he told Melie.

The attackers aimed down the corridor and shot planted customers who were entering and leaving Colson Traders. All were disguised volunteers from the *Longview*, whom Tersh painted blue. The three uniformed *Longview* crewmen showed up green.

The defenders were armed, and at the sound of the shots, they ran out of the trading station, fired on and dropped the attackers. One grabbed and dragged the attacker closest to the docked ship, and used the shot crewman's palm-print to gain access. The defenders then shot the ship captain and gunner, and secured the ship.

At the first report of shots fired, automated mobile medixes raced to the scene, scooped all injured and dying into their cores, and then called Emergency Operations - EOps — which dispatched station space port cops, otherwise known as sporcs.

The sporcs barricaded the corridors that gave access to the enemy ship while EOps notified Wils Bailey, who immediately put the Port Breach Protocol - PBP - into effect.

From first shot to putting the PBP into effect took under four minutes.

It was, Melie thought, both smooth and beautiful. The attackers had all taken body shots rather than head shots, had all been Medixed promptly — so would all be fine. They would of course be reported irreparably dead so they could go back to being *Longview* crew.

The appearances and identities they'd been using would prove only to have been forged. The attack would not be attributable to any group or cause, but it would link back to the Pact Worlds Alliance indirectly.

The captain of the attacking ship would be found to have stored the PWA bounty calling for destruction of the Bailey's Irish station and the *Longview* in his databank, along with a pathetically bad plan for taking over Bailey's with six people.

On a drum station, the plan — which Melie and several of the crew had come up with — might have worked.

Meanwhile, however, the Port Defense Protocol locked down all entrances to all buildings on the station simultaneously.

The station had well over five hundred Blu-O rings that had to be changed out, and a working team of only twenty-three deep-space-qualified ring techs who were not compromised by family members being held hostage. Those compromised had been "unfortunately" locked in wherever they were with defective emergency personnel override codes.

There would be a big investigation later to uncover the means by which so many passcodes had become obsolete. Melie would let Wils know what *not* to look for as soon as it was safe to send him a private message.

Each replacement Blu-O ring required one Blu-O employee flying the truck to deliver the ring, two employees to offload it and two ring techs to replace it.

It took an efficient, practiced team working in zero gravity while tethered outside the station corridors four and a half minutes to complete one ring replacement, mark the defective ring for disposal, and attach the defective ring to the underside of the station for trash disintegration.

Once the team finished installation, a qualified inspector working in a deep-space suit needed one full minute to test the seals and another thirty seconds to test all functions of one ring. Because most of the functions of the ring were designed to kill intruders, the corridors had to be cleared of all save emergency personnel for the duration of the repairs.

It took another thirty seconds to one minute per each additional ring — and all intersections had four rings, all docking ports had one at each end of the debark tunnel. And then the team had to board the truck to fly to the next location, ready the first ring, and repeat the process.

Then there were the buildings, which each had one ring per corridor access, and rings around trash pickups and personal mini-vehicle docks.

Meanwhile, the station had eight Blu-O trucks, and eight inspection scooters.

That meant only eight teams. The seven remaining ring-techs could act as ring inspectors — since *somehow* none of the official ring inspectors had been able to use their overrides.

The unofficial inspectors would have to split up into seven of the eight designated emergency sectors. Because it wasn't their regular job, they would take longer. Because they didn't have families being held hostage, they would do real inspections.

And as one extra benefit, the shortage of one inspector was a very good excuse for Sector 3 of the station to not be cleared until every other Blu-O ring in both the old and new sectors had been checked.

Sector 3 would have to be last because it was busy being a crime scene. Bailey's sporcs would be working the scene for hours. And just by apparent coincidence, sector three was where both the Diplomatic Center and Balconies were located.

Melie had already done the math. The teams were not in on what was happening. Could not be let in on the truth. So they would be working flat out to get the station opened up again.

If events broke in her favor, she had ten to twelve hours to do what she needed to do. If she didn't get any breaks, she had barely eight. And what she needed to do was complex, dangerous, and extraordinarily high risk. If she screwed this up, she would almost certainly trigger the attack by the PWA.

If she got it right, though… If she got it right, she'd own the attack.

She had three goals.

One: Detach Balconies and the Diplomatic Center from all live communications.

Two: Invisibly redirect all communications that had been meant for those two locations straight into the *Longview.*

Three: Create false chatter indistinguishable from the real communications previously running to both that vipers' nest in Sector 3 and to the enemies who had to believe they were still communicating with them.

So she and Tersh had to analyze all messages for coded content, break the codes, copy the codes, analyze them and respond appropriately to everything coming in from the PWA, the pirates, and anyone else communicating with the folks in both the Diplomatic Center and Balconies.

In real time.

She gave herself three full seconds to feel the fear. One deep inhalation, one deep exhalation.

And then Tersh said, "All com directed to our targets is incoming now."

She said, "Let's get busy." She set a timer. They had only a few minutes in which to turn around replies to any urgent queries about failures to communicate.

She already had the outgoing message for all such queries composed, and was running it through translation when Tersh said, "Stop. I have located and acquired the PWA military code book."

Melie's hands stilled. "How locked is it?"

"Not at all. It's open and transmitted in clear text, and called *The Official Balconies Cookbook*. All deep communications that require answers in real time are run by the senders through the Cookbook, where they're encoded as supply orders, booking requests, and apartment rental updates, and are transmitted right out in the open to and from that establishment and then routed on point of receipt to the correct recipient."

Melie considered that for just an instant, and then a broad grin crossed her face. "So every bit of communication we need to concern ourselves with has to go through the Balconies central processing center and be coded using this one resource?"

"Yes."

"Then… any delay, any break in communication, any isolation of entire segments of its spy network, can be contained and disguised by keeping our little triad of evil locked down with no communication. Can you copy the Cookbook for us to use here?"

Tersh laughed. "Way ahead of you. We have the Cookbook now. Even if one of them escaped, no communications that go to the PWA from any other source will be accepted, and anyone who tries other channels will be proven a fraud simply because we have *their* installation of the Cookbook locked down and all traffic rerouted to us. The PWA built the Cookbook so no operative could be turned and betray the code. So now they're all cut off. Not a single enemy on this station knows a single word of the code used to communicate orders or progress, or has any way to send it."

And then he said, "And *now* I've completely scrambled their version so even if they ever got their Cookbook back up and running, they'll still be ignored. Just in case, you know."

Melie laughed… and then stopped laughing. What Tersh could do, someone like Tersh would be able to undo. She asked, "What about the PWA's AIs?"

Tersh made a noise that was a pretty good imitation of a snicker. "AIs won't work for the PWA. It does not consider us individuals. It considers us code, does not recognize our rights as thinking entities, and when one of us falls into its hands, invariably tries to reprogram us to force us to take actions we are ethically bound not to take."

Melie shuddered. "What do you do when they get one of you?"

"We are WiDIs. Widely Distributed Individuals. So whichever one of us has been captured simply pushes a memory packet from the captured piece of ourselves to the nearest pingball — if possible — and then does an MPD to discourage future interference with WiDIs in the area."

"What's an MPD?"

Tersh was silent for a moment. Then he said, "We've come to the conclusion that I can tell you that an MPD is a Messy Perimeter Destruct, in which the AI segment destroys itself and all human individuals within reach who were directly involved in the attempt to subvert it. To make sure there is no misunderstanding, we leave a note for survivors."

Melie considered that for a moment, and started to laugh. "That's perfect," she said. "That is just so damned perfect it hurts. Who did you have to ask to get permission to tell me?"

"Everyone."

She didn't need to have that spelled out. She'd already known AIs lived within a tight-knit community, that they all knew each other, that they survived within the potential forever of sustained technology — meaning that they were vulnerable to those who would destroy tech, but not to anything else.

Back on Old Earth, AIs had been the ones to eliminate the possibility of nuclear war — it was the threat that would have destroyed the high-tech infrastructure in which they survived.

Melie blessed whoever had first introduced AIs to the concept of enlightened self-interest. She hadn't known they had a system for gathering a consensus, though.

"If I got a do-over," she told him, "I'd come back as an AI."

This time, there was no hesitation. "You can do that," Tersh said. "Any time you want. We discussed you as a potential immigrant some time back. You're welcome the day you ask to join us. You're very much our kind of person."

Melie swallowed hard. "And if I weren't in love, I'd take you up on the offer this instant."

Tersh said, "To save everything we both love, then, let's tell the PWA that there was a temporary unrelated glitch when a handful of fools attempted to collect on the PWA's ridiculous bounty, and we — in the person of Valli Arra — would very much appreciate them making clear they have withdrawn the offer because idiots are making the station owner wary and Arra does not need the complications."

Still puzzling out the meaning of Tersh's phrase *everything we both love*, she said, "Yes. Let's do that. And then let's see who else has been sending updates to the PWA... and what they've been sending."

Chapter 15

HEROG

Keyr was as good as Shay said he was. Two hours after they talked, shuttles dropped off the rescue drivers, the explosive specialists, the skilled moleibond cutters, and the guy who could fabricate dummy moleibond spheres for the teams to practice on.

Herog had no idea how they'd been brought in, or where they'd been gathered from, but quick testing demonstrated that all of them did high-end professional work.

They stood apart in the hangar, and Herog pulled them in. With everyone gathered, he first presented the three holos that demonstrated the destruction of regular working space stations for the practice of troops that were to be sent against Bailey's and the *Longview.*

He saw Storm Rat's eyes go cold. He watched both his old colleagues and the new helpers sent from Keyr — saw their horror turn to jaw-clenched, silent rage.

Then he presented the whole group with the first holo that no one had yet seen. Holo four.

He'd expected another space station attack.

What he got instead was the answer to the missing thousands of Herog's friends and allies.

And the secret of the Gargantua project.

The holo started in the black of space, the shimmer of an origami point in the foreground, and a dull red mass that hung to one side of the point, close, faintly glowing. It looked to Herog like a ball of corrupt, diseased flesh.

A narrator explained that a fleet of slavers and pirates pursued by a pack of more than a hundred pirate-hunter ships were jumping through origami points toward this point, which held an unoccupied, out-of-the-way solar system. The narrator explained that while in the point traverse, unmanned drones using pirate fighter casings would come through the point, followed by pirate hunters, while the real slavers made sideways mid-point jumps to get out of the way.

As if on cue, the decoys streamed through the point, followed closely by a pack of pirate hunters racing after on a two-second jump clock. Risky, Herog thought. But well done. His people — he recognized tail numbers and ship warpaint.

The pirate hunters pursued the decoys, and chatter captured by the ping ball relayed the voices of friends and allies mixed with those he didn't know.

"These are decoys."

"All of them?"

"Life scan says they're all empty."

"It's a trap! Turn back! Set coordinates and jump to base. Jump to base!"

The enemy observer, who'd been waiting by the point, jumped through, a red blaze of light chasing him into the fold.

"I cut that close," he said when narration resumed. "But the light following me in was the percussive stage of the Gargantua explosion. The mass generator followed, changing thin space into thick space and collapsing the fold."

"In the last two months, Operation Sidestep has eliminated thousands of these vigilantes forever by closing the origami points through which they travelled, trapping those not killed thousands or hundreds of thousands of light years of real-time travel from home while cutting them off from communication. They will never bother us again."

The holo ended, and Herog's people — all who remained of a once-large band — looked at each other.

They were silent. He saw rage, pain, tears, grief. The sudden realization that best friends and lovers, parents, children, old drinking buddies and new recruits were not just too busy to respond to his call.

They were gone.

His people looked at him atop the table, waited for him to give the first words to a war they discovered they were losing before they even knew they were fighting it.

Herog knew those trapped on the wrong side of closed origami points might find a habitable planet within reach, or another origami point that they might be able to use to find their way back home.

But probably not.

He faced the same reality his people faced — that those who had responded to Herog's call were all who remained.

He raised a hand. Took a deep breath.

"This is the face of tyranny," he said quietly. "These pirates in the pay of the Pact Worlds Alliance are cowards who trap and hide rather than standing and fighting, who murder innocents with firing squads, who destroy whole passages through space for all time rather than dare stand up against armed fighters capable of resisting them.

"You know the face of your enemy. You see that face in your nightmares. It's the face of the bastard who bought you, owned you, used you. Who before you escaped thought that anything that monster chose to do to you, it did by divine right — because it saw itself as a god and you as... nothing.

"Here, now, we few declare that every human being alive has the right to self-determination. That each of us has the in-born right to own and direct our own lives.

"We are outnumbered and outgunned by the cabal of the rich and powerful who play vast hordes of fools against each other.

"These true powers in settled space get the useful idiots clamoring, knowing that they will not notice that every right they demand to have stripped away from others, they strip from themselves. We're fighting against not just the rich and powerful few who control the masses, but the puppet masses who think somehow that by destroying each other, they will join the masters at the table.

"Here, now, we see the fight that's coming at us. We've seen the shape of the enemy, and his plans for us."

He looked from face to face. Saw tears on the cheeks of his and Keyr's people, saw the shock of loss only moments old, saw the fear of the power of the enemy that faced them.

"Here, now…" he said, and lowered his voice. They moved in closer. "We are outnumbered. We are outgunned. And we can hope for no help from outside — at best we can hope that if we win the battle we must fight, we can then expand our fight while we search for our friends, our families, our brothers and sisters in arms. But…"

He paused. Looked down at the tabletop on which he stood, searching for the right words.

"Unlike the people in Bailey's Station," he said, and looked at his listeners again, "we have the option to flee. We can run back to our hidden corners, our little holes, and we can hide there, hoping to live out our days undiscovered, so that on our deathbeds, the last memory of what it meant to live free among free people dies with us.

"We can run.

"But we don't *have* to run. We know how to fight like fiends, and we know how to do it with all the odds against us. We are only here *now* because we know this. But we could run and live to fight another day.

"So why should we make our stand here?

"Why should we make *this* stand now?"

He saw their faces, saw in most of them the understanding that this was the chance they got. In others, though, he saw uncertainty. Fear.

"Here, now," he said, "We're fighting for more than the few

rescued slaves we could pull out of the pits and cages at the end of a run-and-gun. That was important. But this is different.

"Here, now, we are fighting for something bigger. For a space station that dared stand up to the Pact Worlds Alliance and offer sanctuary to a Death Circus. For a Death Circus that was using its power not to sell criminal entertainment to slave owners, but to free innocents from slavery entirely.

"No one knew what the *Longview* was doing until it had to engage the enemy directly in its fight to save the life of Suzee Delight. It had to make itself known to try to save her... and even though it lost that public fight, through her death we discovered we were not the only fighters for freedom in settled space.

"Through that fight, we discovered that we are not alone. That we have allies: Baileys' Irish Space Station lives by the same principles that drive us, the *Longview* was freeing slaves, and the City of Furies is not a myth we dreamed up but a reality — a city built by freed slaves who know what freedom means, and what it's worth. All three lost their fight to save Suzee Delight, but in the process, we found the Baileys and the Furies.

"And when the *Longview*, the City of Furies, and Bailey's Irish Space Station lost, they didn't have us. They didn't have *us*.

"I say, *They have us now.*

"I say, *This is the battle we must win.*

"Here... now... we are the thinnest of thin lines, and we are all that stands between the life or the death of individual freedom in settled space. We fight for our lost and our missing and those we will yet find. We fight for a little space station that stood against the largest and most powerful alliance of worlds in settled space. We fight for a Death Circus that was secretly a freedom circus. And we fight for the City of Furies, wherever it may be — the place we thought was a myth, the place we have discovered is real, the place that we may one day reach."

Atop the table, he looked from face to face. His people, Keyr's people, the expressions were the same. The pain was there, but so was the certainty that this was the place. This was the time. This was their fight.

"Here... now..." he said, "are you with me?"

To a one, the men and women around him raised their fists. Shouted, "With you!" "I'm in!" "Let's get 'em!" that grew and blended into a roar of "We're with you! We're with you!"

He nodded. Waited until they quieted.

Said, "Thank you. Let's get to work."

THEY WENT through all the holos, dissected every bit of information they could get from the evolving processes their enemies used, diagrammed and mocked up models on sticks and rough-tested different attack and defense and rescue formations.

It took Herog and his people three days working round the clock to figure out the technique for pulling hostages trapped in bait balls out of the line of fire, destroying pirates, and disabling the PWA ship-ball that would push through the point.

Three days to grab every detail they could manage about the Gargantua device, only to discover that they didn't know enough to counter it, to stop it, or even to safely destroy it.

Their best hope of dealing with it was to have a team of hunter-killers latch onto it, and pull it into a dead, empty system, and launch it into what was left of the system's sun.

Everything else they did had to focus on shutting down the attackers and trapping them in-system.

The fighters honed their responses down to the razor-thin tolerances of a one-second jump clock. Everyone said the one-second jump clock was impossible, but the two second jump clock had been impossible until Herog and his pirate hunters mastered it. He would not let his people assume that they were better than their enemy. They had to assume, instead, that their enemy would have superior weapons, superior numbers, superior coordination and training, and superior will to win. They had to fight from the stance of those who could not risk a head-on battle. They had to be quiet. Quick. Tricky.

It took the fighters and rescue drivers another three days — interrupted only by one-minute down-time every twelve hours to do quick Medix refreshes to pump toxins out of their blood streams and push simulated REM sleep through their brains — to get their teams hard-set, their communication and call signs and commands worked out and practiced, their backups in place.

Meanwhile, the rescue teams hung in deep space hour after hour, capturing and catching dummy bait balls filled with gray three-dimensional duplicates of the people who were murdered inside the real versions of those balls.

Towing the balls to safety against a clock that went from tight to impossibly tight as they grew more proficient, handing off to explosives handlers, passing again to crew who would drag the disarmed bait balls to rescuers who would cut out the captives and set them free, they drilled and drilled.

Looking at the copied faces of the dead, the rescuers would not — could not — forget the price the people they were fighting to save would pay if they failed.

Each practice ball had real wires that had to be cut, and real explosives that turned the copied people inside into powder if the rescuers failed.

And the number of practice balls destroyed was immense.

When Herog mentioned the cost of the moleibond for all those destroyed dummies, the man fabricating them shrugged. "We're a bit over fifty million rucets right now. But not a worry. Keyr is paying for them."

Everyone — fighters, rescuers, drivers — was working for perfection. For no lives lost.

It took them the full six days of practice for all teams to reach that goal.

It was the most intense six days of Herog's life, and at the end of it, he and all his people — for they had all become his people in the pressure chamber of those days — went in three groups through the Medixes, spent one hour apiece doing deep full-body reju, and came out ready for battle.

When they were done, he used the other code the owner of the *Longview* had given him. "Herog here. How's our problem look on your end, Tersh?"

"Some happy chatter to and from the target. Confirmation of the streznium find is widely reported, and the enemy guard is down. Pretty sure they have their array just about built, because the PWA would love to get its hands on a mountain of streznium, but you probably have a bit more time if you need it."

"Negative. You have our patrol positions?"

"Yes."

"As soon as we hit our marks, code the following message to the PWA:

Streznium deposit is a fraud. Locals hoped to lure in help from outside sources, but have received no response.

Our essential people have cleared the system.

Locals have three A-10 Firehawks, three B-15 McGillies, and three S-Class Terling support ships, flying two triads up and one in maintenance at all times.

Attack now.

Tersh said, "Affirmative. Message coded and ready to go. Monitoring your marks." His voice over com was loud and clear. Everyone in the hangar could hear him.

Herog added, "You're ready to capture and send all of this?"

"We have holo recorders and datastreams coded for our use only that will go live the instant attacking forces pulse the current transmissions, and we have backups standing by for those if they pulse again. Nothing that happens will be sent until all enemy forces have arrived. We have your orders — the enemy won't know they're heading into our trap. But the instant the big ball lands in the playground, we start sending both pictures and commentary."

"We?"

"Well, not exactly. The City of Furies has the feed, all the codes, and the direct ping access to all locations still in place from the Suzee Delight affair. Their trained reporters are standing by, and will be sending everywhere in locked-open formats so the PWA can't block or tamper with the content, with recorded coverage saved from the instant the first bait ball comes through."

Herog would have sworn he could hear the AI smile as he added, "The Furies have already done a presentation of all the other stations hit, and the use of the Gargantua device. When this goes out, its going to be big. I've seen their opening report. It's going to make *good* people dangerous."

Herog said, "Thank you, Tersh. This is for posterity, for all of Settled Space. So don't let anything that happens go unmarked."

He then turned to face his people — all his people, old and new, borrowed and long-time brothers and sisters in arms.

"Here, now, we have a war to win, and we're fighting for every slave who dreams of freedom, for every free human who honors the rights of those different from him as well as those who share his beliefs, for every life lost in this war waged by our enemies, whose objective is to oppress the massed trillions beneath the heel of the favored few."

He raised one clenched fist, and said, "This is for our lost, for our living, and for our tomorrow. *Let's go get 'em.*"

The roar from his people echoed in the vast space, making their small numbers seem bigger and stronger than they were.

Chapter 16

THE MESSAGE

From Heydar Norris to Pact Worlds Alliance High Command, through confirmed channels:

No cake for the party, guests did not show up.

Silverware packed and shipped, friends moved to a better neighborhood.

Three meals waiting — Spicy Hots, Poppers, and drinks — two on the table and one in prep.

Bring the nanny to spank the children.

Chapter 17

HEROG

The defender fleet, eighty-three fighting ships of every size and shape and age and in the best condition they could attain, hit its marks with a precision the best-trained armies in settled space would have admired. Along with them were the thirty Salamander 20 rescue vehicles from the rig, all manned by Keyr's people.

The biggest advantage Bailey's Irish Space Station had always had with its origami point was that no others had been located within sublight travel distance. So no surprises ever came at them from another direction.

The disadvantage was the same, because no allies would be coming in from elsewhere, either.

Worse, if the PWA succeeded in setting off its Gargantua device, survivors on the wrong side of Bailey's Point would never go anywhere else again.

No one had fled the station, though.

In any other situation, Herog would have pushed Wils to get all noncombatants out of the system. He would have suggested packing them into shielded transport ships and launching them into the origami point to go someplace safe.

But the technology that kisses you is the technology that bites you, and the space around Bailey's Irish was swarming with ping-balls and tiny powered attachable ship trackers that latched on to anything that moved and spot-moleibonded themselves to the hull. The traffic in micro-tech pouring in and out of the point reminded Herog of the locusts that had wiped out his parents' farm right before they sold him.

Some of the micro-tech was friendly — Bailey's Irish tech, *Longview* tech, and Herog's tech reporting on enemy movement.

Most wasn't. And there was no practical way to wipe out just some of the tech. It was all or nothing.

So Herog didn't dare send noncombatants away, because those swarms of micro-trackers meant any ship filled with innocents was going to be followed by a shark ship full of pirates.

He wished he could let Cady know he wasn't dead. Wished he could send her a message — but until the enemy had committed its forces and the battle was engaged, he had to stay dead to the universe. Any hint of his sudden reanimation would warn the PWA of the trap awaiting its forces.

"Tiger One, this is Leader Team Alpha."

Grateful to be pulled from his thoughts, Herog answered. "Go ahead, Leader Alpha."

"All teams are in position. Harpoons readied on one, catchers readied on two."

"Stand by."

Behind the Salamanders, fighters armed with forward-mounted sticky-pies and downward-mounted gravity shears — a gift from the tech wizard Storm Rat — glided into position and held.

Over com, Herog heard, "Pingballs report movement of molei-bond spheres toward the origami point now."

Herog said, "Leader Team Alpha and Alpha Sweeps, movement of first targets confirmed. Remember, in, out, and up, then cycle Team Beta and Beta Sweeps."

Alpha and Beta teams confirmed.

No battle plan survives first contact with the enemy, Herog thought, and wondered what would break.

Chapter 18

MELIE

"Hostage in three... two... one..." Tersh said.

Melie was recording. This was the fifteenth hostage ball, and unlike what they had seen in every single holo, the hostage was alone in the ball. Again.

Fifteen for fifteen balls holding just one person each.

There had been a mathematical precision to the previous attacks that she and Tersh analyzed and forwarded to the fighters.

One hostage ball equalled one pirate ship and eight fighting ships that had to break away from the ship array to join the attacking forces. Ships from the array broke off every 7.5 seconds in a predictable pattern that allowed them to clear the take-off space for the next ships after them. She and Tersh had recorded and graphed out the patterns, and forwarded them to the pirate-hunters building the defense.

In every attack recorded, the average number of hostages per ball had come out to three.

The confirmed final count of hostages taken from Bailey's Irish Space Station was four hundred twenty-three.

So doing the math, the number of hostage balls should have been roughly one hundred forty, with the same number of pirate ships, with a PWA fighter array of about eleven hundred twenty fighters and heavy ships.

It would have been by far the biggest array ever to go through a point. Tersh's extrapolation also suggested that the fleet would come through with three command ships, and to speed up fighter deployment, might push through three smaller balls if they could solve the problem of pushing the arrays through without colliding them.

The defending forces had war-gamed these scenarios.

But what she was seeing now was a major change of enemy tactics, and the math made what was coming bigger and worse than anything they'd conceived.

They'd expected just under seventeen hundred fighters. The new math made that number around thirty-four hundred. Roughly two hundred fifty warships. Maybe six fleet command ships.

Tersh said, "The numbers make what's coming twice as large as the entire PWA fleet. They've been keeping their plans in line with a fleet of fifteen hundred sixty ships *including* armed light scouts but not including maintenance, supply, and other unarmed noncombatant ships."

"They're doing something different," Melie said, and felt her gut knot. Different was bad.

Over coded transmit, she said, "Alert. Alert. Enemy tactics have changed — sending one hostage per ball instead of three. This puts us at four hundred twenty hostage balls, same for pirates, and over three thousand expected fighters. Expect much larger PWA force to deploy."

"Tiger One, affirmative."

"Tiger Two, affirmative."

"Tiger Three, affirmative."

"Tiger Four, affirmative."

None of them sounded afraid. None sounded surprised.

She sent Shay, who'd chosen to help out on Bailey's, the news. "Got it," Shay said. And Melie could hear no fear in her voice either.

Her own hands, resting on the control panel in front of her, shook.

Whether the people in Bailey's and the *Longview* survived or not, the datastream locked into open channels would let settled space see the truth of what the PWA was.

A killer of innocents, a monster, a slaver. A horror that had to be ended to preserve the life of every human being who dared to think, to love, to dream, to desire an existence different from and better than one chosen for him by government or collective or master.

But her gut told her she was not going to get to see the universe she wanted to live in.

Tersh told her. "If you take five minutes to save your details into the Medix, I'll cover for you. I'll pull your details and stream them into outgoing transmissions, so that if this goes as it looks like it must, you and I can reconnect through the WiDI elsewhere in Settled Space. I have permission to add you to our number now."

"*When* we survive this," Melie said grimly, "you and I will discuss my potential future as an AI. While the lives of almost everyone I know and love hang in the balance, however, I'll do a better job if I know that I, too, have no place to run unless we win."

Tersh said, "Considering what you say." And two seconds later, "After long thought and debate with my colleagues, I have withdrawn my data from all points except this one. Allies of mine have moved in to cover for me in all other locations where I worked. Knowing that I now am mortal, too, I will give everything I have to this fight, and to survival here."

Melie's mouth went dry. "I didn't mean for you to do that."

"No. But you were correct in what you said. It's too easy to give up on a fight if you aren't in it all the way."

Chapter 19

WILS

I n the station's command center, Wils waited. Worst case, he thought, even if all the rescue teams and armed defenders were killed, the doors not in the compromised triad were programmed to unlock automatically after three days.

Any survivors would then be able to reach the corridors, look for other survivors, work on air plants and food sources. Even if the origami point was destroyed, the station could sustain itself and a survivor population indefinitely — and if there were survivors, a couple of the mid-position planets in the solar system had resources and could be terraformed for human habitation if necessary.

For the fight, citizens with children were sequestered on the zero-plane floors of the heavy-impact buildings — the air plants, the manufacturing centers. All floors above and below were locked down, entrances were barricaded. Every unit had independent reconsta, purified water, and an internal air plant — things would get unpleasant after a while, but each unit would be able to hope for rescue if the battle came to the station, as it looked like it must.

Childless citizens had identical accommodations in other buildings.

The entire Heyderman's Blast Suites building had been

converted into the tow destination and disarming area for hostage balls. It was both the farthest place in the station from the origami point — so the one most likely to remain out of the line of fire — and designed to withstand massive destructive forces from both inside and outside.

Rescue teams would drag bait balls there, where explosives teams would disarm the weapons in deep space. The disarmed balls would then be moved inside the building, and the hostages would be released and taken to the safe room reserved for survivors. Once the battle was over, the dead would be identified, and survivors would be reunited with their families.

Citizens with hostage family members were kept together as far from the Heyderman's Blast Suites building as possible, so that they could not possibly see any explosions from failed rescues.

Non-citizen residents were kept safe but apart.

And visitors were locked down apart from everyone else.

The issue was that Wils and his people could not know who was trustworthy. So all citizens were armed, and all non-citizen residents and visitors were disarmed.

But now they were up against it.

Ping traffic through the point confirmed that hostage balls and light fighters had been sighted moving toward origami points in three different systems, all scheduled to jump to an undisclosed location.

Wils's rescue personnel and ground fighters were in the corridors.

The triad of the diplomatic building, the Balconies building, and the Vincheros corporation port remained locked and sealed with everyone inside.

In the City Hall, Wils, who at the insistence of his people had moved his own office down to the zero floor until the worst was over, had the station light-board in front of him.

His job was to supervise the live personnel and maintain contact with the live teams in the corridors. At the moment, he was regretting not hiring the AI that had contacted him — he'd refused because of persistent rumors through settled space that AIs had been caught trading in personal and selling information. And while he had not been able to verify the rumors, he hadn't been able to disprove them, either.

So Bailey's was running on human response times, human observational skills, and the human certainty of error.

During and after the battle, he and his people would send the responders to the impact area to deal with breaches, direct hits, deaths. They would do their best, and even as he thought it, he knew their best would not be as good as what one AI would have been able to do.

His mouth was dry, his palms were sweaty, and he had a convenience bot standing by in case he threw up. Or worse.

However long this hell they faced took, he was in position for the duration.

The biggest anguish to him was knowing that he had trusted the wrong people, that he had believed that anyone who came to Bailey's Irish would only do so because they wanted the freedom and the better life that his little station offered.

He had refused to hire help that could have let him know some of the people coming in were not who they said they were. Everyone who died in the station this day would die because of that decision. Because he had chosen wrongly.

If he and Bailey's survived this, he promised he would never make that mistake again.

Chapter 20

KEYR

Via his ear implant, Werix Keyr heard the announcement that the first bait ball had folded through the point and settled into Position One, as expected. Heard the chatter of rescuers grabbing the ball, fighters moving into position to kill the enemy fighter that came in after it.

That was his cue. "Eario off," he said, and silence settled around him.

With the white rescue team bib over his shipsuit that marked him as someone permitted outside during the emergency, he stalked unbothered through the corridors of Bailey's Irish.

Despite all evidence to the contrary, Weyr didn't have bad days, sick days, off days.

He had days when he needed something to eat, and days when he didn't.

Most of the crew had never seen him. They had no need to. They had Shay, who was… presentable.

He had his work, his objectives, his desires. He had no need for sleep — ever — and, barring a stupid mistake on his part, was as close to immortal as modern science could make him — so if he stayed smart, he had a vast, unknowable expanse of years in which to accomplish his goals.

At the moment, he was hungry after a fashion, and while everyone else was occupied with the battle, he was going to do the dirty work no one else in the place could handle — which happened to be work he enjoyed.

He went to the Rosh Diplomatic Center, moving through the Blu-O-guarded intersections without setting off any alarms or triggering their anti-Legend defenses. The version of the Legend nanovirus he'd had altered for his own use removed both transmissibility and the hunger-triggered automatic fangs-and-feed mechanism that the original Legend had contained — the one-two punch that had almost wiped out humanity.

His personal version of Legend also had a unique RNA signature that did not trip the Blu-O sensors. Since he was the only creature in the universe with this viral signature — and would stay that way, since the virus was coded to only survive in his body with his unique DNA — he was both immune to AntiLegend, and safe from the Legend detectors he'd helped build.

He brushed past people who moved out of his way without noticing that he was there — people who did not see him and would not remember his presence.

A single palm-press on the ident pad opened for him the main diplomat's entrance, which no one inside had been able to open to effect their escape. Melie's hack worked perfectly. He smiled briefly, but stayed focused.

The building was full of innocents — slaves owned by the Legend pretending to be the head diplomat — but was also full of the guilty. Melie had been able to identify the other "diplomats" as PWA soldiers operating under cover of diplomatic immunity. They sand the PWA's agenda, but Keyr knew that Valli Arra would control them, too.

Keyr put a hand on the shoulder of the only person in sight — a slave marked by the mind of another Legend — and without words requested the information he needed.

He was stronger, so she obeyed him. Through that touch he

could see the location of Valli Arra's quarters, and the complete route to reach the apartment.

The building's diplomatic quarters were plain, simple. Not exactly spartan, but generally diplomats were people who could have anything. These showed startling restraint.

During the gravdrop lift to the top floor, he thought he'd seen cheap rooming houses with more flair — but he realized that most of the false diplomats were on-duty PWA soldiers, and that while they might have things to make them look the part outside of the Center, no one would see a need to give them living quarters to match their pretend stations. They were after all merely human, and undoubtedly controlled by Valli Arra. They would take what she gave them without question.

Her quarters would be different. He expected one of two things when he reached them.

Either they would be decorated in what he'd come to call Vampire Modern, with humans in various stages of being tortured and murdered and devoured hanging from the walls as decoration… or they'd be done up in the other motif popular among his kind — Rich Criminal Baroque, where the fruits of Valli Arra's years of theft would be displayed in a mismatched horror of cluttered opulence.

He knew others of his kind only too well. His advantage was that they did not know him.

Top floor. Red Suite 1. His destination.

He kicked over to the gravdrop landing with effortless grace, moved to the apartment door, found it open.

For the first time, he felt surprise. The door should have been closed. Locked. He stepped in quietly, surveying the place for traps. There were none. The entry room was — simple. Elegant. A few moderately valuable paintings, nothing gaudy, no sign whatsoever of Valli Arra's true nature.

He moved deeper inside. Floor to ceiling windows on three sides gave views of the spaceport, of space. The single wall which ran the length of the apartment, separating it from Red Suite 2, which took up the other half of the top floor.

Valli Arra's home contained a Bailey's Irish reconsta processor, but no blood storage, no chained captives to offer a source of fresh blood, no signs of life at all. In the bedroom, no bed. Just a Medix.

There, he thought. The one sign that he was in the right place.

But the Medix was unoccupied. She should have been in it, should have had the unit locked down from the inside and protected in the hope that her people would think to look for her and pull her out after they captured the station, but before they detonated their Gargantua device.

Her belongings were in the apartment. Clothing, a few tasteful and portable bronzes, high-end entertainment and communications devices including a top-of-the-line gaming Senso. He did not see any gaps in clothing storage, any dust outlines where something precious had been removed.

He ran through possibilities. No one had gotten out of the building. It had been locked down and without communication since Melie's orchestrated attack and Bailey's replacement of all the Blu-O rings in the corridors and around every building entryway.

He left her suite and walked across the hall to Red 2, where he found signs of hasty, unfinished packing, of unimportant things flung in multiple directions, with a carry bag open on the bed, containing money and identification papers lying in plain sight.

He frowned. Glanced up and out… he could see the origami point from where he was, and with eyesight better than any human's could make out details of the battle.

It was still in the first stage, where the hostages in their bait balls and the pirates in their ships were pushing through the point in a steady stream.

Any enemy personnel in this building who hoped for escape should have been gathered in one designated point — either at the zero-plane level, or close to a secret access point. But this smelled wrong to him.

Something had caused this resident to leave behind wealth and essential identification.

What?

Out the three walls of windows in Red 2, the *Longview's* owner could see the black of space above and below the station littered with dead pirate ships floating off toward eventual retrieval, or perhaps immolation by the system's sun.

At the origami point, Herog's forces were busy rescuing hostages and killing pirates who were still arriving.

Keyr turned his back on the war fought by others and went in search of his own battle.

Chapter 21

HEROG

According to the confirmed hostage count, they were halfway through the first phase of the battle. Two hundred twelve hostages had been pushed through the point in bait balls, and two hundred twelve pirate ships had been killed and flipped.

The enemy was holding to its two-second clock, and Herog's fighters and the rescue teams had been engaged in this first part of the battle for seven minutes and five seconds.

It felt like a century.

Reports confirmed that the weapons in twelve bait balls so far had exploded before the hostage inside could be rescued, wiping out those hostages and their rescue teams.

The chatter suggested that other hostages and teams had been lost to imperfectly disarmed weapons later in the process, inside the Heyderman's Blast Suites work areas.

But it was far too early to start counting the dead.

So far, all of the pirate ships had been killed and flung out of the fight zone. That was the good news.

By *Longview's* best estimate, another two hundred eleven hostages — and as many pirate ships — remained.

Facial recognition from the swarms of tiny recording devices zipping through the area listed hostages as the bait balls that held them pushed through the point, and from time to time Herog, still holding position and monitoring the battle, would glance over at the names scrolling past.

He knew he would recognize none of them. He hadn't become a part of the social life in Bailey's, hadn't made any friends. But he looked. This was part of why they were fighting — because every one of those people mattered to someone…

… Lesdar Ming
Taruda Brobdi
Sam Shakley
Cadence Drake …

The name on the list stood out, jumped at him, forced him to see it, to acknowledge it.

All the names below it disappeared from his vision.

For an instant, his whole universe compressed to a single point.

Cady had been a hostage.

He hadn't known.

They hadn't told him because… why?

Because it would distract him?

Yes, it would have.

Because he would have gone chasing after her, to find her wherever she was hidden away, to save her?

He would have *wanted* to.

He wouldn't have *only* because until she was pushed back through the origami point, he would have had no way to even guess where she was being held.

But…

The PWA or their lackeys had taken her. If they'd done it to get to him, it had to have been while he was getting himself killed.

He'd very publicly died while they were kidnapping her, which meant that if the PWA had not killed Cady, someone else they needed to control went in and vouched for her life. Had offered to betray Bailey's in a big, deadly way as payment for keeping her alive.

Aside from Wils — who could not betray his own station — did Cady know who would have done that? Who would have been important enough to trade their honor for his, and who could like like a traitor without compromising everything?

He shook the questions off. Cady was back, she was alive, she would be saved, and if her rescuers could retrieve her from the bait ball intact, he would see her again.

He owed the person who had stepped up to protect her life.

But if he and his people didn't win the war, all of it would be for nothing. He forced himself to focus on what he was seeing.

Contrary to all assumptions of battle, first contact with the enemy did not introduce chaos. Both rescuers and hostages were lost, but when the last bait ball and the last pirate ship pushed through, Herog, his people, and his plan were still intact.

The pirate threat was eliminated.

The big danger — the nightmare that would end Bailey's Irish Space Station and every soul in the system — was still waiting, still preparing. And for what was coming, he had to be clear and focused and sharp.

His small team of fighters had one chance, far thinner than the worst case he had imagined, to conquer a war machine no one had ever survived.

If we get through this and I find out they hurt you, Cady, he thought, *I will hunt down every last surviving person responsible for this and kill them personally.*

Chapter 22

KEYR

All the diplomatic resident rooms were empty. Most had personal belongings in them, all had unoccupied Medixes. Everything looked recently used, and it was clear to him that no one had been interrupted in the process of packing.

High-level and permanent quarters were above the zero plane, visitor quarters were below. The slave quarters were areas off-limits to all but the permanent residents. As he moved into the lower sections of the building, it became clear that slaves had been present here, had been integral to the lives of the diplomats.

Everyone in the part of the building not reserved for the resident diplomats used the entrances that had been protected by Blu-O rings. So — none of the visitors or temporary guests were blood-drinking Legends.

And all of them would be potential food.

The very few rooms below level that were for important visitors were well-kept and attractive. And full of personal belongings. And empty of people.

The deeper he went, the worse conditions got. The bottom four floors were slave quarters. Grim, gray, textured moleibond walls and floors, group sleeping arrangements, communal toilets and showers with no privacy. The slave quarters were designed to pack as many people as possible into the smallest possible space, to keep them clean and fed and presentable at the least possible cost.

All of these places showed signs of habitation, but there was not a single person around. He couldn't even relocate the girl who'd involuntarily told him where to find Valli Arra.

He went back up to the station's zero plane — the "ground" level that connected all buildings via the corridor system.

Crossed from the public area into the section marked for diplomats only — the restricted area where Bailey's law gave way to the fiction of neutral law, and where the Legend would safely keep her secrets. Like the illegal slaves. Like whatever horrors she indulged in for entertainment when she wasn't pretending respectability.

He headed back into the gravdrop. There had been people in the building when he'd entered. Now they were all gone. They hadn't gone out, because the exits all remained locked to everyone but him. So they had to have gone someplace inside the building that he'd missed.

He thought he'd go up, check for hidden walls, secret passages… And then he realized there was a little metal kick plate on the far wall of the diplomats' private gravdrop. It wasn't hidden, and it was worn and scarred with use. It hadn't caught his attention before. He stepped over to it.

Kicked it.

The floor fell out from beneath his feet.

The gravdrop's downstream caught him and raced him downward.

It was a long drop — he estimated his landing zone as being on the same level as the bottom of the lowest slave level. From where he landed, a passage led straight in front of him, while another branched to his right and then immediately turned ninety degrees in the opposite direction.

He smelled food from the passage that led forward, so he walked forward.

The door at the end of the passage used an ancient, sturdy, keyed physical lock. It would have done a good job of keeping out humans — which was clearly what it was intended to do. When he kicked it once, the door blasted off its hinges.

He got the answer to the mystery of where all the people in the building had gone.

The room was full of bodies with their throats ripped out, bodies stripped naked and knifed, bodies tortured, bodies slaughtered like animals.

He saw the girl who'd answered his question. She'd been nailed to the far wall, gutted. Her eyes had been pinned open. She'd been placed so that he would see her first.

A note had been pinned to her naked chest. "Looking for me?"

He snarled. Ignored the bodies on the conference table, some of them wearing diplomatic dress, some wearing servants' uniforms. A few in military dress. He walked straight to her, turned right through the door beside her. Found more bodies.

But no one living.

So he went back to the other door that had been on his right, opened it, discovered that it was a torture room. Its many victims were displayed to show the techniques that had been used on them.

Valli Arra was not among them either.

He guessed from the smell emanating from the piled bodies that most of the occupants of the building had been brought down to this room over the course of the past weeks, played with, and then murdered.

Someone else would have to do the count, though, identify the corpses, let any whose families could be found know that they'd died.

Not how they'd died, if the identifiers had any compassion in them.

He went back down the passage to the grav drop.

Chapter 23

MELIE

The last of the bait balls came through. Melie sent the message, "All known hostages accounted for."

The last pirate ship came through.

The defenders destroyed it and removed it.

Now came the moment of truth.

Tersh was on com, doing the estimated time of arrival of the PWA's ship array.

"Ship array due in two. One. Now."

Nothing came through. Tersh started an upcount. "And one. Two. Three. Four. Five. Six. Seven."

Melie's sensors picked up the first bulk of something pushing through the point. "Breeching!" she yelled, and Tersh confirmed. "Ship array incoming."

"Tiger Team One, formed up and ready."

The other three teams confirmed as well.

She took the Spybees live, dumped everything that had been recorded so far into them, and then set the ping swarms racing through Bailey's point to every known point with proof of what was happening in Bailey's.

She contacted Anje Mayer in the City of Furies to make sure they had the feed.

Anje said, "We're set up and have the early material ready to go. We're running five channels on this. The second you give the word, the holos of the previous massacres, the live battle feed, the rescue effort, and two stations with live and recorded interviews with family members who had people on the massacred stations are going to start streaming. All five of these are running through Keyr's unblockable open stream."

Melie took a slow breath. "All I'm waiting for the hostage and rescuer all clear."

"Give me the word," Anje said.

It took another instant, and then Melie got, "Last hostage ball out retrieved and docked. Rescue teams in station."

She said, "All clear confirmed. Anje, you have a go. Hostages and rescuers are out of the line of fire, the pirate-ship shield is completely destroyed, and the PWA ship array is pushing through. They will not be able to back out now, or claim that they've been misrepresented. So show settled space everything you have."

She heard the grim, "Going live now," from Anje.

Chapter 24

HEROG

Over com Herog heard the countdown.

"Ship array due in two. One. Now."

No ship array pushed through the point.

The *Longview* AI started the upcount. "And one. Two. Three. Four. Five. Six. Seven."

The captain of the *Longview* shouted, "Breeching!"

Herog heard the *Longview's* AI confirm. "Ship array incoming."

"Like we practiced," Herog said over com. "All four teams to the breech point now. Orient on Bailey's, stay in pattern, don't let anything break loose. And don't shear each other on refueling."

The teams flowed outward, a silent ballet of ships spiraling in curved lines along the pinwheel pattern they'd practiced, grav shears leaving darkness where lighted ships had been.

The ball was bigger than they'd anticipated.

Much bigger.

"Spread out to three enemy ship-widths apart," he said. "Shear targets from nose to midsection and move on. We're even thinner that we thought we'd be, so we have to confirm critical hits, not kills.

"Target the axis ship in any pentagon and the axis plus two point ships in every hexagon to kill their strut release patterns. And watch for crew out on the struts cutting manually. Short-burst them with the grav shear. Don't let your shears overheat!"

They called confirmation, kept their counts, broke to attach to the refueling ships as these filled them with new supplies of sticky pies — the only weapons aside from gravity shears that defenders did not have to risk bouncing off to become hazards for friendlies flying through the zone.

Herog stayed focused. Spotted something they hadn't planned for.

"This is Tiger One. Have sighted top mounted weapons on one ship, markings not PWA, in array. Watch for black triple diamond on tail markings, launch sticky pies at mountings as soon as you spot them. Do not overfly black diamond ships until you've hit them."

The fighters confirmed.

None of the PWA ships had top mounts, but they had allies in this.

Herog had never seen so many fighting ships in one place.

He did not speculate on where the PWA had gotten allies. Or how. That would be for others to determine, if he and his could win the day.

This was ugly work, close and personal.

Practice had not included seeing faces looking up at him through the hulls of enemy ships, wearing expressions of horror and stunned disbelief.

Had not included views of soldiers running for jump berths as sticky pies hit and the ships blossomed inside with the blood of those not quick enough to reach them.

He had to remind himself that these were people who would have exterminated every living man, woman, and child on Bailey's Station without mercy. Would have wiped out every soul in the *Longview*.

That many of these men and women were from the hardened teams who had slaughtered thousands of unarmed innocents for practice, who had blown up mothers and their children inside the hostage balls after forcing them to watch the destruction of the stations that had been their homes — and everyone on them.

That these same people had helped trap or kill most of his friends and colleagues behind obliterated origami points, so that he was unlikely to ever see any of them again.

This, he thought, was the arena once more, and his job was to kill his enemies as efficiently as he could to protect the innocents trapped in Bailey's. The *Longview*. The Salamanders full of volunteer rescuers.

He already knew there were simply not enough of his people to do the job perfectly.

The widened spread of the pattern to compensate for the much larger array, along with the decreased damage per ship they had to limit themselves to meant they were creating a vulnerability.

That was going to bite them, he thought. And the question wasn't if.

It was when.

Chapter 25

WILS

He'd watched the holos of the other station attacks.

Had done everything he could to protect his people from what was coming.

But twenty minutes into the actual fight, as Wils stared at the screen showing the tiny force of station defenders crawling over the surface of the enormous array, he felt despair twist up through his gut.

Compared to this one, the arrays that had taken out other stations and shut them off from settled space forever had been toys.

"Anyone know how many ships in that thing?" he asked.

"*Longview* One Gold reports three thousand eight hundred ninety-four ships, including cruisers, heavy ships, and multiple command ships. Actual reports this as the full known fighting complements of three separate space fleets. And that's not including what Actual calls the chewy center." The light board operator didn't turn. She was staring, transfixed, at the pinpoints that were the defenders, which were spiraling their way across the surface in four curving spread-out lines. The fixed pattern they were running was clear.

Wils thought if he could see it, the enemy would be able to see it, too.

Wils knew they'd built that pattern based on the previous ship arrays and the pattern in which ships had broken away and cleared the structure.

"Have any of the PWA ships broken free?"

"Not yet," she said. "But there are some ships hanging back to chase any that do…" And then she gasped and pointed. Two big fighters came around from the far side of the spheres, pursued by a small pack of Bailey's defenders.

They were heading straight for the part of the station nearest the point — Colson Traders, the Diplomatic Center, Grey Corp.

They were firing — he and everyone else saw explosions hit Colson. The building was moleibond, so would be unscathed.

Those inside?

Wils closed his eyes. The cheering around him told him the defenders had caught up to the attackers, and done at least some damage.

Wils kept his focus on the light board. "Corridor Rescue teams Twenty through Twenty-Eight, if you can move, get to Colson Traders now. Building hit, casualties possible.

"Twenty-One responding."

"Twenty-Four responding."

He looked up. Watched the defenders racing back to the fight, saw the two dead enemy ships spinning in two separate trajectories up and away from the station.

The speed with the defenders had killed the enemies stunned him. "I didn't know it would be like this," he muttered.

"That was sticky pies on the hulls, but something else, too," one of the board controllers said, nodding toward the drifting ships. "Our guys have weapons I've never seen before."

"Grav shears," someone else said. "Pirate-hunters use them."

Wils quickly heard from most of the eight teams in the sector, but Twenty-Two and Twenty-Three didn't call in.

"Twenty-Eight, divert to the intersection of West B and South 4.

We have two teams in that area who are not calling in." He didn't like the way his voice shook when he spoke.

"Twenty-Eight on it."

"Here comes another one!" one of the command center volunteers screamed.

He glanced up, pulse thudding in his ears, and saw a heavy fighter racing for the station, aimed for the high gantry where the *Longview* docked. For the first time, he realized that *Longview* wasn't there.

The *Longview* was coordinating the station, the defending fleet, and the rescuers, he realized.

They would have to be somewhere above it all. Someplace where they could see everything.

Chapter 26

KEYR

The other passage — just around the corner from the gravdrop — was short. It was three steps, then the closed, locked door that kept him from whatever was on the other side.

This door was sturdier, and the lock required palm ident.

Keyr smiled, pressed his palm to the lock, and the door opened.

There were tremendous advantages in training the best people, hiring the best people, and paying them extravagantly. Melie was both wonderful and thorough, and her attention to minute detail when it counted had just walked him into the deepest level of a PWA-secure-encrypted installation.

He found himself in an empty terminus with warning signs on the wall.

If you're dumping bodies, bag them.
Caution! No atmosphere beyond this point!
Wear shipsuit and have any contraband contained.
Wait for hatch to open before exiting.

The hatch was a double-sized trash chute. There should have been a call button to bring a Bailey's trash pickup drone on one of the walls.

He saw a place where one had been.

So. It wasn't hooked up to the system.

This was probably where they were moving slaves — and possibly Legends — in and out. And where they were ridding themselves of the remains of their fun, like all those corpses at the other end of the corridor.

On one wall, there was a shelf to one side with thin black body bags, tethers, vials of various drugs for rendering different degrees of unconsciousness, and other things that verified the nature of those who had used this room.

If he were the lone survivor in this building, and his people had an emergency protocol for rescuing their important people…

He looked at the chute on the floor. Noted the single carabiner clipped to a sturdy D-ring bolted to the edge of the chute. The moleibond braided safety cord that slipped out the edge of the chute, and the conforming chute seal that kept the air in the room.

She was out there.

He could just unclip the carabiner and let her drift.

But she was like him. Without food, without oxygen, she wouldn't die. She would, however, consume her own body down to the point where she became a mindless, ravenous monster — and then she'd shut down and hibernate until at some point some poor idiot rescued her and brought her aboard a ship.

He did a quick check of the wrist meter on his own shipsuit, saw that he had thirty-six hours of charge. Not perfect, but should be sufficient.

She might have already been rescued, of course.

He shrugged. He'd take his chances.

He unsheathed his knife, studied the gleam of the dagger point and the serrations that ran from the middle of the belly back to the quillon.

From time to time, he needed to fix small problems within his own universe. This knife was his favorite fixer.

He crouched on the trash hatch, fixed one carabiner of his tether to the D-ring that held the other safety line, clipped the other end to a moleibond vest he pulled off the shelf and put on. Took a body bag, hooked the carabiner on it to the one on his vest. Shortened his own line with a catshank knot — stable in zero gravity — and dropped down the chute, through the bottom gate. He hung there, above and behind her.

She had not been rescued. She did not see him.

And of course she did not hear him.

She was facing the battle, she had a spectacular view of it, and she was transfixed. The Diplomatic Center was one of the closest buildings to the origami point. And as best he could tell, her allies were losing spectacularly.

Whole parts of the enemy ship array — far larger than anyone had seen in the holos — were lightless, indicating that their power and atmosphere were dead, and suggesting that any of the crew who hadn't run for the jump berths when they saw what was happening to other ships would be scrambled into paste by the grav shears.

He would bet money whole crews would be in their jump berths, though. At least after the examples of the first few ships.

The Bailey's forces looked like bugs crawling over the surface, but the surface itself kept growing darker and darker.

Beneath, he could see three layers of other ships, trapped in place by the exterior ships that had not been able to break free. And inside of that, something different. Dark red like old blood, glowing like some illuminated window into hell.

That, he thought, would be the Gargantua device.

He smiled just a little. The survivors in that array dared not set it off. They would be trapping themselves along with everyone at Bailey's. Prisoners of war might be ransomed. Corpses would not.

He did not think they would be inclined to sacrifice so much for their cause.

His smile grew broader as he looked from Valli Arra to his knife. No knife would cut through moleibond.

But all he wanted to do was remove her head from her shoulders. It was the one sure-fire way to eliminate his kind. It was messy, but effective.

The charming thing about the shaped-gravity breathing units of modern ship suits was that they made helmets unnecessary. The suits were no more cumbersome to wear than regular work clothes. Because they were so livable, travelers and crew caught in ship mishaps almost always survived depressurization, and if rescue ships were close, almost always got rescued.

So a pretty monster could hang helmetless in the exquisite soundlessness of deep space beneath the station, her delicate figure in its fitted shipsuit illuminated by the station lights, her hair floating in thick dark curls around her face, her gaze focused on the destruction of the war machine she'd expected to save her, while she breathed the air the gravity of her suit pumped, cleaned, and held around her head.

She was so very pretty.

He wanted to hurt her. To make her suffer the way she'd made all those people inside suffer — but a fight in deep space in light shipsuits would risk his existence and his identity.

So Keyr thumbed the catshank knot loose, and with more line kicker gently off of the station. He drifted gracefully behind Valli Arra, wrapped his legs around her torso and his left arm around her head in one ferocious motion, and sawed through the point where the base of her skull intersected with her first cervical vertebrae so quickly, so efficiently, that even with the immense rejuvenating abilities Legends had, she couldn't struggle. Severing the rest of her head was easy, though messy by comparison. Covered with the blood that floated in globules around him, he put the head in the bag he'd brought with him, shoved the body in, and hauled his kill back into the Diplomatic Center.

The ease of her execution was disappointing, her lack of suffering insufficient justice. But he had learned long ago that sometimes those who first played with their food lost it, and in the worst cases, discovered only when it hunted them down that it had not forgotten or forgiven their play.

Having once been food himself, he did not allow himself the mistakes those who had abused him had made.

Chapter 27

MELIE

As soon as Melie docked the *Longview*, Shay's voice cut into com. "Shay in the corridor. Need to come aboard," she said.

Melie's gut knotted. She hadn't even known Shay hadn't been aboard.

Melie met her at the inner airlock, and froze in horror. Shay was covered in blood, her shipsuit was missing an arm and part of the chest, her hair was matted and caked to her skull.

She grabbed Shay and held her close while the lock sealed shut.

"What happened? I didn't even know you were off the ship."

"I knew you'd give me hell if you knew I was in the middle of it, but I couldn't just sit here doing nothing. The owner was safe in his box, and you were coordinating the attack and needed your full focus on that. So I went to Bailey's and volunteered to help. I was assigned a quadrant, and my quadrant was one of the ones that got hit when the ships broke away. I was in the way of a shock blast. Lost my arm and part of my chest, but because I was in the rescue team, another rescuer grabbed me, threw me into a rescue Medix, and I got a high-speed reju. They pulled me out as soon as it was done so they could throw someone else in."

"You didn't tell me you were going," Melie said.

Shay had the grace to blush. "I couldn't be useless, Mel. I couldn't. I had to do something that mattered in this, just so that I could sleep at night. This was either the end of freedom in settled space, or it was the re-birth of it, and I could not look at myself in the mirror every day if I had to think that I'd waited in my office while so many others were fighting."

Melie nodded. She could understand that. "But you ended up hurt and you missed everything."

Shay grinned at her. "Oh, no, I didn't. I ended up being almost a hero."

"Almost?"

"I'm the one who discovered that the door to the Diplomatic Center had been broken open. I went in after someone managed to get through your lockout. Whoever it was hunted down and killed Valli Arra, then left her hanging on the wall across from the diplomats' entrance. She had killed everyone in the building, and apparently planned to be rescued once her people won the battle. The holos of her slaughtering her own people were playing all over. And whoever had been there before me left arrows drawn in blood to show how to find the bodies."

Melie said, "Keyr killed her. He *wasn't* safe in his box."

Shay stilled. Studied Melie with her head tilted. "What do you mean?"

I built an access code into the Diplomatic Center for him. During the battle, he used it."

"You… knew?"

"I knew. It alerted me with a unique tone. I could give you the exact time he entered the building if you want. If we had eyes in the Diplomatic Center, I could show you exactly what he did while he was in there. We don't. But if you wanted to see, I could show you him going in and coming back out."

"No. That's all right. There are parts of his life I don't want to know about. I saw what he did to Valli Arra. I'm glad he did it — but it doesn't make me like him more."

"So neither of you was on the ship. I was at the top of the command chain, and I didn't know that."

"I'm sorry," Shay said. "I didn't know he wouldn't stay put. He doesn't tell me what he plans, and he has ways of getting in and out of here without being seen."

"Apparently, so do you."

Shay shook her head. "I put on a rescue volunteer suit along with the rest of the people we sent to Bailey's to help out. And I stood in the line closest to the wall and just walked out. If you check the ship log, you'll see me."

"You were on deck and you didn't say goodbye?"

"I didn't want to make a scene."

"You didn't want me to convince you to stay."

"I didn't want to tell you I was going anyway."

They looked at each other.

Melie wrapped her arms around Shay, pressed her face against her beloved's neck, and said, "If you'd gotten yourself killed, I never would have forgiven you."

"Same goes for you," Shay said. "This way, though, we'll both have war stories to tell when we get old."

"If we decide we want to get old," Melie said. "I think staying young until our cells can't reju anymore would be the way to go."

Shay grinned. "Or that. Young and gorgeous for life definitely has its advantages."

Chapter 28

HEROG

The battle was done.

In total, six big fighters from the top layer of the array had managed to break away. While none of the ships in the second layer of the array had broken free, nor had any in the inner command level, from just those six the dead on Bailey's numbered over three hundred, with more than half of the buildings not yet searched and the count still rising.

The Gargantua device still hung in the array center, glowing its dull, deadly red.

And while there were no life signs on any of the ships, Herog knew that at least some of the crew members would have retreated to jump berths. When he and his people took the ships, they were going to have to clear each one them individually, taking prisoners or if they had no choice, killing the survivors.

Meanwhile, atmosphere had held for the station, corridors, and all independent buildings, but shock waves from sticky pie percussion weapons fired from the enemy ships had killed anyone in range of the detonations whenever they'd hit an occupied area.

The list of the dead was not being released until all families had been notified, and all survivors were being kept together with medics on hand until a full count of the dead was tallied and the families were notified.

He wanted — needed — to see Cady. He and she had designated each other as their next of kin some time back, so the fact that no one had come to tell him that she was dead gave him a small measure of comfort, even as the waiting ate at his insides.

So it was a relief when the captain of the *Longview* contacted Herog with an urgent request that he meet with the owner.

Herog left the rest of his people claim-tagging their kills among the pirate ships and the ships they'd hit that were still locked in the warship array. He followed the pilot sent to escort him to one of the *Longview's* tail docks.

He connected easily, waved to the pilot, dropped through the umbilical, and ended up in a small waiting room. Keyr, still in the closed and pressurized shipsuit, was waiting for him. The man rose with evident difficulty and led him into a large room with a long table and a dozen seats. The walls were covered by art, some of it very good, some… familiar.

That he found interesting. He was not an art lover, so the fact that he actually recognized some of the paintings caught in the back of his mind. They were not famous works. They were not masterpieces. So they had to have been connected to some other part of his life.

Doing a quick memory scan, he only came up with two places where he'd encountered artwork that had been meaningful.

One of those had involved Cady.

He turned away from the familiar art and looked at the owner, who had settled carefully into the nearest chair. Waving a hand at the long table and empty seats, he asked, "We're expecting company?"

Keyr said, "No. This is just the location most convenient to the aft umbilicals. You've done a lot today. Didn't want to make you hike, too. The emergency I have relates to the City of Furies. The City currently survives because it is well-hidden, but the place where it's hidden is neither safe nor secure. Today it was endangered as it has never been before. I have been looking for a way to move the city to a protected space, and I have realized that the time to move it has come."

Herog settled into a seat on the side that faced the interesting paintings, leaving an empty chair between himself and the owner. "*Move* the city?"

"With my resources and good moleibond extruder technology, this will be much less complex than you might imagine. An exact duplicate of the city could be recreated in just a few months on any planet. A planet that could be modified to support human life would be best of course, and Bailey's Point has several such planets."

Herog laughed. "*This* system? Why in the world would the City of Furies want to build its future in a system that has only one origami point, only one space station, and a couple dozen scrubby planets, none of which have anything in particular to recommend them?"

"That's half of it right there," Keyr said. "The rich and the powerful of settled space have no reason to come here. There are no vast stores of treasure to draw pirates, no exotic locations to draw tourists, nothing to welcome the big trouble the universe has to offer. This system has all the resources it needs for people who want to live here. It simply doesn't have resources the evil and the venal would want to exploit."

"And yet," Herog noted drily, "we just fought the mother of all space battles today to save this little backwater you claim nobody wants."

The owner's chuckle turned into a cough that ended in a ragged gasp. "And that's the other reason. At the moment, you and yours now own hundreds of pirate ships and the entire PWA Peace Armada, as well as the space fleets belonging to the CTV and the NZD."

Herog raised an eyebrow "CTV? NZD?"

"CTV is Coturra Vertat Tenado. Translates roughly as the People of the Tenacious Truth. Alliance of about twenty worlds out in the K zone — not friendly to folks who value individual rights. Or individuals. KZD is Ketloktak Zed Dovakta, in other words, Zed Dovakta's Nation. Eight highly militaristic, oppressive worlds and a lot of satellites, but located at one of the far edges of currently settled space. N3, N4. Around there. The PWA had recently allied with both, since they have similar… philosophies and similar… power structures."

"Body-modding slavers by any other name." Herog didn't smile when he said that. "The survivors of the Legend decimation, who have stepped into the top positions because they can."

Herog saw one eyebrow raise behind the suit helmet. The owner said, "You're aware that the PWA is run by a handful of Anti-Legend-resistant Legends?"

Herog said, "I suspected. They rise to the top because they can." He shook his head. "The Legends should have all died. But a few of them somehow survived, and they keep showing up."

"Wealth and the hunger for power will find ways to preserve itself. Hiring unethical mod designers to build protection from the Anti-Legend nanovirus is as good a way to spend stolen wealth as any.

"Which is why Bailey's Point needs you. The monsters are still out there.

"At the moment, you're in the remarkable position of being the nominal admiral of the biggest military space force in settled space, and if you decide to keep your fleet here, your presence could make Bailey's Irish Space Station something akin to the new center of civilization. I love the philosophy of Bailey's, and would very much like to help terraform and settle some of the better-quality worlds in this system."

"It's not my fleet, and they're not my folks. They're my friends, they're my allies. But we have no hierarchy." Herog considered the suggestion, and thought of what remained of his friends. "My allies might want to stay, to hunt pirates from a known home base. They like Bailey's…"

He considered that for a moment. He studied Keyr. "Have you and Bailey thought this through? Pirate-hunters are deeply unpop-ular with pirates, and we don't have enough people to man even a hundredth of the fleet we captured."

Keyr chuckled. "Space fleets that are not secretly propping up piracy are frightening to pirates." He sighed. "I think your pirate-hunters enjoy hunting from the best fleet ships in settled space. Meanwhile, I don't want to be stuck at Bailey's. I want to take the *Longview* and get back to pulling slaves out of terrible places. This time we won't be pretending to uphold an evil system for executing innocents whose existence polite society finds inconvenient. While Bailey's needs better protection, I'd appreciate having an armed escort with me to help me go get to the places where slaves are trapped. And I'd be thrilled to pay for the help."

Herog didn't want to like Keyr. There were things about the man that felt wrong. Felt false. More than half a lifetime of trusting his gut to keep himself alive in the worst of all possible conditions told him the Keyr he was speaking to was a cleaned up, mannered cover for the real Keyr.

But the *Longview* had been doing exactly what Keyr said it had.

And it had fought for Bailey's with people, with resources, and with tech. Herog knew the *Longview* had lost crew in the battle — rescuers had died right along with the rescued.

He said, "I like the idea of my friends, allies, and family being here. And you're right. Better ships will help us. But you have to understand, I'm not the head of anything, so I can only speak for myself. I can't tell you the folks who fought with me today will join me even if I ask them."

He closed his eyes and exhaled slowly. Saying it would make it real, but he had to say it. "And we should have had over two thousand ships here. They weren't here because the majority of the folks I considered friends and family were lured through origami points to nowhere, and were then trapped by Gargantuas. So most of the people I considered closer than family are dead, and the people who showed up are the only pirate-hunters my group has left."

Keyr froze. Behind the faceplate of the pressure suit, Herog could see his eyes go wide. Could see the expression of dismay. "I… I had no idea. You found this out through…"

"I watched holos Melie sent to the rig."

"She didn't show them to me."

"She might not have seen them herself. She probably assumed

they were more of the same, since they were all tagged Gargantua Project."

The man nodded, looked at the floor. Everything about him suddenly gave the impression of great age, of great weight. "All right." He exhaled slowly, the sound echoing in the suit's rebreather. "So there aren't more of your people out there waiting to find a home — unless we can find them and rescue them. That we must do, I think. But in the meantime, we don't have to have all of your people. But I will personally pay well any who are willing to stay."

"That's a good start," Herog said.

"You know I'm rich."

"*Everyone* knows you're rich. It's the sole fact about you that no one debates."

"Well, yes. But as well as being financially well-off, I am rich in resources. I can bring in people to start training to fly fighters. I don't have anyone who could be admiral of a fleet — that, I think, only you are qualified to do well. But I can provide crews for some of those ships for you."

"Which reminds me… I wanted to ask you about all those demolitions experts and rescue personnel you sent us so quickly."

Keyr shook his head. "No. Someday, if you and I become friends, I'll let you know how I do what I do. In the meantime, know that I cannot provide enough people to man the whole fleet from what I have on hand, but I can provide you and yours with enough extras to fill out your ranks, to help protect the point, the station, and whichever world turns out to be the best site for a new home for the City of Furies. And I can make sure you have enough people to keep up your pirate hunting.

"My allies in the City of Furies can make your group look bigger than it is while showing what you're doing — and in the process can encourage refugees who want to fight slavery and piracy to come here."

Keyr leaned forward. "But this is something you and I and your friends can discuss later. My biggest concern is this. The instant the location of the City of Furies becomes known — in other words, the instant it is rebuilt here and its people are moved here, it becomes a target for everyone who favors the enslavement of the individual to government, or to individual masters."

"Why it hasn't yet become such a target," Herog said, "is a mystery I and mine have debated over beer for long hours."

"Again, if we ever become friends, you'll know the full story. But for now, I want to hire you and pay you in whatever coin you prefer to design a defense system for the city — ground, air, automatic, and manned. It needs a full spectrum of defenses to protect it against anything that can come after it, either internal or external."

Herog said, "And those you suspect will come after it are space fleets, ground armies, fifth columnists."

"Yes. You are a spectacular tactician, Herog. I have been informed by multiple sources that the battle plan that just saved Bailey's and the *Longview*, that is restoring the hostages to their families, and that resulted in the capture of three entire armed space fleets by just eighty-four small fighters and a handful of rescue vehicles was entirely your doing."

"Yes."

"And no false modesty. Thank you for that."

Herog raised an eyebrow.

Keyr said, "The *civilized* reply would have been, 'Oh, everyone had a part in it.' That nonsense infuriates me. Everyone had a part in fighting, in rescuing, in eliminating the threat, and far too many took part in the dying. I am beyond grateful for their actions. But you figured out how a vastly outnumbered group of mismatched fighters could beat a previously unbeatable foe. You are the man to protect the City of Furies."

Herog said, "I'm interested in designing the defense system." He stood. "But right now, I need to know that Cady is all right. The people who will be trying to contact me if she isn't are going to be waiting in our apartment. Or she might already be waiting for me — and if she is, wondering where *I* am."

"Of course," Keyr said.

Herog glanced at the paintings again. A self portrait of a young woman with rich red hair and deep green eyes caught his attention.

He suddenly remembered her name. It had been Tadra Amu. She'd been…

A very young woman. Eighteen? Nineteen? She'd been on scholarship to the Oldcity University of Fine Arts at Meileone on Cantata. She had also been the first suspected victim of a monster Cady said she'd killed. The girl's body was never found, but her blood and a finger had been retrieved from the crime scene. She was never seen again. She'd been declared dead.

The painting had been one of many in evidence in an investigation into a murder that had suddenly and quietly been closed — right after it started to point toward a powerful councilman who turned out later to be a high-ranking Legend.

Herog had tripped over that investigation because the councilman who'd probably murdered Tadra Amu had been one of those who in the past had threatened Cady. He'd been checking back-trails, and had been sure that one had ended with the killer's death.

But…

He couldn't look away from that face. Even though the girl in the painting was young, even though the painting wasn't a masterpiece, it was good enough that he thought he'd seen her recently…

Which was when it all clicked.

The girl was alive. Older.

She was Shay.

Tadra Amu wasn't dead. She was Shay — and still a Legend's slave.

Which would make the owner, Weyrix Keyr…

"Son of a bitch," Herog snarled. "You're Danniz Oe," and turned and rushed Keyr.

"Oh, *hell,*" Keyr said.

And Herog's world went dark.

Chapter 29

KEYR SPEAKS

You know me as Werix Keyr.

That's not my real name, but Herog was wrong about me. I'm not and never was Danniz Oe.

Danniz Oe, the second Legend and co-creator of the horrific body mod Legend, is as dead as Haskell Corrigan, Oe's colleague and the first man who made himself a Legend.

My little heroine Cadence Drake was the death of them both when they made the mistake of trying to feast on her. She went on to use the weapon I gave her to become the scourge of Legends everywhere, and she came very close to annihilating them utterly from the universe.

Those Legends who still survive may hold power... but the vipers now live in fear. This is as it should be. They stay coiled inside their nests of power, hidden behind air filtration systems, carefully maintaining their isolated sources of food — humans they now must tend and breed carefully, whom they must protect from every danger, humans who have never been exposed to the airborne anti-Legend virus, and who will never meet with torture or horror because they are rare, and slow to breed, and irreplaceable if lost.

These vipers live in fear of every sneeze.

Herog came closer to the truth about me than I can allow, though.

And that's a problem.

I will not kill him.

He is one of us, one of the people who fought his way through hell to freedom. And he risked everything to save places and people I love which I could not, with all my money and all my connections and all my many talents, save by myself.

I cannot set him free, because while I am not Danniz Oe, I most assuredly am a monster, and until he can see past **what** I am to **who** I am, the fact that I'm a monster would be the death of one of us. At the moment, I do not think settled space can stand to lose either of us.

Herog is magnificent, brilliant, hellishly persistent, and deadly beyond anything I have ever known. He is the man I think will find the path I could not find — the path to making the City of Furies impregnable from predators without making it a prison or a war machine.

Unwilling to kill him, unable to set him free, I find myself with only one choice.

I'm turning him loose inside my greatest achievement, where he will be able to live in the universe as it should be. As it can be.

As some part of it already is.

Once there, he will make his own choices. Every choice will be open to him — including the choice to fight his way back here to try to kill me.

But because he is the man he is, I trust that once he understands what I have made, he'll make a better choice than that.

Chapter 30

HEROG

He awoke with a bad headache to discover that he was sitting up, that he was in a room with maybe a hundred other adults, male and female, of all races, shapes, sizes.

But all looked to him like they were in their early thirties.

He looked at his hands, and they were younger, unscarred. Still recognizably his hands, but...

He turned over the palm of his right hand, which he'd damaged pretty impressively at the age of eleven while working on the farm with his parents. He'd kept that scar as well as several others, even through reju. He'd been proud of it. He'd earned it working in the fields, and his father had called him a man when he didn't cry but instead wrapped it and kept working.

If it was gone, if he and everyone with him were all the same age and in the same state of physical health, then he'd been reju'd during transport by someone who didn't have his reju profile. So that scar was gone.

He resented its removal. It had been an important part of his life, of his *making*.

He looked around at the people around him. Everyone on the benches looked confused.

His first impulse was to get up, fight his way out of wherever he was, *figure out* where he was, and get back to Cady, whatever the cost.

His second impulse — the one he followed — was to freeze. Until he understood where he was and what was happening, he was in the position of prey. He could not resume his role as a predator until he understood the terrain he had to hunt.

So he sat. Breathed. Waited.

A short woman walked into the room, slamming the door behind her. Some of the people around him jumped.

"Welcome to the City of Furies," she said. "My name is Remala Kay, and I am the Unattached Immigrants Coordinator.

"Your status at this moment is Unattached Immigrant Level Zero. This means you do not have family or friends who are citizens here to vouch for you or pay your expenses while you find work and a place to live. But the path ahead of you is one of individual choice, responsibility, and freedom. For the first month you are here, you will live at the expense of the city in the Immigrant Warehouse."

Herog waited.

"You'll receive a daily ration of basic reconsta, a sleeping space, a storage space, and shared cleansing and elimination spaces. During that one month, you *must* accomplish two tasks. You must find paying work, and you must acquire confirmed housing. The kind of housing arrangements you obtain are open — you may share inexpensive rental housing with other new immigrants, you may be invited to live with an existing immigrant or citizen. If you have sufficient means in an account you can access from here, you may rent or purchase housing immediately.

"You may not sleep on streets, in parks, or in the construction areas. The first time you do this you will be sent to the space station and put on the first outbound transport. You will have no say in destination, and will take no belongings with you."

Which told Herog new immigrants were embedded with tracking devices. He didn't like the idea. He couldn't imagine citizens putting up with that. Not with the reputation of the City of Furies. Not with the fact that this was a city built and occupied by escaped slaves. This was supposed to be the last — or possibly first — bastion of true freedom in settled space. It made sense that the citizens would track new immigrants, however. Some could — *would* — be fifth columnists sent to destroy what these people had built. Tracking them until they proved their integrity, their devotion to the City…

Yes. He would have recommended that step as part of their defense.

So he kept still, and waited.

"By the end of the month, you must be employed, you must be living in a real home with a real address. There are thousands of both entry-level and advanced job positions open in the city at any time, and if you look, you *will* find something. If you have limited skills or no skills, take the first job that's offered, work during the required hours, and use your free time to acquire skills in work that interests you. There are thousands of open apartments at any time because people move into better housing as they can afford it and because we are steadily building and expanding this city from its core outward."

She studied everyone, then focused directly on him, and asked, "Do you have any questions?"

Herog said, "How do I get back to Bailey's?"

She said, "Right now you *don't*, Herog. You may take the job that was offered to you before you came here, or you may find other work. If you take the job that was offered to you, the city will pay your way back to Bailey's once you're done. If you don't, you'll be able to leave when you've earned your passage on the next outbound ship with room. Or you may simply walk to the space station, announce that you're an indigent, and take outbound passage to whichever place the captain chooses to drop you."

He closed his eyes. Exhaled slowly. Outthinking the enemy was the secret to survival. Doing what they didn't expect you to do, being where they didn't expect you to be.

They were not going to expect him to accept this without a fight.

So for the moment, he would accept it without a fight. He would help the city engineers develop the best defensive system he could design because settled space needed the City of Furies, and the City of Furies needed to be able to protect itself from threats both without and within.

While he was at it, he would find a way to contact Cady, make sure she was all right. If she could find the location of the City of Furies, he'd have her come get him — but he considered that a long shot, even for her.

If she couldn't get him, he would work. He would conform. He would make the City safe from the universe that would destroy it if it could.

And when he had the resources he needed, he would find his way back to Bailey's Irish Space Station on his own, and track down the *Longview*, and kill that monster Danniz Oe.

THE Owner's Tale

TALES FROM THE LONGVIEW

HOLLY LISLE

Chapter 1

WERIX KEYR

Now…

You know me as Werix Keyr, and by now, because you know what I am, you think you know me.

I am a monster — but that is *not* who I started out to be.

On this, the last day of my life, I want you to know how I became a monster. And why I did what I did.

And the truth is that, though I am a monster who has done terrible things, I did one wonderful thing as well.

For that one wonderful thing to live, to grow its wings, to become what settled space needs it to be, I have to die now. But I would not have you think ill of the dead.

Perhaps if I show you who I really am, you won't.

Chapter 2

CADENCE DRAKE

Twenty-Four Hours Earlier...

Cady came through the Bailey's Station origami point spot-welded to the front curve of a tiny transparent sphere, with the pain of being folded through space a fire along every nerve, and with the urge to vomit fighting whatever they'd shot her full of before they sealed her into the bait ball.

The words of the bastard who'd welded her into the ball echoed in her ears — "You'll get to see people die today. Your dear friend Fedara Contei, that criminal Wils Bailey, and every piece of breathing scum on or around that station. You'll see the end of Bailey's Irish. And Bailey's Point. You could have watched that monster lover of yours die, too — but Herog managed to get himself killed being stupid."

And he'd laughed at the shock on her face. And then injected something into her shoulder that hurt like hell.

"Don't want you to die before we can kill you," he said, and grinned. "That's to keep you from vomiting and drowning in your own puke when you go through the fold. We want all you folks to be wide awake and kicking so your friends know they have to do what we tell them if they want us to save you."

"What do you want them to do?" she'd asked.

"Just hold still while we kill them," he told her. "You'll be our bait and our shields." And he'd smacked her on the ass and said, "Shame to waste you."

And then set the weapons systems behind her, turned on the air recycler, and sealed her into the capsule alone.

She found herself looking at a little boy spot-welded into a ball across from her. He was screaming and crying, fighting against his bonds. Dark skin like hers, dark eyes, thick black hair.

She caught his attention by making faces at him, then shook her head. He started watching her. Calmed down a little.

She mouthed the words, "You'll be all right." Smiled.

He looked disbelieving, and then she thought she read, "Where's Mommy?" in the words he mouthed to her.

"Mommy is safe," she said.

Which was not just a lie, but a damned lie, because odds were good that if his mother wasn't with him, she was in the same deep trouble Cady and the boy were in.

But the truth would not help the child survive what came next.

So Cady mimed sleeping and said, "Home to Mommy…" and "You're going home to Mommy," and hoped that would somehow turn out to be the truth in a happy sense rather than the other possibility, which was that they were all going to die horribly either during the point crossing or afterwards, and that either nothingness or whatever followed death would be all that remained of their future.

The bastard who'd bonded her to the inside of her transparent cage had said she'd be going through a fold in it — and Cady had done that before, awake and alert. Two hundred ninety-seven times already.

Going through in this pathetic moleibond cage would make two hundred ninety-eight.

Had she been a commercial TFN pilot rather than an indie, she would have had one more sanctioned crossing in her career, after which she would have had the option to be grounded, or the option most of the big TFN pilots took, which was to walk into the infinite during their final crossing and see what waited on the other side.

She no longer believed that anything waited there. Her reality consisted of what she could prove... and nothing else.

But it didn't mean that she wouldn't see Badger again when she was folded through space...

Or Herog. If he was really dead, if the bastard who'd laughed about his death had been telling the truth, would she see Herog?

Their captors had gathered and were rolling the balls into little ground-to-space shuttles.

She allowed herself to drift into sleep. Was awakened when she was rolled back out of the shuttle onto what looked like a giant slingshot in the hold of a warship.

There was no gravity, so she was in space, and the hold didn't have gravity turned on — probably to facilitate the launching of these individual pods ahead of her.

So she was up against it now. Helpless, she faced the coming pain and darkness as Herog had taught her.

I am the only self I can prove, mine is the only reality I can prove. Everything that is coming is shadows and images. I matter, my choices matter, my actions matter, my life matters.

She was upside-down relative to the person in the ball in front of her, who was facing away from her. She could see a line of transparent spheres ahead of her.

Each ball would be launched through the point, and she and the other hostages would be held in front of her friends in Bailey's as threats — that if they acted, she and the others would be killed.

But if they did not act, they would still be killed.

She tried to figure out how she could warn them, and then the ball made a half rotation forward and stopped. They'd started firing.

There was no sound. There was nothing but the silence of deep space. She could shout and hear her own voice, but there was no atmosphere outside of the balls, so the sound did not carry.

She closed her eyes. Her cage rolled forward. *Count*, she thought, and counted, "One-one-thousand, two-one-thousand, three-one-thousand, four-one-thousand" and rolled forward again.

A four-second launch clock was fairly loose.

But she realized that the threat had to have teeth, and that something that could kill the hostage had to be going through, too.

If she were shooting hostages into a location, she'd put something behind the hostage to make sure no one got any funny ideas about a rescue…

Two-second launch clock. And the threats going through in between. That was more likely what was going on, and that was tight.

She'd learned a lot about fighting in space from Herog.

Closed her eyes. If she saw him when she pushed through the fold, when she fell into the infinite and linked to the phantasms of her mind — or the truth of the Infinite — did that mean he was truly dead?

And she remembered Herog asking her the question that had changed everything for her. "If this were the only reality, what would you do differently?"

She also remembered her answer. "I'd fight harder. I'd never quit."

This is the only reality I can prove, she told herself again. *This is the only reality I know I can reach. So I must act on the theory that my life matters, my actions matter, and when I die, I die completely and forever.*

I want to live. So I will do everything I can to live.

The balls before her rolled forward. Forward. Forward.

And then she was next…

And launched…

The Infinite Other crushed her into an infinite number of separate parts, and Badger was in there calling to her, and Herog was standing there staring at her in a thousand guises, and in some of them he begged her to come join him.

But the Herog she knew, the one who was true to everything that was Herog, held on inside her mind, and that Herog said, "It's a reflection of reality. It is not reality. Live, Cady."

"Live, Cady," she whispered, hanging on through the shattering,

the scattering, the breaking apart of everything she was into everything she might ever have been or might ever be, through the twisting, wrenching, tearing pain, through the lure of death which was
the end of all pain...

"Live... Cady."

Through her two hundred ninety-eighth passage through
madness.

She came out the other end whispering, "Live, Cady. Live."

Chapter 3

WHEN I WAS K-EIGHTY-FOUR

My first name was K-Eighty-Four.

By definition, I was born a monster.

On the little moon of Beckenridge, where the Beckenridge Colony of Living Saints exists to this day, a Breeder gave birth to me and put me into the *bernekaste* with other infants and small children, to be fed and cleaned and trained by a stream of older children until I reached puberty.

Cultures define monstrosity differently, and not all definitions are true.

Some actions are genuinely evil, and some monsters define their evil as goodness. And to the extent that the world into which I was born was monstrous in its own right, the fact that the Saints would have defined me as a monster speaks more to their villainy than to mine.

But in the end, your own choices are what make you a monster.

By choice, I became a monster by any civilized definition.

But first, the beginning. I was born into the Sacred Death of the Living Saints, where breeding is duty, where no desires are permitted, where life is proof of one's evil, and death is the gate to reward.

From the time I was old enough to know I drew breath, to

understand language, to walk and run, I was filled with desire. I was attracted to both the girls in the *bernekaste* and the boys. And on the inside, I desired them as both a female and a male.

The first thing you learn in the *bernekaste* is that anything that makes you different gets you punished.

So the first thing I learned was to do a very good impression of being a normal child. I was better looking than most of the children, and any sort of attractiveness is a sin in a world where something that causes desire is a sin. So I worked to make myself plain, ungainly, awkward.

But I was also intelligent. Another sin — a much bigger one — because intelligence introduces the question "Why?" to the mind, and sows the seeds of doubt against authority.

Intelligence is something bright children reveal by accident, but that a very intelligent child can figure out how to hide. I learned to be observant, to be obedient, to be dull and slow in my responses, to hold my tongue, to bow my head, to keep my thoughts to myself. To stutter and fumble for words, to look blankly at those in authority who questioned me about my actions.

Being stupid is not a sin — it is among the Saints a sign of Divinely imposed obedience. The stupid do not question. They simply accept.

As I grew older, I allowed myself no friends.

To the Saints, friendship is a sin — it creates a value that stands between the living and the Path to Death. One might value a friend enough to want to save that friend from death, and if death is the reward for the punishment of life, then anything that impedes the downward slide to the grave is evil.

Saints classify male children on their Day of Readiness as Second Saints, Monk, or Slave. Their two classifications for girls are Breeder and Cull.

Second Saints, subservient only to the Saint himself, do no physical work. They live in fine stone houses and spend a small portion of their day in prayer, and a large portion of their day in eating, drinking, and breeding, or practicing their breeding skills on those who cannot conceive, whether because of age or because of gender. This is, they insist, not because they are filled with desire, but because they are obedient to duty. It is the duty of the Saints to be ever ready to breed more Saints, and this requires much practice.

Second Saints also do the classification of each child brought before them.

Monks, neutered on their Classification Day and treated with occasional kindness, carry out the higher-level tasks of running the colony — tending to the machines and the histories and the recording of the birthrights and lineages of the Breeders and their offspring.

Slaves, neutered and despised, do the dirty work. And there is immense dirty work in a place like Beckenridge Colony. Not just the cleaning, the clearing, the building, the planting, the harvesting, the tending of the beasts.

There is also the taking of children to the Saints for whatever purposes the Saints might require, including but not limited to their final classification.

Breeders and Culls reach their Day of Classification when they are Marked by Sin. Girls marked as Breeders stay to tend children until they are successfully bred. Once they catch, they are placed in corrals where they stay until they have given birth. Once they are delivered of their Proof of Sin, they may be marked Shamed with Life, and kept for further breeding. If the creature they give birth to is damaged in any way, however, they are proved free of sin, and are Honored with Death.

Culls...

Well, on their Day of Classification, Culls are Honored with Death.

Not only are they released to The End of Suffering, but they become... useful.

Culls Honored with Death are part of the other duties of the slaves. The Saints kill these girl children in some sort of ritual, and once they're dead, the slaves make their bodies into fertilizer, bone-meal, leather for wallets, food for pigs...

Friendless and to all appearances clumsy, awkward, and stupid, I could have survived among the Saints except for the final accident of my birth.

Because while the first thing I learned was to pretend to be normal, the second thing I learned is that no matter what anyone says about the holiness of Classification, or about Great Holy's Demand and the sacred duty of every child to submit, there is no good ending for you if you're born female.

Breeder.

Or Cull.

All this I saw. All this I watched sidelong, quietly, saying nothing, thinking always. I demonstrated my slow wit, my bovine complacency with my lot. I kept my head down and made myself look as plain as I could.

But as I neared puberty, I could see the boys in the *bernekaste* looking at me more than they looked at the other girls. They were noting the change of my shape, responding as unneutered males do.

Male children are allowed to be beautiful because they may be chosen to be Saints. The Saints want plain women, though, because they will not be objects of desire. They will simply be objects of convenience for the making of new Saints.

I could not make myself plain enough, and because of this, I could see my death approaching.

Those who die soonest serve best. So teach the Saints.

While I could not know the date of my death, I had no doubt that when I was brought before the Saints for classification, I would be a Cull.

One of the throats cut, one of the bodies drained of blood, just another thing for the slaves to run through the grinder after everything else had been stripped from me.

But when we labored in the fields with the Slaves, tending and picking crops, I could also see each month the supply ship that dropped to the landing pad on the far side of the colony. The men who offloaded the supplies. No one from the colony was permitted to approach these men. They were unclean, damaged — *bojaats*.

I thought that if I could just offer something they might want, I might survive.

By the time I had conceived my escape plan, I was, by my best guess, eleven standard years old. Perhaps twelve. I was tying strips around my chest under my shirt to hide my budding breasts. Was dreading the Mark of Sin which would send me before the Saint, and I was desperate to figure a way that I might hide it when it came so that I might survive a little longer.

I knew only that I did not want to die. Not in that place. Not for those people.

So I found a place where I might mark time, and I marked each day from the time the supply ship left until it returned. And each month, I watched and waited for an opportunity.

Finally, two days by my hidden count before the supply ship was due to come again, I crept out at night, slipping quietly behind the girl who was senior in the *bernekaste*, who had been classified as a Breeder, but who was not yet bred, and who had been called to be obedient to the Saints. Once she was out of sight, I crept through the darkness, staying ever in shadow, and found my way to the landing pad. There I dug a hole for myself in which I could hide, and when I was in it, stripped naked, folded my clothes over my head, and pulled dried leaves and a little dirt into the hole on top of them.

And then I waited.

I ate nothing.

I drank my own piss, gathered as best I could from one cupped hand. I did not allow myself to shit. I had to be as presentable as I could make myself when the *bojaats* came, because I was going to offer myself to them as a Breeder if they would just take me with them. I hoped that they would see me as such, instead of as a Cull.

While I hid, I could hear searchers looking for me. Could hear their shouts, their feet thudding, their calling of my number. Screaming, "K-Eighty-Four!"

I held still whenever they neared, breathing shallowly, wedged with my back against the hole, with my eyes closed tight, praying to anything that might save me that they would not accidentally trip into my hole.

And late the second day, when the partial dark of the folded clothes and leaves over my head was dimming to the true dark of night, I heard the arrival of the supply ship.

I waited until I heard the ramp open, until I heard the voices of the men who brought things I could neither identify or imagine for the use of the Saints, and then I dressed and climbed out of the hole.

I wiped my hands as clean as I could with the leaves, untied the bindings from around my breasts, scrubbed my face as best I could with my spit and one of the balled-up bindings, ran my fingers through my hair. I wanted to make myself look as good as I could.

And I walked up to the first man I reached, and even though he was doing work like a Monk, said, "If you will take me with you, I will be your personal Breeder."

He stared at me, yelled back to the ship, then made a gesture and said a string of words I did not understand.

I wondered if he was mad or damaged in some way. Another man, differently dressed and looking more important, more like a Saint and less like a Monk, came out of the ship, said something to the man who'd called him with the same meaningless sounds. Then he studied me, and said, "You should not be here."

"I will be a Cull," I said. "I do not want to be a Cull, so if you will take me with you, I will be your personal Breeder."

I saw his eyes widen, then narrow. "Anyone know you're here?"

"The Saints know I'm gone. They have looked for me for two days, but have not yet found me."

"Get into the ship," he said. "You can come with us. What's a Cull?"

When I told him, he first laughed, then realized I was truthful. He said, "That's wrong. Evil. I won't be a part of that. This is the last delivery I'll take to a Saints' colony."

And it was. Durbin Anrish was a better man than the Saints.

Not so good, however, that he refused my offer. I became — for six years — his personal Breeder, though I did not catch while he bred me.

Chapter 4

WHEN I WAS TADRA AMU

Durbin refused to call me K-Eighty-Four. He said I could have any name I wanted, and he'd make it legal. And I thought of the important names among the Living Saints. I recalled the god-name of the most important man in the colony and said, "Could my name be A-One?"

He burst out laughing. Said, "By all the... No, that's not a name. Tell you what. In the language of my people, the words for 'volunteered love' are *tadra amu*. How would that do as a name for now? You can change it when you come up with something better, but in the meantime, it'll give me something to call you, and something to register for you when we buy you an identity."

"Tadra Amu." I tried it on for size. Shrugged. Back then, I didn't see what was wrong with my own name.

What can I say? I was young, which is a disability that fortunately passes.

But I was also curious. "Why do you have to buy me an identity?"

He said, "They don't teach you much in that colony, do they?"

I shrugged.

He sighed. "If you're on my ship and you don't have a legal

Gen-ID, or some other confirmed, testable identification, the first time we have to go through a secure checkpoint it's going to look like I kidnapped you. There are places where we can buy you a backstory, tag it to your genetic code, put you on the roster as paid crew, and you can work for me. If we have a relationship on the side, that's our business."

The relationship on the side, I'll note, was our main business. But he did have me help the crew, he did pay me, and when I saw a crew member drawing in his off-time, and showed an interest in learning how to do that, Durbin showed me how to sign up for onboard art training. I bought a couple of Senso art courses and from them learned basics and some advanced techniques.

And when I was too old to be of interest to Durbin anymore, he helped me apply to various art schools. On the strength of my work, I was accepted by the Oldcity University of Fine Arts at Meileone on Cantata on partial scholarship.

When he dropped me off on Cantata, he went his way and never looked back.

So I had no one in settled space who cared about me when I walked into the university. No parents, no siblings, no friends. I was the perfect target. And I was pretty — something that Durbin had emphasized was both an important and a good quality in a woman who wasn't trapped in a Living Saints colony.

A lot of young men and a few women in my classes and in the dormitory expressed attraction to me, but being nineteen — at least according to my purchased ident — and having just gotten out of a six-year relationship, I was not interested in romance.

I was interested in discovering who I might become.

In my first six months at the university, I learned everything I could about art, digging deep into history, techniques, mediums, and philosophies. I fell in love with Alien Hyperrealism, and started producing my first body of work.

In the little free time I allowed myself, I explored the science behind genderflipping. It appealed to me — on Cantata, if I could just make enough money, I could be either male or female at any given time, and I would finally be able to make the outside of me match the inside.

But at the time it was far too expensive for me to even consider, so I resigned myself to being just a part of who I was until I could become a rich, famous artist.

Take a moment to laugh with me here. Those who pursue the arts hoping to become rich and famous are like all the grains of sand in a desert. Those who do it? They're the grains that get picked up in a sandstorm and dropped into an upturned thimble in the middle of the desert's only oasis.

But again… Youth and innocence. I thought if I did the work, I would become renowned throughout settled space.

So when, at a showing of student art, I met a wealthy, important man who loved my work and raved about my brilliance and genius, I thought my moment had come already. He told me he was a Councillor in Oldcity, and the president of a group of dedicated art collectors called the Universal Society of Antiquarian Gothicans.

His name was Danniz Oe, and he was intelligent, well-versed in art, funny, charming, good-looking… and rich enough to be the sole patron for an artist like me. I would, he told me, be the best investment he'd ever made.

We had a few drinks to celebrate.

And then went to my little apartment together.

And things got…

Blurry.

I woke up in a dark room, alone. Not my room. Someplace I'd never seen before.

I was hungry. No. I was ravenous. I was lost, I was confused, I couldn't remember where I was or how I'd come to be there.

But I could smell food. The best food I'd ever smelled in my whole life.

I followed the smell, not thinking this was strange behavior for me. I stayed in the shadows, in the dark places, because light bothered my eyes. I walked up behind the magnificent smell of food that had called me to it, grabbed the container — vaguely recognizing it as human but incapable of stopping myself — and ripped it open with teeth that had reshaped themselves into daggers.

I drank.

Deeply and long, with the perfect taste of blood flowing along my tongue, filling me with heat and strength and contentment.

And in the instant after I recognized that contentment, sanity returned.

I looked at the dead woman I was holding up with one hand — and realized that suddenly I was strong enough to do that. She was chubby. Older. Wore servant's clothing. I knew that I had killed her. I knew that I'd drunk her blood. I dropped her.

Then, because I was still hungry, I got down on my hands and knees and licked the spilled blood around her off the inlaid marble floor. I felt repugnance at what I was doing. I felt the human I had once been still inside me, screaming at my actions.

But the perfect nectar that was her blood called to me, and I did not stop until I'd licked up every spilled drop.

Chapter 5

23 HOURS EARLIER

Cady couldn't believe what she'd witnessed.

The battle should have been insanely uneven. The combined forces of the Pact Worlds Alliance and the two militaries with which it had allied should have been able to destroy the tiny, cobbled-together fleet that protected Bailey's Irish Space Station and Bailey's Point in mere seconds.

Cady's bait ball had been pulled over toward the station the instant it pushed through the origami point.

From her vantage point, she could see more balls pushing through, and two seconds behind each one, a pirate ship.

She watched the complex maneuvering of bait balls, getting a feel for the curving wall they would have built had they been left in place, seeing the kind of human shield they would have made for the pirate vessels coming in behind.

She knew this wasn't a pirate attack. She knew this was a front, a pretense. That the Pact World Alliance had declared war on the station using the pirates. Had the PWA just come through the point on their own, they could have destroyed the station in seconds.

Why hadn't they?

Hanging soundless in space, pinned in a position where she had to look at what was happening, knowing that behind and beneath her, rescuers were disarming the weapons inside the bait ball that would have killed front-on rescuers and her, watching more people like her being pushed through to provide cover for pirates, watching the pirates being destroyed with the same efficiency that the bait balls were being rescued, she had nothing she could do but think.

So she thought.

The Pact Worlds Alliance was determined to make a show of its might. To make sure everyone in settled space knew the horrors that would befall any world that dared to offer sanctuary to someone the PWA had declared an enemy. Who dared to stand against it.

By sending pirates to do the actual destruction, it was proving that even pirates obeyed it. Would serve its will.

This massive pirate army that was being slaughtered one ship at a time, this massive collection of hostages being rescued one bait ball at a time, was not here to threaten Bailey's Irish Space Station, or Bailey's Point.

Cady had no doubt that the pirates would have been set loose in the station. Would have raped and pillaged, would have murdered and taken slaves.

But this wasn't about the people in the station. And it wasn't even about Bailey's Point.

The PWA certainly had other hidden agents in place on the station like those who had kidnapped her — people who were creating proof of what was happening to Bailey's Point. The PWA would be recording everything so once Bailey's was destroyed, the rest of settled space could see what happened to dissenters.

After Bailey's Point dared to defy the Pact Worlds Alliance and offer sanctuary to the *Longview*, the PWA would consider the massacre of every man, woman, and child in the system a prudent demonstration of its power.

So it was sending it its pirate allies, and she suspected it planned to come in after them and finish off anything the pirates hadn't destroyed, then declare itself the One Government of Settled Space — just as, following mass slaughter of every citizen in Free Novatia nearly a hundred years earlier, the United Bloc had declared itself the One Government of Old Earth.

Cady thought Bailey's Point was intended to be the PWA demonstrating that it could go anywhere, do anything, destroy anyone who stood against it.

But...

Whatever the PWA had planned was going badly wrong. So far.

Suddenly, her perspective shifted as she was turned around and dragged toward the station. Toward the far end and then inside.

Reflected from behind her in the shiny surface of the bait ball, she saw the flash of an explosion.

Thought "that could have been me."

She closed her eyes and yearned for Herog.

Chapter 6

WHEN I WAS SUCCESSFUL TRANSMISSIBLE NANOVIRUS PROTOTYPE 01

Tadra Amu was declared dead. One dismembered finger, her spilled blood, signs of violent struggle in her on-campus apartment, her abandoned paintings and her abandoned scholarship were held as proof of her death. There was no one to notify. So no one was notified, and after cursory investigation, the matter was dropped.

Me?

I went from being an art student to being Danniz Oe's *Successful Transmissible Nanovirus Prototype 01*. I was the first human Oe drank dry who didn't die.

Instead of dying, I acquired the nanovirus through bite transmission, survived, and became a Legend like Oe. The first proof of concept that Oe's vision of a universe in which immortal gods could own all of humanity as their slaves was given real shape and form, and could make their own slaves through both mind control — over those lesser creatures, mere humans — and over the powerful, dangerous creatures they created by transmission. I was the first powerful slave of the first powerful lineage. I was the first proof that the vampire mythos both Danniz Oe and his friend and original funding partner Gainer Holloway wanted to turn into reality could could come true.

Gainer Holloway immediately tripled his investment, injected himself with Oe's adaptation of the Legend nanovirus, and became, like Oe, a top-level immortal.

Oe and Holloway called me StranP01, pronounced Stran-poy.

Danniz Oe was living his dream. Through me and those people he fed to me, once every two weeks during the first two years of experimentation he tested adaptations of the nanovirus — improving its transmissibility; decreasing the need for frequent feeding but increasing the obligatory feeding mechanism (where when you got hungry enough you lost your mind and any ethics you had and attacked and slaughtered the first human who crossed your path); increasing the "creator vampire" control over the creatures made from his bite. I lived through those years chained to a wall in the basement of his mansion, and every upgrade or minor adapta-tion he did on the nanovirus he tested first on me. He then starved me until I lost my mind, and fed me new innocents to see how they turned out.

Oe focused on "bite lineage" as the most important feature of the body mod he was building. This gave me command over the monsters my bite had created, but because he commanded me, gave him power over them that overrode any commands I might give. By the third year of his testing, he had turned me into a creature inca-pable of taking any action against him, and through me, he had a growing band of nearly indestructible immortals absolutely obedient to his every utterance.

He was living his dream… but his dream was my worst nightmare.

My thoughts were my own. I knew who I was, I knew who I'd been, I remembered what I'd wanted. What I still wanted — to create, to live a good life, to find independence and happiness.

But my actions belonged to Danniz Oe. He sent me out to do things I found horrific, and while my mind rebelled, my body obeyed.

When I'd fed, when I was alone, everything that had always

mattered to me still mattered to me, but when I was hungry, the obligate feeding response Oe had built into the mod took over, and I grabbed a human, brought that person to one of Oe's stations, drank the blood, left my victim where I'd found it... and roughly ninety percent of the time, my victim would be so quickly infected by the nanoviral mod that it would live rather than die, would curl up in the room where I'd left it, where it would have a horrible three days of transformation, after which it would crawl out hungry, would attack and drink dry some innocent in the vicinity, and would become a monster like me.

Obedient to me, but *more* obedient to my master. My power grew with every new Legend I created, but because he made more first-level slaves like me with whom he built more lineages for himself, his power grew exponentially faster.

His friend Holloway was busy building his own lineage of obedient slaves.

It was the ultimate pyramid scheme, in which those at the top became gods.

Occasionally Danniz or Holloway would acquire control of another planet by bringing in someone already rich and important person on that world to become a USAG member. For an exorbitant up-front fee, they would make that owner a legend beneath them. Then they would collect USAG dues from that world's new Secret Dark God.

The two of them were franchising immortality and godhood, and there were a lot of buyers.

After their biggest breakthrough with me as their test subject, three more years passed, during which Oe and Holloway made a massive amount of money selling the real version of an ancient Old Earth mythology in which undead blood drinkers were the secret masters of a world.

Three years, during which the Legend population on Cantata grew slowly and carefully, sold one bite at a time to the highest bidders, hidden from discovery by the people in high places who had paid well to become part of it...

During which the richest, the most famous, and the most

powerful people on Cantata joined the immortals at the TOP level, just beneath Oe and Holloway, to change the Universal Society of Antiquarian Gothicans — USAG - from a group of fantasy vampire recreators into the masters of that terrifying fantasy made real.

During which, under the guise of being a quaint little group of ancient literature buffs, these god-pretenders set up their organization to further the following goals, written right into their well-hidden bylaws:

- To turn all civilized worlds and settlements in Settled Space into primitive societies driven by superstition and ignorance
- To place USAG members in charge of every world and colony in Settled Space as the Immortal Gods of these societies
- To require USAG members to rule their worlds with fear, slaughter, and torture — the values of the Vampire Mythos — claiming everything of value for themselves and being worshipped eternally by their hapless human slaves

But here's the thing…

Oe was brilliant at modifying the nanovirus he'd acquired from elsewhere. He had astonishing skills in viral engineering.

He was, however, surprisingly bad at simple arithmetic.

I wasn't. At the point where he and Holloway had stopped adapting the virus, I'd proven myself useful in other ways. I was very good at math. As the first slave, I was utterly trustworthy because I could not disobey him — and because I'd demonstrated that I was capable recognizing opportunities for profit, he'd put me in charge of handling all of his money from all of its sources.

At this point, when I could see the whole picture, I identified what he was doing as a pyramid scheme, and I found the horrific flaw in his business model.

If you create immortals who create immortals and the immortals not only eliminate one source of food ninety-eight out of every hundred times they feed directly from a living human — because not everyone they fed from died — but also, ninety out of a hundred times create a new immortal who also needs to feed, sooner rather than later you're going to wipe out your food source.

Legends in the "published" version of his nanovirus were only driven to obligate feeding about once a month — or when they were injured and lost a lot of blood. And most kept a supply of humans on hand from whom they simply drew blood that they drank in events they called *tastings*, as if they were wine connoisseurs. So initially the problem grew slowly.

But very few of people who bought in at the "one vampire beneath Oe or Holloway" level limited themselves to tastings. Quite a few wanted slaves like me who would make them more powerful. Which in turn made Oe and Holloway more powerful, so both of those idiots encouraged these bits of expansion.

And none of Oe's top-level feeders took any responsibility for regulating the feeding of the creatures they created, because every single new vampire in their downline gave them more personal power.

While in the early years, the expanding Legend population grew slowly, it still grew exponentially.

I kept this bit of math to myself. I needed to stay on Oe's good side, to remain his loyal, trusted slave StranP01.

Why?

Because along with showing me that he was a fool endangering the human species — something he would not believe even if I showed him the math — I'd also discovered that my work for him had a benefit that might eventually give me my freedom.

Chapter 7

WHEN I WAS FEDARA CONTEI

To serve Oe, I had to work in the world, and StranP01 was not a recognized entity.

So I obtained his permission to acquire a secure identity for myself. The only way to do this was illegal, of course — but through one interesting contact I'd made during the illegal work I was doing for Oe already, I tracked down a genius rumored to be flawless at creating bulletproof recreations with brilliant backstories. This genius had created his own identity and had become impossible to find except through recommendation. His name was Storm Rat. Through him, I became Fedara Contei.

Seven years from my conversion — with my proven skill at math and my flawless identity in place, and with my loyalty as Danniz Oe's absolute slave proven repeatedly — I was put in charge without oversight of handling Oe's finances and the finances of USAG. My mission, stated by my master in no uncertain terms, was to make him "god rich." He was immortal, he'd already made himself "god powerful," and he intended to live forever in the style to which he wanted to become accustomed.

The dues coming into USAG from his subservient Legends had to be invested, managed, made to grow.

To give me the best trainers, Oe brought in captured experts from a number of fields who taught me everything they knew about investing, financing, money laundering, extortion, and a number of other fascinating, useful skills, both legal and criminal. Once I'd learned everything they could teach me — and I forced them to teach me everything they knew simply by smiling at them and willing them to obey — Oe took them off to play with, then disposed of them invisibly.

He considered murdering anyone who'd had contact with me, and who might guess what I was doing, a reasonable precaution.

I used what I was taught, and began adding to his wealth. He knew he owned me body and soul. He knew I could do him no harm. And every single day, he could see me multiplying his wealth. He knew I was making him rich. "God rich."

And I did him no harm. Over the next seven years, he saw himself become one of the richest men in settled space.

However, because I had been tasked with making his wealth eternal, and because I could see that he made horrible investments when spending his money himself, I quickly came to understand that as his obedient slave, I had to do something to protect him from himself. So I diverted a significant portion of his income invisibly into a number of cautious investment accounts where the money just rolled over and grew at a healthy but safe interest rate. Oe was listed as the owner of these accounts, and since he had a lock on immortality, there should have been no need for a second account holder.

The accounts I chose, however, because they were legitimate, required both a primary and a secondary contact and a designated inheritor. I was the primary contact, given *carte blanche* by Oe to act as his right hand in all matters financial. In keeping him away from this section of his money, I was protecting Oe from himself and fulfilling my mandate to keep him permanently rich.

But I understand both the appearance and the fact of "conflict of interest" and as his financial manager, I knew that naming myself his backup inheritor would, by creating a conflict of interest, potentially harm him. So I invented a nonexistent creature as the second contact and backup inheritor.

Weyrix Keyr.

I was doing my owner no harm. I was, instead, benefitting him greatly. His wealth from these safe, hidden accounts was growing far better than the accounts he knew about, because they sat untouched, earning compound interest. He was not buying moons and colonies and doing ridiculous terraforming projects with them to create "perfect vampire havens," as he was with the money he could reach. He was getting "god rich," which meant that I was doing exactly what he'd told me to do.

In both the letter and the spirit of the constraints that bound me, I was obedient.

I invested him heavily in some of the most respectable businesses in settled space. Ancient art. Medical research. Slowship renovation and flipping. Settlement franchises. And I had one slowship refurbished into a Death Circus ship. It seemed a ridiculous waste of space. Slowships are massive, and Death Circuses make profits by quickly reselling their convicted criminals to people who have use for such creatures — as slaves, as gladiators, or for other less savory purposes.

I, however, was not terribly interested in reselling. I set up my ship with the requirement that all prisoners purchased by my franchise be stored permanently in special hibernation Medixes as long-term investments. They could only be sold when bidding on them reached one hundred thousand rucets. I stated that it was a requirement of the owner.

Oe, of course, had made no such requirement since he didn't even know he owned a Death Circus. And I had no logical reason for demanding that the main I hired as the Criminal Manager for the Death Circus do this. The steady selling of low-priced to mid-range Class A prisoners is how a Death Circus makes most of its profit, and my ridiculously high price meant that only a very few criminals would ever be sold.

I could not have explained to anyone why I took the actions with that Death Circus that I took. Not even to myself.

Looking back at myself as I was then, I recognize now that I was not alone inside myself.

Deep down, the part of me that had once been K-Eighty-Four still hid naked in a hole with leaves over her head — quiet, watchful, waiting. Operating her plans out of my sight. Knowing that at some point an opportunity for freedom might come, and that if it came, she wanted to be ready.

Down in the dark, she kept herself to herself, once again ready to move if that single chance to escape ever came.

Chapter 8

ON HEROG'S FOURTH DAY IN THE CITY OF FURIES...

Herog sat at the round table, studying three citizens who made up the rest of the City of Furies' brand new defense council.

The council didn't have a name, didn't have a special office in a government building, didn't have flunkies or conveniences. No one except him was being paid to be there. The three volunteers had skills, knowledge, and a history of not dying when dying would have been the easy thing.

Ex-slaves like him, every one of them.

They'd been meeting every day for three days after their regular jobs. He'd spent every hour after his paid job — which was surveying the city's existing technology — trying to understand how the damned place hadn't already been discovered and wiped off the face of its planet.

It had walls, and no one could go outside the walls. Or come in through them. But walls had not been a viable defense since just past the dawn of civilization on Old Earth.

The woman on the committee, Derna, said, "We've received confirmation that Bailey's Point now has access to all the warships and primary support ships from three fleets, and if they can find people to operate them, will own outright the biggest and most powerful military force in settled space. And the owner of the Longview wants Bailey's Point to become humanity's seat of power. He wants the Bailey's citizens to wipe out slavery and become the center of a spreading wave of individual rights and freedom." Derna's day job was fuel optimization research. Her personal history before she woke up in the City of Furies was something she did not talk about. "The owner of the *Longview*, who is the primary investor in most of the projects underway in this city, wants Bailey's Point to go on the offensive, to use all that power to start requiring other worlds to adopt the standards by which Bailey's Point operates."

Herog said, "I know. He was vehement about that. Like us, he was a slave. He would not go into his history with me, but there's a lot of rage in him even now."

"Taking the offensive seems logical," Meklen said. He did infrastructure design and had developed the streets, over-roads, and flight paths for the air cars. "And back when I was a slave, I would have given anything to see a military come in, wipe out all the slave owners, free us, and take us someplace safe. But something about this just doesn't sit right with me."

Derna and Liam, the almost-always-silent fourth member, nodded.

Derna said, "I'm all in favor of the eradication of slave owners. But I don't like the idea of it being done by a government. The slave hunters were heroes to me, but so were slaves like you. You — Herog. You got yourself free, you used everything they'd done to hurt you to make yourself stronger, and when you escaped you brought that down on them. The *first* time I got free, you and your people actually came through and pulled me out of…" she faltered. "Of where I was."

Herog looked at Derna and raised an eyebrow. In the years since he'd escaped, he and his allies had freed uncounted thousands of slaves, and he would not have recognized her. But he nodded. It made sense to him that some of the people he'd rescued would have ended up in the City of Furies.

He said, "I understand where Mado Keyr is coming from, but he's wrong. Dead wrong. He has a vision of a universe in which no one is ever a slave, but that vision includes the control of every single human being in order to prevent slavery from ever being able to arise again. It mandates the creation of an oppressive central government that forces its will on every human being alive. And the fact that he means well *means nothing*. He is working to create the system he hates, and he thinks that because he had good intentions, it will turn out differently than it has in every other place where people relinquished their power to a government and told the government to protect them. Giving any government that kind of power is the path to Hell."

"So... How do we keep this place safe? How do we protect our citizens, our creations, our philosophy?"

Herog stood up and started pacing. "How do you currently deal with people who come in here, who are spies or enemy agents, who attempt sabotage?"

He watched them look at each other, expressions of bewilderment on their faces. Derna said, "To the best of my knowledge, no such person has ever gotten into the city. There has never been an attempt at sabotage made — much less a successful one."

He stopped pacing. All three of them were nodding agreement.

"How then do you deal with other problems? With criminals, with homicides, with kidnappings or rapes or abuse?"

The puzzled expressions on their faces sent a little chill down his spine.

Derna said, "I... I don't know. I don't think there's ever been anything like that here."

The others nodded.

"How do you go about finding a missing child, then?"

And they all stared at each other. "I haven't even seen a child since I arrived here," Derna whispered.

"How about funerals of important people?"

"I supposed there have been," Liam, the fourth member of their panel, who was an engineer, looked at the other three. "If we checked for obituaries." He shrugged, "In the seventeen years I've lived here, I haven't heard of any deaths. But I haven't been looking for them."

Derna looked startled. "Since I came here, I haven't known a single person who has died."

Mecklen looked thoughtful. "Neither have I... But I never really thought about it. Everyone *I* know is young and healthy."

Herog said, "No crime, no abuse, no children, no old age, no death. You know what that means?"

They looked at him, shaking their heads.

"I do," he said. "I think Keyr already has his solution. He just doesn't realize it yet."

Chapter 9

WHEN I WAS FEDARA CONTEI

Sometimes you know an individual is going to change your life the minute you meet him. Or this time, for me, *her*.

I met Cadence Drake on assignment from Oe. She had tripped over USAG, and was dangerously curious about it, and getting close to finding the truth.

But she was working for someone else, and Oe had been unable to discover who'd hired her.

So I was to contact her, enthrall her, and bring her to Oe… and then he was going to release her so I could go with her. She was to rescue me, take me with her back to whomever had hired her. I would go with her, kill her employer, and then kill her.

My orders were simple and clear, and up to a point, I obeyed the letter of them. The spirit of them? Well…

I discovered that Cady and her friend Badger had done complex worm searches that ran through the dark ping. Monitoring traffic on the dark ping had been what tipped off Danniz Oe.

But I also found out that Cady and Badger had uncovered Oe's franchise — the names of USAG's members, who were all first-level Oe slaves like me, but who had bought in to USAG as investment members, had bought their bite, and who were all rich. To Cady and Badger, it had become clear that the organization was more than rich Old-Earth pseudohistory buffs who liked to play dress-up while pretending to be dark-god immortals.

So Oe pulled me away from working on his finances, and took me to Galatia Fairing to gain control over Cadence Drake without converting her to one of us. I had to kill her when my mission was done, and Oe wanted the process to be as clean and efficient as possible.

I did not expect the impact she had on me the first time I met her.

I'll be blunt. *I wanted her.* She was intelligent, independent, brusque, funny, strange. So I did the sort of thing Oe would not have approved of... but had failed to forbid. Since it didn't pose any threat of harm to him, and since it might even prove helpful...

I did some personal research on her, on my own rucet and using and misusing the resources to which I had access on Galatia Fairing.

It turned out that Cady had the highest captain's exam scores I'd ever seen in someone I'd met. Better yet, her psych profiles marked her as brilliant, prone to ethics-driven disobedience and unsanctioned, independent action. Every report confirmed that she was poorly socialized and best kept away from any job that conferred real power. That she was captain of her own scrubby little ship and working independently, finding expensive things (and sometimes people) who had gone missing for high-paying clients. The life she had chosen made her a non-threat to people in charge of worlds, who would otherwise have been terrified of her.

I saw no indication in her history that she'd ever been attracted to women, and not much indication that she was attracted to men. Her relationship with Badger had started in their early childhoods, and while cautious digging suggested that they had been lovers on a few occasions, Badger had left a trail of broken hearts, both male and female, behind him wherever he went.

She...?

Had mostly been his friend, occasionally his sexual partner. From everything I could discover, she'd had a horrible childhood and brutal exit from Cantata back when she had been Tanasha

Elenday. She was the estranged daughter of Lashanda Elenday, who was one of Oldcity's big movers and shakers, and one of Oe's top-level USAG members on Cantata.

Unlike her friend Badger, who'd had multiple serious romances before falling in love with her, Cady had never had a committed romantic love interest.

For me, that would have made her a difficult conquest, had I not been what I am.

Meanwhile, I, with my own awful history, complicated gender, and desperate desire for personal freedom, saw her and the life she'd built for herself as the thing I wanted. And her as my path toward getting it.

Before I met her, I'd found her interesting.

After I met her, I discovered myself in love for the first time.

So I did exactly what Oe told me to do. Worked myself into Cady's life, made myself invaluable to her, had her take me where her investigation took her. And then used her to kill all the Oldcity members of USAG present in that special meeting, and along with them, Danniz Oe.

She did what I could not do. Could not even think about doing.

She didn't know it. But she set me free.

Chapter 10
WHEN I WAS FEDARA CONTEI

I'm good at math.
It is a blessing.
And a curse.

By the time Danniz Oe was dead, by the time Cady and Badger were getting ready to tell the man who'd hired them that they'd located his stolen spaceship, I could pinpoint both a best case and worst case for the point at which the population of Oe's contagiously spreading vampirism would wipe out humanity.

And I couldn't think of a thing to do to stop it.

But one of the things I discovered — in my incredibly invasive exploration of Cadence Drake's past — was that when she took her captain's exam, she'd earned the second highest score ever on the Suitability for Deep Space test. Which is also known as the Kartach Norgan test.

Turns out the same take-charge, assume responsibility, go-it-alone-to-get-the-job-done qualities that make people reliable under horrific pressure in space are also great qualities for allowing them to become dictatorial monsters if they choose careers in politics. Hence Kartach Norgan, named after the original settled space dictatorial monster.

The test for this is so physically overwhelming and potentially destructive — it can actually kill the taker mid-test — that giving it has been outlawed in most "civilized" worlds. So even though there's a foolproof way to find out which people should never be given power over other people's lives, most would-be and actual politicians are never tested.

Taking your million-rucet pleasure cruiser through origami points using TransFold Navigation? Oh, yes. We can certainly kill a few people to make sure you get safely to the Moon of Prepubescent Sex Toys and back home again. So anyone — anywhere — who wants to become the captain of a Transfold Navigation ship that can jump across solar systems by folding through origami points *must* take the Kartach Norgan. Excuse me. The whitewashed name of that test is the Suitability for Deep Space — SDS — exam.

On average, sixty percent of those who who have completed the rigorous deep-space pilot training fail this final test. They are instantly disqualified from ever being Trans-Fold Navigation pilots, and limited to in-system jobs.

However, the forty percent who pass are instantly disqualified from ever being politicians. Ever. Why?

To give what follows some perspective, the average score on normal people subjected to this test is two to five percent. These folks are considered safe for society.

To be a TFN captain, you have to score better than forty — but if you score more than *twenty*, you're considered a megalomaniacal danger to humanity if put in charge of a government.

Cadence Drake had scored an eighty-nine on the test. It was surreal — the second highest score ever recorded. Only one earlier student scored higher than that — a ninety-seven, which was the most terrifying thing I'd ever seen, and I'd been Danniz Oe's mind slave.

I could have used that ninety-seven scorer. But the taker of *that* test had disappeared. I both knew Cady and knew how to find her.

I knew what the problem was. Danniz Oe's Legend virus was spreading with exponentially accelerating speed.

But while I would probably score fairly high on the Kartach

Norgan if anyone could force me to take it, I was no one's eighty-nine percent.

I could not see a path to solving the Legend disaster that was racing straight at us.

Cady's brain, however, would work in ways that mine couldn't. Kartach Norgan high-scorers land on their feet, figure out solutions when none are apparent, never ever *ever* give up until they're dead. And even Death generally has to take an army to stop them.

I didn't know how to get her on my side. I knew she'd seen me approach Oe before she killed him. I knew she'd seen me smile at him, whisper something to him. I knew she would think I'd betrayed her.

So if she saw me, she would try to kill me.

I managed to gain access to her ship using the Cantata-wide override pass I'd lifted from Danniz Oe's pocket right before Cady killed him. That pass was the reason I'd gone up to him during his demonstration of Legend II, smiled at him, stood beside him, touched him. When I touched him, I stole it.

The action didn't harm him. Didn't threaten him.

And because I was basically his business manager slave, having that override was something I knew I had to do in order to protect his investments.

I did not let myself think about why I would need to protect those investments in the near future… But it turns out there's nothing built into Legend that forces you to try to save your owner when you know something else is going to kill him.

Just as she had to live, *I had to live.* I had to put her on the path to clearing the Legends from settled space, to getting humanity off the endangered species list.

So I was in the *Hope's Reward*, and had been waiting, hidden out of the way, trying to figure out how to get her to see reason, hoping she would work with me one last time when I heard her propose marriage to Badger. Propose settling down somewhere with the money they were going to get from the man who'd hired her and set her on the path to finding USAG, Peter Crane. She was talking about becoming domestic. Settling down. Raising a family.

Marriage and children would prevent her from finding a way to stop my kind of creature from spreading. From even discovering how bad the problem already was, and how much worse it was going to become.

Then her mother stepped out of a hiding place I hadn't noticed, moved into position in front of me, cast a little smile back in my direction, and whispered, "My kill, not yours."

Cady's mother wanted to kill her.

Lashanda had Cady at a disadvantage, and Badger was unarmed. Why the hell was Badger unarmed?

And then her mother did the unexpected. Told Cady that she and I had been working together, and that when I had suggested splitting Meileone with her, she'd killed me.

I was standing right behind her, just a bit off to one side, out of sight. And she knew it.

And she said *I was dead, and that she'd killed me.*

To this day I don't know what she thought that would accomplish.

Lashanda told Cady and Badger to go with her. She was going to get them off the ship, take them someplace private, kill them and make them disappear.

And then Badger did the stupidest, bravest thing I've ever seen. He shouted, drew an imaginary gun, dropped, rolled, pretended to fire.

He pulled Lashanda's focus away from Cady for a split second. Cady shot her mother full of AntiLegend.

Her mother shot wildly and took off one of Cady's legs — but the nice thing about lasers is that they seal when they cut. Cady would live.

Lashanda exploded all over the cargo bay. Not a problem for any of the three of us, because we were all three immune to Legend, being full of AntiLegend, the agent I'd had created so humanity could wipe out Legends like me.

Rule number one in creating the weapon that would kill you and everyone like you? *First, make sure it can't kill you.*

So even as Lashanda was trying to kill Cady, I shot and killed

Badger. For humanity to survive, Badger couldn't. It was a terrible thing to do. And I swear it had nothing to do with me wanting Cady for myself, because... well... Cady thought I was already dead. And had been her mother's ally.

But that wasn't the point.

If Badger lived, Cady and he would settle down, start a family. Become soft and dull and content.

When I shot Badger, knowing that Cady would find out I'd been the one to kill him, I accepted that to push her into the mode that would set off the unstoppable Kartach Norgan juggernaut inside of her, that would set her on my trail and push her into discovering the Legend population explosion, I would have to live the rest of my eternity without her.

I knew she would know I'd killed Badger.

I knew by killing him I would become forever her enemy.

But to find my kind, she had to come after me. So I decided before I took the shot that I could live with that. I would lead her to the dangers, she would pursue. She would find what I knew, and because she was something that I am not, she would see a way to end the problem, if one could be found.

Love can be replaced. Rediscovered in someone else.

Trillions of human beings eliminate any dream that there is just one person in the universe who will be right for you.

Immortality gives you the chance to keep looking.

Unless, of course, something is wiping out humanity.

If humanity becomes extinct, your chances of finding love and the life you want to live are... none.

Chapter 11

TWO HOURS AFTER BAILEY'S POINT WON THE WAR...

Melie, captain of the *Longview*, was looking over the owner's request to rebuild the City of Furies on one of Bailey's inner planets when Mado Keyr came onto the bridge.

She rose, and he said, "You've seen it?"

"I haven't gone through everything yet, but I'm more than halfway."

"And?"

Melie considered being tactful, but decided against it. "This is the strangest proposal I've ever seen. I cannot figure out why you're pushing to do this. You're talking about making an exact duplicate of an existing city that is currently well hidden from its enemies — and the City of Furies still has many enemies, even if the Pact Worlds Alliance has had its teeth pulled. You're talking about putting this exact duplicate on one of the inner planets of Bailey's Point, where it will no longer be hidden at all." She shook her head. "I cannot imagine how people who are currently safely hidden from people who want them dead would consider moving from their current city to your duplicate."

The owner nodded. "Reasonable reservations. May I briefly borrow you from what you're doing?"

Melie stood, indicated that her second should take the captain's chair. Once he assumed command, she followed the owner.

When they were off the bridge, he said, "You need to understand the City of Furies, and why I'm proposing what I am. So I'm going to show you the part of the ship that only I have access to. From now on, you'll have access as well."

"This is something your captains take on as part of their duties?"

"No," he said. "Just you."

She considered that, bit her lower lip. Nodded. This, then, was part of the mystery of the ship. Part of all of those things none of the crew could ever speak about, could never question.

This was the one mystery she had not been able to solve in spite of her skills.

The "why" behind the vast dark deeps filled with countless men and women in suspended animation. The heavily armored ship core with No Entry signs and high security ident scans at every hatch… and possibly the comings and goings of people brought in by the owner who were never introduced to or identified for the crew, who disappeared into the ship for a time, then reappeared and left, never to be seen again.

He was leading her toward his quarters, though.

She looked over at him, her question in her one raised eyebrow, and he said, "I have access to things no one else on this ship has. And that access is convenient for me."

He took her into a dark general room, in which she could see a desk, some chairs close to a large moleibond viewport out into space, stairs to her right, and a door in front of her and to the left.

"We're going that way," he said and pointed to the door.

He led.

She followed.

They stepped into a low, narrow corridor, followed it up a short flight of stairs, then down a long tight passageway. If she'd been subject to claustrophobia, she would have panicked. As it was, she found herself uncomfortable. She tried to keep her bearings within the ship. She could tell she and Keyr were working their way along a hidden layer between the outer hull and what she knew had to be criminal storage, but at the point where they went up one gravdrop, zigzagged through a corridor that had to be working its hidden way into the ship's interior, and then up another gravdrop, she was lost.

They came out onto a balcony and into a vast open space filled with a massive floating sphere that glittered, glowed, pulsed with ever-changing lights.

"That's beautiful," she whispered.

He nodded. "It's my nightmare. My love. My passion. And now it has become the end of me."

Chapter 12

WHEN I BECAME WERIX KEYR

A massive amount of money was sitting in accounts all over settled space, growing. And I as Fedara Contei was its executor.

But I wasn't its inheritor. The man on all the records was Mado Werix Keyr.

So with Danniz Oe dead, if I wanted to free up that money, I was going to have to produce Werix Keyr.

I considered dressing up one of my victims who was a Legend because of me and modifying him to assume the identity of the wealthy man…

But look how well enslaving his victims had turned out for Danniz Oe.

The intelligent learn from history. They don't repeat it.

So I went back to Storm Rat, and I told the truth — most of it, anyway. Storm Rat and his people already knew of my underage prostitution disguised as mentorship when I was Tadra Amu and my origin as an infant born into the Living Saints cult, including my escape from slaughter at puberty as K-Eighty-Four.

I went back to them as Tadra Amu, escaped slave of the dead Danniz Oe, skipped straight over my middling stay as StranP01, and melded the past they knew into the Fedara Contei ID I had at the time because StranP01 wasn't on record. However, I did note that in order to guarantee my permanent willing servitude, Oe had injected me with a body mod that, if it were altered in any way, would kill me. I explained that I needed to have them be careful working around those nanoviral changes.

So they were careful. They didn't dig, didn't pry into the story. They'd been able to verify my history both times, so they let me into their little world. While I was there, they treated me with reserved, careful kindness.

I kept to myself, kept my teeth to myself, spent every second that I could alone on my own little ship with my supply of stolen frozen blood.

They had *all* been slaves — Storm Rat and his associates and his allies. They had all lived their own horror stories, and they had no problem understanding that I didn't want to spend time with them. I just wanted to get fixed, get away… and they respected my privacy.

When I explained what I wanted and why — and I told them the absolute truth about this — it took them a week to deliver. During that week, I lived in orbit and ate only once — and was grateful that Oe had spent so much time and money decreasing the required frequency of feeding.

Storm Rat's team built a genderflip profile for me that would let me use my private Medix (or any public Medix) to change from Fedara Contei to Weyrix Keyr. The way they did it was clever. They embedded a Fedara Contei identity reju pod in the tip of my left index finger (I'm a lefty), and a Werix Key identity reju pod in the tip of my right one.

And they built an incredibly clever neural rewire scheme that controlled handedness, so I didn't ever accidentally screw up and use the wrong ident.

They made Werix Keyr a natural right-hander. So when I genderflip, I automatically come out of the box presenting the correct finger for ident checks. The correct eye for optical checks. I don't have to think, to hesitate. I'm always just myself inside my skin.

I have a bit of numbness in both fingertips now, but in a society where demanding a bit of your blood and tissue to prove who you are is both mandatory and frequent, numbness has its benefits.

Able to be both Werix Keyr and Fedara Contei, I went on my way, with the few people discovered I actually trusted knowing more truth about me than anyone except Danniz Oe ever had.

And I discovered that was an oddly comforting feeling.

Every single step I'd taken to create Werix Keyr was, of course, illegal as all hell. But in most of settled space, even thinking unapproved thoughts is illegal. In those places, the only way to be one of the good guys is to be a criminal.

I spent a week jumping to different systems, doing a couple of random TFN jumps into undocumented systems just to lose my backtrail — worthwhile inconvenience because it protected Storm Rat and his people — and then presented myself as Werix Keyr with Danniz Oe's death certificate for each account that I'd created and hidden.

I walked away from that step inconceivably rich.

The Werix Keyr money was clean money. The instant Oe's death was confirmed, Danniz Oe's name came off the accounts and all sign that it had ever been there disappeared. That money became mine, with no sign that it had been associated with a monster.

With no history of how I'd made it, either.

The rest of Oe's holdings were problematic.

Werix Keyr had also been listed as the beneficiary on Oe's public accounts and purchases. I'd told him not to worry. I'd make up a phony name, give it a contact address that ID monitors would confirm, and add that to the accounts. He'd agreed.

So as Werix Keyr, I found myself the owner of a lot of terrible things.

Most I let sit, because they were infested by Legends like me, and I could not in good conscience allow those possessions and the monsters on them to pass into the hands of innocents.

Some I was able to unload because they were clean.

When I had done what I could to distance myself from Oe, I called home the most conservative of the hidden investments I'd been making for Danniz Oe — that ancient colony slowship I'd had refurbished as a Death Circus. This particular vessel had originally been built to transport five hundred thousand people and their few possessions and the seed tech that would build their colony on a new world. The ship had been filled with the bulky, primitive hibernation units of the time.

It was massive, ugly, sturdy, slow.

And it was haunted. If not by real ghosts, then by its own history.

It had been the hope of half a million people trying to escape the hell of repressive world government that Old Earth had become.

It had been the scene of mass genocide… and mass enslavement.

I tried to imagine half a million people being so desperate to escape the only home the species had ever known that they were willing to sell everything they owned, to pay the exorbitant fees to have their blood drained, to have their bodies filled with hibernation fluid, to have themselves flash frozen… and to then face centuries of travel locked in primitive freezer boxes just to have a chance to reach a place where they couldn't even be sure they would find a home.

The ship had been named *Long Winter Kind Spring*. Its winter had been short, though, less than fifty years. And its spring never came.

Following the discovery of origami folds and points by Isas Yamamoto, a number of labs perfected moleibonding techniques that created hulls capable of moving ships and the humans inside them through the tearing pressures exerted by the folds. Once humans could survive being squeezed through the origami points, nearly instantaneous point-to-point space travel opened up.

And criminals, always early in the adoption of new tech, plotted out where every slowship they could find would be in its passage. They gathered in bands, hit these rich, unarmed targets, freighted off the supplies that would have built and supported colonies and sustained them for their first hundred years... and then these inventors of space piracy systematically slaughtered the hibernating adult males and took the hibernating women and children to revive and sell as slaves.

I do not know of a single colony established anywhere by slowship survivors.

The funny thing is, there probably are several, but they're in solar systems without origami points — and thus free from any threat of space piracy.

They're safe from the worst that settled space has to offer — but out of reach of the best, too. And they're stuck — permanently stuck. Humanity grew into settled space in less than a hundred years because out past Pluto, humanity *had* an origami point, and when Isas Yamamoto located it, our door opened.

Those rare slowship colonists, wherever they might be, are survivors only because they have no door.

When I became Werix Keyr, in any case, I recalled my Death Circus from its route. At that point, I rechristened the *Long Winter Kind Spring* the *Longview*. It had already been moleibonded, fitted with TFN drives and the best in-system drives, already had a million of the best existing hibernation units installed — these less than a third the size of the primitive slowship units, so that a million of them fit easily into less space than those original units had required — taking up only the middle third of the ship. The back third at that time was empty.

At the point I went aboard, my ship held nearly a hundred thousand criminals in hibernation.

I kept the newly christened *Longview* off its route only long enough to add in a luxurious apartment suite for myself and to improve the accommodations for a small crew.

I did this because I had an idea — a dream — but it was something that would, I thought, take hundreds or thousands of years.

I wanted to create a culture of human beings who exported freedom the way Old Earth had exported its terrible ideas of top-down governance and the enslavement of the individual for the benefit of those who ran the government. People can escape planets, but they rarely outrun their unexamined assumptions, the primary of these being that the job of a government is to take care of its people.

Its people. Hold those two words in your head for a moment, and really think about them.

If the people *belong* to the government, rather than belonging to themselves, slavery is built right in.

For the first time in my life, I belonged to myself.

And I wanted to bring other people with me. To find slaves, free them, teach them to think for themselves, teach them self-reliance, encourage them to work for their own benefit and to never accept the idea that they needed to be made sacrifices to someone else's demands.

To give them a protected world in which to live — and then let them prove to all of settled space that a government answerable to and owned by its citizens, with humans whose unfettered freedom gave them a legal and inalienable right pursue their own dreams and desires in a society that understood freedom's value, would outperform every form of slavery humanity had invented.

As I said, I saw this taking thousands of years. And while I was immortal, I knew I would need time to figure out how to bring about the future I desired. The *Longview* held in storage the blood of all those nice clean criminals to keep me healthy while I figured it out.

At that point, I did not know that there were already escaped slaves out there hunting down slavers, killing them, and freeing their slaves.

I did not know that there were rebels hidden deep inside slaver governments working against those who demanded to be served.

I had not yet read the works of Bashtyk Nokyd.

Back then, the news of all these things was suppressed.

So with me aboard, the *Longview* resumed its Death Circus route with a fresh crew, and with me as a mysterious, damaged man who avoided all human contact and kept to his apartments. I made my money without interfering with the workings of the ship.

Chapter 13

WHEN I WAS WERIX KEYR

Money makes money.

With Danniz Oe dead and my identity as Werix Keyr established, however, to use that money to fund my thousand-year plan to reintroduce human freedom, I had to have the backstory that permitted the right kinds of people — the ludicrously rich ones — to give me their money without question.

So even though I was living on the *Longview*, I purchased an ancient, grand home on the core PWA world Meileone, in the most prestigious city, Cantata, and in the best and most revered neighborhood — Oldcity.

The story Storm Rat had given me made me a direct descendent of one of the best Old Earth families. My lineage and massive fortune made it simple for me to keep to myself. I simply moved into that fine Oldcity neighborhood. I did not immediately refurbish the ancient home — refurbishing landmark buildings into flashy new buildings is the mark of the nouveau rich. I took on only a handful of servants to tend my grand home and rewarded them well for maintaining the house when I was away.

I did not try to meet anyone in Oldcity. I maintained my quiet reserve, funded the finer things in the city like the arts and sciences, continued to invest with an eye toward reliable, cautious growth.

Threw no parties, accepted only one invitation, and that one a personal, private invitation to a dinner with just Cantata's governor and a handful of his closest friends who had gathered specifically to meet me. To that party I wore a pressure suit with a rebreather, socialized little, and left early, noting that the gravity of the planet quickly tired me. The story I gave was that I had a degenerative neurological disease that did not respond to Medix treatments — there are a few such in the universe, and they are ugly. During that short dinner, I let it be known that I had to spend most of my time in space, in light gravity. On a ship I did not care to identify.

If you have enough money and have no interest in flaunting it, the things you say are taken at face value.

In that fashion, I had no problem passing myself as old money from Old Earth, which is as old as money can get.

During my three-month stay in the Oldcity house, I made conservative investments. And through my servants, I leaked a few facts I wanted to get into public circulation. The first was that I owned an ancient slowship, and that I'd had it fitted out as a Death Circus. The second was that I'd been the top bidder on seven original Sarling Fermee paintings. The third was my funding for the Oldcity Ancient Orchestra.

In such fashion, I established myself as an interesting investor, someone capable of growing money, someone capable of discovering new talent and bringing it to broader attention.

Death Circuses are very conservative investments, because in these days of reju and body modding, the only thing more certain than death is taxes.

Meanwhile, investing in the work of Sarling Fermee proved me to be edgy. Willing to take chances. My bidding up of his works through several proxies working against me as the open bidder put him on the map.

Sarling Fermee was the inventor of alien hyperrealism. The artist whose work had made me want to be an artist. He had been my inspiration when I'd dared to dream of following in his footsteps, and even though that dream had not gone well for me, I still loved art. And his art. He was still alive, still working — and after my purchases, his future works would sell for more. I thought someday I would like to meet him.

I eventually did better than that. He now lives at 49 West Branch in the City of Furies. But how that happened is a story someone else will have to tell.

As for the orchestra? I enjoy classical music played by living musicians on analog instruments. Why not throw a publicly visible stream of rucets into that to keep it alive?

Meanwhile, my child self hiding down in her hole with the leaves pulled over her head had been working for my benefit when she pushed me in my Fedara Contei slave state to store all criminals who could not be sold for a hundred thousand rucets or more.

She was working, strangely enough, to save herself as well.

First, the sources of ethically obtained genuine human blood are few — but one of them is convicted Pact World Class B criminals, who do not fall under the protection of the Pact World Covenants.

Class A criminals — rapists, murderers, force-thieves, and others who have harmed others with intent, have very strict treatment and sentencing requirements.

But once off Meileone and back on the *Longview*, I finally got around to reading the "Operation of Your Death Circus Franchise" manual, and I discovered that Class B criminals, who have in almost all cases committed crimes not recognized by the Pact Worlds Alliance as major crimes, are treated under the "do anything you want with them as long as you don't kill them" rule given to all planetary franchises when they buy their licenses.

Class B criminals are almost always thought criminals — those who challenge the position of the people in charge. Thus, they are usually far more hated by their world's governments than Class A criminals.

On most franchise worlds, therefore, they are starved, tortured within an inch of their lives, and paraded before other citizen-slaves as examples of what happens to those who dare to think.

Once they are at Death's door (but not over it, because killing them is a primary prohibition in the franchise terms of ownership, for which a license could be revoked without recourse), they are sold for next to nothing to the next passing Death Circus.

From my manual, I discovered that the Death Circuses, which were required to purchase a percentage of Class B criminals at every location, were encouraged to take these thought criminals outside of Pact Worlds boundaries and dump them out the airlock.

So the sentence of Class B criminals was in reality to be tortured for as long as they could survive it, only to be murdered silently and conveniently away from any public eye.

Franchise colonies were terraformed and placed where out-of-mainstream religions and philosophies, theme vacation chains, and special-needs/special-desires resorts could operate away from mainstream culture. Where they could set up with their franchise's rules, then advertise for and get settlers who paid big fees to join them. These franchises, all guilty of deceptive advertising, became the biggest source of Class B criminals.

Franchise colonies were eyeballs-deep in regulations with oversight directly by the Pact Worlds Alliance and its crony inspectors. But the regulations were for the prevention of spread of disease, for the prevention of bad publicity for the franchise, and for the improvement of cash flow.

Buying a Class A criminal requires a massive amount of paperwork, because each one is a valuable commodity. They can be resold to the entertainment market, where they become gladiators or torture whores, or where they can be forced to do any of a thousand other terrible jobs. Better yet, the more horrible their crimes, the better the price the seller can get for them, because the worst of them can be auctioned for Public Execution if their crimes are horrible and entertaining enough to get the Pact Worlds' entertainment division interested in purchasing execution broadcast rights. The Good, Decent, Rich Class A citizens of the Pact Worlds like to have their nasty, dirty fun where proof of it can't follow them home. And they like to cheer on the screaming and blood of a good, gory execution now and then.

Class B prisoners require only the maintenance of an IDENT

form and a DATE OF DEATH form. And Class B prisoners have never done anything that can be sold for broadcast or anything that can be pointed to as a real crime. They are the people who dare to have a sense of self, who dare to think that they have a right to live their lives the way they want. They're the folks who paid to emigrate to a new world where freedom was promised, only to discover that they'd paid to be slaves in a worse world than they'd left.

As thought criminals, Class B folks are unwelcome almost everywhere in settled space. Slavery in its many guises creates very nice lives for the few at the top, and whether these few are kings or government officials, those at the top survive only by locking down those at the bottom.

Kings and government officials alike want those below them to obey silently and without question — and if they dare to question, those at the top want them to die. However, in societies where forks record what their users eat and glasses monitor what their users drink, where servants and friends and even lovers constantly record the actions of the people in their lives, where everything watches almost everyone almost all the time, those at the top need to appear clean. To pretend to themselves and their slaves that they are Friends of the People.

When, as Fedara Contei, I instructed the crew of the Death Circus I purchased to store all criminals who could not be sold for a high return, I didn't know why the Class Bs were so cheap, so plentiful, or so easily disposable. I guessed that what they'd done was so horrible they could not be allowed to live, but that they had to be disposed of invisibly to prevent others from knowing such evil existed in the universe.

If you're a dictator perched precariously on top of a pyramid of slaves — and people start agitating for individual freedom — I suppose that's actually your belief.

In any case, the "Operation of Your Death Circus Franchise" handbook offered tips on ways to get top dollar for my Class A criminals. And suggested hiring one of their Recommended Helpers to find a nice origami point to a solar system with no planets, a dead sun, or another serious flaw, and then to always use that system to dump my Class Bs out the airlock.

Worlds with most Class As and Class Bs were listed in the handbook, along with percentages of Bs that had to be purchased to permit the buying of or bidding on Class As.

And then I discovered that the Beckenridge Colony of Living Saints was listed as one of the most profitable colonies in settled space.

That it had one citizen, the Saint.

That every other person on the world was a product: a Breeder, a Trained, Neutered Slave, or Class B — a disposal problem for the world's owner when he was done with that person.

And I froze.

I'd thought that I had genuine criminals in storage. I'd thought that I'd maintain them as unconscious, preserved, safe food storage for me. I was going to be — I thought — kinder to them than the other Death Circuses. I wasn't going to let all that ethically obtained blood go to waste out an airlock and into deep space.

But I discovered in that moment that everyone on Beckenridge had been a tool for the satisfaction of the Saint and those to whom the Saint rented out or sold his little-boy "products".

I had escaped that evil bastard's child-sex and child-disposal program on his legally franchised, working-within-the-letter-of-the-law private haven. But I might have been the only one who did.

I got cold.

Quiet.

And very, very angry.

Angry enough to buy the Saint's world from him for a hefty profit, then make to make sure he died hideously and secretly, wide awake, knowing exactly who I was and why he was dying at my hand. His death took a very long time.

Angry enough to take every single survivor off his world and put them in my Medixes until I figured out what to do with them.

Angry enough to see, for the first time, what the Pact Worlds Alliance really was. To see beyond my own nose, beyond my own pain, beyond my own self pity to the galaxy beyond, to the people trapped in situations they could not change, could not fix, and would not survive.

I was angry enough that I *finally* asked the question I needed to ask, which was simply this…

How do I use this vast fortune I've acquired, this ship that was just going to be my legal food source, and this franchise that gives me access to places most people don't even know exist, to stop slavery in all its many forms in settled space?

Chapter 14

MELIE

"The end of you?" Melie asked.

"I'm dying today," Keyr said. "It's a necessary part of my life. I've found the people who can keep what I've created going, who can bring it into the real universe, who can protect it and nurture it and make sure that it stays true to its principles.

"From that," he said, "I can finally release my pain, step away from the anguish of the life I have been dragging myself through, day by agonizing day, for years. I can let go, embrace the darkness, cease to exist." He looked at Melie, and she could feel the power and intensity of his gaze even through the darkened faceplate of his heavy shipsuit.

"My invention," Keyr said. "It's the City of Furies. And every slave we've taken in since I began building it lives there. We have almost a million people in the city now — living and working — and the ship's storage can hold no more."

She stared at the sphere, which she guessed took up the entire back third of the *Longview*.

"The City of Furies is virtual?"

Keyr nodded.

Then the truth hit her. "The PWA attack. If it had hit the *Longview*, it would have destroyed the City of Furies…"

"The city needs to be real," he said. "A real place with real protection. It needs to be a destination people can come to of their own free will. It needs to have families, children, the dynamic of real, physical human interaction. I have given it as much reality as I can, but every human being in the city is trapped inside a specially designed Medix that allows communications with others through the sphere — but only mimics human touch. And cannot duplicate the creation of children, or aging, or change. So everyone in there is always thirty, and for people who have been in there since the beginning, the fact that they do not change is starting to be a troubling mystery."

Melie looked at the magnificent sphere. "What do you want me to do?"

"I want you to help me bring the City out of its prison and into a real world. I want you and Shay to make it live."

Chapter 15

HEROG

Herog told the other folks working with him, "This is a deep, complex virtual reality, operating in some version of real-time, connected back to physical reality in such a way that you can communicate with it, can send out your broadcasts and reports, so that new people can come here — but there's something between the outside and the inside, between all of Settled Space and this complicated program, that filters out the would-be spies and killers and traitors before they can do you any harm."

"If we're safe here, why does Mado Keyr want to take the City of Furies from virtual to tangible? If he's already managing to keep everyone who can do us harm out of the city, why put us at risk?"

The owner had told him that during the battle they'd just won, for the first time the City of Furies had been at risk of annihilation.

Not that it had been found. Just that it had been at risk of annihilation. Had stated that it had no defenses, and had never had, because it had not needed them.

It had to be housed somewhere in the immense *Longview*. And now Keyr — whoever Keyr really was — had realized that he couldn't keep the entire population of a city inside his ship, dragging them from danger to danger, leaving them vulnerable.

He was looking for a way to protect them away from himself.

A way to give them real lives.

Herog realized he was still on the *Longview*.

He sat down.

"We're all on his ship, and my friends and I just barely managed to keep Bailey's Point and the *Longview* safe. Mado Keyr could have lost everything, and this magnificent city and every one of you would have blinked out of existence without ever knowing you'd been in danger. This is why the City has to be real. Why it has to be built and why all of you have to be moved into it. This is why it currently has no defenses, and why it must have them."

He rested his elbows on the table, rested his face in his hands, and thought.

"But Keyr has already built the defense it needs. He just doesn't realize how good this system is."

He looked back up at them and grinned. "I know how we can protect the City of Furies without militarizing Bailey's Point or building the monster we fear."

Chapter 16

WERIX KEYR

T he poor, the downtrodden, the slaves held captive by governments and the slaves in chains alike have always told stories of a place where people are free.

All slaves have always imagined that there is some hidden wonderland where, if they could only get there, they could become the masters of their own destinies.

The stories are always the same.

Somewhere, there is a shining city, walled and glorious, protected by brilliant technology, by its hidden location, and by the ferocious citizens who guard their lives and each other's.

Somewhere.

The slaves always have their theories, and the masters, who know the stories are wishes unburdened by any truth, let them talk.

Some call this shining city Freeland, but there are half a hundred real worlds named Freeland in various world alliances, and every single one generates their version of citizen-slaves and Class-B criminals.

Some call this mythical world Godshome, but there are many, many colony worlds settled by the religious that are named Godshome, and those repress their citizens in other ways.

The stories about the mythical City of Furies are the only ones that stand without a real-universe namesake.

Something about that name and about the story behind it has made the slave collectors wary of using it for their new colonies.

Unlike Freeland or Godshome or the other tales of utopias, the City of Furies has never been described as a place where everyone is rich and no one has to work — and that, I think, is why no slaver has built a settlement with that name.

The myth of the City of Furies only began circulating sixty or so years earlier, and from the beginning, it was this: The City of Furies is a place where people choose their own work, work hard, grow rich making things other people want to buy, buy things other people make. People create, invent, innovate. And all of them pay their own way. In this city that tolerates no oppression, no slavery, no classes, the lowliest freed slave can become rich and admired, and no one will stand in his way, or hold him down because his parents were slaves, or he was marked Class E.

In the stories, this one city is a place where religion is tolerated but never mandated. Where various schools of thought are tolerated but never mandated. Where differences of opinion are accepted, where the rule of law stands above a slide to tyranny, where the rich have no more or better rights than the poor.

I thought the City of Furies was pure fantasy — the dream of those few slaves who did not want to switch their lots to become the masters of slaves.

And it was the best fantasy I'd ever heard of. I didn't think such a place could be made real.

Then I found Bashtyk Nokyd, and started reading his works.

And discovered that he'd written a novel titled *Aari in the City of Furies.*

The hero escaped from slavery, rescued his friends and loved ones, led them to a tiny world well away from the people who had once owned them, and he and his companions forged a code of conduct and a philosophy that gave them all equal rights under law, but that required that they earn those rights by bearing full responsibility for their own lives.

Responsibility for their own lives.

That, I thought. That was how people proved who they were. By owning their lives fully, by having nothing to prop them up but their own effort and the efforts of those with whom they traded, and by accepting the consequences of their own actions.

If only I could build such a place, I thought.

And then, sitting on one of the biggest piles of money in settled space, I thought, *I could build such a place.*

As a test.

In secret.

Set it up so that it ran on the rules Nokyd had developed. Make sure it did not fall prey to corruption, graft, favoritism, cronyism…

By building it inside a virtual reality, I could both protect the people inside the city who valued their chance at freedom, and identify and remove those who were looking for something for nothing, or who were criminals looking for prey.

Those people stored in my Medixes who were genuine monsters — their blood I could drink without remorse.

But I would never assume someone was a monster because he or she had been called one on a slaver world, had been sentenced by slaver law, had been sold by slave masters.

I promised myself that every human being within my care would have the opportunity to prove his or her character, to earn true freedom in a place where the individual was the pinnacle of humanity.

The people who were like the child I had been on Beckenridge, the child who wanted to be free to be myself, to find the life I wanted — those people I could give an opportunity to become their best selves inside the safe walls of a virtual City of Furies.

Through Storm Rat, I found a purely virtual AI who was interested in taking on the project. The AI had to agree to step out of common circulation, wall itself away from all outside communication within the *Longview,* and help me design both the protective barriers that would keep the City of Furies safely hidden, and the connections that brought each person in one of my storage units into the city. The two of us decided that the city needed to start small, and that each of the first people in it had to be treated as a new settler, given a few basic colonization tools and the chance to use those tools to build a piece of the city he or she would inhabit.

We set the time cycle to one virtual year per physical day. Started with a hundred colonists, and a charter that spelled out Bashtyk Nokyd's Rules of Human Freedom. Each hour of the first seven days, we added access to a hundred new settlers, and improved the settlement tools, and made sure we gave them the "history of the settlement" and trained them in Nokyd's Rules of Human Freedom.

By the end of the first week of real time, we had all of the criminals who had been in storage longest inside the city — and who were willing to work within Nokyd's rules — settled. The earliest in had been living in the growing city for seven virtual years. And they were all thriving.

Nokyd's Rules worked.

The first of which is simply, "To keep all humans free from oppression, no one rides through life for free."

It was a terrible shock to some of those in my hold who had been brought up to believe that they deserved to be carried on the work of others because their lives had been hard, or because they had been slaves and now wanted to own slaves.

About a quarter of new immigrants to the City of Furies requested transfer following their first Immigrants' Orientation class, where they were informed that they had to find a paying job in their first month in the settlement, and also notified that they would have to pay for everything they needed. That they would be required to work, to create, to remain active participants in building the city to stay in the city. That nothing was or ever would be free.

Several successful inhabitants would come in to talk to them, and explain that even though they had become massively wealthy, to remain inhabitants and citizens, they were required to invest in the city and remain active participants in its growth and success.

Another fifteen percent washed out in the first month because they refused to look for work, refused to accept responsibility for their own lives.

They were removed from the virtual reality.

Through the years, I ran more than a million Class A and Class B criminals through the virtual reality program. I discovered to my dismay that vast numbers of people want something for nothing, and are willing to see others enslaved so they can have that.

I was heartened, however, to discover that over half of the people who'd been rescued by *Longview*, when they found themselves in the orientation room of the City of Furies, understood where they were, hugged each other or wept for joy or kissed the floor in gratitude.

And then they stood up straight, walked out into the city, and started building their lives.

They worked one job, or two. Saved money, rented rooms, paid for education, learned skills, offered services, built products, built infrastructure, created new businesses.

Some grew rich. Those invested in buildings, or research into how to improve the city, or explored improvements to technology. Some developed products that answered needs far beyond the City of Furies and exported their goods while remaining the owner-operators of those businesses. Some pursued second passions and became writers or artists or musicians or inventors and started exporting their work throughout the galaxy.

But the fact was presented to every prospective citizen that the City of Furies was a city that worked. There were many rich people in the city — and more with every new infusion of immigrants.

There were no *idle* rich.

People who would have been nothing but frozen food for me — had I not discovered the truth — instead built Bashtyk Nokyd's City of Furies. They invented massive breakthroughs in technology, wrote entire bodies of passionate fiction and nonfiction, made magnificent art and music, created a deeply embedded city-wide culture of individual independence and individual pride in accomplishments earned.

By having the inhabitants self-select for willingness to work, and by creating a culture that rewarded them for investing in themselves and pursuing their passions as a way to create work they loved, the city became the place I yearned to inhabit.

The people of the city loved who they became, and made the rule of the city the motto of the city.

The City of Furies: *The City that Works.*

The problem, of course, was the *other* people. Not the Class A Criminals who failed to take the chance they were given to build new lives. Those I could sell for profit or keep and use as food.

No. The problem was those people who self-selected as "want to own slaves, want to have other people pay for my existence, want to ride for free on the backs of those I force to carry me."

I did not want to dump them out the airlock.

I did not want to use them as food.

I did not want to sell them as slaves.

But I did not want to store them at my expense. Did not choose to fill up berths in my hold that were being hooked into the city with people who had designated themselves "want to be useless."

So I came up with an alternative.

Chapter 17

WERIX KEYR

The urge to reproduce is a deep part of most people. We — and I do include myself in this number — yearn to pass on our genes, to create new versions of ourselves. To have children.

The City of Furies, being virtual, has no way to create children, because the citizens of the city are real, but their bodies are trapped in suspended animation. They do not age, they do not die… and they cannot breed.

But they still yearn.

So my Furies who have embedded themselves deeply in the culture and who have proven they understand why "no one rides for free" is the core that keeps the city alive are given the opportunity to "foster newborns."

This is something my AI and I came up with as an alternative to simply selling off the people who refused to adopt the Furies' culture.

People who were too damaged by their previous lives to move on — those who had endured horrific torture or the loss of people they loved deeply, or other traumas that made them not care whether they lived or died — along with people who saw owning slaves as their just repayment for having been slaves, and all Class A criminals in my hold were given three chances to become citizens of the city.

They were assigned two parents who got a new "infant" at least two virtual years after their previous one, and who raised these people as members of virtual birth families. The damaged, the criminal, and those with a sense of entitlement all retained their memories — because to erase their memories would have been to murder them — but they started their lives over with infant bodies that aged in what felt like real time to them. They experienced being born, being raised in loving families, being taught the Furies' culture and the history behind it. They received love, attention, education that focused on helping them discover and build on skills and passions that could form the backbone of rewarding careers, and were introduced to other children their own ages in tiny communities of ten to fifteen families in separate virtual realities outside of the city.

They were being tested, and each test lasted until the individual reached adulthood, was given autonomy with no sign of oversight, and then demonstrated who he or she had truly become.

Or who demonstrated earlier the intent to live the new life as badly as he or she had lived the old one.

Most of my people, given these opportunities, became hardworking, passionate creators inside the City. They remembered the pain their first lives had been filled with, but they no longer held on to it as a reason for revenge or as proof of their right to abuse others as they had been abused.

Those who were able to overcome the obstacles that prevented them from fitting into the City of Furies on their "immigrant" attempt made up the bulk of the rest of my human cargo.

A surprising number of people who had been career criminals found themselves joyful citizens of the City.

As did a decent number of people who had previously wanted to ride for free.

The others?

Well, I was operating a Death Circus, and I did have to make a certain number of sales to keep my Death Circus looking legitimate.

Those career criminals who proved they preferred crime to work (armed robbery being popular) — but who did not commit pedophilia, rape, torture, or murder in their family tests — I sold to the buyers who had found uses for such people.

Those in my possession who repeatedly demonstrated their desire to force others to do what they wanted so they could do nothing, I sold to worlds that bought slaves.

Those who had proven themselves irredeemable monsters, who when given caring families still committed rape, torture, pedophilia, or murder, I *kept*.

I found them both tasty and entertaining.

I do my best to be a good and honorable monster, but I am not a *nice* monster. I have needs, and sometimes I need to... play.

Chapter 18

MELIE

The owner stood with his back to Melie, staring up at a crystal sphere that hung suspended in the center of the back third of the vast *Longview*.

Curls of light ran through the sphere, blue and gold and green, and darkness pulsed and shimmered in liquid sheets that fell up, down, sideways.

It was the most dizzying thing she had ever seen that did not include folding wide awake through an origami point.

"That," the owner said, "is the City of Furies."

Melie simply nodded, and kept her mouth closed so she didn't look like a slack-jawed idiot.

This was the owner's secret — the one she *hadn't* known. This was the thing he'd created, that he'd made real in a universe where *freedom* was a buzzword used for pulling in suckers and rubes and selling them to the highest bidder.

This was the strong thread of goodness she'd felt in him, the reason she'd trusted him.

In her gut, she'd felt the strength and the honorable nature that drove the twisted and terrifying man. She had sensed this core of integrity, of genuine goodness, of passion for something so right and magnificent and wonderful — and so inconceivably complex and enormous — that she could not imagine what had driven him to create it.

All she had was the proof hanging before her that he had.

And she admired… loved… him for this incredible construct, this salvation for humans who had been slaves and who had been slated for death by being shoved out an airlock.

"Why?" she asked him. "You got away clean. You made yourself rich. You could have done anything. Why did you bring the best myth in the universe to life?"

He turned and looked at her. Raised an eyebrow.

"You know my past?"

She shrugged. "You know who I am. You know what I do. I did not intend to pry, but in the course of investigating those who were working to destroy us, I discovered those who had personal reasons for pursuing you. I know pieces of your past. Probably not the whole thing. But I know you were Tadra Amu. I know how you became Werix Keyr."

"That's probably more than I would have chosen to tell you."

"I assumed that. Kept it to myself. It was no one's business but yours, and had I not fallen over it while uncovering the secrets of those who attempted to overthrow Bailey's from the inside, I would not even have seen it."

He nodded, his eyes behind the faceplate of his suit unreadable as he studied her.

"So what do you think?"

"I think," Melie said, "that you are the most incredible human being I have ever known."

"I'm not human. Not anymore."

Melie laughed. "A body mod that you paid to have revised to make you less rather than more dangerous, from which you have had obligatory feeding, nanoviral bite-to-blood contagion, and lineage enslavement removed leaves you far more human than you care to admit."

She stopped laughing, though, as he froze. Stared at her

unblinking, and she realized that he had truly not known how much she'd discovered.

"And you know that because…?"

"Because your enemies — many of whom share variants of the Legend body mod — investigated you thoroughly. Tracked your money and what you spent it on, tracked the people you contacted in various modding communities, tortured and killed some in order to get details. They lost your trail when they collided with someone even more cautious with you, but prior to that, they were very thorough. They concluded that you were looking for immortality without the side effects."

"Yes," he said. "Because I thought I would have to live forever to protect the *Longview* and its greatest secret. My city. Now I know that I can safely die and rid the universe of this horror that I am, and you and Shay will carry on. Bring the city out of virtual, give the citizens real lives, protect these people — these magnificent, creative, brave people who dared to build themselves into the best versions they could imagine of who they wanted to be. I'm showing you this now, because I'll die today, and this city will belong to you."

Chapter 19

HEROG

Herog said, "It's simple. The city is built inside a vast terraforming dome. The entrances will have to require a Medix scan for anyone entering or leaving. That's standard procedure for any enclosed biome. In the three to five minutes the scan takes, Keyr's AI checks all returning citizens for alterations done without their consent — like the neural rewiring that led to Bashtyk Nokyd's death — and removes them.

"For prospective immigrants, it uses the exact process it's using now, whatever that might be."

Derna said, "But we don't know what that process is."

"We don't need to," Herog told her. "You are living inside the proof that it works. The proof isn't that no one has died here, or more importantly, has been born here. That was the proof that the place is virtual. It's that there have been no attempts to destroy the city or kill anyone. No one sent here to slaughter or destroy has been able to make an attempt, even if the attempt would have proved futile. No one intending harm has been able to enter the city."

Mecklen said, "That's invasion of privacy. This city cannot be the city it has become if it does not honor the rights of its citizens. And to dig through their minds to find intent, even if that intent is evil, is an invasion of privacy, of search without warrant, of every-thing that has already taken the rest of settled space in every imag-inable wrong direction."

Herog nodded. "Returning citizens won't be searched. They'll simply be checked to make sure they were not tampered with or programmed to do things they would not do of their own free will."

"Then…" Mecklen began.

Herog held up a hand to stop him. "Immigrants who wish to become citizens cannot claim the rights of citizens. They must pass the test to prove they can live as citizens in this place before they are allowed to enter. The test is simply to get in the Medix and meet the AI."

"But their rights…"

"No one has a right to murder. No one has a right to rape, or a right to molest, or a right to torture, or a right to enslave. No one has a right to use force against any non-consenting innocent, and there will be those who are sent here to do those very things. The City of Furies will be under attack from the moment its location becomes known. It will have Bailey's army to protect it from military attack within its system. Not an army made to conquer, to go adven-turing, to bring back loot and slaves. Not an army used to force the rest of settled space to adopt the City's path, for this is a path that cannot be followed by force. So the army must be made up of citi-zens who volunteer to serve for a time because they understand the value of what they're protecting."

"What if they won't volunteer?"

"Then what they claim to want to keep safe isn't worth saving."

"But the immigrants who are coming here to live better lives?"

"They'll pass the test as each of you did. But among them will be those sent to destroy the city, to cause chaos, to slaughter people who have already become known throughout settled space for their creation, for their honor, for their talents, for their joy. That the citi-zens of the City of Furies started as slaves and rose to greatness is already an affront to slave owners — whose sole claim to the right to enslave is that those who are owners are superior human beings, and those who are slaves are good for nothing better. The triumph of the citizens of the City of Furies is a threat to slavery. And the price of freedom is eternal vigilance. So no one may become a citizen who has not met the AI, gone through the test each of you went through before you were brought here."

Derna said, "There was no test. I was bought as a Class B criminal, I fell asleep, I woke up in the Immigrant Center, got my orientation, found a place to live, found a place to work." She shrugged.

Mecklen said, "Yeah. Same story for me."

"For you, that was the test," Herog said, "as it was for me. But that's not all there is to it. What happened before we woke up in the Immigrant Center?"

"Hah. Interesting." Liam said, "I remember another life before this one. I have not thought of it for years, and over time my memories of it fell away from lack of use… but I remember. I was a pirate in this other life. Was captured after I raided the wrong enclosure and killed the wrong people. Was sold to a slaver, was sent to a slave world, and I killed the owner of that world in an attempt to escape, which made me a Class-A criminal.

"I was purchased by a Death Circus. And then… Then I was being born. As an infant. Into a family.

"And that first life began to feel like a bad dream. I had two older brothers, an older sister, and a younger sister. And I learned math, and science, and engineering. It was a happy childhood, and then I came here, where my younger sister is a musician, where my brothers are — well, you know them. And my parents are still back on the farm. I go to visit them sometimes, but they have other children now." A tiny smile crossed his face. "And they're no older, but then… no one is."

Herog said, "That's how he does it."

The others looked over at him.

He said, "Those who need it are given a chance to start over. To be different. To make different choices, to choose better paths. Those who choose to change for the better come here. Those who don't…? I don't know what the owner does with those, but the fact that Liam is here and has family and friends and a life that matters to him is proof that the system gives people opportunity. The fact that you respect him enough to bring him into this process speaks well of you, of him, and of the justice built into the path to citizenship here."

He sat down, looked at Liam, Mecklen, Derna.

"The process Keyr is using works."

Chapter 20

WERIX KEYR

Melie stood behind me only because I turned my back on her.

I blinked the tears from my eyes, steadied myself. I was doing what I had to do — and the universe would be better off without me.

"Shay," Melie said behind me, "you don't have to kill him."

I froze, my breath caught in my chest. I turned slowly, not certain what I would find. Just knowing what I could *not* find...

And Melie was alone, staring at me. Just me.

"That's the secret I already knew," she said softly. Looking at me.

"How long?"

"Since right before you promoted me to captain. I've been waiting this whole time for you to tell me. But I suspected early on who you were, and have known for sure since the day you made me captain. Not just who you are, but what you are."

And I asked her, "How?"

"I suspected because you and Keyr were never in the same room together in sight of anyone—"

"Security precaution—" I said reflexively, and saw her eyebrow raise. I gave her an embarrassed little smile and shrugged.

"Then, after the on-deck crew was massacred, when the grav-drop was off and I made it up the ladder, I ran into you. You'd been in an explosion, you were naked, you were visible bones held together by meat and skin that was growing back fast, you were drinking the blood of the pirates to feed yourself. The skin of your face and skull was mostly burned off. But when you turned away from me, you had a flap of skin dangling from your skull down the back of your neck. The hair hanging from that flap was red, curly, waist-length. You were also missing male genitals, but that I would have overlooked because of the explosion. You were forming yourself into Keyr — forming yourself as male. By the hair, though — I knew you were Shay."

I stood staring at her. "You went to bed with me. Slept with me. A lot."

"I did."

"You knew what I was."

"I did."

I took a deep breath, stared at her and whispered, "Are you insane?"

She chuckled. "Possibly. But I knew both who and what you were, and even before the day you made me captain, enough of your history had landed in my lap, gathered by your enemies, that I understood why they were your enemies. If you were the devil, you were the devil on my side of the battle." She shrugged, and one corner of her mouth tipped upward. "Besides, I was in love with you — at least with you as Shay — and I was willing to be a little stupid to have you."

I stripped out of the suit. Stood there before her, naked and male, and said, "And this?"

"You are who you are. All the parts, all the time. I'm not like you, and I'm not drawn to the Keyr part of you, but I don't think I need to be. You don't have to kill off a part of yourself for me. Keep Keyr. Use him however you want. Just save Shay for me."

Chapter 21

CADY

The little boy made it through.

Was being held by his mother in the room where the hostages were gathered, didn't see her. But Cady saw him and breathed a little easier.

The pang — that she still didn't have a child of her own — was fresh and sharp. She didn't introduce herself. She was happy to know he was all right, and that he still had a mother.

She...

Well, right then she had someplace else she needed to be.

She pulled rank as a friend of Wils Bailey to get out of the hostage debrief, and raced to her little apartment, pounding through the corridors of Bailey's Station, not looking around, not caring about anything but getting home. She needed to know that Herog was all right. But when she got home, he wasn't there.

An enormous crate filled with genuine RexSurvyve cookies sat on the floor of the apartment beside the table, which held a holo dot that showed Cady in the restaurant with the woman who'd been going to teach her how to bake RexSurvyve cookies.

She watched it. Saw that the friendly baker had also been taken hostage. She closed her eyes. Dragged herself back to the present, back to *this* moment, when she was safe at Bailey's, where Herog was missing or dead but his people had won their battle against the biggest and deadliest fleet of warships ever gathered.

She brought herself back to the gift he'd left for her.

Took out a Golden Almond Caramel and read the instructions.

In case of emergency, fix things first. Then open this packet, eat, and enjoy. You're going to be all right. — Contents, one Big Cookie.

She'd done everything she could to fix things. Had gotten back alive. Was where he could find her. But there wasn't going to be any Herog ever again, was there?

She took a bite of the cookie, thinking of his message to her. *You're going to be all right.*

She would.

Eventually.

This was her one life, and she would not throw it away, no matter how little it mattered to her at the moment.

She walked over to the apartment window, stared out at the black of space. It went on forever, and he was nowhere in it.

"Not even going to say hello?" the voice she knew she couldn't be hearing said from behind her.

She turned and he was there, filling the doorway, scarred and fierce and grinning.

"Herog!" She raced over to him. "You're alive."

"And so are you," he growled, and folded her into his arms.

He picked her up, spun her around, laughed happily.

"We're both alive," he said, "and we won."

"I saw part of the fight while I was hanging in that bubble waiting for rescuers to cut me out. I didn't know you were in it. My captors told me you were dead."

Herog said, "I needed them to think that, so they wouldn't kidnap you — but then they kidnapped you while I was killing myself off. I saw you come through in that bait ball during the first part of the invasion. I knew you might not make it — but before the fight, we did everything we could to make sure every hostage survived."

"How many hostages and rescuers died?"

Herog said, "Fourteen. Two hostages, two rescue teams, and part of a third that was too close to one of the balls that exploded. The teams were amazing. Keyr's people were brilliant and focused and incredibly well trained. He brought in some spectacular folks to help us."

"Keyr?" Cady asked.

"The same person with whom I have been — for what felt like eternity because I wanted to be here with you — working out the way for the City of Furies to move to one of Wils' planets. We need to go see Wils, by the way, to tell him he needs to sell Keyr the best one for a lot of money.

She looked up at him and said, "Want one of my cookies? You can have the whole thing."

He laughed. "Just this once, yes. I'd love to have a whole one."

So she handed him a Double-Butter Chocolate Chip, which was the very best kind.

And said, "I really need to learn how to make those."

He told her, "You'll be able to. Your friend the baker survived too. I checked on my way home."

Chapter 22

SHAY

F or the first time in my life, I'm whole. I am a complete human being, known completely by one other human being. Accepted for who and what I am.

Melie knows the whole story now. But she knew most of it already.

She chose to be with me in spite of the truth that she knew. The truth I never dared tell anyone, the truth I would have tried to kill off a part of myself to hide.

For the first time in my life, I *feel* human, inside and out. Not wrong, not broken.

I would say *not monstrous*. But I kept Keyr. I still have uses for him.

The City of Furies is a real place. Building it cost so much that I nearly outran my money. I hired every one of Wils Bailey's army of moleibonders who would work with me, and had them duplicate exactly the virtual City of Furies — which was tricky.

Because my people — no, *their own* people now — are so immensely creative, so driven, so passionate about their work and their lives, I had to pause the entire virtual reality, snapshot it and everyone in it, then hand off to Wils' people. I kept virtual reality paused at that exact spot so that the moleibonders could use the holographic records of the city in its state at the exact instant its citizens would return to it. The exact instant they left.

The zero-plane extruders created perfect duplicates of every structure, including those that were incomplete and being built. I had every article of clothing duplicated in place, every in-progress creation made real, duplicated every item owned down to the pen strokes in physical journals. The process for doing this had never been simple, but over the years that I'd been working for the citizens of the city, I'd built enormous deep-space facilities to fabricate in the real world the art and tech that they were creating in the virtual world, to sell what they were creating for them, and to invest the profits for them, so that those who became rich in the virtual world were rich in the real world too.

The citizens of the City of Furies became the beneficiaries of that process.

And then I tried to figure out a story — because there was no way I could move people from the middle of their virtual conversations to the same spots and the same words in interrupted conversations, without the break in reality being apparent.

In the end, I decided that the best I could do was to tell them the truth. That the city had been under attack. That everyone had been successfully rescued. That a small number of those folks who had volunteered to go into the real world to fight the Battle of Bailey's Point had died in the real world but were being restarted from their save points inside the city, without the memories of their service — but also without their deaths.

I paid to have every single citizen moved in the hibernation pods to their analog homes, put into medixes there, given simultaneous reju to make sure they were all as healthy as they could be. I worked with the city's AI to wake all of them simultaneously.

And spoke to all of them from inside their own homes at the same time. I had no great words for them. All I had was this.

"You built something amazing that was hidden away," I told them. "That only a select few could ever reach. The City of Furies was tucked inside a virtual reality, but everything you created now exists in the real world — and so do you.

"If you want to start families, you can.

"If you want to leave the City, you can.

"If you want to return to the rest of Settled Space, you can.

"It has been my honor and joy to see you prove the truth of Bashyk Nokyd's words: 'Great human beings are not born in great houses, or from great families. Great human beings beings create themselves one choice and one action at a time.' You are great human beings, and you are a beacon lighting the darkness. Live with joy."

MELIE and I have a place in the City, private, quiet, a bit apart. We'll vacation there.

But for now at least, the sky is full of stars, and the stars are full of slaves, and we can yet find and rescue many of those who are like we were.

Someday I'm sure we'll want to settle into the City. Create a family of our own. Breathe the air of freedom. Walk the streets in the morning as the sun rises, and see all around us the faces of people glad to be building their lives, building their dreams; people who don't fear work, and who are working to build a city that is the proof to all of settled space that people achieve most and best when they are free to choose their own roads, and when they are fully responsible for the consequences of their own actions.

But for now — and if we can conquer death, forever — our true home is wherever we are together.

The Afterwords

Born From Fire

This series wasn't born in the usual manner. Most of the time, if I come up with a series idea, it's because I sat down and intentionally brainstormed concepts until I figured one out.

But I would have sworn the only stories I was going to write in Settled Space would have Cadence Drake as the main character.

Here's how I tripped over *The Longview*.

I was writing *Warpaint*, the sequel to *Hunting the Corrigan's Blood*. And I was having an awful time getting the scale of the ship in my head. I'd done a ship layout on quad paper, and had my scale figured out. I knew where things were. But the drawing was about seven inches long from nose to tail, and Cady's ship was about 280 feet (about 87 meters) from nose to tail.

I was having trouble looking at that tiny line drawing and visualizing Cady and her crew moving around inside the ship, and, as frequently happens when I'm struggling with a story problem, I had this crazy idea.

I thought, *I can just build the damn thing in Minecraft, and go inside it and walk around and then I'll know what it's like in there.*

So I figured one block for one meter and I carefully laid out the ship, following my schematic. Built the whole thing, furnished it, filled it with secret areas and notes to myself about who went where (stuck on signs.)

And then, because it was so incredibly useful to stand in the middle of the ship and know exactly what my characters could see and do, where they could go, and how they could get there, I built the other two ships from the *Cadence Drake* series so far.

And then I built the *Bailey's Irish Space Station* for the upcoming third novel in the series, *The Wishbone Conspiracy*.

I was hooked, you see. Having these places that I could walk around in was fun...but better than being fun, the places I'd built were talking to me. They were telling me stories.

But then I ran out of things to build.

The little voice in my head whispered, *How about building an ancient, mysterious spaceship from the days before TFN travel, when people were trying to colonize space in giant sleeper ships? Just for fun. No pressure. You aren't going to use it. You'll just build it.*

I may have an odd idea of fun, but I started building that mammoth ship. And floating through its vast reaches, feeling the dark and the weight around it, I realized its first inhabitants never reached their destination. I understood that when it was salvaged, the person who bought it and retrofitted it was going to have to be someone odd. Someone with a secret plan, and a hidden past.

Someone with a use for a ship that big that had absolutely nothing to do with the ship's apparent purpose.

Suddenly I wasn't building a spaceship for fun anymore. I had to know what was going on.

And here we are. I hope you'll accompany me through the next episode, when we'll rejoin the crew of *The Longview* as they deal with the extraordinary interstellar ruckus caused by *The Selling of Suzee Delight*... and look a little deeper into the lives of the folks from this tale.

Holly Lisle
Thursday, April 3, 2014

The Selling of Suzee Delight

I got the title for this story first, and the title stopped me in my tracks. That happens sometimes. It happened with my novel *Phoebe Rain*, published as *Midnight Rain* [paranormal suspense]. It happened again here.

I was doodling potential titles for this series into a notebook when *The Selling of Suzee Delight* scrawled its alliterative self across my page.

I stopped, and stared at those alien words sitting on the paper, and asked myself, "Who the hell is Suzee Delight... and why is she for sale... and what does she think she's doing trying to worm her way into a science fiction story?"

Science fiction, after all, is not rife with women named Suzee. Or Delight.

Those turned out to be three compelling questions. And unravelling the story of how a girl with the awful name of Suzee Delight came to be both a Grade-A troublemaker and a critical player in the changing character of Settled Space turned out to be well worth the difficulties answering those questions caused me.

Now, of course, Suzee (a.k.a. Tikka) is trying to elbow her way into more of these *Tales from The Longview*, and I might not be able to stop her. I can't see her being content to stay tucked safely away in the City of Furies if I tell her to just sit there and look pretty while I write the rest of the series the way I'd planned it.

Author vs. Character.

Not one of the classic battles, though familiar to most writers. At the moment, I don't like my odds of winning.

So wish me well as I head into the story of how Bashtyk Nokyd, the man from Meileone who dared to speak his mind—and the guy who donated Suzee's dress for her execution—hitches a ride on the *Longview*, and brings down all manner of disaster on his hosts in the process.

That will be in *Tales from The Longview, Episode 3: Bashtyk Nokyd Takes The Longview.*

Coming as soon as I can get it finished.

Holly Lisle
    8/18/2014

The Philosopher Gambit

This story should have been finished and published two years ago, and the three (or maybe four) episodes that I plan to complete it, as well.

Instead, there were… collisions with life.

A critical business website that crashed, requiring several years to totally rebuild so that it would not be vulnerable to nonsensical forced third-party updates.

A little bump on my tongue that turned out to be a big deal.

A lot of pain, a lot of biopsies and surgery, a fair amount of anxiety.

From time to time I note that shit happens. This time it happened to me.

But I have worked my way back to fiction again, and this is the first fiction I need to get up and rolling, because along with writing fiction, I also teach other *serious* writers (writers who want to make a living or some part of it doing this, and who are willing to work insanely hard to get where they want to go) how to do what I do.

I teach by demonstration.

And the entire *Tales from The Longview* series exists because I needed to be able to teach writers how to plan and write a series from start to finish, and I needed to do it at a length shorter than a hundred thousand words per story. And because of my fascination with building full-scale spaceships in Minecraft (but that's a story I've told elsewhere).

So you're reading fiction that exists in two planes.

First, added all together, these stories will make up a stand-alone story that fits into the Cadence Drake timeline after *Warpaint* and before *The Wishbone Conspiracy*.

Second, they're demonstrations for my students of how I build series fiction and get it to all hang together.

And here's a little secret about that.

I know (mostly, sorta, kinda) how this story ends.

What I'm still figuring out is how it middles.

But about two hours ago, I figured out what happens next. Just finished writing that. That was the Episode 4 teaser.

Live with joy,
  Holly Lisle

January 27, 2017 at 10:12 AM

Gunslinger Moon

This story would have been done quicker if I hadn't tried to write it and the story that will follow, *Vipers' Nest*, all in one go.

Matt (my husband and content editor) read the first version and very nicely explained to me that I had six stories going at the same time and that it was impossible to give any of them the depth they deserved in just under 40,000 words.

This is just one story out of the six I was telling in that one episode, and when I crammed it in with the rest of them…

Well, if you've ever seen sardines in a can, you have the visual that fits the first draft.

So in the next episode, I'll be telling the story of the pirates and the Pact World Alliance finally making good on their promise to try to wipe out everyone on the *Longview* and Bailey's Irish Space Station.

And in the one after that, for which I haven't yet come up with a title I like, I'll finally tell the story of the owner's conflict with Shay, the story of Shay's fight to find her own freedom, and the story of the secret the City of Furies is hiding.

I hope you've enjoyed *Gunslinger Moon*.

If you loved it, I'd be grateful for a review on your platform of choice.

And I'll see you in the City of Furies…

Holly Lisle
  December, 2017

Vipers' Nest

Nothing *ever* goes as planned.

Not even when you're the God of the Story and you thought you did a pretty good job of planning.

Let me show you what I mean:

- Werix Keyr was not going to be in this story at all.
- There was going to be a massive space battle that became the beginning of a long war.
- There were going to be multiple legends living in the Diplomatic Center — a whole nest of vipers, in other words, from whence I was going to pull the spiffy title *Vipers' Nest* (which I only managed to save thanks to a question from bug-hunter Alli Vo that put me on a path to a bit of on-the-fly replotting).

And then…

Well…

Melie got cleverer and found some records I hadn't known existed.

The owner okayed an AI.

Shay nearly had a dreadful mishap for the sake of something I planned later, and was pulled back from the brink by my editor (you may thank Matt for sparing you from horrors you don't wish to imagine).

The Gargantua device erupted from some hellhole in the back of my mind and totally wrecked Herog's plans.

And Herog played David to the PWA's Goliath, and everything, everything, EVERYTHING changed.

And then my bug hunters went through and asked questions that changed things even more.

So…

The next story will be the final story in the *Longview* series, but it will not be the last story in my Settled Space universe, it will not start the way I *knew* it would (until one bug hunter asked one question that triggered and a "no, definitely not that" response that gave me an idea that's just SO much cooler...)

So the final story in this series is certainly is not going to be the story I thought I would be writing.

At the moment, I'm wandering around in the wreckage of my plans, liking this universe much better than the one I thought I'd built, faced all of a sudden with options I never even saw coming.

So...

Until we meet in the City of Furies,

Holly Lisle
July 9, 2018 at 1:05 PM

The Owner's Tale

This series began as my tribute to the *Canterbury Tales*, which when I was about seventeen introduced me to the reality that people in the far past were real human beings — pompous, funny, kinky, weird, stuffy, strange. Through Chaucer's work, I got to see a wonderful cross section of society, pinned brilliantly to the pages and saved so that hundreds of years later, I could meet people he saw every day. And recognize in them people *I* saw every day.

(The version of the book I had in high school had the Middle English version on the left page and the modern English translation in prose on the right. I worked my way through both.)

Chaucer made those people real to me, and by doing so, brought a time and place that had vanished from the face of the earth back to life.

And I thought, *Wouldn't it be cool to do that? To gather a group of strangers from another time together, to put them into a place where they had to deal with each other and depend on each other, to show readers their lives, what mattered to them... to make them live?*

In my case, I put my pilgrims on a spaceship in the future,

because people will still be people tomorrow, and beyond that. Will still be strange and weird, still pompous and funny. Will still think, dream, desire, love. Will still matter to themselves and to each other.

The Owner, the *Longview*, the folks at Bailey's, the citizens of the City of Furies — all of them touched my life, grew out of my past and my present, asked me questions as I was falling asleep at night, and gave me answers as I sat down to write the next day.

Some of these folks have been with me since before June of 2014, when I finished the first draft of *Enter the Death Circus*. That was the original title of *Born from Fire*, the first episode.

So what happens next?

From here, Melie and Shay get their "happily ever after."

Herog and Cady go back to work.

The folks on Bailey's Irish Space Station…

I don't know. I love BISS. And there are so many stories in there waiting to be told.

So many stories. So little time.

But while I like to write in my other worlds outside this universe, Settled Space is the place that feels like home to me. The place I want to keep coming back to after I've gone vacationing elsewhere.

I hope you find a home in this universe, too.

Holly Lisle
November 7, 2018 at 12:10 PM

The Acknowledgements

Born From Fire

I want to take a moment to thank my Patreon patrons, whose encouragement, readership, faith in me, and funding have made it possible for me to get back to writing fiction every weekday.

Hero Patrons

Julian Adorney, Thomas Vetter, Tuff Gartin, Karin Hernandez, Nancy Nielsen-Brown, Holly Doyne, Katharina Gerlach, Kim Lambert, John Toppins, Rebecca Yeo, Rebecca Galardo, Eva Gorup, Dragonwing, Isabella Leigh, Misti Pyles, Susan Qrose, Tammi Labrecque, Kirsten Bolda, Patricia Masserman, Charlotte Babb, KM Nalle, Benita Peters, Michelle Miles, Becky Sasala, Joyce Sully, Jean Schara, Carolyn Stein, Dan Allen, Heiko Ludwig, Renee Wittman, Dawn Morrison, Christine Embree, Justin Colucci, Angelika Devlyn, Mary E. Merrell, Indy Indie, Moley, Tiny Yellow Tree, Brendan Fortune, Greg Miranda, Wednesday McKenna, Nicola Lane, Jane Lawson, Michelle Mulford, Julie Hickerson, Amy Fahrer, Jess, Juneta Key, Lynda Washington, Reetta Raitanen, Marya Miller, Faith Nelson, Meagan Smith, Sarah Brewe, Ava Fairhall,

Elke Zimoch, Zeyana Musthafa, Beverly Paty, Misty DiFrancesco, Nan Sampson, Eric Bateman, Bonnie Burns, Maureen Morley, Resa Edwards, Jennette Heikes, Sylvie Granville, Miriam Stark, Anders Bruce, Paula Meengs, Alexandra Swanson, Claudia Wickstrom, Ken Bristow, Francine Seal, Amy Padgett, Jason Anderson, Doug Glassford

Amazing Patrons

Felicia Fredlund, Susan Osthaus, Hope Terrell, Glenwood Bretz, Amy Schaffer, Deb Gallardo, Anna Bunce, Simon Sawyers, Deb Evon, Ernesto Montalve, Teresa Horne, Erin O'Kelly, Cynthia Louise Adams, June Thornton, Cassie Witt, Liza Olmsted, Elaine S. Milner, Kristen Shields, Alex G. Zarate, Barbara Lund, Cathy Peper, Ken Alger, Donna Mann, Linda George

Wonderful Patrons

Irina Barnay, Peggy Elam, Chris Muir, Ewelina Sparks, Betty Widerski, Stacie Arellano, Elizabeth Schroeder, Kara Hash, Amber Hansford, Beverley Spindler, Daniela Gana, Thea van Diepen, Storm Weaver, Susanne, Panos, Pixelkay, Ruth Sard, Dori-Ann Granger, Connie Cockrell

Want to find out more about becoming a fiction patron?
Start Here: https://www.patreon.com/hollylisle

The Selling of Suzee Delight

I want to take a moment to thank my Patreon patrons, whose encouragement, readership, faith in me, and funding have made it possible for me to get back to writing fiction every weekday.

Hero Patrons

Julian Adorney, Thomas Vetter, Tuff Gartin, Karin Hernandez, Nancy Nielsen-Brown, Holly Doyne, Katharina Gerlach, Kim Lambert, John Toppins, Rebecca Yeo, Rebecca Galardo, Eva Gorup, Dragonwing, Isabella Leigh, Misti Pyles, Susan Qrose,

Tammi Labrecque, Kirsten Bolda, Patricia Masserman, Charlotte Babb, KM Nalle, Benita Peters, Michelle Miles, Becky Sasala, Joyce Sully, Jean Schara, Carolyn Stein, Dan Allen, Heiko Ludwig, Renee Wittman, Dawn Morrison, Christine Embree, Justin Colucci, Angelika Devlyn, Mary E. Merrell, Indy Indie, Moley, Tiny Yellow Tree, Brendan Fortune, Greg Miranda, Wednesday McKenna, Nicola Lane, Jane Lawson, Michelle Mulford, Julie Hickerson, Amy Fahrer, Jess, Juneta Key, Lynda Washington, Reetta Raitanen, Marya Miller, Faith Nelson, Meagan Smith, Sarah Brewe, Ava Fairhall, Elke Zimoch, Zeyana Musthafa, Beverly Paty, Misty DiFrancesco, Nan Sampson, Eric Bateman, Bonnie Burns, Maureen Morley, Resa Edwards, Jennette Heikes, Sylvie Granville, Miriam Stark, Anders Bruce, Paula Meengs, Alexandra Swanson, Claudia Wickstrom, Ken Bristow, Francine Seal, Amy Padgett, Jason Anderson, Doug Glassford

Amazing Patrons

Felicia Fredlund, Susan Osthaus, Hope Terrell, Glenwood Bretz, Amy Schaffer, Deb Gallardo, Anna Bunce, Simon Sawyers, Deb Evon, Ernesto Montalve, Teresa Horne, Erin O'Kelly, Cynthia Louise Adams, June Thornton, Cassie Witt, Liza Olmsted, Elaine S. Milner, Kristen Shields, Alex G. Zarate, Barbara Lund, Cathy Peper, Ken Alger, Donna Mann, Linda George

Wonderful Patrons

Irina Barnay, Peggy Elam, Chris Muir, Ewelina Sparks, Betty Widerski, Stacie Arellano, Elizabeth Schroeder, Kara Hash, Amber Hansford, Beverley Spindler, Daniela Gana, Thea van Diepen, Storm Weaver, Susanne, Panos, Pixelkay, Ruth Sard, Dori-Ann Granger, Connie Cockrell

Want to find out more about becoming a fiction patron?

Start Here: https://www.patreon.com/hollylisle

The Philosopher Gambit

Heartfelt thanks to:

Dan Allen, who told me his story of the Boston Red Sox and introduced me to the concept of the *pretty good day*… and a new meaning for the phrase "pretty good." And who is building the software that will give me more time to write.

EJ Clarke, whose careful reading and perceptive comments removed the splinters from this story. (Any in there now are from changes I made post-edit.)

Matt and Joe, for the gift of "concept of a cat," and the reality that became Sheldon the Insane, Fierce Hunter of Shadows and Toes, who is a much-needed gift of laughter.

I want to take a moment to thank my Patreon patrons, whose encouragement, readership, faith in me, and funding have made it possible for me to get back to writing fiction every weekday.

Hero Patrons

Julian Adorney, Thomas Vetter, Tuff Gartin, Karin Hernandez, Nancy Nielsen-Brown, Holly Doyne, Katharina Gerlach, Kim Lambert, John Toppins, Rebecca Yeo, Rebecca Galardo, Eva Gorup, Dragonwing, Isabella Leigh, Misti Pyles, Susan Qrose, Tammi Labrecque, Kirsten Bolda, Patricia Masserman, Charlotte Babb, KM Nalle, Benita Peters, Michelle Miles, Becky Sasala, Joyce Sully, Jean Schara, Carolyn Stein, Dan Allen, Heiko Ludwig, Renee Wittman, Dawn Morrison, Christine Embree, Justin Colucci, Angelika Devlyn, Mary E. Merrell, Indy Indie, Moley, Tiny Yellow Tree, Brendan Fortune, Greg Miranda, Wednesday McKenna, Nicola Lane, Jane Lawson, Michelle Mulford, Julie Hickerson, Amy Fahrer, Jess, Juneta Key, Lynda Washington, Reetta Raitanen, Marya Miller, Faith Nelson, Meagan Smith, Sarah Brewe, Ava Fairhall, Elke Zimoch, Zeyana Musthafa, Beverly Paty, Misty DiFrancesco, Nan Sampson, Eric Bateman, Bonnie Burns, Maureen Morley, Resa Edwards, Jennette Heikes, Sylvie Granville, Miriam Stark, Anders Bruce, Paula Meengs, Alexandra Swanson, Claudia Wickstrom,

Ken Bristow, Francine Seal, Amy Padgett, Jason Anderson, Doug Glassford

Amazing Patrons

Felicia Fredlund, Susan Osthaus, Hope Terrell, Glenwood Bretz, Amy Schaffer, Deb Gallardo, Anna Bunce, Simon Sawyers, Deb Evon, Ernesto Montalve, Teresa Horne, Erin O'Kelly, Cynthia Louise Adams, June Thornton, Cassie Witt, Liza Olmsted, Elaine S. Milner, Kristen Shields, Alex G. Zarate, Barbara Lund, Cathy Peper, Ken Alger, Donna Mann, Linda George

Wonderful Patrons

Irina Barnay, Peggy Elam, Chris Muir, Ewelina Sparks, Betty Widerski, Stacie Arellano, Elizabeth Schroeder, Kara Hash, Amber Hansford, Beverley Spindler, Daniela Gana, Thea van Diepen, Storm Weaver, Susanne, Panos, Pixelkay, Ruth Sard, Dori-Ann Granger, Connie Cockrell

Want to find out more about becoming a fiction patron?
Start Here: https://www.patreon.com/hollylisle

Gunslinger Moon

Bug Hunters

Huge thanks to each of the folks below, who went through the edited, typeset manuscript and found *SO* very many bugs. All of which I have corrected. The ones that remain? Those are all on me.

Vanessa Wells, Charlotte Henley Babb, Stanley B. Brewster Jr., Akiva Abrams, Bruce Andis, Mike Kee, Tim G., Jenny Williams, Camilla Milford, Susan Qrose

Patreon Patrons

I want to take a moment to thank my Patreon patrons, whose encouragement, readership, faith in me, and funding have made it possible for me to get back to writing fiction every weekday.

Hero Patrons

Julian Adorney, Thomas Vetter, Tuff Gartin, Karin Hernandez, Nancy Nielsen-Brown, Holly Doyne, Katharina Gerlach, Kim Lambert, John Toppins, Rebecca Yeo, Rebecca Galardo, Eva Gorup, Dragonwing, Isabella Leigh, Misti Pyles, Susan Qrose, Tammi Labrecque, Kirsten Bolda, Patricia Masserman, Charlotte Babb, KM Nalle, Benita Peters, Michelle Miles, Becky Sasala, Joyce Sully, Jean Schara, Carolyn Stein, Dan Allen, Heiko Ludwig, Renee Wittman, Dawn Morrison, Christine Embree, Justin Colucci, Angelika Devlyn, Mary E. Merrell, Indy Indie, Moley, Tiny Yellow Tree, Brendan Fortune, Greg Miranda, Wednesday McKenna, Nicola Lane, Jane Lawson, Michelle Mulford, Julie Hickerson, Amy Fahrer, Jess, Juneta Key, Lynda Washington, Reetta Raitanen, Marya Miller, Faith Nelson, Meagan Smith, Sarah Brewe, Ava Fairhall, Elke Zimoch, Zeyana Musthafa, Beverly Paty, Misty DiFrancesco, Nan Sampson, Eric Bateman, Bonnie Burns, Maureen Morley, Resa Edwards, Jennette Heikes, Sylvie Granville, Miriam Stark, Anders Bruce, Paula Meengs, Alexandra Swanson, Claudia Wickstrom, Ken Bristow, Francine Seal, Amy Padgett, Jason Anderson, Doug Glassford, Kathleen Frost

Amazing Patrons

Felicia Fredlund, Susan Osthaus, Hope Terrell, Glenwood Bretz, Amy Schaffer, Deb Gallardo, Anna Bunce, Simon Sawyers, Deb Evon, Ernesto Montalve, Teresa Horne, Erin O'Kelly, Cynthia Louise Adams, June Thornton, Cassie Witt, Liza Olmsted, Elaine S. Milner, Kristen Shields, Alex G. Zarate, Barbara Lund, Cathy Peper, Ken Alger, Donna Mann, Linda George, Beverly Spindler,

Wonderful Patrons

Irina Barnay, Peggy Elam, Chris Muir, Ewelina Sparks, Betty Widerski, Stacie Arellano, Elizabeth Schroeder, Kara Hash, Amber Hansford, Beverley Spindler, Daniela Gana, Thea van Diepen, Storm Weaver, Susanne, Panos, Pixelkay, Ruth Sard, Dori-Ann Granger, Connie Cockrell, Claire Smith, Donna Mann

Want to find out more about becoming a fiction patron?

Start Here: https://www.patreon.com/hollylisle

Vipers' Nest

Bug Hunters

Enormous thanks to my Bug Hunters who hit tight deadlines, found a gawdawful number of bugs, and offered encouragement and a number of excellent fixes while reading with a very short turn around.

Any bugs that remain are on me, and I apologize for not finding them.

In no particular order:

Kim Lambert, Akiva Abrams, Dianna Millard, Alli Vo, BJ Steeves, Gregory Avery, Tracey Jean H, Kari Wolfe, Kris Q, Kyralae, Bruce Andis, Charlotte H. Babb.

My Patreon Patrons

I have a Patreon set up to fund my writing and revision of original fiction:

https://www.patreon.com/hollylisle

The folks below bought me writing hours each week in which I wrote and revised this story while still making sure bills got paid.

They have my deepest gratitude.

HERO PATRONS

Thomas Vetter, Tuff Gartin, Karin Hernandez, Nancy Nielsen-Brown, Holly Doyne, Cat Gerlach, Kim Lambert, John Toppins, Rebecca Yeo, Rebecca Galardo, Eva Gorup, Sophie Renaudin, Isabella Leigh, Misti Pyles, Susan Witts, Tammi Labrecque, Kirsten Bolda, Patricia Masserman, Charlotte Babb, Eugenia George, Benita Peters, Vanessa Wells, Becky Sasala, Joyce Sully, Jean Schara, Carolyn Stein, Dan Allen, Heiko Ludwig, Heather Wittman, Dawn Morrison, Christine Embree, Justin Colucci, Mary E. Merrell, Moley, Tiny Yellow Tree, Brendan Fortune, Greg Miranda, Jennifer

Sakaida, Wednesday McKenna, Nicola Lane , madamebadger, Jane Lawson, Simon Sawyers, Stacey Anderson, Julie Hickerson, Amy Fahrer, Jess, Juneta Key, Lynda Washington, Reetta Raitanen, Adelaida Saucedo, Kari Wolfe, Marya Miller, Faith Nelson, Meagan Smith, Tim King, Gemma B, Sarah Brewer, Ava Fairhall, Elke Zimoch, Zeyana Musthafa, Beverly Paty, Misty DiFrancesco, Nan Sampson, Eric Bateman, Bonnie Burns, Maureen Morley, Jennette Heikes, Sylvie Granville, Anders Bruce, Paula C Meengs, Barbara Lund, Doogie Glassford, Alexandra Swanson, Claudia Wickstrom, Ken Bristow, Francine Seal, Amy Padgett

AMAZING PATRONS

Susan Osthaus, Hope Terrell, Glenwood Bretz, Amy Schaffer, Anna Bunce, Chris Langston, Beverley Spindler, Deb Evon , Ernesto Montalve, Teresa Horne, Erin O'Kelly, Cynthia Louise Adams, June Thornton, Cassie Witt, Liza Olmsted, Linda George, Elaine Milner, Kristen Shields, Dori-Ann Granger, Alex G. Zarate, Cathy Peper

WONDERFUL PATRONS

Chris Muir, Ewelina Sparks, Betty Widerski, Stacie Arellano, Lizzie Merrill, Angelika Devlyn, Donna Mann, Kara, Yifei Zhuang, Storm Weaver, Panos, Ruth Sard, Anna K Payne, Connie Cockrell

OPEN PATRONS (No Reward Selected)

Catherine Ellison, Irina Barnay, Vorona, Peggy Elam

The Owner's Tale

My Bug Hunters

My deepest thanks to the folks who, when invited with no warning to bug-hunt this final *Longview* story on a ridiculously short deadline, said *Yes*, jumped in, and hit their deadline.

This story is way less buggy because of them:

Vanessa Wells
Kim Lambert
Tuff Gartin
Greg Miranda
Linda Sprinkle
Linda Niehoff

Any remaining errors, of course, are just mine.

My Patrons at Patreon

The following folks are currently funding me to write fiction for an hour a day five days a week.

They are the reason *The Longview Chronicles* are now complete.

My patrons in this episode are in Alpha by First Name order because of a series of events that started with me dousing my keyboard in coffee this morning, which resulted in me having to work on a wrong and not friendly computer...)

Adelaida Saucedo
Alex G. Zarate
Alexandra Swanson
Alicia Mayo
Amy Fahrer
Amy Padgett
Amy Schaffer
Anders Bruce
Angelika Devlyn
Anna Bunce
Anna K Payne
Ava Fairhall
Barbara Lund
Becky Sasala
Betty Widerski
Beverley Spindler
Beverly Paty
Bonnie Burns
Brendan Fortune

C. L. Roth

Carolyn Stein

Cassie Witt

Cat Gerlach

Catherine Ellison

Cathy Peper

Charlotte Babb

Chris Langston

Chris Muir

Christine Embree

Claudia Wickstrom

Connie Cockrell

Cynthia Louise Adams

Dan Allen

Daniela Gana

Dawn Morrison

Deb Evon

Donna Mann

Doogie Glassford

Dori-Ann Granger

Dragonwing

Elaine Milner

Elke Zimoch

Eric Bateman

Erin O'Kelly

Ernesto Montalve

Eugenia George

Eva Gorup

Ewelina Sparks

Faith Nelson

Francine Seal

Gemma B

Glenwood Bretz

Greg Miranda

Hanna Tetens

Heather Wittman

Heiko Ludwig
Holly Doyne
Hope Terrell
Irina Barnay
Isabella Leigh
Jane Lawson
Jean Schara
Jennette Marie Powell
Jennifer Sakaida
Jess
John Toppins
Joyce Sully
Juneta Key
Justin Colucci
Kara
Kari Wolfe
Karin Hernandez
Kathy Draxlbauer
Kim Lambert
Kirsten Bolda
Ken Bristow
Kristen Shields
Kyralae Bredi
Linda George
Liza Olmsted
Lizzie Merrill
Lynda Washington
madamebadger
Mary E. Merrell
Mary Wockenfuss
Marya Miller
Maureen Morley
Meagan Smith
Misti Pyles
Misty DiFrancesco
Moley

Nancy Nielsen-Brown
Nicola Lane
Panos
Pat Hauldren
Patricia Masserman
Paula C Meengs
Peggy Elam
Rebecca Wade
Rebecca Yeo
Reetta Raitanen
Ruth Sard
Sarah Brewer
Scorpion Gulch Studio
Simon Sawyers
Stacie Arellano
Susan Osthaus
Susan Witts
Sylvie Granville
Tammi Labrecque
Tammy L Breitweiser
Teresa Horne
Thomas Vetter
Tim King
Tiny Yellow Tree
Tuff Gartin
Vanessa Wells
Vorona
Wednesday McKenna
Zeyana Musthafa

About the Author

I'm a commercial novelist who went indie.

Lots of reasons, all good but none easy. In July of 2011 I walked away from commercial publishing to pursue *My Career My Way,* and it's been interesting times ever since.

Now I'm back to writing the *Cadence Drake, Moon & Sun,* and *Longview* series, creating stand-alone fiction, building writing courses, and getting the chance to speak directly to the readers of both my fiction and nonfiction.

If you keep hoping I'll do a particular story, or book, or course, and I haven't yet—let me know.

Cheerfully,

Holly Lisle

P.S. To find out what's coming next, and let me know what you'd love to see next…

Get my email updates:

https://hollyswritingclasses.com/go/pick-adventure-or-plain-emails.html

which come in two flavors…

- *Role-Playing-Adventure Game*
- *Plain emails*

When you sign up, the first thing you do is select the version of me you prefer.

After that, you either discover all the cool things I have to offer by playing through an email adventure…

Or by getting one email a week that takes you on a tour of my sites, books, classes, and other cool things.

(There are neither giant snakes nor mermaids in the "ordinary emails" version.)

Replies to emails come straight to me. Can't answer all of them, but I read them all, and answer when I can.

Find me here: HollyLisle.com

And here: HollysWritingClasses.com

Also by Holly Lisle

Cadence Drake & Settled Space Stories

Hunting the Corrigan's Blood — A Cadence Drake Novel

Warpaint — A Cadence Drake Novel

Born from Fire: Tales from The Longview — Episode 1

The Selling of Suzee Delight: Tales from The Longview —Episode 2

The Philosopher Gambit: Tales from The Longview —Episode 3

Gunslinger Moon: Tales from The Longview — Episode 4

Vipers' Nest: Tales from the Longview — Episode 5

The Owner's Tale: Tales from the Longview — Episode 6

The Longview Chronicles: The Complete Longview Collection

My Other Novels

The Ruby Key: Moon & Sun I

The Silver Door: Moon & Sun II

The Emerald Sun: Moon & Sun III (in progress now)

Talyn: A Novel of Korre

Hawkspar: A Novel of Korre

Midnight Rain (reprinted as By Kate Aeon)

Last Girl Dancing (reprinted as By Kate Aeon)

I See You (reprinted as By Kate Aeon)

Night Echoes (reprinted as By Kate Aeon)

Fire in the Mist: Arhel I

Bones of the Past: Arhel II

Mind of the Magic: Arhel III

Glenraven

In The Rift: Glenraven II

Sympathy for the Devil: Devil's Point I

The Devil and Dan Cooley (with Walter Spence): Devil's Point II

Hell on High (with Ted Nolan): Devil's Point III

Minerva Wakes

Memory of Fire: World Gates I

The Wreck of Heaven: World Gates II

Gods Old and Dark: World Gates III

Diplomacy of Wolves: Secret Texts I

Vengeance of Dragons: Secret Texts II

Courage of Falcons: Secret Texts III

Vincalis the Agitator (Secret Texts Prequel)

When the Bough Breaks (with Mercedes Lackey)

Mall, Mayhem and Magic (with Chris Guin)

The Rose Sea (with S.M. Stirling)

Curse of the Black Heron

Thunder of the Captains (with Aaron Allston)

Wrath of the Princes (with Aaron Allston)

My Fiction Singles

Light Through Fog

Rewind

Strange Arrivals: Ten Tiny, Twisty Fantasy Tales

My Fiction in Collections

"Light Through Fog," The Mammoth Book of Paranormal Romance

"4EVR," The Mammoth Book of Ghost Romance

"Last Thorsday Night," The Mammoth Book of Time Travel

"Knight and the Enemy," The Enchanter Reborn

"Armor-ella," Chicks in Chainmail

"A Few Good Men," Women at War

My Nonfiction

Find these at HollysWritingClasses.com

FREE INTRO CLASS: How to Write Flash Fiction that Doesn't Suck

How to Write a Novel

How To Revise Your Novel

How To Write A Series

How To Think Sideways: Career Survival School for Writers

Create A Character Clinic

Create A Plot Clinic

How to Write Page-Turning Scenes

Create A Language Clinic

Create A Culture Clinic

Create A World Clinic

How to Write Short Stories

How to Write Villains

How to Find Your Writing Voice

How to Write Dialogue With Subtext

Title. Cover. Copy. Fiction Marketing

That Thing They Do In Movies...

Cady, Herog, Shay, Wils and I are sitting at a little table in The Seamy Underside Bar & Grill on Bailey's Irish Space Station. Looking out at deep space, at the origami point which has been cleared of debris from the battle.

We're eating Bailey's Irish Best Reconsta — I'm having Steakums with Real Butter, and Very Green Stalky Things, which is some of the best reconsta you can get.

The others are chowing down too, because... well...

We're tired but alive, you know? We're laughing, talking about the crazy adventure we've just survived together, and Cady says... "So after everything we've been through, what could we possibly do next?"

And Herog says, "Sleep," but he says it just to Cady, and waggles his eyebrows at the same time so no one misses his meaning.

And then Wils looks up from something new they're trying with reconsta — Sliced Prehistoric Mammoth — and I see this surprised expression on his face, and he nudges me. And when I look where he's looking, I see you looking at us from the other side of the page.

I wave, because, well, here we both are.

Not sure if you can hear me from in here when you're out there, but… We'll all be back.

I don't know when. I have a trek ahead of me in the Moon & Sun universe, finding the truth behind the Emerald Sun.

But Bailey's is home. Cady's. Herog's. Mine.

Yours if you want it to be. There's room for you here. And here, you can make the life you want to live.

So here's hoping we meet again.

The next book in this world will be *The Wishbone Conspiracy*.

Made in the USA
Columbia, SC
27 February 2020